Jon
Jones, Pauline Baird.
The last enemy

The Last Enemy

The Last Enemy

Pauline Baird Jones

Five Star
Unity, Maine

Five Star First Edition, Second Printing
Published in conjunction with Pauline Baird Jones.

Cover photograph by Gregory L. Jones

December 1999
Standard Print Hardcover Edition.

Five Star Standard Print First Edition Romance Series.

The text of this edition is unabridged.

Set in 11 pt. Plantin by Minnie B. Raven.

Printed in the United States on permanent paper.

Library of Congress Cataloging-in-Publication Data

Jones, Pauline Baird.
    The last enemy / Pauline Baird Jones.—Stand. print
hardcover ed.
        p.   cm. — (Five Star standard print first edition
romance series)
    ISBN 0-7862-2185-2 (hc : alk. paper)
    I. Title.   II. Series.
PS3560.O52415 L37   1999
813'.54—dc21
                                                    99-047793

The Last Enemy

Chapter One

Fear followed Dani Gwynne out of sleep, drying her throat to parchment, turning her muscles to wood and digging up a longing to go fetal and whine.

Where—? It came in a rush. Safe house. Denver. Colorado. The Mile-High City for the afraid-of-heights romance writer. A match made in hell.

She took an unsteady breath. Water would restore the moisture to her throat, but fetal and whining had to be reburied quickly. Things like that got recorded in "The File." After eight months in protective custody, Dani was suffering from an acute case of lost privacy.

"You awake?" Peg's husky murmur drifted on the same cooled air that circulated the smoke from her cigarette. The Deputy US Marshal had gone from occasional to chain smoker in just over two months, but Dani would bet money that wouldn't make it into "The File."

"Yeah." Dani rubbed her face.

"Another bad dream?" Peg asked sympathetically.

Bad dream? The hired killer, Dani called him Dark Lord for lack of a real name, did a brief encore inside her head. She gave a slight twitch. Certainly not a good dream, but at least it hadn't been the one where he held her head under a sea of blood until her lungs exploded.

Now that was a bad dream.

"I just need to pee," Dani said. Dreams made it into "The File," peeing didn't, she hoped.

The Deputy US Marshal, a dark silhouette against the

carefully drawn drapes, gave a tiny, skeptical cough as she checked her wristwatch. "Bang on five a.m."

Smoke made lazy spirals toward the ceiling from her cigarette, then did a sharp right turn when it strayed into the AC current that had just kicked on. The low hum gave a questioning voice to the waiting silence.

Peg lifted the cigarette and inhaled it, then released more smoke from her mouth and nose in a weary sigh. "I've started setting my watch by your bladder."

"My plumbing and I are glad we could help. Really." Dani sat up and peeled the sheet off her sticky body. She felt like she'd run a marathon instead of merely survived another night's sleep in protective custody. Her body was too stiff to get vertical without assistance.

The book-laden nightstand was all there was, so she used it. The flimsy wooden pedestal rocked perilously, then sent her stack of books tumbling to the floor in a jumbled heap. *The Two Towers*, second in Tolkien's *Lord of the Rings* trilogy, landed between her feet with a symbolic thump.

Dani had enjoyed the books more when she'd had less in common with the sturdy, stalked hobbit, Frodo. Probably not a good idea to name the man who hunted her after Frodo's Nemesis, particularly with the sun playing coy in the east.

In her own home, back in the days when no one wanted to kill her, Dani would have immediately stooped to pick up her books. She wanted to be that person now. She hated this drop in standards nearly as much as the endless waiting, but bending wasn't yet on her possibles list this morning.

She plowed doggedly through the mess. In the bathroom she groped for the light switch then flinched as light flooded the small space. The mirror reflected her image without mercy.

Ouch. In the old days, on a good day and in the right light, she passed for attractive. She touched the lines around her eyes. Bad day, wrong light.

Life was hard enough without the added stress of being hunted like Bambi's mother, though it was a good way to lose weight. Yesterday she'd seen her hip bones for the first time in years.

They didn't look as good as she'd remembered.

"Note to myself," she muttered, "never again make a note to myself to *lose weight even if it kills you.*"

If ever there were a time to be in denial, this was it.

Dani draped a towel over the mirror and turned her attention to what had brought her into the bathroom.

Physical relief achieved, she turned on the water, washed her hands, then filled two glasses and carried them back into the bedroom. One she handed to Peg, the other she lifted in a mocking toast. "To the dawn. May it come quickly."

Peg obliged by clicking her glass against Dani's, before edging back the blinds just enough to study the sky. "It's already getting lighter."

"That's good." Dani accepted the lie, despite a brief glimpse of blue velvet untouched by light. She sipped the water, her hand not quite steady. The sense of menace felt sharper tonight, as if Dark Lord had tapped into her fear and was using it to track her.

It's just your imagination. Dani took a long drink of water. It's a *safe* house, remember?

Another drink of water. It didn't erase the acrid taste of fear from her mouth or ease the dryness in her throat, and it tasted woefully flat to a palate conditioned to a Diet Dr. Pepper wake-up call. A pity she drank the last can yesterday evening. Neuman, the special agent-in-charge, had promised to bring her more when he and McBride came back. She frowned. Odd they hadn't returned yet.

She lowered her glass and found Peg watching her. This wasn't unusual. They all watched her, their eyes reflecting varying degrees of professional worry and distant pity. Probably looking for signs she was about to break.

I bend, not break, she could have told them, if they'd asked. Breaking wasn't an option until after her day in court. She'd made a promise to a dead woman.

Dani dropped into the desk chair, propped her elbow on the smooth *faux* wood surface and cradled the cool glass against her aching temple. The furtive light winked off Peg's glass as she took a drink, her hand quivering slightly from the effort.

They made quite a pair—the romance writer and the marshal—brought together by capricious fate. Too bad Peg had the misfortune to look enough like Dani to be her sister, though her recent visit to the ER had made that resemblance closer to a *twin* sister. The dim light deepened the hollows in Peg's cheeks and washed out all color but the bruising under her eyes.

How did Peg do it, Dani wondered? How had she puked her guts out, then dragged her butt back here to play decoy for a killer one last night?

It's my job wasn't enough of an answer. Peg didn't have to be here. In a few hours Dani would be transferred into the care and keeping of the Denver Marshals district. They'd have responsibility for getting her safely into court next week. Peg could have stayed in the hospital. She'd done her duty, above and way beyond.

Instead she'd come back a couple of hours ago, claiming her multiple hurl had been caused by the Chinese they'd had for their last supper together. Even the original OJ jury wouldn't have bought a selective food poisoning theory.

Not that Dani wasn't grateful. It would've been harder to face the dismal dawn with just the men for company. They were good guys and reassuringly competent, but there was something about a "community of women," no matter how small, that made the waiting bearable.

"You gonna make it 'till Neuman and McBride get back?" Dani asked.

"I'm okay."

"Yeah, sure." *You're okay. I'm okay. We're all okay*—and Clinton didn't inhale. "You shouldn't have come back."

"I'm fine," Peg insisted, looking at her watch before taking another drag on her cigarette.

"You didn't tell Neuman, did you?" Dani almost envied her that cigarette. Popping an M&M didn't have nearly the dramatic effect of blowing smoke, which was practically the international symbol for waiting.

"He'll find out when he comes."

"He'll be pissed." Dani didn't mind Neuman getting pissed. She didn't mind anything that relieved the monotony. Who would have thought trying not to get killed could be so boring?

"He'll get over it." Peg hesitated. "And it's only for a few more hours."

"Yeah, a few more hours." Dani set down her glass, splashing water perilously close to her laptop. Surprised at her lack of precision, she moved the glass onto the window sill, then dabbed at the damp with the corner of her tee shirt.

The Velcro edge of her money belt scraped her wrist with yet another reminder of how far from home, how far from normal she'd traveled. Was it petty to miss her purse with all its useful and useless bits and pieces? To sweat the myriad of small things she couldn't do until she testified in court? To be so weary of this portable existence she almost didn't care anymore?

Probably.

Easier to sweat the small things than contemplate the big ones. Like dying before she made it into court—

"So what are you and Neuman going to do once you've handed me off?" Dani asked in a rush.

"Do? Neuman and I? What do you mean?" Peg's voice sounded a little too noncommittal.

"Did you think *I* wouldn't notice the hearts and flowers whenever you and Neuman are in the same room?"

"I suppose you can't help seeing romance everywhere you look." Weary gave way to ironic in Peg's eyes.

"It's one of the main requirements for writing it." Dani turned sideways, trailing her hands across the quiescent keyboard of her laptop. From habit her fingers settled in home position on the smooth, cool keys. The dark screen looked naked without her words scrolling across it, the words that kept her sane and paid the bills after her marriage fell apart, the stories that gave her a place to escape to in the past few months.

"Did you get your story sorted out?" Peg asked. "I was hoping I could read the last two chapters before I leave."

"Like the real people in my life, my characters are proving difficult."

A wan smile edged Peg's mouth. "I expect you'll have *them* whipped into shape before your deadline."

"I expect I will." Dani realized she was tapping out an SOS on the keyboard and jerked her hands back, but not before Peg heard the soft sound of the keys.

"You can't start writing now. They'll be here soon and I'm not hanging out that damn boa," she said, referring to the joke gift the guys had given Dani for her birthday last month, a gift that Dani had converted into a Do Not Disturb sign while working against the double deadline imposed by trial and editor.

Dani grinned. In the past six months, the guys had reluctantly given up a lot of preconceptions about romance writers. They still wanted to believe that romance writers worked naked except for a strategically placed boa. Dani had felt obliged to point out that naked was very cold and most women didn't like uncovering what time and gravity had done to their parts.

They gave her that one, but clung stubbornly to the conviction that romance authors were sex-starved idiots, this despite the fact that she'd failed to jump any of their bones or the long hours she put in at the keyboard. They did seem surprised she could write under the circumstances.

Even with "The File," they didn't understand she'd never missed a deadline. She wasn't about to let a hired killer or her murderous ex-brother-in-law cause her to miss this one. Besides, it was something to do in between getting grilled by Richard's slime ball defense attorney. He'd stopped short of accusing her of the murder, but she expected to be trying on gloves and Bruno Magi shoes when Richard's trial finally got under way. If—

"I'm not planning to work," Dani hurried into speech again.

"So, what are you doing?"

"I'm—" not about to admit she was SOS-ing, Dani improvised, "thinking about going online. I could check out the chat rooms, see if my favorite ex-spy is around." He and her other online friends had, in a strange way, kept her anchored to the real world, been her lifeline to the normal.

"I'll never understand that online shit." Peg shook her

head wearily. "And if Neuman finds out about your little incursions into cyberspace, it'll be my ass—"

"He won't find out. Besides, he's obviously too hot for your ass to care." Dani flipped on the power, waiting impatiently for the machine to complete the booting-up process so she could access her online program. When she was in, she hit the dial command. "Why don't you lie down? Catch a few Zs? Nothing happening for a few more hours."

"Not when I'm on duty."

"You're not on duty. You're not even supposed to be here—" Dani frowned at the screen. "That's odd."

"What's odd?"

"I'm not getting a dial tone." Dani tried the dial command again. Still nothing. "Is something wrong with the phone?" She looked at Peg.

Peg hesitated. In that tiny moment of silence, they both heard a muffled thud in the next room.

Chapter Two

Against the peaceful back drop of the Rocky Mountains, middle-class subdivision and rising sun, the sprawl of emergency vehicles around the burnt-out house looked starkly obscene. Fire hoses snaked across the trampled lawn from the opening where the front door had been. Wisps of smoke drifted out from the blackened interior. Uniformed personnel picked their way across the debris-strewn lawn. Outside the official perimeter, neighbors, still in bathrobes, offered their impressions to a press corps filling time while waiting for an official statement from the Denver Police Department. A gray sedan nosed its way into the mess, moving with determined care through the press of people and vehicles, pulling into a spot between a fire engine and the coroner's wagon. Though dressed casually, the woman and two men who climbed out of the car examined the scene with a more than casual thoroughness.

A DPD officer saw them and approached, his arms extended to wave them off. "You can't park there—"

Matt's dark, detached gaze choked off the effort to stop him even before he flashed his badge.

"Matthew Kirby, United States Marshals Service."

Nature had made Matt a hunter long before the government gave him his license to hunt. Time took nature's gift and honed him into a force to be reckoned with.

His powerful, stocky body radiated raw aggression held in check. Determination beamed out of eyes set deep in a face hammered out of mountain rock. Blunt features neither asked nor gave quarter. He brushed his hair straight back from his high broad hairline, unconcerned by its recession or the lines cutting deep into the weathered skin around mouth and eyes.

Only his full lower lip and a lift in the straight dark brows gave any indication that softness was possible, but not preferred.

A man of nature, part of the rugged mountains at his back, the requirements of civilization on him looked as uneasy as the tie knotted around the strong column of his neck. His conservative suit jacket both confined and contained the broad shoulders that angled down to lean hips and powerful legs. A white shirt threw into sharp relief the tan burned deep into his skin. His booted feet planted, his large, square hands thrust into the pockets of his jeans, he looked immovable. In motion, he was unstoppable.

The police officer read the warning signs and chose not to get in his way.

"Who's in charge?" An undercurrent of annoyance threaded harshly into Matt's husky bass.

The cop gestured toward a woman and two men standing in the driveway. "I guess that would be the fire marshal. Or Henshaw. She's from Homicide. Over there, talking to the coroner's man."

"Right." Matt jerked his chin toward the house. "Let's go."

He started forward, got blocked by two firefighters coiling a hose and hunched his shoulders impatiently. "What a screw-up. Deputy Neuman oughta be shot."

"All right." Toby Riggs hitched up his pants; they immediately sagged back into folds on his tennis shoes. He took a big bite of his Egg McMuffin, chewing it with messy relish.

If Matt was rock, Riggs was malleable clay. He tried to

adhere to the Marshals Service dress code, but some factor in his biology resisted spit and polish. Fortunately his untidy exterior and sleepy-cow-grazing gaze hid a brain designed for solving puzzles and filtering minute details, securing his future in the Marshals Service.

His voice muffled by its passage through egg and muffin, Riggs added, "If he's not a crispy critter."

"Crispy critter?" Alice Kerne's sculpted brows rose. An attractive black woman balancing confidently atop spiked heels, her designer jeans and silk blouse hinted at the crisp intelligence that made her a good foil for Matt and Riggs. Alice was far more than a nod to affirmative action. No one stayed on Matt's team to appease or please.

The marshal's badge suspended from a chain about her neck, swayed between her generous breasts when she shifted her weight from one foot to the other. "Not exactly sensitive, Riggs."

He looked grieved. "I'm the most sensitive guy in the office—"

"Compared to—?"

"Alice," Matt cut her off, "you got those files faxed to us from New Orleans this morning?"

She lifted a leather folder then her brows in reproach that he'd asked. Matt let her look pass. Her punishment waited inside the house. It was part of the job she wanted. The Supreme Court said he had to give it to her. At least Alice didn't whine when she got it.

"You're with me, Alice. Riggs, take the perimeter." Their path finally clear, Matt strode forward. Inside they ran into a wall of heat, thinning smoke and the stench of cooked flesh.

Matt held his ground, breathing shallowly until his sense of smell adjusted, a trick he'd learned from a coroner at his first crime scene. He had no tricks for his eyes or mind to use to aid him in looking at the blackened, barely human forms amid the still-smoking remains of the living room. Around them, like grim sentinels, skeletons of what had been furniture dotted the gutted room, while electric wires dangled uselessly overhead.

"I guess we won't be needing their ID photos," Alice said, a sudden pallor leaving islands of makeup on her face.

"How many?" Matt asked.

"Three." The fire marshal, a grotesque parody of Kris Kringle in grimy gear, rubbed his face tiredly.

Matt looked at Alice, saw his own question reflected in her eyes. They'd been faxed files on five deputy marshals. Dani Gwynne's file had already been in the office in anticipation of her transfer to their jurisdiction. "All the bodies here?"

The man nodded. "Our people found them when they got the fire under control."

"Looks like you caught the fire before it spread too far." Alice's eyes stayed carefully blank as she studied the disposition of the dead.

"Neighbor called it in early." The homicide detective, Henshaw, spoke this time. A sturdy, competent woman with tired eyes, a smoke-smudged face, she had the inevitable chip on her shoulder from surviving in the intensely male world of law enforcement. "Baby woke her up. She saw the glow in the windows. As soon as the fire was out, we moved in. When we found the badges, we called you."

A fireman signaled to the fire marshal, who muttered an excuse and left. Matt looked at Henshaw. "Your people been over the scene?"

Henshaw's gaze passed briefly over the black mounds. "Just a prelim. At least one of them got it in the kitchen.

There's enough blood in there to float a boat. Our guy says—"

She drew her hand across her throat.

"In the kitchen with the knife," Alice murmured, giving Matt a quick look. "Quick and quiet."

"They all get caught napping?" Matt asked. He kept his face cool, but couldn't do anything about the tension that had started a knot between his shoulder blades. Only one man he knew could pull off a hit this thorough, this messy, and get away clean. Ten years since their last meeting. Matt would've been happy to make that twenty.

"Maybe one insomniac in a bedroom." Henshaw nodded toward a hallway to their right, then hid a yawn behind her hand. "Can I get my people started? We've been here two hours already."

Matt nodded. "Have them start in the kitchen. Oh, and tell your guy when he does the blood work to look for the latest in tranqs. This guy likes to neutralize everyone but his target victim before he kills. Let's go look at that bedroom, Alice."

About halfway along the narrow hallway, the scorching marks of the fire faded into light brown carpet, but the choking smell of smoke and death lingered.

"Looks like he dragged them to the living room after he killed them, then started the fire." Alice kept to one side of the rusty brown trail that ran down the center of the hall nearly obscured in places by sooty boot marks. She hesitated, then burst out, "Why move them? Why the fire?"

Matt stepped over the marks into the first bedroom. "With this perp, the why only matters to him."

"You've seen this before?"

"Yeah," he moved slowly about the room, not touching anything. "I've seen this before."

The dawning sun entered the room uneasily, falling on rumpled bed sheets, messy with the marks of recent violence. A service revolver hung in a holster over the edge of the bed, just inches from the blood-splattered pillow. No insomniac here.

Matt moved to the next room, probably the witness's. Like the previous room, rumpled bed covers were tossed back, but the violence that had invaded this room hadn't touched the bed. Looked like most of it went into a crumpled throw rug, except for the bloody trail heading out the door towards the killer's funeral pyre.

A lamp lay in pieces between an overturned nightstand and desk chair. Scattering of books. Whether it indicated serious resistance or just a sloppy landing, he couldn't tell.

If there had been resistance, it had not lasted long.

Hard to believe in God at crime scenes and yet—

A pragmatic man, not prone to imagining things, still Matt felt the difference in a room where death came quietly and one where the victim saw it coming.

This one saw it coming, fought it hard.

Matt stepped into the room through air still thick with smoke and betrayed trust.

Alice propped a shoulder against the doorframe and pulled out the witness's file, scanning quickly for information they didn't need to know. Matt didn't stop her. They all had their own routine for coping. Alice liked to bond with the victim. Probably a female thing. He liked to keep his distance.

"Started here, ended here," Alice said. "She was here in Denver for a book signing when she spotted her ex-brother-in-law and former upstanding citizen, Richard Hastings, pop someone."

"Upstanding citizen with his own hit man?" Matt looked

at her with one brow arched.

Alice made a movement that could have been a nod or a shrug as she studied the page. "The vic is Dani Gwynne, divorced romance writer." She found a photo, studied it briefly, and then handed it to him. "She doesn't look like a romance writer or a murder witness."

What she looked like didn't matter any more, but he was curious to see what a romance writer looked like, so he studied the photo.

Alice was right, she didn't look like a romance writer or like what they'd seen in the living room. Her face looked too alive to be dead, surprisingly attractive. Weren't romance writers frustrated wallflowers or something?

Her face had a mature beauty, as opposed to the walking corpses of fashion runways and Hollywood semi-prostitutes. A charm that owed nothing to youth, artifice or surgical enhancement and everything to character, though he was sure Alice would insist her good bones helped. The lines at the edges of her green eyes and smiling mouth, the fullness time had added to her figure, Matt considered a plus. He'd lost his taste for the young when he quit being young.

Matt frowned down at the photo, uncomfortable with the odd feeling that he had missed something by not knowing her.

Still holding her picture, he started around the perimeter of the room, looking without touching, avoiding the places where her blood had turned brown in the matted carpet.

"Caucasian female, thirty-four years old, five feet nine inches tall, wouldn't give them her weight—with an appendix scar on her right abdomen and another in the hairline above her left ear." Alice looked up. "Seems she fell off a ladder when she was six and is—*was* afraid of heights."

Matt found he didn't want the details of her life, not

while assessing the chaos of her death. Every detail brought her more into focus. *She* wasn't what he should be focusing on.

"Divorced soon after her eighteen-month-old daughter, Megan, was killed in a car accident. Her ex, brother to Mr. Upstanding, was driving when it happened and dedicated himself to alcohol." She looked at Matt. "That sucks."

They ought to know, he thought wryly. They had both done time in divorce court.

"Likes to read—obviously," Alice gave the scattered books a pointed look, "and write, does amateur theater, loves New Orleans jazz and pastries, is interested in computers, likes to surf the Internet." Alice looked up. "We could be soul mates if she'd lose the computer crap. A friend just gave me one of her books to read. I—liked it. It had heart."

"Really?" What the hell did that mean? Matt used the tip of his pen to slide open the dresser drawers. They were all empty. On the desk was a laptop, plugged into both the electrical and telephone plug, the switch in the "on" position. If she had been working that might explain why she had been awake. The telephone line to the computer was interesting—mostly because it shouldn't have been there.

"Let's take the laptop with us after forensics has been over it," Matt said.

"Okay." Alice flipped to the next page of Dani's file. "Hmmm . . . can't live without Diet Dr. Pepper and M&M's. She has good taste in junk food."

"Isn't that a contradiction in terms?" Matt used the pen to sift through the contents of the wastebasket and found confirmation of her junk food preferences. He turned to the closet. On the rod hung a tee shirt with the words, "My life is filled with romance, lust, danger, and dust balls the size of cattle" written across the front. Next to it was a severe black dress, the kind witnesses wear so juries will know they are telling the truth. Next to it was a long, purple feather boa.

Intrigued, Matt held it out for Alice to see. "Standard equipment for romance writing?"

Alice grinned. "Maybe she was planning to wear it at the trial. Wouldn't Sheridan have had a cow."

Her obvious regret at missing the reaction of the prosecuting attorney kept the grin on Matt's face as he stepped into the bathroom. The first thing he saw was a towel, dry but with the indefinable look of having been used, slung over the mirror. What hadn't she wanted to see, he wondered, the grin fading abruptly.

A few personal items cluttered the ledge above the sink, all obviously well used. On the tub was a small bottle of shampoo. He bent close and sniffed, catching the faint scent of—coconut? Not flowers or spice. No, the romance writer chose to smell like fruit. It didn't fit with the image of the boa or the M&M's. But then, what would?

Against his better judgment, he looked at the photograph again, trying to fit her face with what he'd learned and failing. The character in the curving oval of her face didn't mesh with a purple boa. Cool green eyes with integrity and an M&M's addiction? A determined chin, the sunlight striking gold in her hair, and color warming creamy skin defied the unalterable reality of her death.

"She traveled light," he heard Alice say. She moved into his sight line and knelt by the tumbled pile of books, "except for these."

He could have got a dig in on Alice, who was notorious for not traveling light. When he didn't, she looked up, her brows arched.

"You find something?"

"No." He leaned against the doorframe and watched Alice perform a visual catalog of a dead woman's reading material. Maybe it would answer his questions, put his unease—and the romance writer—to rest.

"Interesting mix. JD Robb, Tom Clancy, Tonya Huff, Alastair Maclean, a couple of romances—oh, look, an advance copy of Kelly Kerwin's new historical. Too bad it's evidence." He heard the hopeful question in Alice's voice and grunted in the negative. She sighed. "Orson Scot Card, I've heard he's good. Here's your personal favorite: Louis L'Amour's *Last of the Breed*—"

The romance writer had liked the story about a man who refused to settle for what was possible? Matt frowned. Too bad this was the real world where what was possible was the only option available.

Sometimes not even that.

"—the Bible, and something called *Lord of the Rings*," she twisted her head to see better, "which seems to be two books of a fantasy trilogy about some ring. Oh, there's the other one, by your foot."

Matt read the title through a smattering of the romance writer's blood.

"You all right?" Alice stood up, looking at him in concern.

He rubbed away the sweat beading on his forehead. "It's hot."

"As an oven." She looked around. "Damn shame."

"Yeah." Beyond Alice, Matt saw the bed, the white sheets thrown back, the pillow bunched against the headboard as if she'd had trouble getting comfortable.

Stronger than before, he felt her passionate rejection of the death that life had dealt her. She had not gone quietly into the night in this dreary little room. Like something tangible, he could feel her demanding that he—what? He couldn't change what had happened.

He could only hunt her killer.

He handed Alice the photo.

"We done here?" Her voice carefully neutral, she secured the file and tucked it back under her arm.

"Yeah. Put a call in. Have Henry start pulling up everything he can find on a hit man named Jonathan Hayes—" Matt broke off as Riggs came in. "What you got?"

"Killer did a first-class job of bypassing the security system. Cut the phone lines, too. Fire boys trampled the area pretty thoroughly outside, but I did find one thing that doesn't quite fit."

"What's that?"

"The flower bed outside this room is all torn up."

"Really?" Matt pulled the curtains back and found the window off the latch and ajar. "Show me."

Outside Matt followed the marks in the flower bed to where they stopped by the corner of the house. Had someone stood there, perhaps straining to hear or see in the pre-dawn dark, while the orange glow of fire flickered nearby? They had three members of the team still unaccounted for. If someone had survived why hadn't they phoned home?

Alice came around the corner of the house and Matt turned to her. "Got something?"

"How do you feel about the resurrected?" she said.

"What?"

She shrugged. "Neuman and McBride aren't crispy critters after all."

Riggs looked disappointed. "Does that make them the bad guys or one bad guy and one dupe?"

"Let's go find out." Matt frowned. Two down, one left to account for. Maybe one of them could explain how Jonathan Hayes had found and killed three people as easy as taking a walk in the park.

Out of the mouth of Deputy US Marshal Ricky Neuman, the explanation left Matt's thirst for answers seriously unquenched.

"Two deputies and Gwynne were in the house when we left to take Peg—Deputy Oliver—to the hospital," Neuman said, his clean-cut, nice guy face white with shock. "McBride came with me."

That accounted for everyone. So why was his gut still insisting that something didn't add up? Matt exchanged a quick look with Riggs before he said, "You screwed up, Neuman."

Neuman shoved a trembling hand through his dark thatch of hair, marring the perfect line. "No shit."

Either he was seriously shaken up or a damn big loss to Hollywood, Matt thought grimly. "You didn't smell a rat in your op when your girl got sick?"

"Of course I did! I've been smelling a rat since I got this detail! I asked the hospital to run tests—sent McBride off to arrange a move, but—"

Matt bit back a blistering critique. "Go to the hospital and talk to her, Alice."

Neuman looked up, spots of color coming into his cheeks. "I'll go with you. It's going to hit Peg hard—"

"That's the down side of a blown op." His strangely mixed feelings put a sharp edge to Matt's voice. "Isn't that right, Alice?"

"That's right." Her face was as unforgiving as Matt felt.

"And you'll break it to her gently, won't you?"

"Gentle's my middle name," Alice said.

Right after "castrating bitch," according to her ex-husband, Matt recalled with grim humor. Course, he'd gotten on her bad side. Not a good place to be.

"I want—"

"I don't give a rat's ass what you want, Neuman." Over Neuman's shoulder Matt saw the first body being wheeled out of the house. "You're still on duty. Or maybe you don't care if we catch the son of a bitch that killed your witness and your people?"

"You bastard." Neuman's fists clenched.

"Try it," Matt said, wishing he would. He had been wanting to hit something or someone since he got the call from PD. Maybe Neuman realized it. He didn't try.

The sun climbed slowly at first, finally springing free of the mountains to throw warm light across the park bench Dani had been sitting on since the first rush of adrenaline subsided. Dry air felt cool against her face, the polar opposite of New Orleans in August. It was oddly pleasant to be dry instead of soggy, to sit gazing at a spare view rather than a lush one.

She wasn't afraid. She had seen Dark Lord leave, chillingly confidant that he'd completed his bloody task. No, this was shock. She should know. She'd been here, done this when her baby died.

In a tree above her head, a bird trilled a cheerful morning song. Startled by the sound, Dani looked up at the tree and got blinded by the painful yellow halo of sun behind it.

It shouldn't be there, not after what happened.

"Dismantle the sun, pour away the ocean and sweep up the woods: For nothing now can ever come to any good . . ."

The poem by Auden emerged from the past. Right for

the moment, right to remember it now when she was once more a surprised survivor in life's lottery. Richard had read it at Megan's funeral ten years ago. There seemed a perverse symmetry in linking the poignant past to the painful present. Richard was such an important part of both, more so even than Steven, his brother who was Meggie's father and Dani's ex-husband. Odd to know now, when it was too late, who was important and who wasn't.

Odder to be alive when she should be dead. Three times should be out. Sure as hell wasn't a charm to find herself once again upright and looking at death. The three deaths swirled through her mind on the other side of shock's cushion, beckoning her to join them where fear and pain no longer ruled. Soon . . .

She heard a muted roar as a fire engine trundled the length of the park across from her then turned ponderously into the flow of traffic. She had watched it arrive. Now it was leaving, followed by the ambulance carrying the bodies of the men and woman who had died to keep her alive.

When it was out of sight, she picked up her backpack from the park bench with the same automatic reflex that made her grab it from the closet floor and added it to the weight of their deaths on her shoulders.

Relieved to still be in shock, she turned east, toward the rising sun and the cluster of skyscrapers that was downtown Denver.

Chapter Three

Jonathan Hayes stood at the sink and watched the water turn red as it ran over the dried blood on his hands. It felt almost as good as it had when it was slick and warm, gushing fresh from gaping flesh in a life-stealing surge.

During his time in the CIA he had learned there were two ways to get away with murder—disappear the evidence or disappear the perpetrator. Fate had fitted him perfectly to do the disappearing. Hayes had a pale, malleable face, even paler blonde hair and skin so fair it was almost white. His washed out blue eyes were easy to hide behind colored contacts. His lean length easily conformed to various body types, shapes and even sexes.

For one hit he'd done a version of Victor/Victoria, pretending to be a man pretending to be a woman pretending to be a man when he'd been hired to kill a paranoid and heavily guarded government official. The idiot had been trying to take too big a bite out of the drug profits passing through his country's banks.

A strange little man, Hayes recalled with a reminiscent smile, who sublimated his homosexual proclivities by making his whores dress like men. In the end the little man had been ridiculously easy to take down. Like so many of his victims, he was only as strong as his weakest link. A most satisfying kill.

Though not as beautiful as tonight's kill. How could it match the joy of a nice, clear field with time to enjoy the feel of his knife going through struggling flesh. Time to wash in the blood. Time for the fire that took away his pain. Time to slip away, anonymous once more. Just another Joe on his way to catch the bus. A Joe with blood on the hands shoved in the pockets of his jacket. A Joe with a face no one would remember.

" 'Somewhere, everywhere, now hidden, now apparent,' " he murmured, " 'is the form of a human being. If we seek to know him, are we idly occupied?' "

They could seek him where they would. They would find him nowhere. He was wind. He was water. He was, he smiled again, harder to find than a tax cut—a visible invisible man.

It was so simple. Only the killing was complicated, though he hadn't meant it to be that way the first time. It is said that anyone is capable of murder in the right circumstances. Theory had merged with circumstances when his former employers at the CIA sent the hit squad after him. He'd started the first fire to hide the bloody frenzy, to burn away his guilt, then fled up the rock face of Long's Peak to escape society's retribution.

His fear had been so all consuming that at first he didn't realize he wasn't in pain. Hadn't realized that in killing he'd found a respite from the headaches that had plagued him all his life, something years of doctors and his parents constantly migrating religious beliefs had failed to achieve.

Freedom from pain was something he could believe in and the pattern that brought that ease became his religion. He wasn't some maniacal serial killer. He killed for a higher purpose. With each death his belief in his new religion grew. Strict adherence to the pattern not only eased his pain, but he came to believe it protected him from discovery. Somewhere along the way he started to believe it freed his victims, too.

" 'Let there be light! said God, and there was light! Let there be blood! says man, and there's a sea!' "

Lord Byron understood the nature of man, understood the call of blood, the wonder of light-giving fire. Hayes smeared the water-softened blood over his hands. To-morrow the climb up Long's Peak would complete the pattern. By then, his employer should have deposited his money in the Swiss bank account and it would be available for him to play with.

His religion did not require a vow of poverty.

He liked the things money could buy: his anonymous existence; information about his victims; the expensive, high tech equipment that finally led him to Willow.

The High Priest needed a High Priestess. Abstinence wouldn't be part of his religion for much longer. He had been alone too long. Soon Willow would submit to the pattern. The student would become her teacher.

Hayes turned his hand, letting the water flow across the back where blood crusted in the blonde hairs, turning them dark and stiff. He rubbed up red, thinking how sweet it had been when the woman fought for her life. Blood smelt so much sweeter when it was filled with fear, was more satisfying when it poured out hot and fast. It had been a good kill. A very good kill.

Strange how much he'd needed her death. He'd even dreamed about her in the days before, killing her again and again, only to wake empty with longing for the peace her death would give him.

Now, finally, it was here. It was done. She was dead.

The water ran pale pink now, the blood almost gone. He swirled his fingers in the last traces. He would bathe in it if he could—

He wasn't prepared when his peace detonated. Wasn't

ready when the pain came roaring like a storm over Long's Peak, with about as much mercy. Jagged spikes of agony shot down the sides of his head. He clutched those sides, dug palms into the pain, a low, feral moan squeezed through drawn-back lips.

It was not supposed to happen this way—

" '. . . it is much more than the thorn, it is the *dagger* in my flesh!' " he cried. "She's dead. So perfectly dead—"

She had fought death, fought going into the good night on a river of blood and fire—

No. *She* hadn't.

He dropped in front of his notebook computer, fumbling for the disk that held the data on Dani Gwynne. A few key strokes brought up her picture for him to compare with his memory of the kill. The differences were slight, but so critically important.

The difference between pain and peace.

"Ricky Neuman. Niall McBride. Peg Oliver." Matt finished pinning the last picture on the cork wall to the right side of his desk. Behind him a bank of windows gave a generous view of the uneven skyline that was downtown Denver, with the jagged splendor of the Rocky Mountains serving as a backdrop. Inside, the hum of legal activity made a soothing accompaniment to thought. "The survivors of Gwynne's protection op."

"You think one of them did the dirty?" Henry Robb, the youngest member of their team, had a baby face and innocent eyes that hid a good brain, liberally laced with ambition. His already receding brown hair was pulled back into a ragged ponytail that had taken the place of a failed mustache. He'd come to the Marshals Service straight out of college, attracted by the diversity of the Service's responsibilities and their nearly squeaky clean image. He hated anyone who marred that image more than he hated looking his age.

"Probably." Matt paced back to his desk, dropped in the chair and leaned back with his legs stretched out. He'd shoved Gwynne's file in his out box, but her face refused to be shoved out of his head. She was gone. Her individuality, her humanity had been reduced to a charred bundle awaiting final identification at the morgue.

It didn't help. Ugly reality couldn't so easily exorcise the regret that had dogged him since he walked into the room where she had died or take from his memory the imprint of her questioning face.

"Neuman seems the obvious choice." Henry sat on the edge of his desk, rolling a pencil between fingers beginning to lose their nicotine stain. "His girl was clear when Hayes hit."

"Yeah. Obvious. That's why we're gonna check them all right down to their toenails." Putting Hayes out of business would scratch Matt's itch and remove the romance writer from his head. It wouldn't be easy. They would take all the steps they always did to find Hayes, but unless they could think of something more than that to do—

Hayes knew the routine and hadn't made any of the usual mistakes. So far the most unrelenting search had failed to bring anyone within sniffing distance of him.

Just to make sure that hadn't changed, Matt grabbed the thick mass that was Hayes's file, separated half for Henry and flipped his share open. "Looks like Hayes has been a busy little bastard during the last ten years."

Henry grimaced at a photo from a previous crime scene. "Why does he move the bodies, then torch them?"

"Profiler thinks he's got some kind of skewed religious

fixation, based on the way he arranges the bodies, then starts the fire in a circle around them." Matt flipped quickly through the pages, looking for any indication they had gotten close to catching Hayes since their last encounter. Even some additional personal information might help. There was nothing new except the dead.

Six inches of what he'd done. A millimeter of what he was.

"A religious hit man. Now there's a combo you don't find very often."

"Hayes is an original." Matt shoved the file away and leaned back, clasping his hands behind his head so he could apply some pressure where a headache was starting. "We got a shit load of evidence to convict him if we ever catch up with him."

"He looks—dull." Henry held Hayes's photo at arms length, squinted at it, then tossed it back on the file. "How come we got his picture and fingerprints?"

"He did some contract work for the CIA."

"A CIA killer? Damn."

Matt shook his head. "He didn't kill for them. His specialty was computers. Tracking, hacking and crashing."

Henry looked surprised. "Computer geek to killer-for-hire. Interesting career move. There's not much personal information here. Spooks keeping the good stuff back?"

Matt's grin was harsh. "They'd like you to think that. I got a source inside that says he's turned his computer skills on them, took out his own file and a hefty retirement fund. Basically, he's a thief. His first kill was to protect his own ass. Guess he liked it. The only other solid intel I've got is that Hayes is a fanatic rock climber. Everything else is theory and supposition. Bastard doesn't even have personal contacts that we know of. Does his business by untraceable, coded e-mail and Swiss bank accounts, according to one snitch, just before Hayes popped him."

Matt got up and added Hayes's photo to the rogue's gallery side of his bulletin board, stabbing the pin through paper and cork, then turned his attention to the other three faces.

Ricky Neuman had a good, but not perfect record. His first time working with Peg Oliver, proximity had apparently overwhelmed professionalism. The question was, had his attraction for Oliver distracted Neuman from the job? Or was he a rat who decided to keep her breathing after he fell for her?

Niall McBride had done a decent, though short stint in the Service. Left the New Orleans Police Department because of the residency requirement. Considered a rising star. Getting married before Christmas to a home-town girl.

Then there was Peg Oliver. Picked because she looked like Gwynne in bad light. Top-notch service record. Practically the affirmative action poster girl for the Service. Tough job playing dead ringer for the witness. Dangerous, too, unless she knew she would be hurling at the local emergency room when Hayes came calling with his knife and box of matches.

If he couldn't get at Hayes directly, maybe his accomplice would lead him to the bastard. He turned back to Henry.

"Let's put our three survivors under the big microscope. Toss their lives, turn over every rock. Look down their pants and up her skirt if you have to. I want the rat in the woodpile."

"Right." Henry stood up with a youthful air of determination.

Matt looked at his watch. "How come we haven't heard

anything from Riggs? Or Alice?"

Before Henry could answer, the telephone rang. Matt cut the ring in half by grabbing the receiver. "Kirby."

"You need to work on your phone etiquette."

He tucked the telephone under his ear. "Alice? What the hell took you so long?"

"Unlike you, I'm not part bloodhound." Her voice in the ear piece was strangely breathless. "She's gone."

"What?" If Peg Oliver wasn't at the hospital, where was she? With his elbows resting on Hayes' file, he rubbed the bridge of his nose.

"She checked herself out last night. No one knows when."

"Really." What did it mean? Where did it fit into the little they did know? Three confirmed dead, two in hand and seriously under suspicion, and one missing marshal with footsteps leading away from a window. Whose footsteps?

"That's not all. Oliver did not just happen to get sick yesterday. According to the lab report, she ingested a large helping of ipecac."

"Now that's very interesting. Either someone wanted her out of the way—" Matt leaned back in his chair, rocking slightly.

"—or she wanted very badly to be out of the way. If she did it to herself, she gave herself a rough ride. Doc was surprised she could walk. According to him she almost turned herself inside out and upside down."

"Doc tell her about the ipecac?"

"Late last night, before she went AWOL."

Oliver's disappearance opened all kinds of interesting possibilities. Matt frowned, trying to slow his racing thoughts before they ran out of fuel and left him out on a limb. "I'll put an APB out on Oliver. You head over to the coroner. Squeeze a quick ID on the bodies out of him."

Alice hesitated. "You don't think Oliver went back to the safe house—"

"Depends which side she was on. It's what I'd do if I found out I'd upchucked something rotten in Denmark." Matt kept his voice dryly factual, but couldn't stop his heart stepping up the beats. If Oliver had gone back to the safe house, they were one body short. Now they had to find out which body. Real fast.

Alice was quiet, then said carefully, "From what I've heard, Hayes isn't likely to make—mistakes."

Matt angled his chair so he could see Oliver's photo on the board. "They say everyone has a twin."

He heard her quick drawn breath.

"You see why I need that ID?"

"Hope no one else does," Alice said. "I'm on it."

Dani had been in hiding long enough to feel strange merging with the stream of people moving along the side-walks between the sheltering rise of skyscrapers. It didn't keep her from walking, mostly because she didn't know how to stop, afraid if she did stop, the things she had seen would breach shock's cushion and overwhelm her.

It was an odd sort of panic that spun her forward. A tornado of mixed emotion she was in no shape to sort through. She half-expected to look back and find people and build-ings tossed and tumbled in her wake. So she didn't look back.

A Don't Walk flashed from across the street. Habit stopped her on the edge of the curb. The need to keep moving shuddered through her. She could end the replay of what happened at the safe house before it started. End the one of her baby's dead body in a miniature casket. End it all against the hard metal of moving objects out in the street. No more fear. No more empty arms. No more guilt—

She turned from temptation toward a department store window, seeing without really seeing, the bikini clad figures frolicking in stiff poses.

Dead. They're dead because of me. Knowledge scalded her insides. Worse than that was the relief at not being one of them. Her throat wasn't gaping wide. Flames hadn't licked at her blood and flesh—

The sun eased up a notch, stabbing light down the canyon between the buildings, turning the window into a mirror that reflected her own surprisingly normal image. She had been sure trauma would show on her face like neon.

I bend, not break. It had been her mantra for a long time, but she still had her doubts about whether stubborn survival was a good thing or a bad thing. The oblivion of a nervous breakdown had some appeal.

. . . all dead . . . the rumors of my death . . .

They thought she was dead. They had to. The other marshals, Dark Lord for sure. He'd called Peg by Dani's name in a husky, chilling whisper as he knelt and played in her pooling blood with his long, white fingers. The scream she couldn't let out then, tried to crowd out her throat. Again she fought it back, not out of fear, she realized with shame. She just didn't want to cause a scene. A scene.

She closed her eyes. How pathetic.

How—infuriating. For six months other people had pulled her strings and she'd let them. It had almost cost her life, her liberty, not to mention her pursuit of happiness. When had she forgotten the first rule of writing: never let plot drive characters?

Instead of her reflection she saw two choices.

She could go back to the marshals. Or not.

She couldn't think of one good reason to go back.

That left "or not."

It didn't take much imagination to figure her window of opportunity to self determine was small. The feds and Dark Lord would soon know they had made a mistake. She had to get a little privacy so she could work out a plan—no—she needed a *plot*.

She would plot her own survival.

The beauty of it was no one believed romance writers could plot anything but sizzling sex scenes. With a bit of luck, by the time they realized she was more than her sex scenes, it would be too late.

Chapter Four

"Are you sure you don't mind me crashing with you?" asked Dani, speaking to Rosebud through the microphone that came with her new laptop computer. The Internet telephone connection had been as easy to establish as the salesman said it would. Amazing. Even better, it was virtually untraceable, after she'd routed it through the local university Internet connection thanks to some e-mail tutoring courtesy of another cyberbuddy named Spook. "It's such short notice . . ."

"You think I'm gonna pass up a chance to meet Blossom in the flesh just 'cause I gotta change the sheets on a bed?" Rosebud, aka Carolyn Ryan, answered.

"Ooh, no pressure." Dani grinned, suppressing a wince at the sound of this cyberspace nickname, one of several Dani used to hide her identity, being spoken aloud. Some names should stay in cyberspace. Actually, all of them, Dani decided ruefully. Still, it was comforting to find out that Rosebud was as nice in voice as she was in cyberspace. If all the friends on her list were as helpful, her exercise in hiding was going to be almost easy.

Rosebud laughed. "Twenty minutes, okay? Or do you need more time?"

Twenty minutes seemed like a long time, but Dani agreed and rang off. Like Tennessee Williams's Blanche DuBois, she would rely on the kindness of strangers.

This first contact was a good omen, she decided, taking a last look at the nearly unrecognizable face in the mirror attached to the wall behind the desk.

A shower, minus the *Psycho* victim overtones of the past months, had taken some of the tension from her face and removed all of the grime acquired during her panicked crawl through the bushes outside the safe house.

Without regret, she had discarded everything but her shoes. They were too comfortable to toss aside and were a reminder of a happier time with her friend, Kelly Kerwin. Happy reminders stacked on top of each other put a desperately needed wall between her and the images of Peg's bloody death.

Her black power suit was short enough to be distracting, yet conservative enough to blend. She'd bought and applied cosmetics, but opted for a smart little hat rather than give her hair into the care of a strange hairstylist. She was desperate, not crazy.

She looked at her watch, then quickly began to assemble the stuff she was taking with her. She'd already been in one place too long. She could almost hear her hunters, lawful and unlawful, baying in the distance.

If Hollywood was even half right, public accommodations were easy to check. If they failed to pick up the scent, they would head straight for anyone she was known to be acquainted with. Thanks to the inventors of the Internet and Spook, they shouldn't find the ones that mattered.

Under the impression he was helping her research a book, Spook had been tutoring her via e-mail about the byways and sly-ways of the hacker milieu. Reputed on the boards to be former CIA, Dani had "met" him shortly after going into hiding. A lucky find, possibly even a life-saving one.

Dani smiled slightly, thinking about the cyber-pass he'd made last month. At the time, she'd thought it a funny coincidence that he actually lived in the Denver area, but she didn't plan to contact him unless she had to. She wasn't working on a romance plot this time.

Before calling Rosebud she'd taken the time to assemble information about the city. She had to be able to move around quickly. Hesitation could be fatal.

The hardest part of her exercise in independence, besides the not getting killed part, would be finding ways to fill the long days and longer nights. She had to polish up the last two chapters of her book, but that wouldn't take long. If necessary, she could play tourist—her hunters wouldn't expect that.

She packed her computer in the briefcase she had bought to go with the suit. The floppy disk containing her book and the personal items she had bought followed. The list of friendly strangers and places went into the pocket of her suit.

One thing remained.

She'd almost left it where it fell when Peg went down. She still didn't know why she had picked it up. Now Dani extracted it from her backpack, the metal of the handgun striking a chill to her heart and her palm. Tears burned the back of her eyes, but they failed to cleanse away the hard reality of why Peg and the others died.

Betrayal.

It had always been there. She would have realized it before now if her senses hadn't been dulled by the waiting. What other reason was there for the sense of foreboding that had hung so palpably over the safe house? Or her nightmares dripping with blood? The killer had *known* Peg was supposed to be gone or he would have looked for Dani and found her.

No, Dani didn't wonder *if* she had been betrayed. She wondered *who* had betrayed her. Neuman who had loved

Peg? How could she not wonder about Peg's sudden illness or forget he didn't know Peg had come back?

What about Niall McBride, with his shy, dark eyes and his high society fiancée in New Orleans planning their fancy Christmas wedding? The differences in their income bothered him. He had asked Dani if she thought it would be a problem—under the mistaken impression that romance writer was synonymous with advice columnist.

She couldn't put a traitor's face on them or trust them until she did.

Weighted with that awareness, she studied Peg's revolver, turning it in the light, adjusting to the feel of it in her hand. It was weightier than she'd expected. Could she point it and pull the trigger? Could she do it knowing the bullet would explode from the chamber, flying straight and true to the target? Watch it enter without mercy, tearing through skin, flesh and bone, spilling blood—

So much blood.

She shuddered. Was violence the only defense against violence—

Moral musings fragmented when she saw the safety. It was "off." Of course it was. Peg had been ready to use it. No hesitation in her mind about bullets flying into bodies.

Dani's hands shook as she changed the setting, then tucked the weapon in her briefcase. She sank back on her heels and thought about her mad dash from the burning safe house. The backpack with the unsafe gun bouncing against her back.

Kelly always said that irony was her strong suit.

Heck of a time to almost prove her right.

Although Matt's case wasn't the only ongoing operation, most of the desks surrounding Matt were empty. Some people actually thought weekends were for play. Courts and judges still needed protection. Prisoners still had to be transported, and fugitives always required rounding up. The wheels of justice ground twenty-four hours a day, three hundred and sixty-five days a year.

Maybe that's why justice was so screwed up.

Paper drifts covered his desk, getting worse as reports began to filter in from the various tentacles of the investigation. He read each one. Unlike movies, most breaks came from the boring grunt work. It wasn't fun. It certainly wasn't glamorous. The waiting was the hardest.

In his youth he'd dogged cows and ridden broncs to the buzzer. Getting repeatedly tossed on his ass had taught him how to keep a rein on impatience. Now it took all his honed-under-pressure control to keep reading and making notes when he wanted to be out hunting a woman who read Louis L'Amour and may or may not be dead.

When Alice's call finally came, he barked into the receiver, "Talk to me, Alice."

"It's not her, Matt. Coroner double-checked, then checked again."

"Hot damn. Get your ass back in here." He dropped the telephone in the cradle and leaned back.

She was alive.

Regret for Peg Oliver tempered his elation. She'd died knowing she'd been betrayed by her own. If she was watching somewhere, he hoped she knew she'd kept her witness alive. Surely there was a special place in the next life reserved for the line-of-duty dead. And one in hell for the people who sent them there.

Matt jumped up, unable to sit now that he knew she was out there. That soon he would see her, not her picture. Soon he'd know if her eyes were a trick the photographer had played with the light or—*damn*. What was wrong with him?

He couldn't do this. He had to stay detached, stay focused to be effective. Neuman had made a lot of mistakes with his op, but the biggest, in Matt's opinion, had been getting involved with Peg Oliver. Neuman should have moved Gwynne immediately, not taken his girlfriend to the hospital. He sure as hell shouldn't have lingered to hold her hand while she threw her poisoned guts up. If he'd led with his brain instead of his dick, his girl and his men might be alive and Gwynne wouldn't be missing. No way he'd be following Neuman's primrose path to failure.

He spun around in his chair. Neuman would have to be told about Oliver, but not yet. Not a good idea to let a suspected rat in the woodpile know the cheese was still out there for the taking.

"Matt?"

Matt hadn't noticed Henry approaching. "Yeah?"

"Jogger saw someone answering to Oliver's description sitting in that park at the entrance to the subdivision early this morning."

Matt muttered an expletive. They probably drove right by—while she sat and watched. "Did he see where she went?"

"Said she headed down the road towards the bus stop. Riggs has got the PD checking transportation and hotels. We heard from Alice?"

Matt nodded, said as if it didn't matter, "We still got a witness."

"Holy shit."

"She could still get dead if we don't reel her in fast. Contact known associates, check her finances. Does she have walking around money? If so, how much?"

Henry looked up from his notes. "What about phone taps?"

Matt hesitated. "We shouldn't need 'em, but let's get the warrants just in case. Get on the horn to Anderson." The complex process of witness protection wasn't Matt's purview, but he knew Anderson. A good man and honest, he did protection better than anyone Matt knew. No surprise Hayes made his move before Gwynne got tucked under Anderson's wing. "Tell him his protection detail isn't a bust after all. I'll let Sheridan know."

Henry grinned. "How did our esteemed attorney general take the loss of his witness?"

"With the trial starting Monday morning? Same way democrats took losing congress. On a long, slow whine." Matt grinned, then turned it to a frown. "About our boy Neuman—"

"You're not letting him back in the loop, are you?"

"Hell no. We need to let him know about Oliver, but not until Gwynne's safely back in the nest." And then? A spurt of eagerness was firmly flattened. "Let's keep him and his guy on hand, just in case we need them."

Henry looked up with a frown. "Why would we need them?"

"Hayes will have to complete his contract or he'll have his employer on his ass." It was as inevitable as death and taxes that the mob punished failure quickly and permanently. Local mob boss, Bates, the man suspected of footing the bill for Richard Hastings, was not known for making exceptions to this rule.

Henry arched his thin brows to his receding hairline. "Anderson ain't gonna let you set his witness up as a clay pigeon. Or our excitable attorney general."

"She's already a pigeon." Matt shrugged. "And Anderson's got a wife and kids he's gonna want to see again."

"Hayes is that good?"

"Read his file again. Show me where he's ever missed his mark and then tell me he's not that good. Besides, we don't have to put Gwynne in harm's way, just make him think she is."

"You think he'll decoy twice?" Henry looked doubtful.

"If we control his source and Bates keeps the pressure on him, what are his options?"

Henry looked thoughtful. "It could work."

"Anderson needs to take a good, hard look at the logistics of the safe house they had on tap for Gwynne. And we need to find something like, well—"

"A—web?"

Matt smiled. "Yeah. A web." He leaned back in his chair, his body tense with the anticipation of action. Hayes was so close he could almost reach out and touch him. They wouldn't even have to hunt for the bastard. Hayes would come to them. Once they had Dani Gwynne.

The romance writer and the hit man. Now there was a title for a book.

Hayes was a man with a mission. He had to find Dani Gwynne and finish the job and he had to do it quickly. Bates did not like failure. Hayes didn't like what Bates did to failures. He couldn't let Dani Gwynne escape her death. Each piece in the puzzle of his existence fit into the other. Remove one piece and the whole came apart.

She was his missing piece.

" 'There is a passion for hunting . . . deeply implanted in the human breast,' " he murmured. With every fiber of his instincts he knew that hunting her was about more than *a* death. He needed *her* death. As long as her blood pumped through her veins he would be in pain. He had to kill *her* if he was to survive.

He worked with calm intensity, marshaling all his resources, all his will, using his pain to fuel his drive and directing it toward tracking Dani before she could go to ground or be picked up by the marshals.

He had tapped his sources inside law enforcement and knew she was on her own. It pleased him to have her so— took out the middle men. Made the hunt just between them, the way a good hunt should be.

Hayes looked through her financial accounts, his fingers stabbing the keys as he put a trace on her bank and credit card accounts, a "cc" on her e-mail. If she tried accessing her money, he would know when and where as soon as the marshals did and he could mobilize faster than they could. Bureaucracy was a bitch.

Not that he thought it likely she would use them. He studied her bank account on his screen. Either her agent was stealing from her or she was carrying a lot of walking around money. A whole lot.

"Money's a horrid thing to follow, but a charming thing to meet." He looked forward to that meeting.

The first instinct of a hunted animal was to go to ground. He turned his search to local hotels. Child's play to look through their systems for a recent registration by a female paying with cash. On the fifth try he hit pay dirt. Louise? He made a note of the name and room number she was using. As in *Thelma and Louise*, he wondered with a grin. He noticed she had made some telephone calls, all of them to numbers he recognized as Internet lines.

What was she up to, he wondered, then shrugged. Whatever it was, he would soon put an end to it.

A message that he had e-mail appeared on his screen.

Hayes glared at it, was tempted to ignore it. Bates, the man behind Richard Hastings, the man footing the bill, had a hair trigger temper. If he thought Hayes couldn't complete the contract, if he lost his fear, then he would focus all his resources into hunting Hayes down. He would give Gwynne's contract to someone else. Hayes couldn't let that happen. So Bates must be placated. For now.

He pulled up the e-mail, and read the short, vituperative message, then stabbed the response button and typed a kiss-ass reply. When it had been sent, he logged off. He had an appointment to kill.

Where would she go? Matt stood next to Alice, studying a map of the city. A few meager pushpins marked the places Dani had been spotted. Around the room there was an assortment of electronic surveillance equipment. Faxes, printouts, and the remains of breakfast, lunch and enough Styrofoam coffee cups to breech a landfill littered the massive conference table.

When Riggs' call came in, Matt settled near the speaker telephone, rubbing the chin he had obviously shaved too fast this morning and said, "I hope you have good news, Riggs."

"Some. We got a trail. She surfaced downtown at Saks Fifth Avenue, bought some clothes—"

Matt looked at Alice. "Shopping?"

She arched her brows. "It's been six months."

"—a new laptop, had a makeover—"

"A makeover? No—" He held up a hand as Alice opened her mouth. "I don't want to know."

She grinned as Riggs said, "Hold on. I think we got something." There was a muted rumble of voices, then Riggs came back, "She checked into the Hilton—"

"We'll meet you there." Matt was out of his chair and halfway to the door before Riggs finished the sentence. "Come on, Alice. I'm sure I'll need your insight into the weird workings of the female mind when we get there."

The drive seemed to take forever. Matt held excitement in check, but it was not easy. They were close. So close he could almost smell her coconut shampoo.

Fifteen minutes later he walked into her hotel room— and inhaled coconut. And precious little else.

Matt stalked to the center and looked around with a frustrated sigh. "You got the list of what she was wearing, Riggs. See if she made any calls or if anybody saw her leave."

"Right." He slid out the door with his characteristic slouch. Off to one side Alice peered into the trash can. "Diet Dr. Pepper cans and an empty M&M's wrapper. I'm starting to feel like a hound dog on a junk food trail. I'll check the bathroom." In a moment she called out, "Wet tub and towels. Not much else."

"What? She paid two hundred bucks to take a shower?" Matt made a restless circuit of the room. The bed had clearly not been slept in, though the cover was rumpled. Otherwise the room looked undisturbed, phone books, paper and pens still neatly stowed in the desk drawers, the closet bare of occupancy. Matt turned as Alice emerged from the bathroom, then stopped abruptly.

"Well, look at what we have here." He crossed back to the desk and crouched down, lifting up the telephone line lying free of the wall plug. He fingered it for a moment, re-membering the laptop in the safe house plugged into the telephone line. She had bought a fully loaded laptop. That meant it had a modem.

Pretty high-tech for a romance writer. He would expect

her to know more about bubble baths and aphrodisiacs than computers. He didn't give voice to the thought. Alice had strong opinions on stereotyping, even of romance writers. He showed the line to Alice. "Is the other phone line in or out?"

Alice checked. "In."

Matt stood up. He had one of their computer people going over Gwynne's safe house laptop, but had considered it a footnote in her file, something that might dot some Is or cross some Ts. Apparently Gwynne didn't see it that way or she wouldn't have moved so quickly to replace it. "She had her notebook modem hooked up at the crime scene."

"Yeah." He could hear the question in Alice's voice, but he wasn't sure he had the right questions, let alone any answers. "What's going on in her head? She was almost killed this morning. I can understand her panicking, taking off. But this," with a sweeping gesture he indicated the bland empty room, "this isn't panic."

Alice turned slowly, studying the room as if it might give up more information if she just looked hard enough. "No, it isn't." She frowned. "She's decided on some course of action and I don't think it includes us."

"She doesn't trust us." If she had tarred him with Neuman's dirty brush—well, she ought to have more sense. He saw amusement in Alice's face. "What?"

"It isn't personal, Matt."

The hell it isn't, he wanted to snap back. Couldn't because Alice wouldn't understand. Which left him nothing to say that made sense. Luckily Riggs came back, looking more melancholy than when he left. Matt snapped at him instead, "What you got?"

Riggs looked surprised. "Not much and bad news."

"Give me the bad news," Matt said.

"We're not the only ones who've been asking questions about Louise."

"Damn. Hayes?"

"Probably. Doorman couldn't describe him. Neither could the desk clerk. They weren't much use identifying Gwynne either. Doorman says she left in a private car. He doesn't remember the tag, though he was pretty sure it was local. Apparently the romance writer has great legs." Riggs leered good-naturedly as he held out a computer sheet. "Here's a list of her calls. I dialed them on my way up."

"Who'd you get?"

Riggs shrugged. "What, not who. Computers. You ever had one of them whine in your ear?" He stuck a finger in the offended orifice with a pained look. "I faxed the list in. We should have something by the time we get there."

At the door Matt hesitated, then looked back. The late afternoon sun shone in the windows at a cruel angle, bleeding what little color there was out of the room. Dust hovered in the beams of light. The coconut scent had faded, leaving the pervasive smell of hotel to reclaim the air. The room felt more empty than the bloody, burned out safe house he'd stood in—was it only this morning? It felt longer. A lifetime longer.

He felt all of his forty-five years, plus some. Maybe it was running into Hayes again. He didn't want to think about the past, sure as hell hated postmortems on it. Just reminded him of what he couldn't change. What was gone. The lives of friends. His marriage. The confident idealism of the young man he had been.

Odd that Dani Gwynne was clearer in his mind right now than his ex-wife. He hadn't seen Judith for almost ten years, but they had been married for eight—long enough to find out how wrong they were for each other.

Judith hated Matt's career. Despite her sleek image and high profile job, she had kept her sixties prejudice towards cops and feds. Matt thought she'd get over it. She thought he'd get over being one. Instead they got over each other. Hayes's entry into the ranks of hit men—and Matt's problems in dealing with it—had helped speed the demise. Judith's infidelity had hastened the end.

Ironic to think the day his divorce was final was the high spot of that year, what he remembered of it. His brothers had taken him on a drinking binge that cost him three days and gave him the worst hangover of his life. He had returned to his work free of distractions to face the ugly reality that there were things he couldn't change no matter how he did his job.

He shook his head impatiently. This case was messing with his head big time. There was an itch he couldn't scratch between his shoulder blades. Maybe it was because of that bastard Hayes popping up on the horizon or Gwynne dropping off it. It didn't matter. A man couldn't live half his life around horses and not know a serious pile of shit when he saw it in his way or wish he knew a way to avoid it.

Alice touched his arm, bringing him back to the present. "Find something else?"

Just some old memories. He hunched his shoulders impatiently. "No. Let's get the hell out of here."

Chapter Five

A pity that traffic delayed him and he missed Gwynne by mere minutes. Was she very lucky or very clever, Hayes wondered, as he slipped into her empty hotel room. The doorman couldn't remember much besides her legs. He should have left then, not hung around until the feds had swept her room. He should have, but he didn't.

What was it that drew him to the center of the room? Had him standing quietly, while the sight, sound and smell of the room seeped into his senses?

He felt her fear first. Smiled as it burned its way into his soul. Usually he only felt it at the moment of kill. He usually didn't dream about his victims either. He frowned, suddenly uneasy.

What was so different with Dani Gwynne, about this particular kill, that disturbed him so? He had only to close his eyes to see her here. See her moving about, thinking, planning, and trying to escape the sense of *him* getting closer.

Yes, she felt him, too. How curious.

The idea unsettled yet intrigued him. It was also dangerous. To him. To his future with Willow. For a moment he hesitated. Should he just disappear? Let Bates give the contract to someone else to complete? Sure Bates would be after him, but Hayes knew how to disappear.

It would be the sensible thing to do.

He knew, even before he turned to leave, that he was not going to be sensible. If he crashed and burned on this one, so be it. He had to kill her or die trying. It was as simple as that.

He had his hand on the door knob when he heard the fumble of someone using a key card to enter. He retreated to the bathroom, pulling the door to an almost closed position just before the maid entered. The longing to kill her was so strong he shook with it. He shouldn't—he leaned against the wall trying to fight through it, to fight back the pain. It was too dangerous to do it here, where Dani had been—

The woman pushed open the bathroom door and saw him.

So, she was meant to die. He quit fighting the need, smiled as he moved toward her. It wasn't the main event, just the prelude.

His elbows propped on a littered desk, Matt rubbed his weary eyes with the heels of his hands. He didn't try to hold back a sound that was half sigh, half groan. It was long after midnight, long after the retreat of the summer sun. Behind him the mountains were hidden, the city at their base a myriad of patterned lights. He dumped another cup of coffee down his throat, but despite the rat-a-tat of his heart, he got no lift in spirits or energy.

After the setback at the hotel, Matt had returned to the office determined to be optimistic. Only Alice had expressed doubt in a speedy resolution.

Riggs was immediately derisive when she voiced it. "Of course we'll find her. We're the marshals, Alice. She's a *romance* writer. No damn contest." Hours later, his face lined with exhaustion, Riggs had obviously been forced to reassess the mettle of the romance writer. He'd paced into the room, passing Alice's desk with a snapped, "Don't say it."

"What?" She had looked a bit too innocent and Matt found he still had a grin in him.

"You know what." Riggs dropped down in the chair in front of Matt's desk. "Nada. Zip. Zero. Sorry, Matt."

"Wonder how Bates found out Dani was still alive?" Alice voiced the million dollar question.

"The coroner promised to sit on the ID until tomorrow," Matt said. Which meant zip. Bates was a wise guy with longevity because he had sources inside the law enforcement community. It would be stupid to assume they could keep anything from him. The Marshal's Service had not got its reputation by being stupid—though there were exceptions, he had to admit, thinking of Neuman.

Matt gave Riggs a quick rundown on their lack of progress in finding the rat in Neuman's woodpile. About Neuman's debts and McBride's rich fiancée. "Both our boys have reasons to sell out. Both could use an influx of cash. For all we know, they could be working together. Once we knew Hayes was hunting, we told Neuman about Oliver's death. Bastard has no clue where Gwynne might go for help."

"So far," Alice said, "they both appear too shook up to have ideas, let alone good ideas."

"Great." Riggs's mouth opened in a jaw popping yawn. Before it was completely finished, he asked, "What about Gwynne's laptop? Anything helpful there?"

Alice propped an elbow on her desk, then her chin on her hand, caught his yawn and passed it on. "Maybe. We found out she's been using the modem in her laptop to surf the Internet almost from the moment she went into protective custody."

"Oh?" Riggs subsided deeper in the chair, lowering his chin to his chest. "What does it mean?"

"We're not sure," Matt admitted, fighting against the insistence of the shared yawn. Tired was not an option.

"She could just be doing research—" Alice began.

Riggs lifted his head. "She writes romance novels. Only thing she'd need to know—"

"Don't say it, Riggs, until you've actually read one just—don't."

Riggs studied her face and decided not to. "Any indication she's left the area?"

Matt shook his head.

"What about who picked her up? We figure out where and how Gwynne contacted someone?"

Matt let Alice answer that one, while he finally gave into the compulsion to yawn. He quickly passed it back to Riggs.

"You know that fancy laptop Gwynne bought?"

Riggs nodded.

"Well," Alice continued, "it seems she can also use it as a telephone."

Riggs blinked, opened his mouth, closed it, then opened it again to ask, "What about the wire-taps? Anything there."

"No—" Matt stopped. "Son of a bitch. She doesn't have to phone home. She's been e-mailing half the country. Alice, get someone back on her agent. Riggs, get with Sebastian. I want to know if Gwynne contacted anyone she's been e-mailing regularly."

"I'm on it." Alice picked up the telephone. Riggs nodded, dragged himself out of the chair, and shuffled out with the yawn in tow. It lasted at least until he was out of sight.

Matt leaned back, his hands beating on the arms of his chair. He already had people running a cross-check to see if any of the people she had been chatting with online were local. Their computer guru, Sebastian, had been quick to point out she might have more than one way onto the Net. It might not be possible to get a complete list of her online contacts.

"Like death and taxes, networks go down. All the web's surfers gotta have alternate access." Sebastian, a spare cartoon with a stand-up shock of red hair, had sat bonelessly in his beat-up, government-issue chair as he tried to explain the unexplainable. A genius with computers, he'd started hacking as a teen on a Commodore 64. He'd eventually been caught where he wasn't supposed to be, then recruited by the Marshals Service since it takes a hacker to find one. He had not disappointed.

Access costs money, so Matt directed Henry to sniff out her money trail and then turned back to Sebastian for some more bad news. There might not be a money trail. New Orleans offered free Internet access and there were ways locally to get free, anonymous access to the Internet. Matt heard a "but" in Sebastian's voice and straddled a chair across from him. "So?"

"There's more than one way to search the Internet for information and people. I know this guy, Boomer Edison, a real character. Looks like a football player, thinks he's a cowboy and is a computer genius with a nifty little program that searches for online identities."

"Identities?" Matt knew what the Internet was not—a person, place, or thing. He had a vague idea of what it was—the name given the monstrous cyberspace frontier of computers, networked world-wide into a faster-than-the-speed-of-light information exchange. What did identities have to do with that?

Sebastian leaned back in his chair, his hands with their extra long fingers moving in a version of sign language. "A lot of surfers like the Net because it's a place where there are none of the usual visual cues that people use to pigeon-hole each other. No one is fat or thin, short or tall, young or old, you don't even have to be male or female. There's only your handle—the nickname you choose—and your words to define who and what you are. Some people create different handles and identities, for different gathering places on the Net. It's not as strange as you might think. We're all different things to different people. Net surfers just admit it."

"Okay." Matt could understand the concept. His ex-wife had been a lot of things to a lot of men during the decline of their marriage. Matt rubbed the bridge of his nose. "And this Boomer's program does—what?"

Sebastian spun to face him. "It takes a known identity, analyzes written posts associated with it, then searches for similarities in writing style, content, word usage to produce a list of possible matches. All we need to give him is a good representative sample of Gwynne's style—which we have right here in her computer's output file."

It sounded like a long, long shot, but Matt gave him the go-ahead. Anything to add a new strand to the net he was trying to throw around Dani Gwynne and, by extension, Jonathan Hayes.

Hours later with nothing new on the horizon, Matt silently admitted to rising concern. He shoved aside the last of the reports and stood up, stretching his aching back and cramped muscles before turning to the window. With his hands in his pockets, he stared down at a city laid out in lights. The dark sky was moonless, the stars hidden by a drifting cloud cover.

Tomorrow would be a good day for climbing if the cloud cover held. Keep the temperature down, long as it didn't rain. He wished he were up at the cabin, waiting with his brothers for first light. Attacking a rock face, feeling for cracks and fissures, fighting granite and gravity. In motion. Anything but standing still and wondering what the hell to do next. Wondering what the romance writer would do next. Wondering, most of all, what Hayes would do next.

He heard the low hum from the air conditioning, felt the rising chill now that there was only his body heat against a thermostat set to cool a crowd. The place even smelled deserted. Old sweat. Stale coffee. Staler perfume.

He didn't mind being alone, had made it a personal choice. After his divorce an almost female-free life had seemed a blessing. When had it become a habit? Something he had stopped thinking about?

He hadn't stopped looking. He wasn't dead, just unwilling to climb the slippery slopes inside a woman's head. When they asked and he was around, he went. Which wasn't often. The job was a parasite persistently eating away at his free time. He had done nothing to cut it back. Why go home, when the apartment he shared with his brother was usually empty? More entertaining to be out kicking bad guys' butts.

He felt her eyes boring into his mind, digging up his secrets. Would her real eyes be as penetrating? He gave into her insistence. In the safe house her eyes had entreated him. Now they mocked him. How could a pair of photographic eyes make him wonder if he had missed something? He had been happy before he met her, would be happy again when she was filed away and back in New Orleans. She was a romance writer, so of course she wanted a girl for every guy.

The mockery in her eyes seemed to deepen. With a muttered curse, he turned back to his desk. He was too damn tired. That's all. The day had started too early and gone on way too long. Now it was too late to go home. Probably meet himself coming back. He rubbed the back of his neck.

He could stretch out on the couch in the employee's lounge long enough to take the edge off tired.

He should have gone to sleep the minute he lay down. Usually he could sleep anywhere, even on a couch that was too short and as comfortable as a slab of cement. This night he stared at the ceiling with sleep-gritty eyes while bits of Dani's online posts played in his head.

. . . Men think we can't live without them, but it's chocolate we can't live without . . .

. . . I think GHOST was a hit because we all want to believe evil will be punished in the end—though it's hard to believe good will triumph when you're sitting in the dark and out of M&M's . . .

What was she doing, what was she thinking? He had gone over every detail in her file, got a glimpse inside her head through her online posts that Sebastian had printed out for him. What did it mean? There was no logic in them that a guy could hang his thoughts on. They were all awash in feelings, in emotions. Emotions didn't put away bad guys. Emotions left big gaping holes in your flanks and got your friends killed because you weren't paying attention.

He sat up, then stood up, found himself looking out the window without a conscious decision. She had guts, he'd give her that. What was it she'd written to one friend?

Like the willow tree, I bend, not break, though sometimes I wish it were the other way around.

Was that the easy answer to the romance writer with a purple boa, who surfed the Internet under the noses of her protectors, left Sebastian eating her cyber-dust, and vanished into the city night lights like a seasoned pro? She bent, but didn't break?

A fire engine siren wailed in the distance. He could see the flicker of its red lights heading east. He leaned his forehead against the cold glass and wondered which light shining out of the dark was the one she was standing in.

Dani would be the first to admit that going to a country western bar probably wasn't the best decision in her present circumstances, but it wasn't the worst either. Getting blind, stinking drunk would be the worst choice. No matter how appealing insensibility was, it would not happen.

The soda, sadly not her usual, cradled between her hands lacked the ability to blunt the feel of Dark Lord hunting her. Thank goodness the honky-tonk country band was playing loud enough to ease the sensation. With a killer and the feds on her heels, she'd wondered about the wisdom of going out with Carolyn Ryan and her writers' group, who were now out on the floor pushing their tushes with a care-free confidence that Dani could only pretend to feel.

She would envy them if they weren't such a friendly bunch. There was no room for envy in the midst of their kindness. No room for anything but the need to hold it all together. It helped that there were different stages to trauma, just like there were differences in an ocean when you were drowning. Dani had seen all those stages when Meggie died, knew each one intimately.

That first, knock-you-overboard, white-edged wave is quickly followed by a shell-shocked disbelief at finding yourself in deep water. Then there is a period of helpless floundering. Luckily the shock sets in fast, providing a mea-sure of protection as the body accustoms itself to this new order of existence. This semi-numbed period is sometimes marked by an efficient coping that lulls you into thinking rock bottom could be avoided, or at least well managed.

Unfortunately, there is not a dignified or graceful way to drown. In the end, grief fills you up, weighs you down

without mercy. The collision with rock bottom is so overwhelming, you almost don't notice that there is no way left
to go but up. When you do, the decompressing trip to the
surface is a dreary and an endless exercise without shock's
buffer to blunt the pain.

After Meggie's death, Dani had made it back to the surface of her life. Instead of landfall, she had found herself
bobbing on the surface of a world forever changed. One
where grief was an ocean surf that sometimes knocked her
down with its wildness. At other times it seemed content to
lap a melancholy reminder that memory was all she had left
of her little girl.

Dani knew the drill. Knew where she was in the process.
She didn't know how long she would be there. Only time
would tell that, time that was friend and enemy. She
couldn't speed it up or slow it down, couldn't control what
others would do with their allotment. So she sat in the
honky tonk, inhaling the scent of booze, sweat and tobacco.
Exhaling the stench of blood, fire and flesh. Letting the
pounding music fill her up. Using the chattering crowd as a
buoy to stay afloat.

A cowboy at the other end of the bar lifted his beer can
in her direction. After a slight hesitation, Dani mirrored the
move. She'd played this part on the community theater
stage back home, knew just how wide to force her plastic
smile when the cowboy, a cop—she was very familiar with
the breed by now—exchanged his bar stool for the one next
to hers.

"So, little darlin', would you like to take a turn around
the floor?" He leaned close, his breath puffing warm and
beery into her face.

"I don't really know the steps." Dani spared a brief,
longing look at the milling dancers, the brisk music prom-

ising an appealingly, thoughtless motion. "Is that a problem?"

"Not to me, darlin'. I'm a good teacher and you look like a fast learner." He held out his hand with a wide, good ol' boy grin.

Dani set her drink down, let him lead her onto the sawdust strewn floor. His arm hooked strongly around her waist, pulling her against a chest that was country hard and scented with Zest soap and Brut aftershave. She had forgotten how nice it felt to be held by a man.

"Just follow my lead," he said.

She nodded, hoping he was right about her being a fast learner. She needed light feet for more than pushing her tush if she was going to dodge the Marshals Service and Dark Lord until she got her day in court.

Step . . . kick . . . step . . . days . . . cross and kick . . . nights . . . step and push that tush.

One step at a time, it would eventually be over. No problem, she told herself sturdily, then stepped on her partner's toes.

Matt had so much coffee in him he was surprised he wasn't buzzing the room. He had finally managed to catch a few Zs, all of them taken in his chair. He tossed back a couple of ibuprofen to take the edge off his stiff neck, chased them down his throat with more coffee, and turned his restless impatience back to his study of Gwynne's paper trail.

A report from the Denver PD about a murder and fire in the hotel room Gwynne had used sat on top of the stack. So they'd missed Hayes and he'd missed Dani by mere minutes.

His headache tightened its grip on the sides of his head.

He gritted his teeth and kept reading.

According to Sebastian's report, Gwynne had been in touch with her agent about some chapters she still owed on her book. The contact had occurred during her stay in the hotel, but it didn't mean she was still alive. If she was, they might be able to trace her when she sent the chapters over the Internet.

It was progress of a sort, but Matt didn't want to know where she'd been. He needed to know where Dani Gwynne was right now. If she was still alive. He was halfway down the stack of morning reports when Riggs slouched in.

A yawn that looked like a leftover from yesterday twisted his face. He held a fistful of papers as if they were a security blanket he wanted to curl around. When he had assumed his usual slouch in the chair in front of Matt's desk, he deposited the papers, then helped himself to some of Matt's coffee.

"I should have been a romance writer."

Matt blinked. "What?"

"You wanted to know how much walking around money she has?" He looked at a computer sheet with a look as close to awe as his hangdog face would allow. "How about fifteen thousand?"

It wasn't an easy figure to bend his sore brain around. Matt dug his thumbs into a knotted pain spot. "Dollars?"

"She ain't toting pennies."

Matt considered some more. "How come we didn't know about it before now?"

Riggs shrugged. "Seems Neuman didn't know. Her agent slipped it to her a couple of months ago, layered in some galleys for her new book that Gwynne had to proof. Asked her why Gwynne asked for the moolah, but she didn't know."

"You believe her?" Riggs shrugged and Matt frowned. What had prompted her to ask for money? Had she been planning to bolt before Hayes struck? "What's she going to do with it? Where's she going?"

"I don't know where she's going." Alice had approached unnoticed. "But I know where she's been."

"So?" Matt asked, impatient when she didn't continue. "Where's she been?"

"You aren't going to like it." Alice propped a hip on the edge of her desk and crossed her arms, her damn Cheshire cat grin back in place.

Matt scowled. "I don't like much anyway. What you got?"

"A cop saw our APB this morning. Swears he was with our girl last night at a country dance club on the south side. Seems he taught her to tush push."

Riggs choked. Matt didn't blame him. Alice wasn't trying near hard enough to control her grin. Matt didn't give her the satisfaction of hearing him choke, too, but it wasn't easy.

"Dancing?"

"That's right."

"The tush push?"

"So he says."

Matt rubbed his forehead. It didn't help. "I'll never understand women."

"Good." Alice's grin broke free of minor restraint.

"Don't—just enlighten me. What the *hell* is she doing?"

Alice sighed. "If she'd gotten drunk, would you be surprised?"

"No." Matt looked at Riggs. He shrugged, shook his head. "So what? This is the female equivalent of a bender?"

"Sort of. Though the parallel is weak because women

don't consider insensibility a viable route to problem solving."

Matt stared at her from under lowered brows. "I have so much to thank affirmative action for. Just think what I would've missed if I'd never met you."

"Don't." Alice gave a mock shudder. "It doesn't bear thinking about."

"Then don't think. Find out who the hell she went to that club with."

"Already on it." She dropped behind her desk. "My guy at the PD thinks he's knows someone who knows one of the women she was with, so it shouldn't take long. He's gonna call me back."

"Good." The back of his neck prickled. He felt like a hound dog picking up the scent. Too bad Dani was acting like a damn fox. He wasn't the enemy. He wished he could tell her a few home truths. "Son of a bitch!"

He could tell her anything he wanted to.

Riggs lifted his head from his chest. Alice looked at him in surprise. "What?"

Matt grinned. "E-mail. Instant communication."

Alice got it before Riggs, but then Riggs hadn't finished Matt's coffee yet. She smiled. "Tell her how much I liked her book."

Dani slept restlessly, woke early with tears on her cheeks, the grim remains of yet another nightmare digging into her emotional reserves. The tears were easy to brush away. Exhaustion dug in its heels, refusing to be dislodged by mere willpower. What had possessed her to think she could take on the forces of law and disorder for who knew how long? Rosebud had asked the same question quite forcefully last night when her gentle question had loosed the brakes on

Dani's tongue. It had helped to talk about it and Rosebud did have a point. But Rosebud hadn't stared into Peg's dead eyes, hadn't fled a burning house that was supposed to be safe. She hadn't seen a killer at work on a friend that was supposed to be her—

If Dani went back, she would be back to square one, wondering where and when Dark Lord would strike.

And who would lead him to her.

Dani rubbed her face. "I need my soda."

She carried the cold can into the bathroom to wash away the morning. It took her halfway through a second soda before the caffeine level in her blood got high enough to fuel something besides an inclination to whine.

Dani sat down at the kitchen table with a pencil and her trusty idea notebook. She flipped through the pages, looking for a blank one. A couple of sentences on one page caught her eye.

A wish before—

Dani remembered the night she had made it. A dark one. Heavily laced with foreboding. She bit her lip, then with conscious intent, filled in the blank.

A wish before *dying*.

There, she had faced it. She couldn't compute the odds of surviving, not while she was sleep deprived. She did know they weren't good—though still better than the odds of getting her wish. She looked at the wish, her mouth twisting in a bitter smile.

Fall in love again.

The romance writer dreaming of romance. She had a better chance of being taken hostage by terrorists and not just because she was over thirty. She tore the sheet out and deposited it in Rosebud's circular file. Thoughts were not so easily tossed away. A romance writer with no hero was not grounds for expulsion from the league of romance writers.

It was a pity.

With a sigh, she connected her computer to Carolyn's telephone line and logged onto the Net as an anonymous user. Once inside, she began threading her call across the worldwide network as carefully as she had once placed stitches in a baby quilt.

" 'Oh yet we trust that somehow good,' " she muttered, as she typed in commands, " 'Will be the final goal of ill!' "

When she realized what she was doing, she grinned. Spook, the online spy, had a lot to answer for. He had started a veritable epidemic of quoting across the boards. What was it he'd said, that a good quote was almost as good as a swift kick if properly applied? He sure knew where to apply them. Let's hope he'd come through with the information she needed—

She saw Spook's e-mail address come up. With a file attached. Bless the boy. She might have to look him up and thank him for his help in person. What was it he said about friends? Some people go to priests. I go to my friends. Something like that. She couldn't nail quotes like Spook.

When she finished her thanks to Spook and sent it on its way, she re-logged on as Blossom, hoping for something from her agent. The missive waiting for her wasn't from Pat. She had knocked around the Internet long enough to recognize it came from the Justice Department.

Well, well, they had found out faster than she expected. If they had this e-mail address, they could be tracing it to her real time address while she sat marveling at the obvious. She picked up the letter and cut the connection the quick way, by pulling her line out of the wall plug. They could not have traced her in that brief instant, but she fought the urge to look over her shoulder as she pulled the letter up onto her screen. Her gaze went first to his name at the bottom of the note.

Matt Kirby.

At least it wasn't Neuman or McBride. She scanned the missive quickly, her eyebrows and blood pressure inching higher with each word.

"—stupid to stay away. He was in your hotel room and killed a maid. Get your ass back in protective custody and help us stop Hayes permanently—"

Hayes? Did he mean Dark Lord?

"—and do what you came here to do." He ended his terse summons with a business and home address, several telephone numbers, and no emotional shorthand. Not that he needed smileys or frowns to get his point across.

She was stupid. He was smart.

She hoped he *was* smart and not just arrogant. Smart meant he could still be taught a few things.

Like when to tell someone where to take their ass.

And when not to.

Chapter Six

"We got an address on Gwynne's friend yet?" Matt asked. He stopped in front of Alice's desk and tossed a couple of folders onto her in box.

"I'm on hold for it." Alice lowered the telephone to answer Matt. "You finished your peerless prose already?"

He arched his brows. "How long does it take to tell someone to get her ass back in here?"

"And I was afraid you wouldn't take the diplomatic approach." She shook her head and almost dropped the telephone.

Feet planted and arms crossed, Matt looked at her derisively. "We don't have time to be diplomatic. Besides, thought you women wanted to be treated like equals?"

Alice arched her brows. "Your concept of equal treatment needs some fine tuning—yeah, I'm still here," she spoke into the phone, then straightened and grabbed a pen so she could scribble an address across the file cover. "Got it." She tossed the telephone in the cradle. "Let's saddle up. We got an address."

"About time." Matt grabbed his suit jacket off his chair and shrugged it on as he followed her out the door. This time he knew better than to let confidence run ahead of him and was glad he hadn't when they were facing Carolyn Ryan. First they had to connect the dots between Dani and Blossom. Then she told them they had missed Dani by thirty damn minutes. When Ryan told him where Dani had gone, he choked. Hayes on her ass, she takes time to go to—"Church?"

"People do." Ryan, an attractive brunette with a slim silhouette starting to smudge with age, looked grimly amused.

"People do a lot of things they shouldn't," Matt shot back.

"Like betraying a witness they were supposed to protect?"

Matt opened his mouth to deliver a blistering rebuttal, but Alice grabbed his arm and held on. He gave a grunt that was part disgusted and part "ouch." Alice had long nails.

"If our people had been guarding Ms. Gwynne, we wouldn't be here, Ms. Ryan." Alice slipped smoothly into her "good cop" role to ask, as if they were friends sharing a cup of coffee, "How long have you known Dani?"

Ryan shrugged. "I didn't know Dani. I met Blossom online eight or nine months ago. Wish I'd known. I've been reading Dani Gwynne's books for several years now."

"Is she as funny as her books?"

Ryan nodded warily. "You read her books?"

"I just finished *Can't Call It Loving*. I swear, I cried at the end."

Matt gave a strangled protest, but Alice's gambit worked. Ryan's face softened. "Caroline and Daniel were great lovers—" She stopped, was quiet for a bit, then said, "I'm afraid she's set on doing this without your help."

Matt gritted his teeth, said through them, "I'm sure Ms. Gwynne has this *romantic* idea of beating the odds—"

"Murder isn't very romantic, Inspector. Or have you forgotten that Blossom saw Dark Lord kill that woman who looked like her?"

He hadn't forgotten because he hadn't stopped to think what Dani had seen that night. Abruptly he was back in that room looking down at a brown blood stain with splatters all around. Where had she been while Hayes slit Peg Oliver's throat?

He realized he had lost the thread of the conversation and gave himself a shake.

"—from *Lord of the Rings*. It's her favorite book," Ryan was saying. "You'd have to read it to understand."

He fought back a burst of frustration. He didn't want to understand. He just wanted to find her and stop Hayes. End of story. "Did she tell you where she was going? What she was going to do?" he cut in to ask.

Ryan's feline smile held a warning of what was coming. He didn't say anything to Ryan. He had his pride. Three minutes later, Matt slammed the car door shut and grounded out, "The zoo?"

"Even Ryan didn't think she meant it."

"We still have to check it out."

"At least it's a nice day for it."

The firing of the engine drowned out the substance of Matt's growled response.

Dani was glad she had taken time for church, not just because she had a surfeit of time on her hands, but because she so desperately needed an infusion of peace. *Lead Kindly Light*, the closing hymn had been her favorite since Richard's wife, Liz, sang it at Meggie's funeral. Now the music lingered, a balm for her bruised heart.

> *Lead kindly light amid the encircling gloom.*
> *Lead thou me on.*
> *The night is cold and I am far from home.*
> *Lead thou me on.*
> *Keep thou my feet.*
> *I do not ask to see, the distant scene.*
> *One step enough for me.*

She dug a hand into the peanut sack and tossed it to the

waiting elephant. She hadn't meant to go to the zoo when she made her offhand remark to Carolyn, but she had finished her business at the flea market early. It wasn't like she had a lot of options. She had too much time to kill—pass—time to pass.

She needed to work on her vocabulary if she was going to get through this reasonably sane.

With his leathery, flexible trunk, the elephant reached for more. She dug into the nearly empty bag and tossed him a handful. I should be depressed, she thought, with a sigh, but how could she? The sun hung high in a sky too blue to be real. The air she inhaled was so crisply clear she felt a guilty euphoria.

Must be John Denver's *Rocky Mountain High*. Apparently a modest dose of altitude could be beneficial, even to those with acrophobia. Or maybe she was just tired of being down and out.

She tossed the last handful to the begging pachyderm, then tipped the empty bag to show him she really was out. To escape the gentle reproach in his eyes, she stood to leave.

A small girl darted around the corner of a side path, trailing an irate echo of her mother's voice. Before Dani could brace body or heart, the girl wrapped herself around Dani's legs.

Even as Dani knelt to hold the small escapee, an older version of her appeared, followed in short order by the harried mother, holding another small, struggling boy body.

The young mother's face lightened into a smile when she saw Dani holding the truant. "Thanks."

The little girl smelled of powder and baby lotion. Her tiny body was soft and strong, and determined to impose her will on the big people in her life. So like Meggie.

Her arms full, her heart empty, Dani said carefully,

"Sometimes you need another hand."

"Not just sometimes," the young mother said, ruefully. "I don't know what made me think I could handle them all, but it was such a lovely day, anything seemed possible."

Maybe it was this echo of her own thoughts that prompted her next words. She usually avoided the painful pleasure of getting too close to other people's children. "I was just heading the same way and I've got two free hands—"

The woman hesitated, her eyes assessing Dani's worthiness. Dani's "grandma" get up, purchased at the flea market, helped tip the scales and the woman said with real gratitude, "Thanks."

Dani turned with them, the little ones held firmly between the two adults. The older girl, Jenny, walked by Dani, sharing the family secrets in breathless bursts. Her mother looked embarrassed and apologetic. Dani found she could chuckle.

At the lion cage, Jenny told Dani she was ten years old. The age Meggie would be, Dani realized. Looking at Jenny's face, Meggie's baby face blurred, then turned older. Would she have been like Jenny? Dark hair instead of light bouncing with each skipped step? So eager to see the world, not afraid to meet it head on?

Not still and alabaster white in a coffin in the ground.

In a haze of painful pleasure, Dani toured the zoo with them, but her soul was with Meggie. When it was over, hugs were offered and gratefully accepted. The sweet, baby smells of the little ones, their wet, sugar-laced kisses smeared against her cheek, were manna in Dani's wilderness.

Dani fought back the urge to cling, to hold on tight and not let go when Jenny wrapped her thin arms around her neck and squeezed. Holding on didn't work. You had to let go, even when your heart left, too.

Resolutely solitary in the golden light of a lowering sun, she watched the little family make a meandering path across the parking lot, board a minivan, and drive away.

Leaving her alone again.

Her path stretched long and empty toward night. Her shoulders slumped, weary from the weight of returning fear.

> *I do not ask to see, the distant scene,*
> *One step enough for me.*

One step. That would be a place to stay tonight. Okay. Then finish those chapters. Oh yeah, and don't forget to respond to Matt, the oh-so-opinionated, Kirby.

"Okay," Matt straddled one of the chairs that circled the conference table, "let's get down to business, lose the frustration and try to find our witness before we all turn gray."

Alice, who had taken a seat on a small table off to one side, arched her carefully sculpted brows. "Funny she hasn't turned herself in, especially after your well-reasoned request."

"Don't mess with me, Alice. I'm not in the mood." Matt hadn't been in the mood for much since their abortive visit to the city zoo. That it had been a perfect day for a stroll merely added insult to injury. "We can't wait for her to pick up her mail. Hayes is on the move. So let's have your ideas, suggestions, intuitions. I'll even accept revelations from God and hallucinations that aren't drug induced."

His gaze swept the table, stopping briefly on each member of his team. Sebastian had chosen the chair at the table's head, but lacked the authority without his computer keyboard. He shrugged and looked apologetic. Riggs straddled a chair across from Matt and was using the chair back as a pillow. He did open his eyes long enough to look despairing. Henry was too restless to sit. He paced back and forth between the surveillance equipment and the table "smoking" a fountain pen and muttering to himself.

With some reluctance, Matt angled his body to face Alice. She frowned into space and didn't immediately realize she had his attention. When she did, she straightened and said uneasily, "What?"

"Give us some of that famous women's intuition, Alice," Riggs muttered, relaxing an impossible inch more across his forearms. He covered a yawn by lifting his elbow, then added, "Or could you get us men some coffee?"

This feeble jab in their friendly, ongoing battle of the sexes earned him a quick, resigned glance. "I'm fresh out of both, I'm afraid."

Matt rubbed the bridge of his nose. "Do we even know what Gwynne's wearing right now?"

"Probably not." Alice lifted a sheet. "When she left Ryan's she was wearing the Saks suit. When she walked away from church, she was wearing the Saks suit. But—"

She didn't have to finish. No one had arrived at the zoo wearing a Saks suit. They didn't even know if she had gone to the zoo. They didn't know squat.

Matt didn't like it. As Riggs had pointed out yesterday, she was a romance writer and they were the marshals. This was not the way it was supposed to be.

"I've got a description of her watch and shoes," she offered with the same hopeful air she'd probably use giving sand to a thirsty man.

"A watch and a pair of shoes. Why am I not excited? Hell, Alice, she could have already dumped them."

Alice's smile showed some teeth. "Since you're a man and couldn't possibly understand the irresistible appeal of *comfortable* shoes, I'll cut you some slack, Matt. It's just—" She gave a frustrated sigh. "She's not just changing her clothes. She's changing *herself*."

Henry stopped his pacing and looked thoughtful. He liked to think he had a sensitive side. "She has done community theater back in the Big Easy, Matt."

"Then let's find out what parts she's played. Like I said, more brains, less frustration." Matt had a thought. "Ryan mentioned some book—Alice?"

"*Lord of the Rings*. We found it at the crime scene, remember?"

Matt nodded. "I want to take a look at it. And her books. The ones she reads and the ones she writes. You're a fan, Alice. You got copies?"

"A new fan. I have one. Plan to get more."

"Fine. Plan to do it now. Make a list and give it to Henry. You don't mind buying some romance novels, do you?" Henry obviously did, but he couldn't say so without appearing insensitive. "Check local bookstores. If you strike out there, try the library. The sun's going down on day two, people. I want a lead before it comes up again." He turned to Sebastian. "Speaking of leads, you got anything on any local acquaintances she might contact next?"

Sebastian rubbed his bony chin. "Well, I got a damn long list of local people who are online. Having a little trouble deciding who she'd turn to. It's not like we have time to call them all."

Matt looked at Alice. "Librarians? Writers? Booksellers?"

Alice shrugged. "It's a place to start. We can cross reference by hobbies, interests, occupation, eliminate the obviously non-compatibles."

"And level of contact," Sebastian put in. "I can identify the ones she's talked to a lot under her known identity. I should have something on any other identities from Boomer by tomorrow afternoon at the latest."

"Good. Go to it, people." He leaned back in his chair as they filed out on their separate errands. He was the only one with nothing to do but think. Had she received his e-mail? What would she do when she did?

"Rushdie was right," Hayes muttered, "our lives do teach us who we are. Even better, your life will teach me who you are, Dani Gwynne. Once it has, I'll end it."

For a moment his temper had almost gotten away from him when his contact inside the police department had let him know too late for him to reach Gwynne at Ryan's house. He would have enjoyed killing her in the suburbs. He had always hated his parent's milieu. Lucky for his snitch the feds had gone away empty-handed, too.

What would she do next, he wondered, fingering his knife in anticipation. It was an interesting problem. Absently he tested the blade, leaving a beaded, red trail along the edge of his finger. He sucked the cut as he read a photocopy of Gwynne's file detailing her interest, among many others, in the Internet.

The first thing Gwynne had done was turn to someone she'd met online. Quite a clever idea really. It added an interactive dimension to the hunt. If she stayed connected he could hunt her *and* talk to her. Assault her mind while he hunted her body.

He turned to his computer and logged on to the Net. He had already arranged to read her e-mail, to get any replies she sent. Now he read Kirby's e-mail with interest. How would she respond to it's commanding tone? It would tell him a lot about her when she did. Then he would know how to act. Where to act. Another bead of red blood formed along the cut he had made on his finger, hovered briefly, then dropped onto the keyboard in a perfect, quivering circle.

He smiled, thinking of her blood falling like rain. It would flow softly at first, but soon it would turn into a rushing red river sweeping her life away. Then the fire would lick at the river, swallowing red moisture in a flickering, healing flame. Heat made a shaft through his middle, quickening his breathing.

His hands settled on keys slick with sweat and his own blood. Breath came in short, panting gasps as he formed his first words to her. In a sharp crescendo, he finished and sagged back in the chair, his thoughts centered on the two women in his life.

Dani Gwynne. The one he had to kill.

Willow. The one he had to love.

Soon he would have both where he wanted them.

Dani had exchanged her grandma attire for tattered jeans and a Stones tee shirt before approaching her next kindly stranger. The smart little hat was now a "gimme" variety put out by the Denver Nuggets. The briefcase was now a ratty backpack.

With the sun beginning a hurried decline in the western sky, she studied the junkyard/garage combination across the street from her, then checked the address against the one on her printout. This was the place.

She just hoped the stranger was more kindly than his digs.

After hitching her backpack to a more comfortable spot

on her shoulder, she crossed the dusty street and cautiously pushed the rusted door. She winced at the protest the sagging metal hinges made against movement, then slid through the gap. Before her eyes could adjust to the light change, her nose identified—and wrinkled against—a pungent mix of grease, paint, dust, beer and old sweat. Dani took a step back, then stopped. If not here, where could she go?

"I'm closed," a deep voice rumbled at her out of the deep shadow. It took her a minute to separate the massive figure lovingly polishing a Harley-Davidson motorcycle from the shadowy chunks of equipment.

"Meathook?"

"Who wants to know?" He stood up, sending an already impressive shadow spreading across the clutter floor.

She grinned, recognizing the "voice" of her online friend, even if the figure wasn't familiar. "I want to know."

He started toward her, getting bigger with each step. The meager light outlined each bulging muscle and the bush of a beard that obscured the lower half of his face.

"Who the hell are you?"

She held her ground. "Willow, that's who."

"Willow? Internet Willow?" She nodded. Like a spring thaw, a smile cracked the severity of beard and face, splitting his battered face into less menacing lines. "Well, I'll be damned."

Chapter Seven

Matt could tell from Alice's carefully demure expression as she wove her way between desks that she had more bad news for him. He stood up and stretched his back. It eased the painful kink from another long night spent in the office, made him feel like he was doing something besides pushing paper.

"What?" What now, is what he meant.

"Dani answered your e-mail." The amusement in her eyes told him it was personal.

Matt looked past her. "I thought Sebastian was in charge of e-mail?"

"He was afraid." Alice handed him the sheet, then put her hands on her hips, a look on her face that reminded him of his mother when she was about to deliver an improving lecture. "We're all afraid of you, you know."

"Yeah, I noticed you shaking in your high-heeled shoes." He unfolded the sheet. Under the usual e-mail header gibberish were four words: *I don't think so.*

He rubbed the bridge of his nose. It didn't bring enlightenment. "What the hell does this mean?"

Alice shrugged elegantly. "Uh, no?"

"Damn it." Matt dropped into his chair, tossed the note onto the desk top, picked it up again and scowled at it for the sweep of a second hand, then threw it down again. "What's her problem?"

Alice looked amused. "Maybe you shouldn't have told her to get her ass back in here—"

"Why the hell not?" He shoved his hands through his

hair, trying not to tear it out. He didn't have that much to spare and sure as hell didn't want to waste it on a capricious romance writer. "Don't you think she should get her ass back in here?"

"Yes, but—"

"No. No buts. Right is right. Right?"

"Not if she doesn't know it. For Pete's sake, Matt, she doesn't know us from Neuman." Alice sat down across from him, her expression sympathetic but still openly amused. "To her, we're just a new set of feds who may or may not get her killed."

He knew that. No, he didn't. If he was feeling weird, she should be, too. He rubbed his face. "I need coffee. Has anybody made any?"

Alice started to get up, but Matt stopped her with a shake of his head. "I'll get it. Wouldn't want to be accused of committing a non-politically correct act. Besides," he stretched his back, twisting his shoulders left and right, "I could use the exercise."

It felt good to be in motion, however brief the duration. Back at his desk, he handed Alice a steaming cup, before settling in his chair again. His back protested, but subsided a bit after he'd downed half his mug. Calmer, he asked, "So how do we convince her we're the good guys?"

Alice took a careful sip before she said, "The good news is, Carolyn Ryan came down on our side. She e-mailed Gwynne shortly after we left."

"Let me see it." Matt held out his hand, unease returning at the slight, though obvious, reluctance with which she handed it over. He read it. His brows arched. He looked at Alice. "Cute-assed fed? Fine hunting hound dog? Is she talking about me?"

Alice grinned. "I don't think she'd call me a cute-assed

fed. And you do hunt people, Matt."

"I hunt a lot of things, but last time I looked I only had two legs and don't howl—very often. What the hell is this stuff?"

He turned the sheet so Alice could see the strangely configured punctuation at the end of the letter: :-).

Alice craned to look. "I wondered about that, too. Sebastian says it's called a smiley—"

"A what?" He barked the question at her.

"A smiley. You have to tip your head to the side—"

Matt's eyes narrowed sharply.

"—or not." Alice got her grin under control before adding, "They're called emoticons—emotional punctuation used to add emotion to plain text. Sebastian's getting you a dictionary—"

"There's a whole dictionary of these things?" He leaned back. The one good thing about computers, in his opinion, was their total lack of emotion. So someone gets the bright idea to add emotion? What a world. "If being called a cute-assed fed is the good news, what the hell's the bad news?"

"Hayes has e-mailed Gwynne, too."

"What?" Matt straightened in his chair, but it wasn't enough. He jumped up and paced to her side of the desk, grabbing the last sheet she had in her bag of tricks.

Death hath many doors to let out life, Dani.
Soon I'll open yours and send you through.
How are you sleeping nights?
Still dreaming about me?

"Nasty, isn't it?" Alice said.

"Not nice." Urgency went from a steady clip to a hundred in a heartbeat. "Any indication she's picked this up?"

Alice shook her head. "And, no, we can't stop her getting

it. I already asked. Sebastian says that, based on Hayes's record as a computer whiz, he's probably reading her mail, too—including what we send her." She hesitated. "We're going to have to let her know our communications with her aren't secure, Matt."

"Re-enforcing her belief that we can't be trusted." Matt leaned against the edge of his desk, thinking about Dani. About Hayes. Instead of a lover's triangle, they were a killer's triangle. The hit man, the marshal and the romance writer, bound together by the greed and ambition of Richard Hastings, accused murderer with some still unknown tie to the mob. When the hit man was Jonathan Hayes, it was weird enough to make a guy wax philosophical—if he had the time or inclination for that kind of shit. He looked at Alice. "Do it. Tell her Hayes is listening in. Hell, she's probably already figured it out. Maybe we can get some points for honesty. You women like that, don't you?"

"Yeah, we just love it," Alice said dryly as she stood up, "especially when you're so sincere about it."

"I don't have time to be sincere. Have Riggs give a copy of this to Sebastian's identity friend, what was his name?"

"Boomer Edison?"

"Yeah, him. Maybe he can find Hayes out there, too." He crossed round to his chair and leaned back, steepling his hands into a triangle. As Alice walked away, he brought two points of his triangle together. The action pushed the last point away. Good thing he didn't get off on symbolism or believe in bad omens.

Riggs poked his head in long enough to say, "Boomer Edison called. Says he'll have something for us right after lunch."

Matt nodded, leaning back with his hands clasped behind his head and rocking the chair in time with his thoughts.

See, no good or bad omens. Just patient hard work by people following a time-proven process. He could do patient. He picked up a report and leaned back, his body carefully relaxed in the chair.

His fingers, in pointed defiance, beat impatiently against the arm rest.

"Mornin'." Meathook, aka Meat, filled the doorway of his bedroom from frame to frame and then some. His eyes were still groggy, his body stripped down to a pair of hip-hugging leather pants that left his massive chest bare—though bare wasn't the best description for a body so thoroughly furry. He was a walking, talking biker-with-a-heart-of-gold cliché—something Dani usually tried to avoid in her life and her fiction. He was also a thoroughly nice guy, who had done two tours in Vietnam, lost a child to death, his wife to denial of that death and dealt with it all by writing nonsense rhymes for children. A stereotype with a twist, she thought. She needed him, his innate goodness, more than she needed her soda or M&M's, though she was happy that his house had both.

He roughed up his beard and stretched. "Thought you'd still be getting your Zs."

She hadn't slept much, but it was easier to agree than explain she'd finished her chapters and cruised the Internet most of the night. "Been checking my e-mail."

And wishing she hadn't done that part. She lay slackly against his mama's Naugahyde couch, her laptop with Dark Lord's e-mail still on the screen resting on her knees, her feet resting on the scarred, biker magazine-buried coffee table. On one side was a purple lava lamp, on the other a full size street sign from Las Vegas, in front of her, a fake fireplace mantel covered with an array of photos that started with a wrinkled newborn and stopped with a bright-eyed little boy of seven.

Meat rubbed his face vigorously, then crossed in front of her on an intercept course with the refrigerator. He held up a carton of orange juice. "You want some?"

"No thanks. I already had a soda." She held up the can, but the caffeine in it hadn't helped. She was tired right down to her soul. If she was about to break, she was too tired to know it.

Meat drank out of the carton, carried it with him to the mantel where he stopped by the last picture in the row, a photo of a little boy in uniform kneeling by a soccer ball. He stroked the picture lightly, as if he were stroking his son's head.

Dani had a feeling this was a daily ritual. How well she understood the compulsion. Even after ten years, she would be somewhere and suddenly panic wondering where Meggie was. Or she'd see a toy she knew Meggie would like and be up to the checkout before she remembered.

"He's beautiful," Dani said, huskily. She hesitated, then asked, "How's—Opal?"

Meathook hunched his shoulders, turning from his son's picture to the window that overlooked the junkyard. "Piss poor. Can't stop blaming herself. I—don't think she's going to get over it."

"Getting over it isn't possible, is it?"

"No. It ain't." He looked at her. "But we ain't sitting in a hospital staring at a blank wall."

Dani smiled wryly, thinking about Meggie's father who spent his days staring into a whisky bottle. "Maybe we should be."

His laugh was surprised, edged with loss. "Yeah, maybe. How come we're not?"

What made it possible for some people to absorb the body blow of loss, while it was a knock-out punch for others? Why was she trying so hard to keep going when it would be so much easier to quit? For answers to these and other questions, stay tuned, she thought wryly. Aloud she said, "I don't know. I know if I sit for too long, I have to pee. Once I'm up—" She shrugged. "I just keep—going. I guess I don't know how to stop."

Was going forward progress, she wondered suddenly, or just a different form of denial? She looked up and realized he was looking at her, his dark eyes uncomfortably penetrating.

"What?" she asked.

"You want to talk about the deep shit you don't know how to stop?"

She had known before she met him that he wouldn't be clueless, but thought she was putting on a good show. Apparently she thought wrong.

"It's pretty deep, Meat. Deep and—dangerous."

He dropped down next to her, making a crater in the Naugahyde surface. She slid down it and thumped against his side. He wrapped his arm around her and squeezed. It was like being hugged by a tree trunk.

"Tell your Uncle Meat all about it."

Dani chuckled, even as tears pricked at her tired eyes. Telling was too hard, so Dani turned the laptop with Dark Lord's letter front and center toward him. She didn't have to read along with him. She had it memorized after the first read through.

Are you sleeping nights?

If she had been sleeping, which she wasn't, she wouldn't be now.

Meat inhaled sharply. "Why's this bastard got it in for you?"

"For him, it's a business transaction." Amazing as it seemed, it wasn't personal. He was a supplier, her death the demand. "You been following the Richard Hastings case?"

Meat frowned. "He's that do-gooder that plugged some chick last year?" At Dani's nod, he frowned. "What's that got to do with you?"

"I saw him do it. I knew him. His bad luck. My bad luck. He doesn't want to go to prison. This guy," Dani nodded at the screen, "is gonna make me forget what I saw."

"Bastards." Meat's forehead creased. Finally, he asked, "What's a do-gooder doing hiring a hit?"

Her laugh was sharp and unamused. "They tell me the FBI is wondering the same thing. As far as I know, they haven't found out. I've known Richard since I was sixteen and I don't get it."

And what had all that knowing added up to? Nothing. Even now, with the picture of him killing burned in her brain so it could play and replay in her nightmares, some part of her couldn't quite believe it. Was she that gullible or was he that clever? Would she live long enough to find out?

"Sucks, don't it?"

"Dead toads," she agreed.

Meat grinned, then grew serious. He tapped the screen lightly. "Isn't this kind of weird? I admit I'm not up on hit men protocol, but this is pushing the envelope. I wonder—"

He stopped, obviously following a line of thought she couldn't see. Dani waited a bit, but finally prompted, "Wonder—what?"

"I bet this guy is a regular on the Net. See that crap at the top?"

"Yeah?"

"The right person could use it to trace him back to his dirty, little hidey-hole."

"I knew that. But Spook told me you can counterfeit that stuff."

"Spook would know," Meat conceded. "But you can't hide your personal style. If he's on the boards, Boomer Edison can find him."

"Really?" It was an interesting concept. "Could I talk to him?"

"If you can throw a leg over a Harley, I can take you to him."

Dani smiled. "I've always wanted to throw a leg over a Harley—as long as the leg was still attached to my body."

Meat chuckled. "Can you wait for my lunch hour? Gotta get a Hog ready for 11:30."

"No problem." It would give her time to come up with a Harley-compatible persona suitable for public viewing.

It was easy, but time consuming for Hayes to cross-reference Dani Gwynne's online posts with the people she chatted with then sort them by locality. The program had run most of the night while he tried—and failed—to sleep. Now the printer spit out a series of lists comprised of the people she'd chatted directly with, then cross-referenced by the different places she visited regularly. Contact wasn't always public. "Going private," taking a discussion to the privacy of e-mail, was a common practice throughout the Internet. He and Willow had gone private soon after meeting, though she'd continued to politely but firmly resist the intimacy Hayes was determined to have with her.

How could she fight fate?

The printer finished its work and Hayes gathered up the sheets, shuffling quickly through them for anything that might stand out. Much of what he did was through a finely honed intuition. Nothing jumped out at him. This kind of research wasn't part of his normal procedure. When he got a hit, the research had been done by Bates people. All that was left for him was the kill. This time he was willing to make some effort, as long as it was the right kind of effort. The kind that would lead him to Dani Gwynne.

Effort is only effort when it begins to hurt, Hayes recalled the phrase culled from the "quote wars." It was hurting, so he must be close. He pulled up the lists, removed the first five names from one, then faxed the rest to Bates with instructions at the top to have some of his people check them for signs of Gwynne. Wouldn't hurt Bates to exert himself or his people.

His short list consisted of four women and one male. The women were romance writers with a high probability of contact. The male was a biker, fairly low probability, name of Meathook. Hayes knew him online. He and Willow chatted with him. There were no outward signs Gwynne had talked to Meathook, a remote chance she'd seek him out. Hayes almost crossed him off the list, then stopped. It wasn't likely, but he couldn't afford to pass up even remote chances with just five days left until the trial. Bates was getting restive. Only his very real fear of Hayes kept him in check. If he thought Hayes could fail, that fear would fade. He didn't need Bates complicating matters right now.

Hayes looked at his watch. He should be able to hit all five names before lunch, sooner than that if he was lucky.

He was feeling lucky.

Chapter Eight

Boomer Edison's office was so awash with paper and technology, Dani almost couldn't find him. She found a shock of orange hair moving in the mass and used it to home in on where he'd hunkered down, typing at two of three computers. A third whirred with the effort of making a printer spew pages in a continuous feed. Except for bifocals perched on the tip of his nose that gave him a vaguely mad scientist air, he looked like a football player who'd taken a wrong turn on his way to the field. His tee shirt even sported a number: infinity.

He didn't fit into Dani's notion of a computer whiz. But then she no longer fit anyone's idea of a romance writer. Meat's Mama had played fairy biker "motha," but instead of taffeta and glass slippers, Dani now sported black army boots, shiny black leather shorts, a bandeau top that doubled as a push-up bra—more than doubling her available assets—with a black vest pulled over. In her neon beauty salon, conveniently attached to Meat's junkyard, Mama had trimmed and planted a pyrotechnic bomb in Dani's hair, then did her face in a combination of slut and Elvira that somehow worked.

After a bit of coaching on her attitude, Dani had thrown her leg over the back of Meat's Harley and hung on. They stopped once so she could mail her chapters to her agent, then headed for Boomer's office. She got off the Hog feeling like she could kick some serious ass—a feeling she liked. It made a nice change from whimpering and cowering.

Dani propped her shoulder against the doorframe, raised

her voice to be heard over the technology, and asked, "You Boomer?"

"Yeah, I'm—" He turned to look at her, impatience melting into a look of shock when his gaze collided with the biker babe interrupting him.

Dani chewed the gum Mama had insisted was mandatory and let him look his fill while she studied the scarlet tipped, acrylic nails Mama had applied. If Shakespeare was right and life was a stage, then timing was everything. She wanted him to be capable of thought—but just enough to help her without asking too many questions.

"Can I help you?" The question emerged minus some of his bass tones.

"Meathook said you could, like, help me with a little problem I'm having?" Dani felt the particularly lethal point of her index finger, while studying him through her outrageous lashes. He looked to be simmering nicely.

"Meat—hook?" He dabbed at the sweat popping out across his forehead.

"Big guy, tattoos, nice Hog?" she prompted gently.

His grin was edged with sheepish. "Oh yeah. Meat. What can I do for you?"

Dani smiled back, hoping it was as smoky as it felt. "I been getting this, like, shitty e-mail crap from some jerk. Meat says, like, maybe you can tell us who it is, so he could, I dunno, kill him or something?"

She could almost see his knight in shining armor genes kick in. He straightened. "I might. You got copies?"

"Yeah." She worked her way through his paper stack maze so she could hand him the print-out, then propped her elbows on a chest high pile to watch him at work.

It wasn't until he blinked and swallowed so dryly she could hear it that she realized the movement had put her cleavage on display. The romance writer inside cringed, but biker babe licked her lips, then watched the sweat on his skin sizzle like water on a hot skillet.

"I—uh—usually need several posts for a good match—" he stuttered. Biker Babe looked disappointed and he rushed to add, "—but I can try."

She made eye contact, held it for two beats, then said, "I'd be real grateful if you would." She parted her lips slightly, waited another beat, and added, "Real grateful."

His glasses fogged over. He took them off and turned to the computer, his hands visibly shaking.

Cool. Dani straightened, glad she wouldn't have to deliver on that gratitude, though not unhappy with his response. She'd have to seriously consider adding a leather scene to her next book.

While his fingers fumbled on the keys, she looked around. The high-tech clutter of Boomer's space was interesting, particularly to someone with her cyberspace habits. The up side of being hunted like a dog was that she got to learn so much. Idly, she thumbed a stack of print-outs—

She stopped, her gaze caught by a name at the top of a list on the first sheet. Willow? She tipped her head to read what turned out to be a nearly complete list of her online handles. As far as she could tell, he'd missed only one. It didn't take much imagination to figure out she wasn't the only one who'd availed themselves of Boomer's special ID hunting skills. She ought to make sure. It could be Dark Lord.

"So, what's all this Willow stuff?"

Boomer looked up, trying to look modestly proud. The effort put a twitch at the edge of his right eye. "That's a search I did for the feds."

"Bitchin'." Dani smoothed back her heavily moussed hair. "So you think you can find my guy?"

He sighed, fiddling with the stack of papers closest to him. "Less I have to work with, harder it is."

"Oh." She chewed her gum, trying to find a way to exit stage right. She had run a check on Matt Kirby, Marshals Service tracker. He was good. Not the type to let sleeping lists lie. She'd bet her leather brassiere he or his guys would be here any minute to collect. Did she hear baying hounds getting closer? Absolutely. "So, when do you think you'll, like, know?"

Boomer shrugged. "Tomorrow?"

"I'll check back then. Thanks." It was all he was going to get, so she gave him her sultriest smile. Instead of smiling back, he jumped to his feet, a look of dismay marring the stupor she'd worked so hard to put on his face.

"Inspector!" he croaked out.

Dani stiffened. The hounds, it appeared, were closer than she'd realized. It didn't matter, she told herself with all the bravado she could muster. She was Biker Babe. She wasn't afraid of no fed. No way.

She turned. The fed filled the doorway, giving Dani no choice but to study him.

It wasn't a hardship.

What hit her first was how large and solid he looked, how safe it made her feel to have him looming over her. He was as broad as Texas and solid as the Rock—which is what he looked like he'd been carved out of—pure granite, except for his molten, brooding eyes. They'd been poured in under the wide forehead and then given the power to cut through flesh and sinew in search of buried secrets and hidden desires. The only softness she could find in his whole face was the dark hair brushed back from his face and the slightly full under lip of his straight mouth that no amount of iron control could harden.

She recognized the weakness in her knees and the warmth that started in places that had been polar since her marriage bit the dust. She should. She'd written about it often enough. Warmth flickered to flame when her gaze found the place where his conservative suit jacket met sexy, well-worn jeans, wrapped around narrow hips and powerful legs planted firmly in her path.

Wow. Her hands curled into fists against the urge to fan herself. She shouldn't be surprised there was life in the old hormones, or even that this man was stirring them up.

His raw, barely leashed energy wasn't just physical. The rock had a volcano at its heart. She was looking at an alpha male—in the finely formed flesh—or she wasn't a romance writer in biker babe drag.

No wonder Carolyn had waxed lyrical about his assets. It was a wonder she could wax anything or do anything but drool.

From the heat moving like thick honey through her midsection came an instinctive urge to seek the safety of his sturdy body, to trust in the self-confidence he wore as comfortably as his jeans. He wasn't just sexy as hell. He was a law man. A hunter. He wouldn't go around obstacles. He'd go through whatever stood in his way and over anyone keeping him from what he wanted.

He wanted her.

The idea did nothing to cool her jets until she reminded her unruly libido it was what she *knew* that he wanted, what she'd *seen*. He needed her to get to Dark Lord.

Trying for detachment she studied the scuffed cowboy boots he wore. They'd be laying a track right over her if she didn't get out of here before he turned his hunting dog nose and laser eyes on Biker Babe and saw Dani cowering underneath.

Hmmm. Biker babes walked, they didn't get walked on, she reminded herself. She took a steadying breath, hoping Mama's work was as good as she'd thought it was, then asked in a carefully calculated drawl, "You putting down roots, cowboy, or just coming in real slow?"

As soon as he looked at her, she knew it was a tactical error to demand his attention. She'd watched the surgical steel in his eyes cut through Boomer. She might be Biker Babe on the outside, but inside she was still romance writing woman who should have kept a low profile and hoped he'd get what he came for without seeing what he was looking for.

Stark naked in a stadium full of men would have felt less exposing than being caught in his gaze. Time to go. She took an unsteady breath and stepped toward him. If he was a gentleman, he'd move.

He wasn't and didn't. Let's try that one again. He had to move, didn't he? She took another step. Nothing. Was he made of stone? A single stack of paper separated them. Even worse, she was close enough to see the smooth-rough texture of his skin, the different variations of brown in his eyes, and the lines fanning out from those eyes and his mouth—wait a minute. Was that a twitch at the edge of his mouth? Was she imagining—no, there it went again. Definitely a twitch.

Was that good or bad? She did one sidestep, then one forward step. Now she was close enough to see, not just feel the banked fire behind the cool control in his eyes, close enough to see the jump of the pulse at his neck just above the crisp white shirt.

Well, well, the hunter wasn't all cold, hard rock. Like a fire changing direction in the wind, embarrassed heat turned into pleased elemental flame. Had she thought him safe? He wasn't. He'd be dangerous, even if she wasn't in trouble. He stirred the ashes of her past, reminding her of what it felt like to want, to need, to feel that first surprised shock of desire. To recognize that this man was different from all the others. That even if she walked away, she exchanged something in her for something in him.

Dani wrote books about desire. She'd heard songs sung about it, read poems crafted for it, but she still didn't have a clue why one particular pair of eyes could make bones go soft as butter. Why one man's smile could tempt a woman to step out of the safe zone into passion's battlefield, even when she knew it could mow her down.

His dark gaze took her to the knife edge of knowing why Eve chose knowledge in Adam's embrace over that pretty Garden. It tempted her to surrender lonely autonomy for the shared warmth of his molten gaze.

She'd been cold a long time.

If he knew who she was, if he knew who he was looking at, she'd be on the fast track to bait city. Desire wouldn't turn that jaw from pursuit of Dark Lord. She had to get away before her hormones effected a *coup d'etat* on her willpower.

Her throat was dry with longing as she forced out, "You make a better wall than a door, cowboy."

He heard her words, knew he needed to move, but Matt was wound so tight he didn't know if he could. She wasn't his type. She wasn't on the same planet as his type. His body didn't seem to care. It registered only that she was long and lean, except where the leather fell open to frame her round, full breasts. That she was giving off enough bravado to bring out the beast in any guy with a beating heart and working equipment didn't help.

His parts were doing what nature intended them to do,

despite a determined rearguard action by his common sense. His blood supply was draining south faster than a cowboy's first beer, taking the oxygen he needed for thinking. Sweat beaded his brow. A red mist formed in front of his eyes. His chest went tight from the scent of warmed leather, warmer woman, and something he should recognize, but couldn't because of that blood shortage handicap.

Riggs, straining to get a look over Matt's shoulder, accomplished what Matt couldn't do for himself, bumping him aside, and leaving a small channel for her to pass through, one so small her body brushed excruciatingly against him as she edged past.

Her lashes hid her eyes from him. The makeup was heavy on her face, but it couldn't hide the clean, strong foundation of her bones. Her hair was a wild halo around her face, wild like she'd just been prone and seriously physical. At the last minute, her lashes lifted, her gaze catching his, holding it captive while she cut the ground from under his feet without blinking.

Her eyes. Deep in his brain an alarm went off. As if she heard it, she broke the contact and stepped past him into the hallway. Hands on leather hips, she looked over her shoulder, her gaze flicking down, then up, the depths slumberous with "come hither," her smile weighted with warning. "Thanks, cowboy."

"You're welcome," he said, wanting to match her grin and raise it. Wanting nothing more than to escalate this sudden battle of the sexes with his own salvo. He didn't. He was an adult. A professional. He almost forgot both when her eyes called him coward. Then she turned and headed down the hall, each swish of her leather-covered hips packing a prizefighter's punch to his gut.

"Hot damn," Riggs said in his ear, adding reverently,

"Kinda restores your faith in a higher power, don't it?"

"Yeah." Matt watched her pause at a bulletin board covered with flyers. She paused very well.

"Do you think she's reading that or just looking at the pictures?" Riggs asked, awed.

Dani heard the question as she stared blindly at the board. The chilled air in the hallway stroked goose bumps across her heated skin. She could still feel the way their bodies had brushed together, still smell him with each unsteady breath, but when she heard Matt snap, "Does it matter?" she knew she'd made the right decision.

Damn him. Damn both of them for not seeing Dani underneath Biker Babe. If she got out of this alive, she was going to put the alpha hero in her next book through total hell. She stared at the flyer hard enough to burn a hole right through it, felt his eyes boring into her for an endless moment. The urge to turn and challenge him was almost overwhelming.

She almost sagged with relief when she felt his attention shift away. Her heart pounding in her throat, she took a cautious peek and saw him start into Boomer's office. Then he stopped and stepped back, his back to her, so his partner could go in ahead of him.

She still wanted to rail at him, but she did have to admit one thing. Carolyn was wrong. His ass wasn't just fine. It was *really* fine. Jeans ought to be illegal on men who already had the corner on sexy.

She sighed, turned to go, when she caught a familiar name out of the corner of her eye. She stopped, more closely examining the flyer. Kelly Kerwin, listed as the featured speaker for the writers conference the flyer was promoting.

Kelly. It was like finding land in a storm. Course, Kelly

would probably tell her to get her ass back down the hall and jump that man's bones.

Dani grinned, felt Biker Babe make a come back. Just in time, too. Matt started to follow his partner, hesitated, then looked back at her, like he couldn't help himself. She gave him a cheeky grin, then turned and headed down the hall away from him, taking each step like the song said, one hip at a time, reveling in knowing he watched every one.

Matt didn't, couldn't move, until she turned the corner out of his sight. What the hell was wrong with him? He couldn't blame this on Dani Gwynne. Maybe she wasn't the problem. Maybe he needed to get out more, chase some women instead of fugitives. He shook his head sharply, trying to break free of the keen bite of lust brought on by swaying hips, endless legs and those cutting eyes—

He stepped into Boomer's office, frowning, his unease returning in a pointed surge. What was it about her eyes—

Riggs held up a printout. "We got ten possibles with the five mostly likely matches near the top. The list of people each handle chats with is attached."

"Let me see." Matt took the sheet, blinked twice before the first name came into focus. *Willow.* Again he felt the kick of instinct—her posts. Something he'd read in her posts—*like the willow tree, I bend, not break . . .*

It was almost too obvious. "That's her. I'm sure of it. Did you give him the e-mail from Hayes?"

"Not yet." Riggs pulled the sheet out of his coat pocket and handed it to Boomer.

Matt looked at the list of names again, then lifted the sheet, and quickly scanned the list of people Willow chatted with—a biker called Meathook? Biker? Biker's babe? Pieces were falling into place around him as lightly as boulders, but it couldn't be that easy—or could it?

The moment they'd been chest-to-chest came back to him. Leather. She'd smelled of leather but there'd been something else, something too elusive for him to be sure—

Boomer looked up. "I've already seen this e-mail—"

"Coconut. And her eyes. Son of a bitch." Matt turned, his boots slipping against the tile floor as he dived for the door. Riggs made a plaintive sound behind him. Matt ignored him, too intent on getting down the hall. It took forever until he skidded around the corner and slammed into the railing. Lucky for him it wasn't too low. Matt was only winded when he looked down and saw her in the heart of the stairwell, her hand on the door.

"Dani Gwynne!" She started and looked up at him, Biker Babe fading abruptly from her upturned face. He couldn't believe he'd missed it before. Maybe the leather had confused his thinking. And the legs. And the breasts. He shook his head sharply. Her body was tense with a fight-or-flight wariness that was as disturbing as her cocky stance had been. His was tense with lust. Her eyes flashed a warning he couldn't ignore. It took effort to ask with tight calm, "Can we talk?"

She hesitated. "About what?"

About what? Control be damned. "Oh, I don't know— how about the guy trying to kill you?"

Her gaze narrowed. "You want him bad, don't you, cowboy?"

"It's my job to want him bad."

"Funny," she said, looking suddenly sad, "I thought it was to protect me." She pushed the door open.

Trust a woman to turn it around. "Damn it—"

She was already sliding out the door, calling as she ran, "Meat!"

Matt jumped the rail as Riggs ran up beside him. He

landed hard, slid down four steps before he got his balance again, heard the roar as a bike was kicked to life. He plunged recklessly to the bottom, taking the steps in threes and made the door just as she was throwing her leg over the back of a nice looking Hog. He just had time to make the license plate before they wheeled in a circle and roared down the street.

"Son of a bitch!" He started for his car, remembered Riggs had the keys. "Keys, Riggs!"

Riggs, puffing like he had asthma and patting frantically, joined him in a dash to the car. "You sure I got 'em?"

Matt stared at the Hog getting smaller and smaller. "Just find the damn keys!"

"Uh, Matt?"

"What?"

"I found the keys."

He turned, saw Riggs pointing inside the car. "You didn't."

Riggs shoved his hands in his pockets and contemplated the sky. "Oops."

With a low moan, Matt leaned on the car, mentally cursing fate, Riggs and the romance writer, while a moving picture of her long legs and leather-covered ass settling on the back of the Hog played repeatedly in his head.

Hayes watched the Hog pass with his prey, then pulled in behind them. Who would have thought that she'd go to the biker Meathook for help? And yet, why not? Both of them had lost a child in accidents. Learned their first lesson in that ultimate democracy called death.

Like a shadow he followed each turn they made until they stopped in a convenience store parking lot. They were splitting up. Good. He saw her look up at Meathook, her face shadowed. Did she sense him? Perhaps. It didn't matter. She was about to get her last lesson in death. Like the proverb said, "Death is a shadow that always follows the body." He was, Hayes thought with rising pleasure, that shadow for Dani Gwynne.

There'd be no escape for her this time.

Chapter Nine

"You sure you're gonna be all right? Don't like leaving you here." Meat stared down the dreary street with a scowl. "Mama ain't gonna like it neither."

"He made your plate, Meat. They could be at your doorstep by now. Biker Babe is too hot."

Meat's gaze flicked down to her legs and back. He grinned. "Can't argue with that, sweet thing."

Dani smiled, but it wavered at the edges, then faded. "I can't thank you enough, big guy."

He looked down, shuffling his feet. "Shit. You ain't gonna get mushy on me are you?"

"Yeah. Deal with it. It's the price you pay for being there for me. Now give me a hug."

"Well," he opened his arms wide, "if you insist."

When his arms closed around her, she closed her eyes, absorbing comfort from him, drawing strength from his sturdy male body while the iron rings of his leather vest dug into her cheek.

It hurt to step back alone. With the sun westering in the sky, she felt her will to go the distance waver.

"Willow—" Meat frowned, as if he sensed her indecision.

"I'm gonna be fine. Really." She didn't convince herself, probably didn't convince him, but it didn't matter. It couldn't change what she had to do.

"Yeah." He slung a leg over his machine. "Tell Oxford I sent you. He'll make you a good deal."

"Sure."

"Watch your back, babe." He gave a vaguely frustrated shake of his head, then kicked his Hog to life, put it in gear and made a slow, wide turn away from her before picking up speed with a roar and a final wave.

Dani watched until he was out of sight, then turned and pushed open the door of the convenience store. Inside, she could hear Mary Chapin Carpenter singing about taking chances. Easy for her, Dani thought sourly. She didn't have a killer stalking her waking and sleeping and a very short list of strangers to call for help.

She studied her list, then dialed, unreasonably annoyed when there was no answer at his number. How like a man to tell you to let him know when you're in town, then not be there. Dani couldn't think of any message that wouldn't sound paranoid, so she hung up without speaking. She should have left then, but instead she stared at the pay phone like it held the answers to her problem.

She was adrift in the city, night was approaching fast, and she was desperately in need of contact with someone solidly on her side.

Think, Dani. You've got yourself out of plot dead ends before. Use your noodle.

A pity her noodle, even with a Diet Dr. Pepper charge, was mush. She couldn't fight temptation, not now. She reached for the telephone, dialed, waited for a pick up and said, "This is Dani. Let me talk to Pat."

It was a short wait before her agent came on. "Dani! What the hell are you doing?"

Dani leaned against the dirty wall, using both hands to hold the telephone against her ear. "I'm calling you on the phone. Why?"

"What's wrong? You back with the feds?"

"No. I—needed to hear a friendly voice."

"And you called me?"

Dani smiled and leaned against the wall. "Yeah, well, I had to settle for bracing, okay?"

"Feeling sorry for yourself?"

Dani's laugh broke in the middle. "Yes, damn you."

"What happened?"

"What hasn't happened?"

Pat was quiet. "You in trouble?"

"Trouble? Me? Why would you think that? Just because the bad guy wants to torch me and the good guys want to turn me into a target? That's not trouble, is it?"

"Can the pity wallow and do something. When have you ever choked over a plot?"

Dani smiled shakily as tears stacked up in her eyes. "Do you always have to be right?"

"Yes." Pat hesitated. "Call them, Dani."

"Call who?"

"You know who."

Dani hesitated, opened her mouth to protest, then closed it. Talking to Pat put you solidly in the no bullshit zone. Arguing with her would use up scarce energy. "I'll think about it. Better go now. They're probably tracing this call."

"Take care, Dani." Pat's voice didn't sound quite so brusque, until she added, "I'd hate to lose you when you finally started making me some real money."

"Don't get sentimental on me. I wouldn't know how to handle it." Dani hung up the telephone, but didn't let go of the receiver, unable to break the contact.

"You done?" a woman asked impatiently behind her.

"Yeah." Dani stepped back awkwardly, relinquishing her spot in the gritty hallway. She wasn't Baker Babe anymore. She was pathetic, an embarrassment to her leather shorts. She straightened her shoulders. She may not have a plan, but she did have the next step: Meathook's friend, Oxford.

Hayes had almost decided to risk going inside after Gwynne when the door of the convenience store opened and she came out. Her biker babe getup was looking rough around the edges, her face pale and drawn. She was weakening even as he grew stronger. He smiled, one both feral and anticipatory, his thoughts lingering pleasurably on the e-mail he'd sent her earlier. She wouldn't get it, but it was nice to know how prophetic he'd been.

Do you flee and cry out, Death? Say farewell to hope, and with hope, farewell to fear. Have no hope to live, but prepare to die. Be absolute for death, for life will be sweeter thereby. If you lose life, you do lose a thing that none but fools would keep.
You're no fool, are you, Dani?
Do you miss your baby?
Well, weep no more, sweet lady, you'll be seeing her soon. Fit yourself for the journey. Make yourself worthy. I am coming to set you free.—<—<-(@

As if everything was an effort, she looked both ways and then stepped off the curb, crossing the street in the center of a knot of people. Despite her in-your-face swagger, she looked around, studying every face as if she sensed scrutiny.

A pity she'd seen him. Stalking wasn't nearly as much fun when the victim could make your face. No time to change that now. He studied the crop of bums lounging against a seedy building, picked one looking woefully at his empty bottle.

"You want a full one of those?" Hayes asked. "You follow my wife, tell me where she goes, and I'll give you enough cash to buy you a case."

The bum considered his offer. "Your wife?"

"That's right." Hayes pointed Gwynne out and handed him a card and a quarter. "Call this number when she stops moving."

The man studied the card, then his empty bottle. He scratched his dirty hair with a dirtier hand, tossed the bottle and said, "Sure. Why not."

Alice met Matt at the door to his office. "Hayes has e-mailed her again. And she called her agent. Sounded pissed. Any idea why?"

"I'm the one who should be pissed." Matt thought about his interview with Meathook's Mama. Chalk another one up to what he owed the romance writer, double for the pat on the butt from the biker's Mama. "What did she say?"

"Come listen."

In the conference room, Matt threw himself in a chair and nodded to the tech to start the tape. His frown lightened somewhat as he listened. The agent had weighed in on their side. It had to help. "They get a trace on it?"

"Public phone in a convenience store off Colfax," Alice said.

Matt looked at Riggs. "Tracks with where Meathook said he dropped her off."

"Sent the DPD over to check it out, but—" Alice said.

"She was gone." Henry looked glum. "Never stays anywhere for two minutes. How'd she get onto Boomer?"

"Following the same tack we were. She asked him to do a compare on the e-mail from Hayes." Matt frowned. Was it possible that she knew her Dark Lord from cyberspace?

"She's had us chasing our tails from day one. If she doesn't contact any of the people we've worked so hard to uncover, how are we gonna track her?" Riggs tossed the computer sheets from Boomer onto his desk and dropped into a chair, his shoulders slumping in defeat.

"Maybe she'll contact the people we do know about." Henry tossed another file onto the growing pile on the table. "I found her money trail—for all the good it does us now."

Alice rubbed her forehead. "If she's on the hop, she's liable to make a mistake."

"Well, let's try to be the ones who cash in on it." Matt rubbed his chin, then turned to Riggs. "I want you to get the records off the pay phone. If she called her agent, maybe she called someone else, someone who wasn't there. Or someone who was. Check the numbers on either side of her call within, say, ten or fifteen minutes?"

Riggs brightened. Phone numbers had names and addresses associated with them.

"Henry, get back onto the DPD. See if they can scare up a snitch or two in the area to watch for her. If she's slumming we got our best chance to spot her."

"So does Hayes." Alice looked sober.

"Let's e-mail her again. Send it to all the addresses we suspect are hers. She sounded open to an offer. Alice, you write this one, apply some pressure with that special woman's touch." Alice nodded. "Oh, and the list of her online contacts? Anything there?"

Alice looked at the sheet. "We've got people out checking them, but I'll have to admit, I didn't have the biker on my list."

"Riggs, call Judge Kincaid. Let's get phone taps in place on the most likely ones. She may still try to contact one of them by phone since she knows we're watching her e-mail addresses."

"Right." Riggs looked unenthusiastic. "What would you consider a likely?"

Matt ignored this as he looked around his group. "Any

other ideas? Suggestions?"

"It's too bad," Alice said, thoughtfully, "there's no way to anticipate the unexpected." She looked up at Matt. "It's what she does best in her books."

"Funny you should mention her books." Matt gestured to his assistant Karen Tebbs, holding a stack of books. "Pass them out."

"What?" Riggs asked, suspiciously.

"I want everybody to take one. Read it. Note names, occupations, interests, hobbies, information, anything that you think she could use or might hint at what she'll do next. Let's see if we can anticipate the unexpected."

Riggs looked at Henry. "Shit."

Matt grinned as he held up one and read the back. "Not according to *Romantic Times*. They called this '. . . delightful, a keeper to be revisited again and again . . .' You can start your visit now, Riggs."

Oxford's place was an innocuous little shop in the corner of a seedy strip mall. A buzzer hailed her entrance into the shop and a small, brisk man emerged from a back room and leaned on a glass case filled with tiny, electronic gadgetry. "Can I help you?"

"I hope so." Dani adjusted her backpack on her shoulder and tried to maintain her bravado. "My friend, Meathook, said you were the man."

"Meat? How is old Meat?" He looked at her curiously.

"He's cool." She looked around. "Like this place."

"So what can I do for you?"

Dani hesitated, almost too tired to tell him. Oxford looked at her, his light eyes blandly expectant. She dug up the words and forced them out, "I need a portable motion detector. And some pepper gas, in a size I can keep in my pocket."

"Okay." He didn't look surprised or curious. "What's your price range?"

"Money—isn't a problem."

"I only take cash."

"I only pay cash."

Oxford unlocked a cabinet, slid the glass back. "I think you'll like this one—"

They did business and then Dani was back out on the street, being jostled by passersby. She wasn't just out of ideas, she was out of energy. She clutched the strap of her pack and her biker babe persona as she made her way through less than welcoming streets, careful to avoid eye contact with youths lounging in doorways and hucksters outside strip clubs. The rim of the sun barely showed in the west between rising peaks. Night came faster when mountains loomed to block the sky, she'd learned. Another reason to hate heights. A better reason to find cover. She couldn't do night in the open, not even in this neon jungle.

A blinking sign pointed down at a massive woman squeezing her breasts together and calling to a man passing by, urging him to sample her wares. The man shrugged without stopping. *Lead kindly light?* This was nuts.

Ahead of her, a cryptic notation over a seedy establishment flashed FOO, the D darkened. Half a kindly light? Worth a try, anyway.

The door resisted, then whooshed forward, sending her stumbling inside. The reek of grease, sweaty bodies, and mildew filled her nostrils as a roomful of red rimmed eyes swiveled her way. She resisted the urge to duck her head, swaggered over to straddle an empty stool, tucking her pack securely between her legs and the wall. The plastic was cold and sticky against her thighs.

"Coffee?"

Dani shook her head, peering past the waitress to the soda fountain. She wasn't surprised that Diet Dr. Pepper wasn't featured. It rarely was. She sighed. "A Diet Pepsi, please."

She found a bill in her pocket and tossed it on the counter, watched the waitress add a couple of ice cubes, then some watery soda to float them, before setting it in front of Dani.

"I'll get your change."

"That's all right, keep it." Dani didn't fight the impulse, finding in the sad eyes and blank face of the waitress a distraction for her own dreary thoughts.

She fingered the bill, a half smile edging the cynical mouth. "Thanks."

Dani sucked up the cold, bland fluid, her hands circling the cup to keep them from shaking. In the dirty mirror behind the counter, she saw a bedraggled biker babe with frightened eyes.

"Can I get you something else, honey?" The voice of the waitress was warmer now, touched with sympathy.

Dani looked at her and found that same sympathy softening the cynicism in the woman's eyes. Was this her kindly light? She managed a stiff smile. "Well, I could use a room with no one humping next door."

"Couldn't we all." She studied Dani for a long moment, then leaned forward to murmur, "My landlady might put you up for the night. But she don't take no free loaders. It's cash up front."

"I got cash. If it's not too steep." The story, the character came naturally, from the memory of a part she'd played several years ago. She was too tired to do anything original. "My boyfriend's pissed at me, says he's going to cut me. Asshole thinks I cheated on him. Like I'd dare. Thought I'd give him a day or two to cool off."

"Bastard. They all are." The woman propped her elbows on the counter in front of Dani. "Name's Cloris."

"Louise. I'm—Louise."

"Order up!" the man behind the counter intoned, his eyes as dead as his voice.

"Yeah, yeah. In a minute." She glared over her shoulder, then looked back at Dani. "I been there, honey. My ex used to slap me around. Look, you just sit tight. I get off in thirty. But you'll have to order something. Bart don't let no one sit without ordering."

"I was going to anyway. How 'bout a salad?"

"Lettuce is as limp as my ex's dick. Soup's only thing he don't screw up."

"Okay. Soup. Do I want pie?"

"Apple won't kill you."

"Okay. And a refill on this." Dani shoved her cup across the counter. Whether from the caffeine or the kindness, she felt better. In the mirror she saw a derelict shuffle in behind her, his body swaying with the effort to hold the door open.

Cloris reared back. "Get your ass outta here—"

"Wait," Dani grabbed her arm, "give him some dinner. I'll pay."

"Probably through the nose, honey. No wonder your old man thinks he can knock you round." Cloris shook her head, poured the man a cup of coffee, and shoved it at him, then moved away, still muttering.

"Thanks," the man said as he settled on the stool next to her. The acrid smell of sweat and urine briefly overpowered the stink of grease. The hands he slid around the coffee cup trembled and he spilled some. On one "Mother" had been tattooed with hearts and flowers. "Give me the meat loaf!" he called after the waitress. He turned back to Dani. "So what's a nice girl like you doing in a shit-hole like this?"

There was, Dani remembered with a sort of awe, a Garth Brooks song about friends in low places. She'd bet her royalties this wasn't what he had in mind.

Later Cloris became almost loquacious when she was out from behind her counter. About the same age as Dani, she looked years older, was also divorced, trying to make ends meet with an interrupted education and fading stamina.

"I'm saving up for night school. Figure on being one of them physical therapists." She filled the short walk to the boarding house with the minutia of her life while the warmth of human contact filled Dani's cold places.

Her landlady, small and mean, was inclined to be suspicious, but quickly became revoltingly amiable when Dani paid her fifty for the night and made it clear she didn't expect anything back. The room she led Dani to was a tiny box with dark, water-stained walls, a few pieces of sad furniture, and a dirty window that looked out on the alley. It smelled of damp and enough ammonia to make her nose burn. When no one was looking, Dani checked for dust, found none, but did pick up a greasy film that wouldn't rub off her fingertip. Furtive scrabbling came from the corners when the pallid light was switched on. The fire escape and toilet were down the hall. The lock on the door wouldn't have stopped a terminal senior citizen. Breathing a silent prayer of thanks for the portable motion detector she'd bought from Oxford, pepper gas, and an illegal handgun, Dani ran a hand over the sticky surface of her hair and longed for a towel. Maybe Cloris would lend her one.

"Looks good." Dani smiled determinedly as night crept across the floor toward her. *I'll see you in your dreams.* She'd never been so tired or less ready to sleep.

Cloris waited until the landlady shuffled out of earshot. "It ain't the Ritz, honey, but no one gonna put a fist through your face neither."

"Hey," Dani produced a shrug, "it's better'n what I left. I'm cool with it." *Numb* with it, her writer's brain corrected, always looking for that right word.

Cloris made no effort to hide a wide yawn. "Gotta hit the rack. See you in the morning. You need anything, I'm right next door."

"Thanks." I'll slip a fifty under her door in the morning, Dani decided, closing her door after her. Careful to not look too closely at her surroundings, Dani opened her pack and dug out her new toy. Oxford had explained how to set the range, how to place it for optimal protection of the area. All she had to do was figure said range. He'd cautioned her against setting it too wide. She didn't want alarms going off just because Cloris happened to make a midnight trip to the john.

"Math," she muttered, trying to figure the range. "I hate math." Especially when she was tired—so damn tired. Four days. How many hours was that? She couldn't do that math either.

"No, not a flophouse," the derelict said into the telephone. "A rooming house. The address?" He hesitated. "You ain't gonna hurt her none, are you? Cause she was nice to me. Bought me supper." A short silence. "Well, that's all right then. Husband needs to talk to his wife." He gave the address. "When do I get my money?" Another short silence. "Yeah, I'll wait here for you." He replaced the receiver and settled across the street, his eyes on the rooming house the woman had gone into, dreaming of the full bottle of booze he was going to buy with the money.

Chapter Ten

Matt eased a finger around the inside of his collar. The words on the page showed faintly through a haze that was part tired, part something he wasn't willing to acknowledge in a room full of his co-workers.

The sweet musky scent of her cologne dug into his senses as soon as he opened the door, one so completely hers, he could have found her in the black of night. He didn't have to hunt for her. The lamp on the nightstand pitched frail light against the shadows, falling on her where she sat cross-legged in the center of the big bed.

Carolyn. His wife. His love.

His enemy.

Even knowing she wanted to bring him down failed to stop the slow, hot burn of desire from twisting in his gut. Not when the strap of her satin nightgown had slipped off one shoulder, exposing the lush curve of her breast. Not when her dark eyes were filled with a mixture of hate and need.

He hesitated, his control tenuous as he waited for her to speak, to tell him to get the hell out.

Only the steady click-click as the clock metered the minutes passing and the languid rustle of leaves against the window broke the heavy silence in the room.

He pushed the door closed and saw her shiver at the sound, but whether from desire or anger, he couldn't tell. He started toward her, increasing the rise and fall of her chest with each muffled beat of his feet against the thick carpet. When he was close enough to see the dew that coated her skin, he stopped.

"I'm sorry I hurt you."

"Are you?" She lifted her chin higher, opening to his gaze the long, pure line of her neck and the enticing, shadowy valley between her breasts—

Next to him Henry coughed or choked—it was hard to tell—breaking Matt's concentration. Matt looked up. Henry's eyes were wide and intent on the book in front of him. He flipped the page, leaning closer to the words. Next to Henry, Riggs unabashedly tugged at his tie, a finger holding his place as he paused to look hopefully at Matt.

"Will real woman do these things?"

"Just read the damn book," Matt snapped.

"Yeah." He dabbed at the sweat beading his forehead. "Read it."

"I need a cigarette," Henry muttered, turning a page.

Matt didn't smoke, but he knew how Henry felt. All too well. All he had to do was close his eyes to see Dani's biker babe. Unending legs, shadowy valleys, all wrapped in a bit of leather. What was leather anyway? Cow skin. Why should stretching it across a woman's butt make him want to sit up and beg for mercy? He wanted to throw the book across the room, tear the city apart until he found Dani Gwynne in her hot pants and—what?

Nothing. She was Anderson's problem, not his. Hayes, he reminded himself, is your problem.

Only it wasn't visions of Hayes that were dancing like Christmas sugar plums in his head when he searched for his place on the page. He took a deep breath and started again at the *shadowy valley between her breasts—*

The boarding house was on a street that was never completely quiet. A knot of toughs clustered around the doorway, their hard faces intermittently lit by a neon bar sign. Across from the bar was a twenty-four hour market with bars on the window and an air of being hunkered down for another long night. Druggies, bums and hookers dotted the street. Anyone with legitimate business had long since sought refuge behind security barred doors and windows.

With an intentional stagger, Hayes lifted the closed bottle in the paper sack to his lips, using the movement to disguise a thorough examination of the tenement layout. When it was clear in his head, he turned and shambled toward the alley that led to the back.

He never entered a room that didn't have another way out, not even when his body throbbed with the lust for blood.

Patience, he reminded himself, then added with a quick feral smile, *Beware the fury of a patient man.*

Now that he knew where she was, he could contain that fury. Do it right. Do it slow. The derelict he had hired to follow Gwynne was waiting right where he had said he would be. He had been helpful, so Hayes gave him a long drink, then took him out quick. When his body quit twitching, Hayes dumped it in a trash container by the rear door.

There would be no loose ends this time.

As night closed in without mercy, the sounds from the other boarders faded into an uneasy quiet. Dani sat curled in a semi-fetal position against the rusted headboard with Peg's gun nearby, her ears tuned for some indication the bathroom was free. Not that she was sure she had the nerve to step into a shower in this Bates Motel clone, no matter how bad she longed to rid her hair of its many colors and thick coating of hair gel.

With no sensation of passing into sleep, Dani found herself back in the hallway of the safe house, only this time it was lined with doors, hundreds of them glowing faintly in a dark, drifting fog. With that peculiar certainty of dreams, she knew Dark Lord was behind one of them. The realization had barely formed in her mind, when one of the doors began to open. She turned to run but she had waited too long. He was coming—

She jerked in her panic and came awake to a reality only slightly less awful than the dream. It was dark in the room, so dark the outlines of the furniture were shadowy, the window only slightly less so. A feeling of dread thickened the air already nasty with the stale smell of grease and old food.

Stiffly Dani straightened her back, then her neck, her muscles and the bed springs creaked in protest. Pain snaked up her spine when she reached for the light switch, followed quickly by panic when it didn't work.

Just get a grip, she told herself severely. She massaged her neck, until it moved semi-normally, then checked her watch, not surprised the glowing dial showed five a.m. Even worse, she needed to pee. No way she was walking down that nasty hall in the dark. Looked like she would be counting the minutes until dawn in heartbeats and droplets. How fun.

Outside the noise had abated a bit with the approach of the dawn, but she still might not have heard the furtive scrape outside her door if her ears weren't conditioned to strain for furtive sounds. Panic restarted a fast crawl up from her gut. She slid off the bed, crouching on the cool, gritty floor on the side away from the door. Her hand closed round the butt of Peg's gun just as the door swung silently inward with a tiny squeak of protest.

When Matt stretched out for yet another night on the office couch, he didn't expect to sleep, not with his brain playing mouse in a maze going nowhere. Luckily his body knew when to quit even when his brain didn't. The next thing he knew, Riggs's voice was calling him out of a deep, dark well. He shook his head, muttered groggily, "What?"

"Police snitch thinks our girl's in a boardinghouse off Colfax—"

"Cops been called?" Matt rolled off the couch, despite a pointed protest from his back. Riggs nodded. Matt's back straightened with an unhappy crack. He headed for the door and was running when he passed through it.

The menacing silence pressed in like a pillow over Dani's face, even as a slight lightening of the sky softened the darkness. She eased back until the wall stopped her, felt for the gun's safety, and then hesitated. What if it was Cloris or one of the other tenants making a trip to the bathroom? She couldn't shoot. Not until she knew—

Then what? Just pull the trigger? Send bullets thudding into a human body? Just like Richard? Could she kill—even to save her own life?

While she wondered, Dark Lord came in. No wings beat the fetid air to herald the arrival of Death's messenger—just the muted rasp of breath and a slight groan as the wooden floor gave under his weight. She knew it was him, even before she separated his dark silhouette from the framed opening of the door.

Hayes paused just inside the door, listening to her faint, panicked breaths coming from deep in the room, taking in a scent that might have been coconut drifting on the stale air. It mingled with the intoxicating scent of her fear. His blood sang with eagerness. Soon, very soon her blood would spill across his hands, then evaporate in healing fire. Every fiber of his being strained towards her, his muscles bunched to spring at the first hint of a scream.

The silence drew out. He smiled his pleasure. She was strong, but he already knew that. That's what made her blood so sweet, so necessary to his survival. It was why his pain wanted her. He took another careful step forward and heard her inhale sharply.

"I have a gun."

Her voice came to him on a slender thread of terror. He inhaled it greedily. "I don't believe you."

He fingered the shaft of his knife, felt the warm, wet slick of recent bloodletting harden his need for more, for hers. He had entered three rooms before hers, but it wasn't enough. It was never enough. Only her blood would take away his pain. Only her blood would give him Willow. Another step toward her and he heard the double snap of a bullet being loaded into the chamber.

"Okay. I believe you." He chuckled softly as delight speared deep in his groin, loosening a shaft of heated pleasure. Foreplay for the climax of fire. "Do you dread Death, sweet lady? Do you fear that last, insensible sleep?" His body had no weight, no substance. Let her send her bullets his way. How could they hurt him anymore than he already hurt? They might enter, but they couldn't stop him. "You shouldn't. Dying is your destiny. Run to your new lover's bed. He's waiting—"

"No!" The first cry was sharp and high. A short silence filled only with the intermingling of their panting breaths. "I'll shoot. I will."

He felt her hesitation, felt it feed his lust. She moaned and the heat in him quivered in pleasure. Now. He must have her right now. He shifted, his body light like a dancer's, homing in on the sound and feel of her terror like a guided missile. "Go ahead. Pull the trigger. You can't touch me, can't escape Death when it wants you—"

In the darkness, he heard a small, guttural sound, the next to last sound she would make in this world. He smiled as pain prepared to retreat.

"You for the fire," he gasped, his sweat-slicked body tensing to spring. He added as his personal vow, "and Willow for me—"

"How did you know I'm Willow?"

Her words cut through his intent, reverberating like the thunder on his mountain. He cried out, staggering from the new pain exploding inside his head as Dani's alarm shattered the night with a raucous scream.

How did you know I'm Willow?

No, it wasn't possible—

His cry fell on Dani like the howl of a wild beast in pain. It drowned out the harsh one forced out of Dani's throat as she cowered at his feet. Outside the first pale strand of morning sun put a halo around the steel in his bloody hand. He cried out again, a savage sound that told her this was the end. She had lost the toss. Richard and his dark killer had won. Death had arrived. She looked into it's heart for her baby—

She stared in shock when he pivoted, turning his spring toward her into a leap away. His shadow grew large against a wall touched by the burgeoning dawn, then vanished like an image in her nightmare. Only this wasn't a dream, was it? How could it be when the shriek of her alarm was all around her?

I'm right next door.

Cloris. She must get to Cloris . . .

Driven by the pounding alarm, Dani staggered into the black hall, still tainted with the passage of evil and found Cloris's door. She lifted her hand to pound it, but at the first touch it swung open. Pale rays from the window lit the bed and the still figure on it. Light fell without mercy on the place where a neck had been. Gleamed dully in the pool of red soaking into white sheets.

Dani didn't decide to run, had no sense of movement or passage from one place to another. One moment she was staring at Cloris, the next she was in the alley with the chill morning air hitting her in the face.

In either direction was rank road, the stink of garbage joining the scent of blood in her nostrils. In the distance the wail of police sirens joined with the alarm in her room. They would help her—

How did he know about Willow?

The question wouldn't go away. It demanded an answer. Something brushed against her bare neck. She reached up to brush it away, touched something cool and smooth that felt like—

No, she didn't want to know. Too late. Her head had already turned. Her eyes saw the hand hanging down from the garbage bin. The tattoo was clearly visible, despite dried blood caking on flaccid skin.

A harsh scream tried to force its way out her fear-dried throat. Blocked, it turned to flight. Out of her chaos one thought emerged with macabre clarity: how awful that meatloaf had been his last supper.

"Shit." Matt stood in the center of the dreary room Dani had almost died in, holding onto rage with a weary grip. He wanted, needed to say worse, to swear until the frustration gnawing away at his gut was gone. They had come so close, so *damn* close. He could still feel her panic and the chill of Hayes's evil quivering in the air. All around him was the smell of death that hadn't entirely missed its mark.

"She didn't stop to pack this time," Alice said, holding up a box of floppy disks she had found in Dani's abandoned backpack still hanging from a crooked chair. Her hand shook slightly and she dropped it, then shoved her fisted hands into the pockets of her suit jacket. "Left her book this time."

"Only smart thing she's done," Matt growled, turning as Riggs displaced the cop in the doorway. "What you got?"

"One dead outside, found him in the trash bin—probably a snitch—and three dead inside. All done the same way," he said, pulling his hand across his throat in a graphic demonstration. "Looks like Hayes worked his way down the hall until he got here."

"Where he tripped over Dani's new toy." Alice held up the motion detector. "Must have scared the hell out of him."

And Dani? Matt wondered. She had been seen leaving the scene alone and alive, but no one knew if it was before or after Hayes's arrival. Where the hell was she? Surely she knew now that she couldn't hide from Hayes? That the only way to end his threat to her was to help them catch the bastard.

He tried to see the scene through the detached eyes of an investigator, uncolored by the painful mix of feelings in his gut. It wasn't easy. Maybe because he had looked in her eyes, breathed her woman's scent, watched her breasts rise and fall and her pulse pound against her neck while raw lust twisted in his gut. No matter how much he told himself this was just another op, he knew it wasn't. He wasn't the same. Never would be again. Why had she chosen to come here and risk other lives besides her own? There was no peace in the knowing she had brought this on herself. Only a bitter regret that she appeared willing to trust everyone but him.

Riggs turned from conferencing with the cop. "Look, Matt." He held up a pistol in a clear plastic evidence bag. "This looks like service issue. They never found Oliver's weapon at the last SOC, did they?"

"No—" If she had had a gun, why the hell hadn't she used it?

Riggs answered his unspoken question. "She never even took the safety off."

Henry edged around Riggs.

"Any sign of them?"

He shook his head. "I got people combing the area, but so far we've found a big, fat nothing."

"Keep looking," Matt ordered. "She can't have gotten far."

Like a gothic heroine, Dani ran through mean streets and meaner alleys until adrenaline and stamina abruptly ran out. She stumbled, then sagged against a graffiti-marked wall, her eyes closed, waiting for her breathing to even out, her thoughts spinning around the million dollar question.

How did Dark Lord know about Willow?

Even as her mind asked the question, she wanted to avoid the answer.

Betrayal.

What other explanation was there? How else could Dark Lord know she was Willow? The alarm had startled him, driven him away this time, but it wasn't over. Wouldn't be until she died or testified Friday morning against Richard Hastings.

Richard. Did he know what he had unleashed in his drive

to save his worthless hide? Did he care? The Richard she'd loved as a brother would have cared. Did that Richard exist? Nothing she thought she knew about Richard added up since the moment six months ago when she saw him kill.

She had felt a lot of things since then. Shock. Dismay. Fear. Exhaustion. Sorrow. Pain. Determination.

With a distant surprise, she realized she wasn't feeling any of those things right now. She had been there and done all that. What she felt was—

Pissed. Royally, completely, totally pissed off.

It swelled up from her bend-not-break core in a wave that curled her hands into fists and filled her heart with iron. She wished she had blown the bastard away. Dark Lord wasn't mankind. He was an aberrant animal. So was Richard. And whoever else had chosen money over the lives of the innocent. The bad guys weren't going to win this one. She refused to die until she had walked into that courtroom and told her story—until the whole world knew exactly what kind of person Richard was, knew the kind of scum he had aligned himself with.

And Matt Kirby? She didn't want to think about him. The feelings he had stirred up just clouded the issue. If only he wasn't so hard to push away. She had seen a lot of things in Matt Kirby's face yesterday. Strength. Determination. Even ruthlessness. She hadn't seen evil, had felt no compromise mixed into the power his strong body emitted, seen no quarter in the stubbornly carved out jaw. Her heart told her he hadn't betrayed her.

What did her heart know? It had trusted Richard and Steven. Both had let her down. When had she decided she was so wise? When had she decided she could discern someone else's heart and mind? What did she know about hearts or minds? Nothing. Less than nothing about her federal hunter. Just because her hormones wanted him to be a good guy didn't make him one. There was too much at stake to trust her life to a hormonal response and a fine ass.

She looked at her watch. According to the papers, the jury selection was done. The first round of witnesses would begin giving testimony in the morning. Her turn would come after police and forensics. If everything went like it was planned that gave her—it was surprisingly easy to do the math when her brain was churning with pissed—something like seventy-two hours until she was due in court. If events didn't go like they were supposed to? Well, she would deal with that when it happened. She would deal with all of it without dying trying. She would not give Richard the satisfaction.

The first step was to figure out where she was. She looked around, suddenly uneasy. The alley was shadowy, the sun not yet high enough to top the buildings on either side of her. The still air was weighted with the stink of garbage, car exhaust and hopelessness. A car out in the street backfired and she jumped. She'd better get her ass in gear before someone unfriendly from either side of the equation found her. A man thrust open a door and dumped some trash into a bin. His curious glance was an added spur. She shoved her hands into the pockets of her shorts, one hand closing around the pepper spray can she had forgotten was there. She lifted her chin and started away from him towards the light, the street, and the people she could see passing by.

Pepper spray wasn't a gun, but it was something.

There was no warning. One moment she was walking forward. The next an arm had hooked around her waist, a knife was pressed against her throat, giving her no time to resist being dragged into a darkened doorway.

"Don't make a sound or I'll kill you right now." Dark Lord's voice rasped in her ear, edged with a rage more terrifying than the knife nicking the skin over the frantic pulse at the base of her neck.

For a moment terror crawled back up out of her gut. Then rage did a comeback. Who the hell was he to be angry? She had had it with this crap. His rage fueled her own, sharpened her thinking to a knife-edged precision. She didn't flinch from the bite of steel against her skin, didn't shiver when a warm trail started down her neck. Instead she eased the pepper spray out of her pocket and felt for the trigger.

"Tell me about Willow."

Willow. Why didn't he just wave a red cape at an enraged bull? This was not an all-powerful killer. This was a creep. A scummy, slimy life-taker. She tensed and the knife pressed close again.

"Tell me about Willow!"

"Not until you tell me how you knew I was Willow."

His body jerked like she had shot him and the knife bit through another layer of skin. Her anger rose to challenge his. She lifted the spray and depressed the trigger. His howl of pain mingled with her own cry as pepper stung into the slice on her neck and got her own eyes in the process. His hold loosened. She used her elbow in his gut to break it and heard his knife clatter against the pavement. She whirled. Her fist shot out and caught him imperfectly on the jaw. It hurt. His head snapped back. He crashed loudly and untidily into a row of garbage cans.

Through a blur of tears she glared down into his shocked, streaming face. "Tell Richard I'll see his ass in court."

She turned and fled.

"You think you saw this woman?" Alice crouched beside the drunk, holding the photo of Dani close to his bloodshot eyes.

Matt closed his senses to the rotting garbage the man sat in, to the filth that coated his body. All that mattered was what he knew.

"Yeah, she was running. Woke me up."

Matt didn't blame him for sounding aggrieved. Waking up couldn't be pleasant when your home was an alley behind a trash bin. "How long ago?"

"Mebbe an hour. Mebbe longer."

Alice looked at Matt. "It was probably less than that. Hasn't been an hour since we got here and we were practically on her heels."

"How long did she stay in the alley?" Matt asked.

"She start walking, then someone grabbed her—"

"What—"

"I hear him yell, she clips him a good one, then books out of here, rubbing her eyes like crazy. He gets up, heads other way, rubbing his eyes, too, and laughing like a crazy man."

Matt looked at Alice, felt an insane urge to laugh himself. "Pepper spray?"

She shrugged. "She could have got some at the same place she got the motion detector."

"Where'd she go? Which direction?" Matt asked.

"To the mission." He pointed toward the street and Matt could see the sign. "She stop and see the sign, then she walk that way, probably because of the blood."

"Blood?" That took away all the desire to grin.

"She was bleeding and they got someone what does first aid there."

Bleeding. She was bleeding. He felt almost lightheaded for a minute. Hayes had damn near finished her off. His head cleared. She was alive. That's what mattered. She had punched Hayes. Knocked him down. The romance writer had gone three rounds with one of the mob's most notorious hit men and walked away. He wanted to laugh. He wanted to find her and—

The drunk grabbed Matt's leg as he turned to leave. "Something for my trouble?"

Matt hesitated, he would probably just drink it up. What the hell, he had earned his bender, almost wished he could share it with him. He tossed the man a crumpled bill, then turned to follow Alice.

"You have to admire her ingenuity," Alice said.

"Yeah." He felt like he was climbing at fourteen thousand feet. His breath was ragged and shallow with shock and hope. Inside the mission the slope got steeper, the air thinner as hope gave way to reality. "She's gone?"

The thin, serious mission director pushed back a coarse mop of hair. "I'm afraid so. She was wired when she came in. We thought she'd got some bad crack or something. Bleeding from a cut on her neck. Claimed a trick tried to cut her and she sprayed him with pepper gas. Some of it got her. We rinsed her neck off, and her eyes, then put some stuff on her cut. Must have hurt like hell. She calmed down after a bit, then Carol gave her—"

"Let me guess. A Diet Dr. Pepper," Matt said, dryly.

"Didn't have any. She settled for water." He grinned, tiredly. "And some aspirin. She wouldn't take anything stronger. We tried to get her to let us call the police, a doctor, but—" he shrugged, "if she was turning tricks, cops would arrest her, so we didn't push it. She sure looked like she'd been hooking."

She was still wearing leather. He wasn't ready for the surge of lust at the memory of how she looked wearing leather. The smooth soft skin, the curve of body and mouth—his mouth went dry thinking about how she would taste and feel. Damn it, he was a fed, a pro. And she was getting further away. He fought his way to a kind of calm, held onto it with a thin rope as he asked through gritted teeth, "Where'd she go?"

"She found out one of our workers was heading home and she asked if she could hitch a ride downtown. Said she had friends who would help her."

"How long ago did she leave?" Alice asked.

"Maybe fifteen minutes? Not much longer than that."

Matt felt an unaccountable urge to howl, but he was afraid Dani might hear him.

Dani didn't care when the clerk looked at her like something that had crawled out from under a rock. She almost had. Let her hold her nose while she looked down it, as long as she took Dani's money when the time came. The dress Dani eventually chose was an in-your-face scarlet red that lovingly hugged the pared down lines of her body with a sleek and sexy elegance. It seemed appropriate to wear red, since she was seeing red. As an added bonus, she didn't have to change her nail color to match it. The hat she put on her head was so smart it had it's own degree. Her high heels weren't made to run in.

She was through with running, through with looking back, with retreating or anything like it. There was only forward, no matter who she had to walk over with her spiked heels to do it.

She left all the manifestations of biker babe in the dressing room to be dealt with by the snotty clerk. She had better things to do, like finding and adding a Marilyn Monroe wig to her ensemble. Then she would need to start on her new plot and find a place to implement it.

Matt Kirby's face rose in her head, maybe because she was dressed to take on an alpha male of his caliber. He had his own agenda, just like Richard, just like Dark Lord. They all wanted something they thought she could give them. Well, they could take their separate agendas and stick them up their collective asses.

Tough talk, her alter ego sneered, for someone who only knows what she doesn't want. Just how do you plan to get from point A to point Z?

It just shows what you know, she sneered right back. Have you forgotten my ex-spy, Spook? If anyone would know how to beat the feds and baddies it was a former spy. It wouldn't be easy. The feds probably had his name on their handy-dandy list of people she had talked to online. A large problem—if Dani didn't have an online handle up her bright red cap sleeve they had missed. Delphi could e-mail Spook right under all their sniffing noses and only she and Spook would know who she really was. He'd thought it a hoot when she'd asked him to help her create her first alter-identity, had helped her set it up.

It was perfect. Once she got her hands on yet another laptop with a modem and arranged a meeting.

"So, he failed again." Bates hung up the telephone and turned to face the two men waiting for orders on the other side of his mahogany desk. He smoothed back dark hair which reflected what the cut had cost. His Italian silk suit was custom tailored for a body just starting to thicken at the waist, his silk shirt underneath a discreet pinstripe, the tie an original. His face was narrow and neat, his eyes so dark they absorbed the light without reflecting it back.

He was a wise guy who started out on the streets, stealing stereos and tires, moved into dealing drugs, then clawed his way up the ranks on the heels of fellow punk, Paul Orsini, who had put him in charge of all their Midwest operations. Denver was out of the criminal mainstream of either coast, but Bates didn't mind. His wife liked living near mountains and it was a better place to raise kids.

Hayes was out there, but there was no unease on Bates's face. He hadn't gotten where he was giving up his thoughts or feelings to underlings. That didn't mean he wasn't worried. Hayes had played an important part in Bates's success, making Bates look good by eliminating the competition so efficiently. In his business, success meant enemies, but he hadn't cared. His enemies had been partly held in check by their fear of the whacked-out hit man's reputation—a reputation that was now in a nose dive.

What Hayes had done for Bates in the past was irrelevant. He had failed now. Bates regretted the necessity. Hayes had been the perfect weapon—when he was pointed at Bates's enemies. Now he must be eliminated before his failure ricocheted in Bates's face like spit in the wind. Before his enemies scented weakness or failure and came at him. Before Orsini got any doubts about how effective he was at managing his interests.

"Hayes is gonna bolt. Stop him—permanently. Understand?"

The two men, his best muscle, exchanged looks, their nearly identical faces mirroring a mutual unease.

"We're working it. Not even the acid heads are eager to roll over on a bopper like Hayes—" said the muscle on the right, known locally as Bad Trip because crossing him was worse than a bad acid trip.

"—but we gotta snitch we can apply some muscle to," finished Bum Trip, so named because an encounter with him was as unpleasant as one with his twin.

"The sooner the better," Bates said. "He's a loose cannon. We don't take care of him, Orsini'll have our asses." He wanted them to be properly motivated to complete the task. In his business, motivation was everything.

They exchanged glances that told him they'd got it.

"We'll get him, sir," Bad Trip assured him.

"Get going. And send Davis in on your way out."

They left as silently as they had arrived, leaving Bates frowning thoughtfully until Davis appeared.

Donald Davis was a large man with a deceptively vacant face. He looked like a thug, but had the brains of a think tank. He was useful—and dangerous—for both those reasons. Behind Davis's vacant gaze lurked the same ambition that had driven Bates up the wise guy ranks.

"What's the word on Richard Hastings?" Bates leaned back in his leather chair, careful not to disarrange his hair when he clasped his hands behind his head.

"The feds are closing the gap fast—may already have closed it." Davis dropped his bulk into a period chair. It gave a small squeak of protest.

Did he know how much it irritated him, Bates wondered, that he always chose the smallest chair to inflict his magnitude upon? Somehow he was sure Davis did. "I thought our man inside the Bureau was being paid to keep the lid on the Hastings shit?"

"He's gone mute on me. I figure he's been smoked by the feds and turned. If I'm right, Hastings will roll over next."

"You sure?" If Davis was right, it was all coming apart. He cursed internally. This was Orsini's baby, entrusted to his care. It wouldn't matter who had fucked it up, only that it was.

"Hastings is an arrogant bastard," Davis shrugged, "or he wouldn't have toasted his on-the-side broad in the first place. Should have taken him out then, I guess."

"If the asshole had just kept his head, he'd have walked. Or got probation. No priors. Only one witness who might have a grudge against him. Why Orsini chose to save his worthless hide—" Bates bit back his ire with an effort. Twisted, his words could be turned against him. He was getting damn sick of the politics and ass kissing.

"Yeah, well, we both know Hastings will try to save his own ass—at our expense. Thinks he can beat the whole world. In the end he'll squeal, long and loud."

What neither of them said, but they both knew, was that if they went down, Orsini wouldn't wait to see if they'd keep their mouths shut. Bates could admit to himself he might talk, with the right incentive. Who wanted to go to prison when you could be set up in witness protection somewhere with the money from his Swiss bank account to make up what the feds didn't pay? Orsini would take them out to stop the domino cascade before it knocked him down. Who talked, who lived, was all a matter of timing. Best case was not to have to worry about any of it. They were locked into their present course.

"That's what we get for working with an amateur. No ethics." Bates picked up his coffee cup and sipped the rapidly cooling brew.

Davis shoved his hands in the pockets of his tailor-made slacks, stretched his legs out. "If the laundering deal had worked, it would've been a sweet deal for Orsini."

"Yeah, well, the only sweet deal he'll be interested in now is damage control." Bates was quiet, thinking. Finally he said, "If Hastings would do his time, we'd make sure he doesn't lose by it."

"Not a chance of that. Guy's a pansy. Think's he can play dirty and still keep his lily-white rep. Prescott's barely holding him together."

"We can't afford to wait for him to roll. Let's move on him now." Bates set his cup down and stood up.

"Shouldn't you clear it with Mr. Orsini?"

Bates felt a flash of anger, fought it back before it showed on his face. "I'm calling Orsini right now." Bates dropped the "mister" to remind Davis that he and Orsini had a past together. A flicker of Davis's lashes told him he got it.

"Who you want to hit Hastings?"

Bates cussed silently. "This would've been a perfect job for Hayes. How the hell did he let a damn romance writer get the drop on him? Boys will be busy with Hayes—"

Davis half grinned, shrugged. "There's Copeland. He's in New York, but I could have him here by tonight."

Copeland was almost as good as Hayes had been. He hated Hayes for being better. "Get him."

Davis nodded. "Thought Hayes was too whacked-out to be a real pro. Only as good as your hold on him."

Bates shrugged. "A fanatic kills just as thoroughly as a capitalist—and sometimes he'll take more risks. He was useful, but not anymore. Let's end it quickly."

"Right." Davis turned to go, then stopped. "What about the romance writer? I've got Dent on call if she's spotted but—"

Bates hesitated. Dent was a messy killer, couldn't spell finesse, let alone define it. Her threat was to Hastings, not him. His wife did like her books, but how would it look if he backed off a contract? "Make it official. The hit is his. And put some pressure on our snitch at the DPD. I want to know what the cops know before they know it."

Davis nodded. "Just wish we knew what the feds know. McBride's being kept so far out of the Marshal's loop he's no damn help. We're flying blind there."

Bates shrugged. "He'll have to be taken care of, too, when the dust settles."

"When the dust settles he might be useful again," Davis pointed out.

Bates shook his head. "He's tainted. I wouldn't trust him, why should they?" He looked hard at Davis. "We gotta get clean here, Davis, or Orsini takes us both out. We stay together or we die together. Clear?"

Davis nodded easily, comprehension of the implied threat in his placid gaze. "I'll take care of it. I'll take care of it all."

He eased out of the room, leaving Bates convinced he had better watch his back. This was just the kind of situation he had used in the past to rise another notch in the organization.

Chapter Eleven

The sign outside the bookstore was big enough to catch the eyes and attention of even the most preoccupied person, but it wasn't size that stopped Dani. It was what the sign proclaimed so enthusiastically: BOOK SIGNING TODAY! Romance novelist Kelly Kerwin signs her newest release *Love and Lust*.

Kelly? How was that possible? Then she remembered seeing the flyer about the writers conference when she was assessing Matt Kirby's sexy body outside Boomer's office. Dani smiled slightly. She'd only had to go through blood, fire, and excessive altitude to make wild child Kelly look like a better prospect than an ex-spook with a crush.

Her plot was taking an increasingly macabre turn, she decided, with a distant fatalism that could be the by-product of her pissed off vantage point. Inside, the sense of the fictional was further enhanced by Kelly, who was seated at a table stacked with books, positively awash in organza ruffles and lace, with a Scarlet O'Hara floppy-brimmed hat, languidly signing her books with a feather pen.

Apparently Dani wasn't the only one loaded for bear this fine summer day. She lifted a book from a stack and set it down in front of "Scarlet."

"You want this personalized or generic, sugar?" Kelly's voice was heavily weighted with a sultry, southern drawl.

"Oh, Miss Kerwin, most definitely personalized," Dani gushed, "to Louise?"

Kelly stiffened, lifting her flawlessly sculpted chin up until she could see out from under the floppy brim. With no trace of southern and a boatload of skeptical, she said, "Louise?"

"Yeah. Wanna see my ID?" Dani sat on the edge of the table, the action hiking the already dangerous hemline higher on her silk-covered thighs. She leaned close enough to confide, "I made it myself."

Kelly gave two men who'd stopped to stare at Dani's legs a severe look that sent them on their way, before asking, "What the hell are you doing here? I thought you were in solitary confinement or something?"

"I was. I'm out now. You have a break any time soon? I need to talk to you."

"If I didn't deserve a break soon, I'd take one anyway." Her limpid blue gaze narrowed in scrutiny of Dani, what she could see of her hair under the brim of the smart hat, her red dress. All she said was, "Why don't you plant it here and sign with me for a bit?"

"*Louise* isn't an author."

"Oh, right. Well, plant it anyway." Kelly patted the chair next to her. Dani took it with a wriggle that stopped another male customer in his tracks. She ignored him and waited for Kelly to sign a book, then asked, "What's with the Scarlet ensemble?"

Kelly shrugged elegantly. "I had an interview before this signing. Some jerk at the local paper was obviously expecting Scarlet, so I gave her to him, but good." She smiled wickedly, then did a quick switch to charming when a woman approached. When they were alone again, she said, "Red is your color, but the blonde locks are definitely plagiarism. Do tell, who pissed you off?"

Dani laughed, leaning back and crossing her legs at the ankle. "Just about everyone. How could you tell?"

"Because that dress could fry men's brains and turn

some of their parts to stone. Not exactly your normal style."

Dani smoothed the skirt a millimeter closer to her knees. "Maybe I'm tired of my normal style."

"Well, well. Better tell Miss Scarlet all about it so I can exploit it shamelessly. I'd hate to see a long overdue kick-ass mood go to waste."

Dani's eyes narrowed, her mouth curving in a dangerous smile. "Don't worry. It won't."

Later, in a quiet little bistro deep in the mall, Dani filled Kelly in. Kelly, being Kelly, took notes and offered a stringent critique. Still feeling removed from the crap and yet strangely normal in a very surreal but comforting way, Dani studied her friend over the top of her drink cup. "I thought you were holed up finishing your book?"

"That was last month. This month I'm here for the conference."

"This is what—Tuesday?" It was getting harder to keep track. "I thought the convention didn't start until Thursday?"

"It doesn't. But *our* publicist thought it would be a hoot if *I* did some signings and an interview or two."

"Ooh." Dani grimaced wryly. "I guess there are some benefits to being hunted like a dog."

"Yeah, no one's gonna be asking you at seven a.m. tomorrow morning how you research the sex scenes in your book." Kelly sighed and fluttered her false lashes wistfully. "So where are you staying? Or aren't I supposed to ask?"

"I was hoping I could stay with you. I'll clear out in the morning. And before you say yes, be aware you'll have my fed on your ass if they figure out you're helping me."

"Really? Your own fed. Cool." Kelly leaned back in her chair, her pose sultry. "Is he cute?"

Cute? Matt was too easily conjured up and replayed feature by feature, right down to the jeans and boots. "Oh, yeah." She smiled. "Damn annoying, totally opinionated, definitely—cute."

"So why are you running from him instead of jumping his bones? You know better than to mess with the basic plot."

Dani gave her a Look. "This isn't a romance."

"Everything is a romance. Don't you read our PR?"

"All I've been reading lately are bumper stickers," Dani shot back. "According to them, life's a bitch."

Kelly grinned. "And here I thought I was the bitch."

Dani grinned back. "No comment. I'm not obliged to incriminate myself."

"Smart girl. So, now that you're out and about, you gonna do the conference? Lots of our friends around. Not to mention the tax benefits."

"Have you forgotten my fed isn't the only one after me?"

"No, but you've already wailed on the hit man. If he's got half a brain, he won't be back."

"Richard can't be too happy he missed again," Dani agreed thoughtfully. It was the main reason she felt comfortable seeking temporary asylum with Kelly. It would take them some time to regroup. What would he do with that time? That was the question. Would he try to find someone else? Could he? How many hit men could he know?

Kelly straightened, "You need a place to stay with someone who isn't known to know you." Kelly's mind tended to run along plot lines, too.

"Well, that would be nice, but the problem is, people who don't know me, don't know me enough to give me aid and shelter."

"Yeah, but if they know me—"

Dani didn't take advantage of that big opening. It was

too easy. No challenge. Kelly gave her a suspicious look
that Dani met with one of innocence. It left her friend nowhere to go but on with her thought. "My ex-mother-in-law
is from here. We're still friends because she thinks her son
is an asshole, too. And, even better, she has this little guesthouse on her property."

"Really?" It would have a telephone. Guesthouses did.
Kelly would have a laptop—she loved expensive toys—so
Dani could make contact with Spook without seriously de-
pleting her money supply. And Matt the marshal hunter?
Oh yeah. She had some things to say to him, too.

"Yeah, and Dobermans," Kelly said, still following her
own line of thought.

"Really?" Dobermans would discourage any killers
Richard hired, wouldn't they? "My mother-in-law *was* a Do-
berman."

Kelly grinned. "No kidding. I'll call her. Mine, not
yours. If no one's visiting, I'll bet we could move in tonight." She shoved her chair back. "Let's get out of here.
Suddenly I'm suffering from Southern Belle overdose. I
gotta get changed before I'm forced to slay someone with
my eyes." She slid her arm through Dani's. "Damn, I'm
glad you showed up. Was wishing I had someone to go out
with me tonight."

"Out?" Dani asked, not in protest, but because it was
their routine.

"That's right. Out. Time you kicked up your heels, girl.
Did the wild child thing."

"Every time we do the wild child thing—"

"—we have a great time."

Too true. Dani smiled. "I can't afford to get arrested this
time, Kel."

"Trust me." Kelly crossed her heart. "There is absolutely

nothing that can go wrong in my tender care."

Famous last words Dani thought in a detached way. They usually are uttered just prior to the shit hitting the fan. Only the fan had already received a boatload of the stuff. How much more could there be out there? "I need to buy a toothbrush."

Kelly looked mock serious. "Won't get any argument from me on that one. I'm committed to good oral hygiene."

Dani grinned. "So how is your dentist?"

Kelly licked her lips. "Showing no signs of decay."

Dani's grin expanded into a laugh. It felt good. It was a scientific fact. "I don't care what anyone says about you. *I* think you're a treasure."

"I know. And I sell more books than you, too."

"Bitch."

"Damn right." Kelly looked at the parking lot. "Now where did I park my stupid rental car? Last time I let them give me a white one."

State Attorney General Dennis Sheridan bit back a sigh as he watched Richard Hastings's lawyer wear an agitated groove in the carpet in front of his desk with his expensive leather shoes. Sweat glittered like diamonds in the places where his graying hair had given up trying to cover his large, round head. Greedy, hunted eyes peered out of indentations in his bread dough face. Beneath a pug nose, his nauseatingly pink, cupid's bow mouth twitched with an uncontrollable tick.

Agitation wasn't a good look on Digby Prescott. Not that Sheridan had seen an emotion that was good on him in the six months they had been on opposite sides of the case of State of Colorado vs. Richard Robert Hastings.

The saint-turned-accused-killer had been an interesting

problem. If Dani Gwynne hadn't seen Hastings kill the Jane Doe, his ties to organized crime would have stayed hidden, lost in the glare of his "good works" foundation. Now that the tangled, mob money-laundering web was beginning to unravel for Hastings—and become a political bonanza for Sheridan—he could lean back in his chair and enjoy the sight of Prescott caught in the cleft stick of his own greed.

Prescott would have taken on the Hastings case at the request of Paul Orsini, the man who controlled organized crime activities from the West Coast to the Mississippi, a man who always had more money than places to launder it. At the time it had probably seemed like a simple matter: stall the case until the sole witness of the crime is dead and the feds admit they couldn't find anything in Richard Hastings's closet.

Except the witness hadn't died. And the mob's man in the FBI, bought with a truck load of money he hadn't been near as good at hiding as Orsini, was getting ready to cut a deal. The whole package was coming apart and Prescott's short legs were straddling the crack. No wonder he was twitching like he had St. Vitas's dance.

Orsini would take him out for what he was saying, for being here when Richard Hastings began his roll, though Sheridan had a feeling that Hastings hadn't told his attorney until they were safely inside, knowing the only place his legal advisor would take him was to a quiet meeting ending in a shallow grave. Prescott was going to have to do some fancy footwork or request protection for himself. He wasn't light enough on his feet for plain footwork, let alone the fancy kind.

This weekend, when Sheridan thought he had lost his witness and his case, had been the worst in his career. It wasn't often he actually liked a witness, but it would be hard not to like Dani, harder still not to desire her, particularly after he'd read one of her books. Who would have thought that much passion lurked beneath her quiet exterior? He had felt regret when he got the news she was dead.

Amazing what a few days could do for his prospects. The way things were going, it wouldn't matter to the case if Dani testified or not, though he'd always regret the sex he'd been hoping for when the case was concluded. Sheridan's smile widened as he studied his perfect manicure. He was in the catbird seat and enjoyed it.

Prescott finally stopped talking and looked at him. "Well?"

Time to toy with the mouse. Wouldn't do to appear hungry. "Bullshit. Your guy's up to his ass in it. Why would I want to pull him out?"

"Because he can give you Vernon Bates." Saying the words out loud moved Prescott's twitch another notch up the Richter scale. "And Bates can give you Orsini."

"I thought Richard Hastings didn't know Bates?"

Prescott's little mouth worked for a minute before he said with controlled rage, "We gonna talk deal or not? You know you've got nothing without your witness—"

Sheridan straightened. It was almost too easy. "Who told you I don't have my witness?"

Prescott's tiny gaze narrowed to nearly invisible. "I could go to the judge and force you to produce her."

While Dani was living, Sheridan had no compunction about bluffing. Prescott was holding the worse hand. He shrugged. "Do it. Dani's more eager than ever to nail your client's ass. The sooner the better." He smiled reflectively. "I can't wait to see her in action. She's a dream witness for a prosecutor. She has that extra something that plays well with a jury."

Prescott stared at him, indecision written large across his florid face. "You—she—I don't believe you. She's dead. We both know she's dead."

Sheridan adopted mock surprise. "Who told you she was dead?"

Prescott saw the danger too late. "Client-attorney communications are privileged—"

"—and apparently incomplete. I wonder why Bates didn't tell you she's very much alive? That his expensive killer missed his mark?"

Prescott's mouth opened, then closed. He dropped in a chair, his shoulders rounding in defeat.

"You're right," Sheridan stood up. "It probably isn't a good idea to say anything else. You've already incriminated yourself enough for one day."

Damn, he loved it when a plan came together.

"Tell me what you got, Riggs." Matt paced restlessly away from the speaker telephone on his desk, whirled around and headed back.

"Not much. She was here at the mall, Saks Fifth Avenue again. Bought a red dress."

"Red? That's a red dress?" What the hell? Trying to figure out what was going on in her head was like trying to work his way out of a maze—in a damn blizzard.

"Affirmative. Clerk showed it to me. All I can say is, it's definitely kick ass."

Despite clamping down on his thoughts, Matt felt a pang at missing the dress. With her legs—he frowned. Kick ass? Whose ass was she targeting? He almost looked behind him. He didn't know how he knew. He just did. She was pissed at *him*. Not all the other people, good, bad and ugly, she should be pissed at. Him. It wasn't fair. He hadn't caused the mess at the boardinghouse. She had. She had no right to put him or his ass in her sights. "If it's so kick ass, then it ought to be easy to track her."

"You'd think. She doesn't exactly look like the picture I'm showing, but I still have a few places left to check. Oh, and just to stay with the bad news/no good news theme, I talked to that guy, Adams at the DPD?"

"Yeah?"

"His snitch claims Bates has put Dent on Gwynne and called Copeland in from New York."

Matt wheeled around. He'd be perfectly happy to have Copeland take out Hayes, but—"Dent? Holy shit. He's almost as bad as Hayes." He saw Sheridan approaching. "Let me get back to you, Riggs. Sheridan's here." Matt broke the connection and watched Sheridan approach. His face was impassive, his pace relaxed, but Matt could tell he was both satisfied and excited. Matt's senses went to full-blown wary when Sheridan sat down without asking for news about Dani, a small smile flickering the edges of his narrow mouth.

"What's up, Sheridan?"

"Before I talk to Anderson, I just wanted to let you know the case is breaking wide open."

Matt's gaze narrowed sharply. Only one reason Sheridan would need to talk to Anderson. He needed a witness protected.

"FBI's finally starting to unravel the mystery of Richard Hastings," Sheridan went on, oblivious to Matt's knife-narrow gaze pinned on him. "Seems Bates had a friend in the ranks muddying the waters for him or we would have had Hastings months ago."

"What's the scam?"

"Money laundering through his charitable foundation.

They tell me it would have been a damn slick deal if Hastings hadn't screwed up the works by toasting our Jane Doe. Which is why Bates was so willing to provide a hitter to clean up his mess. Course now Hastings is crying dupe and seriously worried about his own worthless hide."

"Oh?"

"Yeah, Prescott claims he was manipulated, but my call is, he was panting to be in it."

"Prescott?" Matt looked at Sheridan. "Hastings is planning to roll over on Bates, isn't he?"

Sheridan didn't look at Matt, the first sign of discomfort blunting his satisfaction. "That's right. Requested protection this morning."

"What'd you tell him? You gonna let him plea down?" Matt didn't try to keep the disgust from his voice and Sheridan reacted defensively, "I don't have a choice. He delivers Bates, we have a shot at Orsini."

"He must have been in deep if he can deliver Bates."

"Yeah," Sheridan gave a short, sharp laugh. "Asshole. We'll get Davis, too, in the deal, maybe Orsini himself. As an added bonus, Prescott incriminated himself in the plot to kill Dani. He's looking for a lawyer and deal for himself." For the first time, Sheridan looked warily at Matt. "They'll need protection. I've got sources that say Bates has already put out a contract on Hastings."

"The FBI should be able to handle that for you," Matt didn't hesitate, although technically it wasn't his call. They were responsible for the deaths of three marshals and the corruption of at least one more. He wasn't interested in getting them off the hook they had put in their own mouths.

Sheridan didn't misunderstand. "I'll get a court order if I have to."

"Do it. Neuman and his boy are available. One of them

probably isn't holding a grudge."

"Damn it, Matt, if he helps us—"

Matt's eyes and voice were laced with steel and pointed right at him, "You know how we feel about our own, Sheridan."

"Yeah, I know." Sheridan's face turned red with his struggle for control. "Don't mention the deal to Dani."

"I wondered when you'd get around to Dani. But then you don't need her anymore, do you?"

Sheridan's gaze slid away again. "Of course I do, to keep the pressure on Hastings. Prescott's legal problems will mean a postponement, but I doubt she's in the mood to hear it—"

"No, I don't think she is," Matt said, thinking about the kick-ass red dress. "Doesn't change her situation or our responsibility to protect her. Hayes will still be after her. And word on the street is, Bates has assigned Dent to complete the contract—"

"Dent? Damn, that's not good. He's a messy killer. Why isn't Bates dropping it with Hastings turning on him?"

He actually looked concerned, Matt thought with disgust. "He'd lose face if he backed out on a contract. Be a laughing stock if a romance writer got away from him."

Though the romance writer was going to cost Bates more than the price of Dani's contract if Prescott and Hastings fingered him, Matt mused. Bates would be dodging bullets himself before he was through. It was not an unpleasant thought.

Sheridan nodded thoughtfully. "Be useful if she could lure Hayes in for us. I wouldn't mind putting him out of business with the rest of them. Course Bates'll probably take care of him long before we catch up with him. I hear he's called Copeland in."

The words sounded more cynical and a lot less high-minded coming out of Sheridan's mouth than they had when he'd thought about using Dani to draw Hayes in. It gave him an unpleasant jolt as the window of Sheridan's ambition turned into a mirror thrust in Matt's face. It was his job to get the bad guys by whatever legal means possible. More times than not, it took turning them on each other, letting some minor fish off the hook to snag the sharks. A trade-off, but an acceptable one, he had always thought.

"You'll call me if you find her?" Sheridan asked, standing up and shaking the creases from his expensively cut pants. "Naturally we're keeping the trial going until the deal is set."

"Do that." Frowning, Matt watched Sheridan leave. With visions of bagging Orsini dancing in his head, the cold-hearted bastard was trash-canning Dani and the last six months of her life.

It was an imperfect world they operated in, one of shifting grays, too little white, and a boatload of black, with right and wrong under the jurisdiction of lawyers and judges who used to be lawyers. He had lost his idealistic virginity early. To keep from getting screwed again, he adopted a big picture pragmatism, learned how to keep a tight focus on realistic objectives, not to sweat the details more than absolutely necessary and how to come to terms with what couldn't be changed. He would take what he could wrest from the system and walk away when the fat lady sang.

He was one of the good guys.

Using Dani to catch Hayes wasn't nice. The mob didn't deal in nice. Someone had to stop Hayes. Easier to do if they had something he wanted. Hayes didn't just want Dani. He needed her dead. If she didn't die, he would be dodging Bates and his friends for the rest of his life.

Dani didn't like the situation. He didn't blame her. He didn't like it either. This wasn't fiction. No possibility of a tidy ending, just a lot of unappetizing, carefully considered compromises. Welcome to the real world.

Of course there was some risk. Collateral casualties were inevitable. Matt was confident of his people and trusted Anderson to fulfill his part. The kicker was, Dani had to trust *them* for it to work. She had to come to terms with reality. Hayes would find her. Better if he did it on their terms, than on his.

He leaned back in his chair, but couldn't get comfortable. He stood up and paced to the window, stared broodingly down at the city. He liked her, well, liked what he'd learned about her, he admitted, though it made about as much sense as her taking the battle onto Hayes's turf. Worse, Matt hunched his shoulders trying to escape discomfort, he had felt something even before he knew she wasn't dead. Before he had seen her biker babe persona. He had felt something the first time he looked at her picture.

How could she look like that—he looked at the picture pinned on the board—and pop up as biker babe? Made him woody just thinking about it. If he'd known who she was then—

He would still be standing here wanting something he couldn't have. This wasn't about sex. It wasn't about what he would like or what she wished the world was. This was life and death. Right and wrong. Justice and punishment. Good against evil.

Hayes was evil. This guy liked killing, liked burning what he killed. He got off on it and had to be stopped. Not just for Dani's sake, but for the people he'd kill if they didn't stop him.

No matter what the cost? Matt frowned, not seeing the

city below, but himself against the backdrop of the office, against the backdrop of the Service and country he had taken an oath to serve. He was just one part of the process. Behind him Sebastian was still hunched over his keyboard, following her trail in cyberspace. In other rooms and out in the city, other men and women worked on leads, using every resource they had to follow up. It was his op. In the end, the buck stopped with him. They accumulated data, he made the calls, decided when and how to act, where and when to put people in jeopardy, when to take them out. He decided how far they went to catch Hayes, how close Hayes got to Dani—if they got close enough to her to make the call.

He had been at the apex of a breaking case before, could feel the pace picking up, like a car speeding forward. He had no way to stop it, no way to know if he was a crash test dummy heading for a wall or Mario Andretti about to cross the finish line of the Indy 500. Normally he would get a rush at this point, as his training and instincts merged into a razor-sharp readiness for action. This case wasn't playing out like normal. He had to get his head clear, tighten his focus on the essentials. The last thing he could afford to do was a "Neuman," and screw his timing. There was too much at stake.

It wouldn't help anyone, least of all Dani, if he choked. And being out there somewhere in a kick-ass red dress doing who knew what, with who knew who, wasn't helping either. It was dangerous and downright stupid. He would tell her that if he got the chance.

If he got the chance.

It was going to be another sleepless night. He rubbed his face, but he was gonna spend it at home. Take a shower, shave—his chin was bristling unevenly from the shave in the men's room with a dull razor this morning. He looked at Sebastian. "I'm going home. Call me if we hear anything."

Sebastian looked up, flexing his long fingers. "Why don't you take one of her laptops with you? I'll show you how to hook it up, then if she shows up on a chat line somewhere, you can keep her busy talking while I track her."

Matt nodded, too tired to be daunted by the idea.

Whatever it took.

That's how the game was played before he met Dani. That's how he had to play it now. End of story.

Chapter Twelve

It was well into a new day when Dani helped a seriously impaired Kelly to one of the twin beds in a bedroom of her mother-in-law's guesthouse. Niles, the butler, who had arranged for them to use the guesthouse while Kelly's ex-mother-in-law was away, was an interesting case study in contrasts. He looked like *The Addams Family*'s Lurch, talked like an Oxford don, and was a former basketball player for the Denver Nuggets. Dani had to agree with Kelly's suspicion that Niles' duties as a butler were a cover for a more intimate involvement in Ana Terril's life.

Whatever else Niles might be, he was a good stand-in host. He made them more than comfortable in the homey guesthouse, then directed them to let him know if there was anything else he could do for them. His air of competence almost induced Dani to unload her problems on him.

As if he sensed her longing to confide, he had drawn his thin lips out in a wide, and surprisingly charming, smile, then reiterated his desire to help. It was probably a good thing that Kelly asked him to bring them chocolate chip cookie dough. The request diverted his attention from Dani and provoked a homily on the dangers associated with eating raw eggs.

With considerable amusement, Dani watched the immovable object debate the irresistible force to a mutual standstill. She came down on the side of the irresistible force when they took a detour to buy a package of cookie dough. Dani needed both the sugar and the chocolate boost for what had followed.

"I can't believe I actually went to a place called Buns 'n Roses," Dani said, watching Kelly fall back on the bed, a reminiscent smile still curling the edges of her lipstick-smudged mouth.

Dani had exchanged the red dress for something less conspicuous, but the red dress's ambiance had lingered, carrying her into the male strip club with her chin defiantly high. A pity the smoky atmosphere, sensual pounding beat of the music, and assorted men didn't get a certain marshal out of her head, despite the fact she was still pissed at him.

"Frankly, I can't believe you went either." Kelly rubbed her face, then looked at her hand as if wondering where it came from. "You were never this fun before people wanted to shoot your ass."

Dani grinned, half guiltily. "It has kind of altered my perspective—though I'm not sure it was for the better. I should have spent the evening preparing to meet my maker, not watching naked men swiveling their hips for tips." She sank down on the edge of the other bed and, out of habit, grabbed Kelly's heel-shod foot and began undoing the strap. "Though it was almost a religious experience when that guy stripped to ABBA."

"Yeah." Kelly's smile widened to lascivious. "Made me want to kneel and give thanks."

"You did kneel and give him a tip," Dani said dryly.

"Oh yeah." Her face blurred, her eyes losing focus as she settled deeper into the soft bed. "Gave thanks, too."

"I believe you." Dani pulled off her shoe and tossed it in the corner, then started on the other foot. "I just hope your seven a.m. interview doesn't hear about our foray to the fleshy side of town. We already get too much bad press."

"Honey, I figure if he wants to talk about sex, why fight it? Besides, that was research."

"Is that what you're going to tell your dentist?"

Kelly's smile went past lascivious. "Ain't gonna *tell* him squat and he won't ask when I jump his cute bones. Oughta see him in his scrubs."

"Slut." Dani pushed Kelly's bare foot away and tossed the other shoe over with its mate, then bent to detach her own shoes. For feet that had only had to tap and curl all evening, they sure were complaining. Course, they hadn't had the view her eyes had.

"Compliments will not sway me from my purpose." Kelly lolled her head in Dani's direction and yawned widely. She blinked a couple of times. "What was my purpose?"

"To go to sleep."

"Oh, right. Night." She rolled into fetal position, muttering, "Damn fine ass . . ."

"I hope you're talking about your dentist," Dani said, trying to sound severe and failing because of the giggles trying to bubble up. She pulled a blanket over the supine figure, tucking the edges securely around her. Kelly muttered something. "You're welcome."

Dani sank down on the other bed, then fell back, staring at the ceiling for a long moment, her mind turning with a kaleidoscope of faces. Dark Lord, dead Cloris, the hot brown eyes of her personal fed, all of them circled by bare rotating butts. It didn't make for a pretty picture. "How many more days of this do I have to get through?"

In the middle of subtracting and adding she slid into sleep and her nightmare without passing "Go" or collecting what she was owed. Everything was happened faster now. The replay of Richard killing. The moment when he realized she'd seen him. Dark Lord's arrival, his cold, pale eyes lusting for her death. He laughed wildly as a circle of fire flared around him in an unholy nimbus.

"I am Death, Willow," he told her, and she saw he held a knife. It dripped blood that smoked when it hit the ground. The knife sliced toward her in a deadly arc—

The frightened flinch of her body freed her from the dream. She stared at the lace draped canopy over head, briefly baffled by its presence, then Kelly give a gentle snore in the dark to her right and yesterday came flooding back, in all its good, bad, and embarrassing detail.

Had she really gone to a strip joint? Yes, she had to admit, she had gone. At least she hadn't tipped anyone, though it had been a near miss during that ABBA routine. She lifted her arm and peered at her watch. The illuminated numbers inevitably showed five zero zero.

"Great." Dani sagged back with a groan. When would the horror end? Maybe she should be hunting Dark Lord so he could put her out of her misery. With another groan, she rolled out of bed and headed for the bathroom, after a quick detour past the refrigerator for the Diet Dr. Pepper that the highly efficient Niles had found for her. The man was a positive treasure. How much did a butler cost, she wondered as she popped the top and poured that first reviving stream down her throat. If she lived, she wanted one just like Niles.

A short time later she emerged from the bathroom carrying a glass of water and two Alka-Seltzers. She sank down by Kelly and gave her a nudge.

"Come on, girl. It's plop, plop, fizz, fizz time. Your jerk awaits. Oh," she nudged the limp body again. "Can I borrow your laptop?"

Matt rarely remembered dreaming, so at first he didn't realize he was dreaming, despite a smoky haze hanging in the air outside Boomer's office, not to mention an elongated perspective that made Riggs taller than him.

"You putting down roots, cowboy, or just coming in real slow?" he heard her say. *Dani.* He turned and found her, biker babe with soft, sad eyes. "You make a better wall than a door."

"I know who you are," he said thickly, blinking the smoke from his eyes as he strained to see through the haze.

"Do you?" She laughed, but it was a man's laugh, deep and evil as she turned into Hayes, his knife slicing the air on a collision course with Matt's chest. He came awake with a jerk that sent pain shooting down his back. Briefly panicked, he put his hand on his chest, then realized it was his back protesting the fast change in position. He rubbed his eyes and looked around, wondering why he was in the living room of his apartment and not in his bed. It all looked oddly unfamiliar, as if he were still dreaming. Or hadn't been home for three days.

He straightened his back, more slowly this time, so the pain could crawl down his spine instead of shooting like a rocket. Damn, shouldn't have sat down "for a minute" when he got home—he looked at his watch—only three hours ago? Five-thirty was his usual time to get up, but it had never looked or felt so bad.

He stood up, intent on finding coffee as quickly as humanly possible, followed by a shower. His cell phone gave his heart a faster jump-start than the strongest coffee or coldest shower. He grabbed the phone. "Kirby."

"She's online," Sebastian said in his ear. Didn't the guy ever sleep? Matt wondered.

"She passing her chapters to the agent?" Matt rubbed his neck.

"No. It seems she just snail mailed those."

She used the post office? "Great. So why is she on?"

He could hear the grin in Sebastian's voice when he said, "She wants to talk to you. You get the laptop set up like I told you?"

"Yeah." Matt crossed to his desk and opened the top. "You tracing her?"

"Of course. But she knows her stuff. You sure she's just a romance writer? So far I've been to Toronto, then headed across the Atlantic for a tour of Switzerland. It's probably going to take me longer than she's going to give you, so you'd better hurry and say what you want to say while you still can."

"Shit." Matt shook his head to clear it as the program logged him online. "How the hell she'd get access to a computer? We know she didn't buy one."

"Don't know. Doesn't matter." Sebastian sounded laconic. "You about here? She's getting impatient."

"Pretend you're me—"

"—tried that, but I made the mistake of using a smiley. She seems to know you're not the type. Sure you two haven't met before?"

Matt could hear the grin in Sebastian's voice as his computer took him to the chat lines where Dani waited. With something that was almost awe, he watched words scroll down his screen. *Will the real Marshal Kirby please come chat?—This year?* was the last sentence, right after Sebastian's ill-advised smiley. Matt ignored Sebastian's question and rubbed his eyes again. "So I just start typing?"

"And hit enter when you're done."

"Keep me updated on the trace." Matt tucked the telephone between his ear and shoulder, flexed his hands, settled them on the keys and typed: *You wanted to talk to me?*

Grandma was slow, but she was eighty, Deputy. We're almost out of chat time.

It's a little early—for both of us, don't you think? Matt typed, recalling from her file that she had had trouble sleeping and was definitely not a morning person. It didn't take much in the way of sleep deprivation to quickly impair judgment, but he didn't tell her that, even without Alice there to coach him. There were some lessons he didn't have to learn twice.

I had to rouse my friend. She's got an appointment to talk sex with a jerk.

Matt glared at the screen. "What the hell do I say to that?" In lieu of an answer, Sebastian choked. "Thanks a bunch. Are we even getting close to finding her?" he snapped as he typed: *Oh?*

"Not even on the same continent yet," Sebastian said.

<g> Did I make you blush? So sorry. Tell me, are your guys enjoying their visit to Sweden? All those willing blondes must make them want to linger. <g>

"Sweden?" Matt said aloud.

Sebastian chuckled. "Don't worry, I'm not getting distracted. Looks like we're heading for—oh, Iceland, that's an interesting choice."

If they were, Iceland has cooled their jets, Matt told her, hitting the keys with more sureness as his brain clicked into alert status. The chase was happening out of sight on a world connected by fiber optic phone lines, but that didn't lessen the pulse pounding tension of matching wits with the surprisingly clever romance writer. He added, *Did you have something in particular you wanted to say, or did you arrange this little chat so we could take a modified world tour?*

A writer strives to make every scene do double duty, Deputy, popped quickly up on his screen. *Since you brought it up, which one of you told Hayes about Willow?*

"What the hell—"

"She can't hear you, Matt," Sebastian reminded him, then added, "We're stateside again. Passing through Florida with our sights on Texas."

We didn't tell Hayes anything! Matt told her, finding the exclamation point not nearly emphatic enough. No wonder onliners invented those damn emoticon things. Before he sent this to her he added, *I give you my word it wasn't us. We did warn you he was getting your e-mail, didn't we? Maybe he found it the same way we did?*

The cursor blinked her lack of response. "She still on?"

"Yeah—we're getting closer—I think," Sebastian told him, "We're in Utah now."

Maybe. Matt sighed his relief when the cursor moved to make room for the single word. She didn't add emoticons, but he felt how grudgingly she had typed that word, felt her lack of trust as clearly as if she was sitting across from him.

How do you know Hayes knows about Willow? Matt asked her. He frowned while he waited for her answer. "There been any activity on her Willow e-mail address, Sebastian?"

"Just chat from her friends. Whoa, we're in the outskirts of our fair city now. Might just have her—"

Why didn't she answer? Had she already cut off the connection? Matt quickly asked, *Why did you take off? Hayes found you once, he can find you again. He'll have to try again. I know this guy and you don't—*

Are you always this negative or are you just not a morning person? I figure two misses are an out for him, don't you?

Matt bit back an impatient exclamation and typed: *They've already hired someone else. Someone every bit as nasty as Hayes.*

"We got her!"

"An address! I need an address!" Matt half stood up,

then hesitated when her words bumped aside his cursor again.

You're just full of good news this morning, aren't you? And I have to go. I can practically feel you breathing down my neck. The answer to these and other questions later. In Australia, maybe? I hear the beer packs a wallop—uh, duck!

Duck? What the hell did that mean? "I want that address, Sebastian!"

"No you don't," Sebastian said in his ear, excitement replaced by reluctant admiration. "She smoked me, Matt. Sorry."

"Smoked you? How? Where did you trace the call to?"

Sebastian gave a laugh that was wry and frustrated. "To me. I don't know how she did it, but our trace came back on me like spit. Damn, I've seen some fancy footwork out there, but nothing like this. Either she's an inspired amateur or she's been tutored by an evil genius."

Like an echo, one last line of text scrolled across his screen. *Did you duck?*

It was, Matt realized, possible to be pissed to the eyeballs, amused—no, way past amused—and admiring at the same time. It was possible. It was also uncomfortable. A verbal response started low in his gut, rose toward his throat in swell. Even he didn't know whether it was going to be a yell or a laugh. He felt Sebastian bracing at the other end of the line. Braced himself, too.

When it erupted, strained and slightly grim, but still recognizable as laughter, he was as relieved as Sebastian, who quickly joined him.

"Sebastian?"

"Yeah?" he managed to gasp out.

"If we ever get a case involving a romance writer, we run as fast and far away as we can."

"No argument here."

"Damn, I'm getting too old for this. Let's see," he ordered his thoughts, a strangely easier process in the aftermath of a good bout of laughing, "can we print out what was said and have Alice look at it? Maybe she'll notice something we clueless males can't."

"Righto."

"Thanks." Matt broke the connection and sagged back in the chair. He knew so much about Dani from the files, had heard her voice from tapes of her pretrial depositions, seen her thoughts from the online posts, read one of her books—

He had to admit she had made him feel things he hadn't felt in a long, long time. Surprise. Admiration. A longing to wring her neck until she begged for mercy. A desire to be in the same room with her.

Was she a flesh and blood woman with a bit of biker babe and romance writer? Where did grieved and grieving, a wicked sense of humor and a stubborn heart fit in? When he did come face to face with her, what then?

He thought he had felt all the regret he could when he had stood in the safe house and thought she was dead. This was worse. He had told her she could trust him and she could—to save her life, to stop Hayes. She couldn't trust him with anything else. Betrayal had dogged her from the beginning and now he got to be a tacit conspirator in administering the *coup de grace* when Sheridan let Richard Hastings off the hook so he could go after Orsini. Sometimes justice wasn't just blind—it was also stupid—and so damn wrong.

Richard Hastings would lose a lot in the process. He wouldn't lose enough. There wasn't a thing Matt could do about it. If he warned her, it wouldn't change anything. Hayes wouldn't go easily or quietly into the night. Even if

Bates managed to get him snuffed, there was Dent waiting for his chance to take her out. It was like having the best seat in the house for a gigantic train wreck. All he could do was sit here and wait for it to happen.

It took away all desire to laugh and recoiled the tension into a knot around his head. He rubbed his face and wished he could go back to sleep. Instead he headed in to the office. First that shower and shave he had promised himself. He stood up and his back protested again. Okay, first aspirin, then the shower.

Dani pushed Kelly's laptop away, feeling a guilty exhilaration at smoking Matt's experts in cyberspace. It had been close, a real squeaker, according to the status window in the corner of the screen tracking the trace, made closer by that last jab. Not a wise move, but a satisfying one. It was a known fact that alpha males needed to be thwarted occasionally—for their own good.

"The interview," Kelly called from the bathroom, "won't take me long. What say we do the tourist thing?"

Dani looked up. "I've already been to the zoo."

"I don't even want to know." Kelly propped a shoulder on the doorjamb and briskly rolled one leg of her pantyhose. "We could go see those mountainous, rock-like things looming over the smog. I've always wondered if the late, great John Denver's *Rocky Mountain High* was from mountains—or mountain grown."

Dani grinned. "Too high for this girl."

"Oh yeah. I keep forgetting you have that height phobia thing." She balanced on one foot and inserted the other into her panty hose. "Actually, I might have one, too. I've never really done anything seriously up, other than flying. And that doesn't really count, does it?"

"With a little Valium prior to flying, it doesn't." Dani hesitated, reluctant to take the first step away from Kelly, but knowing it needed to be done. The death that stalked her had a way of grinding up those around her.

"With a little Valium, little does matter," Kelly said dryly. She gave that final wriggle that was so critical to wearing hose with a semblance of comfort, then grabbed her silk tee and pulled it on. When her face popped through the neck, she added, "Quit stalling, Dani. I've known you for longer than I'm old. What's cooking in your far-too-devious noodle? If it's a new book, you know I don't allow you to get ideas in my presence."

She sat down beside Dani, a smile on her red mouth that didn't erase the worry in her blue eyes.

Dani shook her head. "Nothing bookish going on there right now."

"So what is?"

"You been reading the paper?" Dani handed it to her. "The trial is going forward very—briskly."

Kelly took it, read the first few paragraphs about the trial, then looked up. "Looks like it's about over."

Dani nodded. "I'm guessing sometime tomorrow they'll call me to the stand."

"And then?"

Dani gave a half laugh. "I don't know. I never thought past the trial. Just focused on getting to it." She shrugged. "Maybe they'll let me go home?"

"Works for me. All we have to do is get through today—"

Dani shook her head, looked down at her clasped hands, then at Kelly. "I've made alternate arrangements for tonight. Don't—" Dani cut off Kelly's protest. "You know as well as I do, that I need to keep moving. It's too dangerous for you, your mother-in-law, her staff, even the Dobermans."

Kelly stared at her, her signature pout slightly marred by resignation. "Don't tell me you're really gonna meet with your lovelorn ex-spy?"

"All right, I won't." At the look on Kelly's face, Dani added, "It's not like I have that many options and we're meeting at the mall. If I don't like the look of him, I'll walk away, still anonymous and think of something else."

"Like what?"

"I don't know!" She jumped up and paced away. "Something."

Reflected in the window, Dani saw Kelly stand up, pull on her jeans, and then stamp into her shoes. Her arms crossed, she stared at Dani's back for so long she hunched her shoulders.

"I'll think of something."

"Look, Dani, I'm all for making the alpha guy suffer torments. I love putting them through hell—in my books. But this ain't fiction, girl. This is real life. Your life. Your—death. Put the spook on hold and call the fed."

Dani could see the telephone without turning her head. All she had to do was put out her hand, dial some numbers, and they would all come running. They would lift the burden of living or dying off her shoulders. Let her lapse back into a semi-terrified limbo, going where she was told, doing what she was told—

"They can't all be dirty. If you can trust some cyberspace spook you've never met, you can sure as hell trust the feds for a mere twenty-four hours, can't you?"

"It's not me they want, Kelly. They want Dark Lord. They think I'll draw him to me and they can catch him."

"Sounds like a better proposition than facing him alone again. If he's not dead, he will come. And you're using up your luck." Kelly stalked over and pulled her around. "How the hell are you gonna get into that courthouse without their help? If Richard really does have mob connections, they'll have the place covered so tight an ant won't be able to get past them. You gotta know when to fold 'em." She gave a crooked grin. "Kenny Rogers said so. Hey, a guy that cute can't be wrong. Unless—"

At the change in her tone, Dani looked at her sharply. "Unless—what?"

There was only concern in her face. "Unless you've changed your mind about all this? Unless you don't want to get into that courtroom? Unless you don't want to face Richard? Is that it? When it comes right down to it, that you can't do it to him and Liz? Or their kids?"

Dani shook her head once sharply, then hesitated. Was Kelly right? Was she choking at the gate? She couldn't, wouldn't forget the horror of seeing Richard kill. She couldn't forget the other memories either. He was the brother she never had long before Dani married his brother and he married her other best friend, Liz. He was the one who had come to tell her that Meggie had died. The one who held her while she cried out her first shock and grief. Stood by her, with Liz on the other side, at the cemetery when Steven wouldn't even look at her. Protected her from Steven's drunken grief. Helped her navigate her messy divorce. Rejoiced with her when her first book sold. When Liz had her cancer scare, Dani was the one he had called to share his worry. She'd waited with him, then rejoiced with them both when the tests came back negative—

And the kids? She couldn't think about the kids without flinching. She was their godmother—

Why would she want to do this? She was losing as much or more than Richard in the deal.

Dani wrapped her arms around her middle, cradling the

hurt that was as fresh as the day she had watched him pull the trigger and shatter her illusions. "Did you hear what they're saying? That I'm accusing him of murder to get back at Steven for killing our baby."

"I heard. The bastard." Her touch was light at first, as if she was afraid Dani didn't want it. Dani covered the hand on her shoulder and Kelly slid her arm around Dani's shoulder in a warming hug. "It sucks big time dead toads, girl. But he did this to himself. He did this, not you."

It was the right thing, she knew it. Why did it feel so wrong. "So why do *I* feel guilty?"

"It's a woman's lot in life, according to Erma Bombeck, a lovely gift that just keeps on giving—kind of like the Energizer Bunny. Only way to beat it is to plow through it. Put his ass in jail and get on with your life."

Kelly was right. Dani knew she was right. He had started it by killing. She couldn't let him walk away. Not because he had tried to kill her, but for Peg and Cloris and all the others who had died.

Dani looked at Kelly, gave her a smile that tried to be brave, but was shaky at the edges. "I'm going to be there tomorrow. I'm going to testify if I have to do it postmortem."

Kelly hugged her again. "Good. I was starting to worry."

Dani arched her brows. "You? Worry?"

"It was getting hip deep in maudlin in here. You know how I hate that."

"Yeah." Dani gave her a gentle shove. "You'd better get going. Don't want to keep your jerk waiting."

Kelly turned to leave, then stopped and looked back, her face a mix of relief and worry that was strangely reminiscent of the look on Meathook's face when they'd parted company.

"What now?"

"That was it, right? Just the guilt thing about Richard?" Dani stiffened. "What else would it be?"

Kelly looked uneasy. "It's just that, well, when Meggie— at first, I was worried you wouldn't make it, then you did okay, but . . ."

"But what?" Dani asked, tensed.

"Now I'm not sure you did—get over it," Kelly admitted.

"I didn't get over it. No one does, no matter what they say. I learned to live with it. It was that or—" Don't even go down that road, she cautioned herself. "What does it have to do with Richard?"

Kelly looked like she wished she hadn't started this. She shifted uneasily on her heels and rubbed her upper arms convulsively. "Well, you can't blame me for wondering . . ."

"Wondering what? Come on, spill it, Kel. You've never spared me your keen insights before."

The words came out sharper than Dani intended and erased the hesitation from Kelly's face. She slung her purse over her shoulder and looked squarely at Dani.

"Well, I did wonder if you wanted this Dark Lord guy to kill you. You're not the type to commit suicide, but if someone did it for you—no guilt, right?"

It would have been kinder, Dani decided, if she had just pulled her beating heart out of her chest and stomped on it. Much less painful. It hurt to breathe, hurt more to ask, "You think I have some kind of death wish?"

Kelly looked away. "Think about it, Dani. Your angst-ridden heroes practically writhe with life and death themes in your books—even the funny ones."

"Which they resolve by choosing life," Dani pointed out with a hint of desperation. "Always life."

"Yeah." Kelly opened the door, looked back. "But those are books. This is real. This is about what you choose."

Instinctively Dani shook her head. "I've never even thought about—"

She stopped. It was a lie. Of course she had thought about dying. No one could lose a child without wondering if they could live in a world their baby wasn't in anymore. Once, a couple of months after the accident, she had cut herself shaving in the shower. It hadn't hurt. She'd stood for a long time with water pounding into her back watching the blood run down her leg.

"Damn you, I don't know, okay?" Dani glared at her because she had to be angry. Anger was easy. It didn't involve thinking or deciding. It just was.

"It's not okay! Figure out what you want before someone comes after you again, Dani. I'd hate like hell for Richard to lose the battle—and win the war." She left then, closing the door with pointed care that was more dramatic than slamming.

"If a world full of people couldn't agree on when life begins or ends," she said, "how am I supposed to figure it out?"

She sighed. Maybe she should ask Niles.

Instead of heading straight into the office, Matt took a detour into Commerce City to meet Riggs. Their interest had become focused on the suburb of mostly blue-collar families by the telephone call that had immediately preceded Dani's call to her agent from the pay phone in the convenience store Monday evening. Though the name listed with the phone number, one Joshua Heywood, didn't match any of Dani's known contacts, Matt's gut told him it was worth checking out—since their other leads were going nowhere fast.

On the drive over, he had a conference call by cell phone

with his team. It strengthened his conviction that Heywood could be important. Alice, acting on a hunch that Boomer's magic program couldn't have found all of Dani's cyberspace identities, had done some cross-checking of the online information they'd collected on her, then cross-referenced it with her real time life and identified several more online handles that could be Dani's. One in particular was an actress known as Delphi. Alice made a convincing enough case for Matt to direct Sebastian to monitor her e-mail traffic. Before the call ended he hit pay dirt. Just prior to Dani's online meet with Matt, Delphi had e-mailed some joker called Spook. The message was innocuous enough, a reminder that they had talked about meeting at "their" place if she ever got to Denver. She was here, did he still want to meet? The signature was followed by a quote that had probably been tampered with, since it was followed by an emoticon grin: *"There is only one passion, the passion for chocolate."*

Dani's posts certainly reflected a passion for chocolate, but so did a lot of the other romance writers' musings. More important in his view was that this Spook was near the top of the list of people Dani chatted with regularly and extensively. CIA agents were called spooks and Dani had mentioned an ex-CIA agent making a pass at her in her posts on a romance writers bulletin board a few months ago.

This bit of information was strangely annoying. Because, he told himself, it was crazy for her to be approaching some weirdo ex-spy for help. Of course, his annoyance was on a purely professional level, with maybe some professional jealousy mixed in. How could she choose the CIA over the Marshals Service?

The final piece of the puzzle fell into place when

Sebastian linked this Spook to Joshua Heywood and the address they were approaching just as he and Riggs turned onto the street from opposite directions. Matt pulled into the curb several houses down. Riggs parked directly across the street. Still talking by telephone, Riggs asked, "So do we set up a surveillance or talk to the guy and hope he throws in with us?"

Matt frowned. What was the best approach? If the guy really was ex-CIA and infatuated with Dani, would he be likely to help them? Spooks were unstable, ex-spook's notoriously so. A misstep now could put them back in the dark double quick. He tried to relax, to mine his instinct, but his gut was giving off mixed signals with his pride complicating the mix.

"I'd like to get a read on him before making that call," Matt admitted slowly, annoyed with himself for being indecisive. "Can you get me something from his records, Sebastian? I'll settle for an unpaid parking ticket."

"You don't think an ex-spook will smell a rat," Riggs said, dryly, "when a couple of US Marshals wake him up at seven a.m. to ask him about a parking ticket?"

"I don't care what the hell he thinks," Matt snapped, "as long as he doesn't make the connection with—"

Matt stopped abruptly when a car cruising slowly down the street turned into Heywood's driveway. Two men got out and started up the walk.

"Now where have I seen you two?" Matt muttered as they reached the door. One examined the street with an alertly casual air. The other bent to unlock the door. Or to pick the lock, Matt thought with a frown. They looked suspiciously like mob muscle. He looked across at Riggs. "Isn't that Bates' favorite muscle? The Trip boys?"

"What the hell they doing here?" Riggs asked, pulling his

gun out from under his coat and checking the clip.

There was only one reason Matt could produce. Dani was already here. "Send backup," he snapped into the telephone. Without waiting for confirmation, he tossed it onto the seat. Moving in sync with Riggs, he slid out of his car and started up the street, keeping low, moving fast.

A quick look told him they were still trying to work the lock. Matt signaled for Riggs to start working his way around to the back. Riggs nodded, dropped to the street, and crawled under a parked car.

The lock gave, followed quickly by an explosion that unleashed a ball of fire. It engulfed the Trips, then roared across the car Riggs was under and headed toward Matt.

Chapter Thirteen

Smoke still drifted in fragments of white against the deep blue of the morning sky when the bomb squad's investigative team moved into the wreckage. It was both easier and harder to navigate than the safe house had been. This one lacked the unstable overhead beams due to the roof having been completely destroyed in the explosion, but there were more pieces of wreckage to sift through this time, with hidden hot pockets that threatened to flare anew when uncovered.

The Trip boys, Bad and Bum, had been blown across the street, making a messy landing on the hood of one car and the roof of another. Screens now shielded curious onlookers from their remains.

Not too surprisingly, their initial inspection failed to turn up any fatalities beyond Bates's two boys. The door had to have been booby-trapped. The question was, why? Who was this guy that Dani may have turned to for help?

An hour after the blast Matt still didn't have an answer, though the ringing in his ears was beginning to subside. He'd been lucky. He was still breathing. The car he had been behind had afforded him a measure of protection from the blast, if not the flying glass and debris. The EMT finished patching the wide variety of lacerations and contusions on his exposed skin, luckily, all of them superficial, then stepped back to survey his handiwork.

Matt didn't ask how he looked. If it was close to how he felt, it was better not to know. He tossed aside the cold pack and fingered the lump caused by a flying door knob. It felt smaller. The headache it had spawned felt worse, though he had a feeling he felt better than Riggs.

He had been closer to the source of the explosion than Matt. He might have a concussion and possibly internal injuries, according to the EMTs, who advised transport to the hospital for further examination.

Matt hated to lose Riggs to the injury list, just when the operation was accelerating so lethally. Riggs protested he was fine. Matt wanted to believe him, but it was hard when Riggs's eyes kept crossing. Matt gestured for them to take him away, then turned to Henry and Alice who'd arrived on the scene shortly after the house blew.

"Anything?"

Alice shook her head.

"Right." He had had time to think while he was being doctored. His bell had been thoroughly rung, but he could still add two plus two and get a solid four. "We gotta move fast. Give me the short version of what you've got while we're in transit."

Alice and Henry exchanged puzzled looks, then Alice asked carefully, "In transit?"

"Someone needs to tell Bates his boys are toast. I want it to be me." He pulled out his car keys, his car had been luckier than all of them, with only minor dents and a layer of soot. He tossed Henry the keys. "You drive. I'm not seeing good yet."

This time their exchange of looks was distinctly uneasy. Matt ignored them and slid in the back seat, grimacing as his butt protested both movement and contact with the seat. Getting knocked on his butt was no longer an abstract expression. He had been offered a painkiller but refused it. He couldn't afford to fog his thinking with the situation jumping to critical mass. He could admit to himself that he hurt like hell, that he was seriously shook up—this one had been a little too close for comfort—but he couldn't let it stop him.

"Let's start with Dani," Matt directed. "What's her status?"

"I looked over your chat this morning and had a bit of luck," Alice said, resting her elbow on the seat partition between them. "I had my radio on this morning when I was driving in. Romance author Kelly Kerwin was being interviewed. She's in town for a writers conference this weekend. All the guy interviewing her wanted to talk about was the sex."

"Go talk sex with a jerk," Matt said softly. "I'll be damned. I never thought of that."

"No reason you should." Alice grinned. "I called the agent. She almost shuddered when she heard Dani had hooked up with Kerwin. Their chemistry, when combined, is a bit—incendiary, her words toned down a bit. She suggested we check packaged cookie dough sales and canvas strip joints. Kerwin is writing a book about a male stripper and has been doing a lot of research."

"And did we do that while I was getting blown on my butt?" Matt asked dryly.

"We did the strip joints." Alice's smile was deficient in demure. "Tuesday night. Buns 'n Roses. The clincher? Kerwin was signing books that day at the mall where Dani bought the red dress. I checked the hotel she's registered at and there's no sign of either of them. Room wasn't slept in last night."

"They have to be somewhere. Let's add Kerwin's known associates to our list. They may be bunking with someone Kerwin knows but Dani doesn't." When, he wondered, had he started calling her "Dani" instead of "Gwynne?"

"Already working on it," Alice said. "But based on her latest e-mail traffic, she's getting ready to move again."

"Which brings us to Heywood." Matt frowned. He was having trouble focusing. Every turn they took hurt just enough to be distracting. "I can understand Bates sending his hit squad in if he thought Dani was there. She probably wasn't. So where does the bomb come in? You don't send a hit squad into a location you've already booby-trapped."

"We have a theory on that," Alice said soberly. She extracted a folder from her briefcase and held it out.

Matt shook his head impatiently. He wasn't sure he could read yet. "Just give me the details."

"As soon as Sebastian penetrated the first layer of information on Heywood, red flags started flying. It's bogus, Matt. Not even a deep cover bogus, though good enough for a cursory examination. Once he knew it was a fake, it was easy to find a death certificate for the infant Joshua Heywood."

"A bogus." Matt rubbed his aching head, not liking the direction his thoughts were heading. "Birth year?"

A crease of worry put a sharp line between her brows. "The same as Hayes."

He didn't have words, profane or otherwise. Times like this he really envied Sarge from the *Beetle Bailey* cartoon. He had a whole keyboard of symbols to use. All Matt had was the dictionary. It wasn't enough. "Hayes is Heywood. Heywood is Spook. Spook is—"

"—the man Dani thinks is her friend and is planning to meet," Alice finished for him with an air of calm. She had had more time to get used to the idea.

"Is it a coincidence?" Matt asked, then answered himself, "How could it be?"

The implications were staggering—and sobering. If

Hayes was chatting with Dani online, then it was entirely possible she had inadvertently engineered the compromise of the safe house. Which meant that Neuman and his team might be in the clear, except for being too stupid to know what was going on under their noses.

"Coincidence doesn't seem likely," Henry agreed, stopping for a red light.

"When's the meet?" Matt asked. "And where?"

"High noon. Looks like they suspected their mail might be monitored. They both allude to a favorite place of Dani's, but no mention of where that might be. I put some people on to reading through her posts again for any reference to a place they could meet." Alice looked at her watch. "But we've got less than two hours."

"We tried to warn her by e-mail?" Matt tapped out a beat on his knee. It hurt, but the movement kept time with thoughts twisting and turning for a viable plan of action.

"Yeah, but if she's on the move, she's not likely to risk logging on—particularly since she's found out what she needed to know."

Matt uttered an unamused laugh. "What she needed to know. Where to meet her killer. What a mess." Hayes was running true to type. Nothing he was involved in was ever simple.

"This is it," Henry said, pointing to an open gate. Beyond the gate, visible through the trees that partially shielded the house, red lights flashed a warning of a new problem. "Looks like someone beat us to the punch."

"No, this is something else," Matt said, looking at the coroner's wagon parked among the police cars. They flashed their ID's to the uniform guarding the open gate. "Bates?"

"Bates and Davis, sir."

"Bang goes Richard Hastings plea bargain," Alice said.

At least there was some good news. He asked the cop, "Fire?"

He shook his head. "Throats slashed."

"Really?" Matt frowned. He had been sure that Orsini hired Hayes to do the hit. Orsini was heavy into that kind of irony. "Anything else unusual?"

"Well," the man hesitated, then added, "there's talk they found a message pinned to Bates's chest."

"Message? What'd it say?"

He looked almost embarrassed. "Not worthy."

"That's it?" Matt frowned.

" 'Fraid so."

Not worthy? What—he looked at the cop. "Were the bodies moved and arranged?"

He looked surprised. "How did you know that, sir?"

"Just a wild guess," Matt said grimly. If this was his handiwork, why hadn't Hayes done his usual torch job? What were Bates and Davis not worthy of?

His pattern was screwed. Totally screwed. Dani emerging as Willow threatened to send Hayes over the edge of his own madness. He had wanted to deny it. How could he live with the knowledge that he had almost killed Willow? It didn't fit the pattern. Still he could not deny it. It made sense. It was entirely logical. It explained why he had felt her, seen her in his dreams. His heart had known what his mind had not. Had tried to warn him. It broke the pattern. When he had Willow, they would fix it. Or make a new pattern.

"Order eventually restores itself by psychic equilibrium." He had to believe this to survive. Together they would forge a better pattern. One that couldn't be destroyed by anyone.

First he had to secure her safety. There were too many players in the game. That's why he had taken Bates and Davis out of the equation only hours after they had put the contract out on his head. The irony of it pleased him, soothed the itch to kill and keep killing again until all who threatened his future with Willow were dead.

The meeting at the mall was complicated. He hadn't dealt with all of her enemies yet, but he couldn't ignore her summons. He knew how much she needed him to protect her. So he came. It was as simple as that. She would be frightened, but when she realized he was her destiny, she would accept him—accept his heart—his protection. She would recognize, as he had, that they were meant for each other. Once she was safe, they would start creating the new pattern by climbing his mountain together.

With her his pain would go away. Not just until the next kill. Forever. Willow was the cure, the final solution. Nothing must stop their coming together.

"I can't believe what I'm about to say," Kelly said, stopping her rental car at the mall's entrance and turning to look at Dani. "It's against my deepest shopping beliefs, but—don't go into the mall, Dani."

Dani grinned, amusement momentarily diffusing her own unease. It was certainly a first. It tracked with her own feelings. Right now the last thing she wanted to do was go inside and meet another person she knew by words, but not by sight. Her mind was total goo. She had passed tired days ago. Even pissed off had faded, leaving behind a thick exhaustion that made even one step at a time too hard to contemplate, let alone execute. It would be so easy to stay in the car, drive off with Kelly, go to the convention. She belonged at writers conventions. Not meeting an ex-CIA agent in a mile-high mall.

Every decision she had made, except for hooking up with Kelly, had ended in disaster. If she stayed with Kelly, disaster could catch up with them both. How could she live with herself if something happened to her best friend? Practically the only friend she had left? All because she didn't go into a mall? She couldn't. She opened the door and lifted one, then the other foot out. Now all she had to manage was standing up.

To postpone it, she looked at Kelly. "I'll be fine. Really."

"I don't buy swamp land in Florida, the Brooklyn Bridge, or desert in Arizona. Do you seriously think I'm gonna buy that?" Kelly asked. Dani didn't answer, just looked at her. Kelly sighed. "Look. I can't believe I'm saying this either, but how about I wait out here for, say half an hour? If Spook turns out to be a drip, you'll have a fall back position."

Dani smiled her relief. "Sounds good to me."

Too good actually, but she didn't have the energy to resist, especially when Kelly was being logical. What she knew about Spook seemed okay. He was smart and funny, but so sensitive it was hard to believe he could be for real. This wasn't a good time for unpleasant surprises. All she needed or wanted from Spook was help in getting into court this afternoon.

"Why don't you circle around? We're meeting in center court. If he doesn't look promising, I'll just walk straight through without stopping."

"Works for me," Kelly said. "Let's synchronize our watches." She grinned. "I've always wanted to say that."

"There's too many things you've always wanted to say and do, girl." Dani slid out and stood up. Her legs wobbled slightly, then held. She looked doubtfully at the cowboy boots Kelly had talked her into buying. They were so shiny she felt like a real greenhorn, especially with the cowboy hat and western stitched shirt. You've gone to Mardi Gras dressed like a romance novel bookmark, she reminded herself. How can you possibly feel ridiculous? The stiff leather did seem to help steady her ankles. Hopefully they wouldn't remove yards of skin in the process. She took a deep breath. "Half hour. If I don't come out, save yourself."

She opened the door, stepped into mall air and music. It was her spiritual home. So why did the door swishing closed behind her sound so—final?

Chapter Fourteen

It was like watching lines of dominos going down in every direction, Matt decided. He had to figure out which one would lead him to Dani using a brain that was still ringing from the explosion. Just in case that wasn't difficult enough, all they knew for sure was that she and Spook had a "place" and they were going to meet there at noon. A relentless search of their common online posts had failed to hint at a place, let alone turn up a mention of it. Nor had their APB on Kelly Kerwin's rental car turned up her or her car.

No wonder he had a headache.

"It has to be some place public," Alice said, pushing aside her share of online posts and arching her back. "She'd never meet someone she didn't know anywhere but in public."

"Wouldn't she?" Let's see. There was the biker, Meathook. She had showed up at his place unannounced, then spent the night with him and his neon mama. What about that waitress from the greasy spoon that she followed to the tenement like a lamb to slaughter? Or the male stripper-obsessed romance writer. Sure, she was going to be sensible. And the democrats were going to quit whining about losing congress tomorrow.

He didn't share his reservations with Alice. She would think he was being sexist. Which said all that was needed about the contradiction that was female logic.

Matt exchanged pointed looks with Henry and Sebastian—who obviously were on the same page as he—

behind Alice's back. They all knew they were right, but if she caught on, they would pay for it.

He shoved back his chair and stalked over to the coffee machine for some chemical energy. He added three sugar cubes above normal, stirring them in while he tried to stir up his thinking. He should be able to think his way through the problem. Should be able to take available information, add equal parts experience and intuition, let simmer until a conclusion formed, then act on it. End of situation. Move on to the next problem.

Only it wasn't working in the case of the romance writer and the hit man. She wasn't reacting the way she should. When he tossed in Hayes, who wasn't in the same universe as normal, it was a recipe for disaster. Hayes must be in high cotton. Dani was coming right to him. She wouldn't know it until it was too late.

Matt lifted the cup and tossed half of it down his throat. The coffee was as bitter as his thoughts. He paced back to his desk, slopping coffee with each frustrated step. "Damn it, there must be something we can do to stop the meet!"

Alice opened her mouth. Closed it. Then she frowned. He recognized the look. Her wheels were turning. If anyone could figure out what the woman was thinking, it was another woman.

While he waited for her wheels to spin, a clock ticked in his head, getting louder the closer it got to high noon.

"Maybe," she finally said, "we've been looking at this the wrong way."

"What do you mean?" Henry asked.

"Well, we're acting like their original meeting was this intrigue thing they were trying to hide," she said, thoughtfully.

"Oh?" The puzzled crease in Sebastian's brow deepened.

Alice ignored him. "Hayes couldn't afford to sound mysterious unless he wanted to arouse Dani's suspicions. When he made his offer, it was just a pass between a guy and a girl. Let's meet for drinks—"

Henry sighed. "She doesn't drink."

Matt stiffened. *"Chocolate chip cookies. The only perfect food."*

That earned him blank looks from both men, but an approving one from Alice. "Good for you. We might just turn you into a sensitive guy yet."

"Why does a compliment from women always sound like an insult?" Sebastian asked.

"I don't get it." Henry frowned. "Are you saying, they're meeting for—cookies?"

In unison Matt and Alice turned toward each other.

"The mall."

The closer she got to center court, the more uneasy Dani became. The question was, why? She was taking an online friendship into real time. She had done it with Carolyn and Meathook. That neither of them had made a pass at her was a slight, but surely unimportant difference? What mattered was that Spook was someone she liked. Someone she trusted. Someone who liked *her*. Not her face, her body, her testimony, or her ability to die. That he was ex-CIA was a positive, sort of, if she didn't think about it too much.

She didn't have to make contact with him. If she didn't, the problem of how to get into court today remained. She was fresh out of good ideas and running out of time. The trial was scheduled to resume at one. She could be called any time after that. She had to be there or all this was for nothing. Richard would win by default.

An ex-spy would know how to get into all kinds of

places, wouldn't he? She hesitated, her hand sliding into her pocket to the sheet with the addresses Matt had sent her. The marshals or the spook, Dani? Which is it to be?

She checked her watch. Five minutes to twelve. She hesitated. She had asked him to come. It would be rude to leave without a word. Just ahead of her was the bright, high dome of center court. She had to pass through it to reach Kelly anyway. Couldn't hurt to check him out. This was her chance to find out what an honest-to-goodness sensitive guy looked like.

She was late. Hayes looked at his watch again. Found it one minute later than the last time he looked. Sometimes the waiting, the anticipation, was the better part of the hunt. He wasn't hunting now. He was waiting for Willow. He had waited too long to finally be face to face with her. Now she was coming. He couldn't wait anymore.

Why didn't she come? She said she would. Willow didn't, wouldn't lie. It wasn't in her nature to lie. He scanned the center court area again, then turned toward the cookie counter where they were supposed to meet.

In Willow's Book of Life, chocolate chip cookies are the perfect food group. <g>.

He smiled. He would have to cure her of her obsession with chocolate. It was so unhealthy. If it brought her to him, he could live with it. For now. His smile turned to a frown when he saw the empty counter. She wasn't there either. He could feel their window of opportunity shrinking with each passing second. Could feel the ripples of pursuit coming closer. He couldn't let them get trapped here.

Why didn't she come?

Willow. Her name whispered across his mind and became an ache of longing. Henry Miller wrote that "the aim of life, is to live life, aware, joyously, drunkenly, serenely, divinely aware."

He was aware. It was her turn. Once she was aware, she would understand. She had to, it was their destiny.

Matt ejected from the car before it came to a complete stop. Police cars, lights flashing careened into a ragged circle around the mall entrance, releasing a flood of uniformed officers in SWAT gear. No one was taking Hayes's possible apprehension lightly. The SWAT commander intercepted Matt before he reached the door. Matt resisted sweeping the man aside.

"Alice, handle this, I'm going in."

Both of them said, "—not a good idea—"

"Don't try to stop me," he snapped. "I have two minutes to stop this meeting—maybe less. I have my radio. I'll stay in touch."

The commander looked at Alice, who hesitated, then nodded. They both stepped back and Matt jumped forward. He jerked the door open, aware on some level that he was acting out of character. It wasn't like him to be out of control, to go in without careful thought, without a plan.

He hadn't felt like himself since he got mixed up with the romance writer and the hit man.

Dani stood in a shadowy area just outside the bright reach of skylights criss-crossing the ceiling. The area was a typical mall milieu: the artificial trying to look natural; bright, open counters, lots of stone tile; green and growing things and scattered wooden seats breaking up the traffic patterns so shoppers couldn't take a straight line through, but were directed toward possible impulse purchases.

The scent of cookies drifted past on recycled air. Dani

turned towards the smell like a flower to the sun. That's where he would be. By the cookies.

She almost stepped out into the light. Something stopped her. No, not something. A feeling that someone was looking for her. Someone?

Him. Dark Lord. Here?

She shrank back against the wall. How could that be? The only people who knew where she was were Spook and Kelly. She was getting paranoid. Not too surprising when she counted up how much sleep she'd missed.

Across from her a man moved around the perimeter toward the cookie counter. Was this her Spook? With his loose-limbed body and bland face, he kind of looked how a CIA agent would. Weird if he actually did look like she expected him to.

He bent down, a natural enough action when you have just dropped something. But the movement, the way his head angled as if listening, his eyes sweeping the area with probing insistence, was almost a mirror for Dark Lord when he'd crouched over Peg's fallen body. All that was missing was the knife.

And the blood.

She pressed back into the wall, but the hard stone refused to yield even an inch. She wanted to run, but she was back in her nightmare. Afraid to run. Afraid to breathe.

He stood up, tossed what he had picked up in the air, and caught it with a fluid ease that made Dani flinch. He tucked it in his pocket and left his hands there as he strolled in the direction of the cookie counter.

He was a chameleon. She had seen him become Dark Lord with her own eyes. Seen him vanish into normal. How could she believe her eyes now? He looked so innocuous, so much a part of the mall scene it was eerie. She would be hard pressed to pick him out of a line-up.

She eased along the wall, keeping the man in sight, then slipped inside the store behind her. The plate glass on two sides helped her see; the racks of dresses provided cover.

"Can I help you?"

"I'm just looking," Dani told the clerk with perfect honesty. She moved around to one side, stopped when Dark Lord propped a shoulder against a pillar. Her nerve endings jumped in time with the question playing repeatedly in her head.

How did he know I would be here?

There was something, some realization hovering at the edges of her mind that she wanted to flinch away from. Why had it made Dark Lord so angry to find out she was Willow? Why hadn't he killed her either of the times he had had the opportunity? If only Kelly and Spook knew she would be here, then—

Dark Lord must be Spook.

There was no other explanation. Kelly sure as hell wasn't. Cyberspace had brought her and her killer together in a bizarre scenario. One doomed from the beginning, with the punch line to be played out in a real, killing time.

Stupid. I've been so stupid.

"You looking for a size? I can help you—" the clerk tried again.

Dani looked at her as the full enormity of it crashed over her. "No one can help me."

Matt slowed as the cookie counter came into sight. Cookie counter. He couldn't believe he was about to stake out a cookie counter.

On the radio he heard Alice deploying their resources and mentally placed them in his head. The exits were covered and men were moving his way. The evacuation of the mall had begun.

Dark Lord suddenly straightened, his head up, his body tense like an animal sensing danger. Dani could feel him reaching out toward her. Knew that he knew she was here somewhere. She wanted to run. She wanted to cower. Wanted to postpone the moment of discovery.

"You all right, ma'am? You're kinda pale," the clerk said, her young voice uneasy.

She would never be all right again. Dark Lord turned in a circle, his piercing gaze following where his senses led, both on a collision course with her. Everything slowed, even her heartbeat, it's frantic pounding echoing in her head. Her life didn't flash before her eyes. Instead, she heard Kelly saying, "You wouldn't do it yourself, but if someone did it for you—no guilt, right?"

Had she brought this on herself? Had she chosen without choosing? Had she drawn Dark Lord to her? Had she felt death and invited it in? Had others died protecting someone who didn't want to live? Because if the answer was yes, then she deserved whatever happened.

He turned abruptly away from her, several long strides taking him quickly out of sight. Why? The answer to that question strode into view bare seconds after Dark Lord disappeared.

Her hound dog hunter, Matt Kirby, looking big and angry with his body coiled tension.

How did he know she would be here?

It was almost—annoying. She was going to die. Now she wasn't. Somebody needed to make up their mind. She didn't want to mess with this anymore. She wanted to whine, loud and long. To sleep without nightmares. To go home. Instead she walked forward until the plate glass got in her way. She leaned her head against it because it was there.

At least the view was good. His jeans were inspiring.

She was too tired to flip a coin. Let him decide. If he wanted her, she would go with him. If he wanted Dark Lord, well, there was still Kelly waiting outside.

"Wow, wonder what's happening," the clerk said behind her, snapping her gum with noisy enthusiasm.

Dani ignored her, waiting for Matt to see her. The killer or the romance writer? Who did he want to find the most? Maybe it wasn't fair, but she didn't have to be fair. She was a woman. He was a man—with the power to hurt her. He wouldn't mean to, but he would.

Even knowing this didn't stop her wanting him to choose her over the killer. There was no law that said she had to be logical. No rhyme or reason to explain why one man made her burn, another chilled to the bone. She should leave. She stayed, waiting for him to see her. Waiting to see what he'd do when he did.

Matt was in the zone. The place where it all came together. Training. Experience. Instinct. This was what it was for, what made it—the paperwork, the waiting, the politics, the lawyer crap—worthwhile. This was why he did it. To catch criminals.

It was too simple for some people. He liked it simple. Liked it straightforward. A to Z. Making the world safe for the people who had no idea how bad it could get. For his mother. For Dani—

He stopped in his tracks. There she was. Looking at him through a damn store window not at all surprised to see him.

His gaze narrowed, zooming in to absorb the small signs indicating she wasn't shopping: her pale face, trembling mouth, eyes wide and shocked. She had seen Hayes. He was here somewhere. Where? Matt scanned the area and found nothing. He turned back. Now her eyes had a question for him. What, he wanted to ask, but there wasn't time. They could still get Hayes. He had to move now.

"Hayes—" he mouthed. She hesitated, then pointed down one of the wings. Matt pivoted, avidly searching the shadows for his quarry. Still nothing.

He turned back toward Dani. He needed to find out how long Hayes had been gone. She wasn't there. Had he been smoked? Had Hayes made her—no. There she was, walking away from him like he was nothing. Matt turned, lifting his radio as he headed in the direction she had pointed.

"Alice, Hayes is heading your way. Be very careful. Alert the DPD and let's try to cut him off. Oh, and Henry, Gwynne's walking your way. Pick her up. When we're through here, we'll take her to the trial."

Harold Dent sat in his car, tapping the steering wheel impatiently. Only slightly less wide than he was tall, he had a misshapen head, created by nature, and misshapen fingers because of his nature. He had started life as a boxer, but had quickly taken the path of least resistance and big money by hitching his wagon to Bates's dark star. He was not a bright man or a particularly brave one. He didn't need to be. He was very strong. His only instinct besides killing was survival. It was as strong as he was and it kicked in as he studied with narrowed gaze the lights flashing on the top of police cars positioned crookedly in front of the doors of the mall.

He had left his broad in bed for this crap? The snitch at

the PD shoulda told him how hot it was gonna be here. This wasn't a hit. It was a short trip to stir and dating guys again.

Even if he could find the mark, he couldn't take her out with the joint crawling with cops and feds. He was too bright to be that stupid. He reached out to restart his truck. He was getting the hell out of here. Not like he was gonna get the rest of his scratch for this hit with Bates and Davis biting the big one. Unless Orsini came through with the dough.

Dent frowned. Hard to see what could be in it for Orsini. Sure as hell couldn't figure out why Bates was so set on toasting the romance writer. Maybe he didn't like her books or something. He kinda liked the idea of his broad reading about getting it on. She didn't like watching anyone getting it on. Women. Who could figure 'em out?

Take that broad over there in the white car. Couldn't park straight to save her life. And the way she kept popping out to look around, like she was looking for someone or something, then ducking like she don't want the cops to see her. Totally weird.

He straightened. It was more than weird. Why wouldn't she want the cops to see her? She was demonstrating what the cops called highly suspicious behavior. He oughta know. His snitch had said the writing broad was hanging with some other writing broad. Blonde. Built. She could be a writing broad. Kinda looked like she had an active imagination. Sure enough got his imagination working.

Maybe he'd just hang tight. See who she was watching for. If he got the chance—introduce himself.

He pulled his gun out from under his jacket and checked the clip, then screwed on the silencer. With a little luck, he could do Gwynne fast. Do her friend slow.

Stupid to be angry with Matt. She should be angry with herself. She knew the score. Had seen where his priorities were by the rock hardness of his face that day in Boomer's office. She didn't have the right to be disappointed. He had never promised anything. Not even to be kind.

She looked at her watch. She had ten minutes to maneuver around to where Kelly waited. Directly ahead of her she saw people being ushered out the doors by cops in uniform and a man wearing a US Marshals jacket. He hadn't noticed her yet. Without missing a beat, she turned into a department store, weaving through the almost empty aisles toward the outside exit, but stopped short when she found it.

More police. Fight or flight, Dani. What's it going to be? They weren't the enemy. I can't do this yet. I need time—as if they heard her, they scrambled into their cars and roared away with multiple squeals of tires.

The hunting hound dog whistled and the rest of his pack came running. She was glad they were about to catch Spook.

She was. Really.

A man opened the door and she slipped out ahead of him, his exclamation of annoyance following after. It was irrelevant. She was irrelevant. A detail among a multitude of details.

She emerged from shadow into sunshine, but the chill from the mall stayed with her as she crossed to the curb and stopped, trying to decide which direction was the fastest route to Kelly.

Dent couldn't believe his luck. It wasn't just good, it was great. Not only had the cops pulled out, the mark was delivering herself to him on a freaking platter. Dent smiled, thin lips spreading to reveal discolored and crooked teeth. Unbelievable.

He pushed open the door and climbed out, pulled down his jacket and adjusted his belt over his belly, then strolled forward. This was gonna be a walk in the park.

Chapter Fifteen

Dani didn't have much time before Kelly was due to leave. She had to get around the mall . . . A horn honked imperatively in the parking lot. It took her a minute to find Kelly's arm waving out the open window of her white rental car. She smiled. Good old Kel. Trust her to size up a million cops and come to the right conclusion. She was a truly devious person. No wonder they were friends. She was parked part way down the row and Dani started toward her, but stopped when a man stepped in front of her. No reason to worry. No reason to be scared.

Until she saw the gun in his hand.

How hard to drag her gaze off the large, very steady hand pointing it straight at her heart. She had to tip her head way back. A big man, his shoulders were just getting started where her height ended, with a face that was coarse and puffy. Small cruel eyes were shoved in on either side of a bulbous red nose.

"This way, babe."

Articulate, too. If she had thought nothing could be worse than Dark Lord, she had thought wrong. Desperately she looked over her shoulder where the cops had been.

"Gone. I can get you and your friend before anyone can stop me. Some of them, too, if I have to." He smiled. It wasn't a pretty smile. It lacked charm and good teeth. Kelly's dentist would have had a field day inside his mouth—an odd thing to think when she was about to die.

"Let's go join your friend. I like blondes . . ." He stepped toward her, reaching for her arm.

Maybe it was the mention of Kelly, the implied threat in his evil satisfaction. Maybe it was instinct. Maybe she just couldn't stand the thought of his meaty hand on her. The why didn't matter. There was barely time to act.

With a distant awe, Dani saw her leg kick out. Saw the pointed toe of one of her new boots thud solidly home where it would cause the most damage. The thug's tiny eyes got larger as they bulged briefly out of their sockets. Air hissed into his lungs between his clenched, misaligned canines. The eyes sank back almost out of sight. His breath gushed out in a low, foul-smelling moan.

His massive fists clenched. The gun coughed a bullet that shattered the window next to Dani. She jumped, but stayed cool—no cold, like ice. She waited until his fingers twitched and the gun dropped free, then she kicked it away. He didn't try to stop her. Just stood hunched over, his hands tucked protectively over his manhood, while he moaned and muttered an impressive array of swear words.

Kelly edged cautiously around him. "You all right?"

"Yeah." Dani rubbed her forehead, not surprised her hand was shaking. Her nerve endings were jumping with enough adrenaline to run Chicago for a week.

Side by side, they studied her handiwork. Finally Kelly looked at her and said in an "I told you so" voice, "And you were afraid you wouldn't get your money's worth out of those new boots."

Dani made a sound halfway between a gasp and a laugh. "Let's get out of here."

Kelly lifted her hands in mock terror. "I ain't gonna argue with you." She gave a last admiring look at the preoccupied goon. "You sure do good work, girl."

When they reached the car, Dani sagged into the seat.

"I think I'm gonna be sick."

"You don't have the time. You gotta be in court in less than an hour."

She closed her eyes. "Now I know I'm gonna be sick."

Hayes quickly pulled on the dead cop's black flak jacket and helmet, adjusted the brim, then his gun belt. With the radio in his ear to keep him apprised of his adversaries' movement, he ran purposefully around the corner and merged with the other cops waiting for him to come out and be gunned down. He loved the irony of it. Irony was one reason he loved Willow. She had a nice touch with it.

The disguise would be perfect for his appointment at the courthouse. He looked at his watch. Richard Hastings would be arriving in just over twenty minutes. It's where Willow would be heading. If the fates were kind, she would be in time to see his next gift to her.

Matt rubbed his face wearily. His arm felt like it was on fire and his head had a determined drummer playing taps on the inside of his skull. No Hayes. No Dani. A dead cop and a shooter nursing his dick.

"Dani do it?"

Alice looked up from her notebook. "That'd be my guess. He isn't talking yet."

"No, I don't suppose he is." Matt tried to remember how long it took, but was too tired. He wasn't in the zone anymore. He hadn't stopped Hayes. He hadn't even stopped this goon. The romance writer had. The world wasn't a slightly better place. There would still be a boatload of paper work to fill out. There was no justice in this world for the just. Maybe this was a sign he should retire. He was too old to be staking out a mall. A mall. Made him twitch just thinking about it. It was all Dani's fault. He didn't belong here. He shouldn't be here trying to figure out how he was gonna explain what went wrong. He should be hunkered down waiting for a fugitive to visit his girlfriend or tracking whacked-out drug dealers. Anything but the mall. There was a lesson to be learned here, but damned if he knew what it was.

"Word on the street is Hayes has put out the No Trespassing sign on Gwynne," Alice said. "Wonder who Dent thought he'd collect from if he did do it? Had to know Bates has bitten the big one and that Hayes probably helped him do it. Why risk pissing off a fruitcake like Hayes?"

Henry shrugged. "Maybe he thought Orsini would make good on the contract. Bates was his man."

"Probably just too stupid to know better." Matt did not care. He talked so he wouldn't have to think about all he had to do before he could crawl into bed. A cop beckoned Alice. Matt watched her walk away. Her back was still straight, but he could see the effort it took to keep it that way. They were all too tired. No surprise they were making mistakes. This should never have lasted this long. If Dani didn't show up in court this afternoon—

Alice finished her confab with the cop and walked back. Bet she was wishing she hadn't chosen heels today, he thought.

"What now?" he asked.

"Looks like she's still with Kerwin. Someone noted down their license plate number after they saw her kick him." Alice grinned tiredly. "The bad guys are oh-for-two. Not bad for a romance writer."

"Would you try not to enjoy this? You're supposed to be on our side." He stared off in the distance, trying to look like he was thinking. "The courthouse?"

Alice shrugged. "If she's keeping track of the trial, it's the obvious place. Sheridan was keeping things going until they'd hammered out a plea, but now that Bates is dead, Sheridan's gonna want to get his full pound of flesh out of Richard Hastings—"

"Matt?" Henry leaned out from their car. Matt hadn't even noticed him leave. Sure as hell hadn't heard the telephone. "You'd better get over here."

Matt sighed. "What now?"

"All hell just broke loose at the courthouse."

"What?" he barked.

"Don't know. Sounds like a real mess though."

The wail of sirens bit into his aching head. Worry ate at his insides. The ride was a slow motion nightmare that took too long. When they finally arrived, information was sketchy, somewhat less than satisfying, though it could have been worse. As far as they could tell, only Richard Hastings and his lawyer, Prescott, were dead. They had been bumped out of protective custody, their deal with Sheridan rendered null and void the minute Bates and Davis turned up dead. At twelve-forty-five, just as they were pulling up in front of the courthouse, a bomb in their car ended the trial and their lives.

At least, Matt thought grimly, he wasn't the only one who would be making explanations to superiors later today.

It was almost like coming full circle, Matt decided, looking at what the bomb had done to the vehicle. The smoky smell of fire and death was a familiar reminder of what had begun at the safe house five days earlier. It was hard to feel sorry for Hastings. His end had been quick and probably painless, if a bit messy. Better than what he had arranged for Dani. Better than he deserved.

Two explosions in one day. It made him wonder. What reason could Hayes have to kill Hastings? Bates had put Copeland on the job before he died. Someone must have forgot to tell Copeland the party was over. He waited for Alice to pick her way to his side. "Any sign of her?"

"Coherent witnesses are a little hard to come by."

"Yeah." He rubbed his face. "I've been trying to calculate the time—"

"I know." She sighed. "It's too close to call it either way. We'll just have to—"

"Wait. I know." He shoved his hands in his pockets and hunched his shoulders. "I hate waiting."

Alice smiled wearily. "No shit."

Dani smoothed the edges of her black dress down to her knees, then curled her icy fingers into the palms for something like the hundredth time since they left the courthouse. A stop in a McDonald's parking lot so Kelly could run in and get them coffee hadn't helped her to warm up, not even a drink of coffee as hot as Richard's last stand.

Kelly picked up her cup, brought it almost to her lips, flinched at the heat and set it down again. "What now?"

Dani blinked, then frowned. "I won't be going to Disneyland."

Kelly's grin was relieved, though she still looked shocked around the eyes. "Not the way you'd choose to win your point, was it?"

"No, it wasn't." She was cold, but she still felt the heat of the explosion, could still see the way the car heaved skyward, then slammed back against the pavement, it's interior gutted, engulfed in flames. She could still see Richard's face, looking so much like himself it hurt, just as he prepared to step out and meet the press. She could still see him disappear in flame. "You didn't see Liz, did you? She wasn't in the car?"

Kelly shook her head. "I don't know."

"I have to call—"

Kelly looked relieved. "It's about time you called him—"

Dani frowned. "Called who?"

"Your cute-assed fed. Who else?"

"Oh, yeah. Him." He stayed in her head, some place where she couldn't see him. Not now. Now she could only see Richard.

"Who—oh no. Oh no." Kelly gripped the steering wheel and shook her head. "You're not thinking of calling—"

"I have to. I—just have to."

Kelly snorted, then sighed. "It's your funeral. Here, you can use my cell phone. But don't ask me to stay and listen to this, because I won't." She opened the door. "You want something else?"

"Yeah, thanks, something with sugar?" When Kelly nodded and shut the door, Dani dialed. By the third ring, she was sick to her stomach. This was nuts—

"Yes, hello."

It was Steven's voice, laced with irritation. She hadn't expected him to answer, but she should have. Surely Liz was here in Denver for the trial—

"If this a crank call—"

"It's—not," Dani got out in a rush. "I was just surprised to hear your voice."

"*You're* surprised to hear *my* voice?"

"I—was worried about Liz. And the—kids."

He didn't answer. Her hands tightened on the telephone until the knuckles went white. Please don't let Liz be dead, too. I couldn't bear it. "I'm sorry I bothered you—"

"She's there. Liz is in Denver," he said brusquely.

Dani inhaled sharply. "Oh no, not—"

"No! She wasn't—feeling well. Was going to catch a cab later—we haven't—told the kids. Liz wanted to—" His voice broke. She could hear his heaving breaths. "Why? Who would do this to him? I don't get it."

Dani sighed wearily. She couldn't handle his grief. She could barely handle her own. "You never did get it, Steven."

"I know that if you'd just—just—"

"Kept my mouth shut? Let him get away with murder?"

"He was family, damn it!"

Dani almost didn't notice that Steven didn't deny Richard's guilt. Almost.

"You knew, didn't you? You knew all the time." Steven didn't answer. He didn't have to. "Did you kick in something on the hit man he hired to kill me, Steven? Because he's family?"

She had thought he couldn't hurt her anymore. Just shows how wrong a girl could be. He started to say something, but she wasn't in the mood to listen. "Just—tell Liz I called. That I'm sorry it ended this way."

She broke the connection and leaned forward, resting her head on the dashboard. Why did it feel like Richard was the lucky one?

The car door opened and Kelly slid in. "You aren't crying, are you?"

"No." Dani sat back, taking a shaky breath to steady her voice. "I'm not crying."

"Good. Real women don't cry." She handed Dani a baked apple pie, then opened hers and took a bite.

Trust Kelly to kill the angst. Dani looked at her. "It's real men that don't cry."

Kelly paused in mid-bite. "I thought they did now?"

"That was the eighties. Now they're just tough in a very sensitive and caring way."

"Oh. I guess that's what I get for spending so much time with fictional men. And my dentist." Kelly munched quietly for a bit. "We still doing that 'I am woman, hear me roar' thing?"

"I have no idea." Dani was quiet for a moment, then sighed. "What do you do when your ex-husband wants you dead?"

Kelly shrugged. "I went to a movie."

Dani thought about that. "I wonder what's playing?"

Chapter Sixteen

It hurt to move. It hurt to think. Matt did not want to get out of his truck, let alone tackle the stairs to the second floor apartment he shared with his brother Luke. He was no masochist. The treelined, gently sloping street was almost empty, a soothing sight in the half-light left by the recently set sun. He could just put his head back and sleep sitting up if it weren't for the fact that it also hurt to *not* move.

He slid out, moving like the old man this week had made him, then looked up at the converted Victorian house. According to his mother, it was mellow and charming. She was probably right. Tonight it just looked high and all stairs. He climbed the outside stoop, then the inside stairs, not enjoying any of it, not even making the landing. He still had to drag his tired ass and aching body down the hall and around the corner.

Vaguely, he noted someone at the end of the hall, sitting in the window well of the old-fashioned window. It meant he couldn't groan. He still had his pride—somewhere down there under the bruises, the tired, and the pissed off. He had his door unlocked and open before his brain registered who the someone was at the end of his hall.

Only the quarry he'd hunted all over the damn city.

Not dead.

Not blown up.

Actually, the opposite of blown up. Neat as a pin with her hair up and wearing sober black, a long string of white pearls, and a reserved expression that made her look honest and earnest. The perfect prosecution witness. All dressed down and no jury to charm.

So she had come to him.

Better, he supposed, to be the last resort than no resort.

He had a lot of things to say to her. A lot of questions to ask her. He didn't want to say or ask anything, he realized, looking into her tired, wary, green eyes.

He wanted to wring her neck.

Dani slowly stood up. She had known he wouldn't be happy to see her here. She just didn't know he would be quite so unhappy.

"Where the hell you been?"

"You really don't want to know," Dani said, careful to keep her distance. She watched his eyes narrow dangerously.

"I've never hit a woman."

She couldn't blame him for the "yet" she heard at the end of that statement. She admired his control. His face was scored with exhaustion, but his body was erect, his restraint made out of pure iron. She was too tired to stop her nerve endings from becoming emotion receivers for what was behind the control. The heat wasn't all from rage and frustration. She was cold enough to be glad for the warmth.

His cellular telephone rang. Without letting her gaze off the hook of his, he flipped his telephone open. "Kirby."

"Matt," Alice said in his ear. "We got confirmation our girl is still above ground."

"Really?" He watched Dani's eyes widened slightly, then slide away from his, as if she knew they were talking about her. She seemed to know a lot. He didn't like that in a woman. He didn't like the way her eyes sized him up, rooting out his secrets, taking her ill-gotten knowledge and tucking it away to use against him at a later date.

A woman looks at a guy and sees an open book to write in. A guy looks at a woman and sees a puzzle with breasts, legs and an ass. If the breasts, legs, and ass are good, a guy can't even spell his name. If not, he still didn't have a chance in hell of figuring her out.

"Yeah," Alice went on, "seems she called her ex. FBI had the phone tapped."

"Really?" He listened while Alice ran the tape for him, then said, "Interesting."

"Yeah. Kerwin's surfaced, back at her hotel. Claims Gwynne's heading your way. Thought you'd want a heads up."

"Thanks." Matt didn't know why he didn't tell her Dani had already arrived. Instead he asked Alice to keep him posted and rang off. He shoved his telephone back inside his jacket and looked at Dani. The romance writer and the lawman. He could see the wheels of her mind turning in her big, green eyes. He liked green eyes. Beneath the bravado of her defiantly angled chin, she looked exhausted, brittle, ready to break.

He was tired. He was pissed. He wasn't a hammer.

He nodded towards his open door. "I don't have your soda, but I can probably rustle up a cup of java for us."

Until this moment she didn't know how much she had needed him to be kind. It wasn't politically correct to need a man, but she wasn't ashamed to need him. The sisters would just have to deal with it. "Thank you."

He flicked on the light and gestured for her to enter. She stepped past him, careful not to let their bodies touch. There was too much tension in the air. He was tired. She was tired. Touching could be dangerous to their health.

His hall was short, but it still took concentration to put one foot in front of the other, like a drunk trying to walk a straight line. She stepped around the loop of rope reaching out to snag her dragging feet, noticing in a vague way that it was attached to some climbing gear piled to one side.

Behind her, Matt shut the door, wood snapping against wood, the lock snicking in place with finality.

The hallway opened onto a living room with a high ceiling. She stopped in the doorway. The light from the hall made a circle that reached part way into the room, but even without the sun outside, there was enough light from the streetlights shining in the uncovered windows for her to see the layout of Matt's home. In the spirit of "know thy adversary," she looked at it for what it would tell her about him.

On her right a low bar partially exposed a shadowy kitchen that didn't look big enough for Matt's shoulders, let alone his whole body. It was clean, without even the smell of old food to indicate use. In the other direction, three long windows did double duty by giving a view to the street and breaking up the white expanse of wall. Between two of the windows was a square, serviceable desk. Matt moved past her and closed the blinds, then turned on a table lamp sharing desk space with a laptop computer that looked suspiciously familiar. There was also a stack of mail, several gun clips, and a scattering of loose bullets.

Probably not a liberal.

Straight ahead was a doorway to a bed and bath. Other than the desk chair, the only place to sit was on a massive, manly gray leather sofa or one of three stools lined up in front of the bar. In front of the sofa was a battered coffee table that looked like it doubled as a footstool. It was covered with magazines devoted to sports and law enforcement. One inside wall was covered with shelving fashioned out of planks and cement blocks. In the center was a fancy television and stereo setup. Rows of books and videos marched off in either direction. As far as she could see, the videos weren't of a salacious nature, but if Richard had taught her anything, it was that looks could be deceptive.

It was a testosterone-only zone, the quintessential bachelor's pad, though cleaner than one not acquainted with the lonesome lawman's terse smile might expect. She and her estrogen felt an urge to add flowers in vases, curtained windows, and pantyhose drying in the bathroom.

Matt thumbed briefly through the stack of mail on his desk, then looked up, his brows drawing sharply together.

"You'd better sit down before you fall down."

Despite his blunt delivery, he had a point. Her knees were losing structural integrity with each passing second. She tottered the short distance to his man-size couch and sank gratefully into its cool depths. It felt good, even if had been made for a man-size body.

For a few seconds she tried to resist the compulsion to shed her shoes, but even the most comfortable shoes wore out their welcome eventually and her feet were in full rebellion. She simply had to kick them off. To ease the cramps in her insteps, she stretched her legs out on the coffee table and rotated her sore feet with a soundless sigh of relief. Something, a quality in the silence, a current in the air, made her look up. She found Matt staring at her, his expression too controlled for comfort. What, she wondered, was going on behind those eyes?

Dani looked good on his couch, her stocking-clad legs stretched across his table for easy viewing. She reached up and freed her hair, shaking her head slightly, and pushing her fingers into the mass to massage her scalp, the thick strands catching light as she moved.

It was bad how good she looked. He felt the gnawing bite of lust do a slow crawl in his gut. His control was under attack by the sheer black nylons on her nearly perfect legs, not to mention the lift of her breasts against the soft fabric of a dress that wasn't as demure as he had thought.

She leaned forward and massaged one foot, then the other. Her long necklace fell forward, clanking against the table. She pulled it off and tossed it on the table. From where he stood, he could now see the bare, smooth nape of her neck. He rubbed the nape of his neck and wished the room wasn't so hot. Damn August.

Her gaze found his. The room got so quiet he could hear the clock in the kitchen ticking. A car honked outside and she jumped, then hastily pulled her legs off his table. Her feet didn't quite reach the floor.

"Sorry," she murmured.

A dangerous feeling wound into his want.

Tenderness.

He would rather face a truck full of Uzi-toting wise guys than a woman that made him feel tender. Tender was the disguise weakness wore. He would not do weak again. No way.

"Not a problem. Do the same thing myself." He wasn't ready for her smile. It flowed across the tired landscape of her face, briefly lighting it with something almost as dangerous as tenderness. He picked up the beads. "Nice touch."

"Mardi Gras," she said, a hint of strain in her voice that told him he wasn't the only one suffering from August heat. "Can't wear them in New Orleans because everyone would know."

"Everyone would know what?"

"That these are the good beads. The kind you show your—" She stopped abruptly, color rushing into her face. The flush was almost as good on her face as the smile.

"Show what?"

Dani looked at him. His face was still carved out of rock, his mouth a straight line above his give-no-quarter chin, if she had stopped there—but she didn't. She had to look at his eyes. They gave him away, spilled his deep, dark secret.

The lonesome lawman had a sense of humor.

She couldn't remember which hobbit in *Lord of the Rings* had tossed a rock in the pool blocking the gate to the Mines of Moria. She did remember it caused the band of adventurers a boatload of problems. Knowing trouble was waiting didn't always blunt temptation nor could it stop her from wanting to make ripples on the hard surface of Matt's face.

She wriggled her butt deeper into his couch, lifted her legs back on the table and crossed them at the ankles. His face didn't change but his throat rippled when he swallowed hard. Tough audience, but not tough enough. She crossed her arms behind her head and arched her back in a mock stretch. He ran a finger around the neck of his white shirt and blinked once.

She could tell him she had gone to the movies this afternoon, but he would probably kill her, with the same stone face.

"Skin," she said, then gave a mock sigh. "You have to show skin. Lots of it. The more skin, the better the beads they throw you."

"I—see."

His face didn't change. The temperature in the room did. From his direction, she felt enough heat to make a furnace jealous. The siren call of passion tried to stir up her sluggish body, tried to blind her to the fact she didn't know him, despite the persistent feeling that she knew him better than she'd ever known Steven.

She was too tired to sort it all out, but not too tired to worry. Pressure plus heat had to explode somewhere. It was the only scientific law she remembered, probably because she blew up a beaker in high school chemistry learning it. Singed her eyebrows, too.

Her one foray with love had singed her mind and damn near broke her heart. Dangerous things, heat and pressure, action and reaction, love and hate.

She ran a fingertip along her eyebrow. It had grown back. Her heart thumped out a caution. It healed, but it wasn't as brave as eyebrows. It had more to lose in desire's arena.

Dani took a shaky breath, gathered her thoughts together and said lightly, "That's what Kelly says. These are her beads."

"Oh." He hadn't moved or altered his stance, just stood there with his hands shoved in the pockets of his jeans watching her with his dark neutral gaze.

He gave no quarter, but unlike Steven, he didn't compromise or give up. Unlike her, he didn't bend. She had recognized the quality outside Boomer's office, seen it in action when he went after Spook at the mall. Because he wouldn't turn or be turned aside, he would be very cautious about what—or who—he chose to commit himself to.

The vigorously male surroundings made it pretty clear where matters of the heart stood in the queue of his life. If she mistook his kindness for something more, she was going to lose more than eyebrows.

It was as if he had followed her thoughts and agreed with them when he said in a carefully cool voice, "I'll see if I can scare up that coffee, unless you'd like something stronger? There might be some Scotch—"

"I don't—drink." Watching Steven's slow spiral into alcoholism had pretty much killed any desire to imbibe.

He stopped beside the couch, said without looking at her, "I'm sorry. I should have thought—"

"Don't." She looked up at him. "I'm not a hothouse plant who can't deal with reality. I'm—"

"Willow?" Matt looked at her then.

She flinched. "I think I'm going to give that handle a permanent rest. I'm not feeling too willowy right now."

He felt like a bastard for reminding her of Hayes. He vented it by banging his cupboard doors as he assembled cups and spoons. They were both wound so tight the air in the room vibrated with it. Tired and tense. Bad combination. He didn't kid himself that lust wasn't part of the tension. Hell, he wasn't made of stone—well, ninety-five percent of him wasn't—and she was a damn sexy woman who needed something he couldn't give her. It was unprofessional to get involved with her. Not fair either. He had already screwed up one woman's life. Dani's life had been worked over real good before he met her. She didn't need him administering the breaking blow.

He wiped at the sweat beading on his forehead, then wet a towel with cold water and applied it to face and neck. He would have applied it lower if he could have.

"I'm sorry I invaded your space," she said, her voice richly drowsy, like a woman sounds after sex. "I didn't know how to get around the police tape and bomb squad—"

"Don't worry about it." He hesitated. There were things he needed to know, but was she up to it? "Can you handle a few questions?"

There was a short silence. "Sure. What do you want to know?"

Did you see him die, was the first question that came to mind, but he couldn't bring himself to ask. "How did you plan to get inside?"

"We had a plan." She sounded defensive.

He didn't tone down his disbelief. "Really?"

"Really." Another short silence. "Kelly was going to jump up on a car and do a striptease."

He stopped what he was doing, thinking about the picture of Kelly Kerwin Alice had shown him.

"Too bad it got called off," Dani said, dryly.

He grinned. "Yeah, too bad." He leaned against the counter, watching the coffee bubbling in the pot. "The explosion came before one. It's now closing in on nine. Where have you been?"

"I'd feel safer telling you if you weren't wearing that gun."

"Not another strip joint?" He might have to use his gun if she had.

"Movies."

"Movies? At a movie theater?"

"Yeah, three of them, one after the other."

She saw Richard Hastings get blown sky high, called her ex-husband, and then went to the movies?

"It was quite cathartic, actually," Dani said.

"Cathartic?"

"What would you do if you found out your ex wanted you dead?" Dani asked him.

Matt didn't hesitate. "I'd live."

"You would, too." Dani chuckled softly. It was a husky, tired sound, not unlike a music box winding down. "Well, I plan to live, too."

Matt's grin faded with her words. She planned to live. Hayes planned to kill her. He wouldn't stop now. It wouldn't matter that Bates was out of the picture. His reputation was at stake. The hit man couldn't be beat out by a romance writer. Not if he wanted to kill in this world again.

The coffee pot finished bubbling. Matt wasn't sorry for the distraction. He poured two cups. "How do you take your coffee? I have sugar, but we're out of milk." Only silence from the living room. "Dani?"

He stepped round the bar and found her asleep. Not in a relaxed sprawl, but curled nearly fetal where the back met the side, her head turned to one side, her cheek resting in the palm of her hand. The tenderness started in again. The only way to stop it was to get pissed off. It was hard to drum up pissed when she looked like that. He could kick bad guy butts till the cows came home, but one look at a sleeping woman—

He turned abruptly away from her, went into his bedroom, turned back the covers on the bed and closed the curtains over another set of long, narrow windows. Back in the living room, he hesitated. It was one thing to look, but to touch? To gather close? Insert in his bed?

He could take the coward's way out and cover her where she lay. He wasn't a coward. That was against regulations. His problem, he decided, was that his focus was wrong. Instead of thinking of her as a soft, warm female, he needed to think of her as a package that needed to be moved from point A to point B. That settled, he bent and picked her up. She made a small murmur of protest before settling against his chest with her face pushed into the side of his neck. Her soft bare skin rubbed against his. Her warm breath stroked the side of his neck.

She didn't feel like a package. What he felt he refused to think about. He lowered her to the bed and she muttered again, a soft, distressed sound that put another dent in the armor of his detachment. She relaxed against his pillow with a small sigh. He arranged the blanket, taking care not to touch her again. She shifted slightly, turning her cheek towards the pillow, one arm curved above her head as her chest rose and fell. He should have turned away then.

How long had it been since he had watched a woman sleep?

Too damn long.

If he wasn't careful, he would be in coyote position again, howling for the moon. He didn't get the moon before, wouldn't get it this time. It was harder to turn away from her this time.

He did it because he had to. He checked the locks, downed a cup of coffee, very black, and then carried another cup with him to the bedroom. He shed his jacket, loosened his tie and put his gun close at hand on the table by the bed. After adjusting the bedside lamp to a low setting, he pulled the easy chair close and dropped into it, his body going slack with a weariness that caffeine couldn't blunt anymore. It went too deep.

He blinked, rubbed his eyes, knowing he had to stay awake. He sipped the coffee, then picked up the book on the nightstand—hers. He settled deeper in the chair and opened to where he had left off last night.

. . . Daniel stood by the bed, watching her sleep. The body that had given him so much pleasure the night before was relaxed, enticing in unguarded slumber. She murmured, then rolled to her side, pulling the sheet taut across her naked body. With a sigh she lifted her arm over her head exposing the smooth, erotic line from breast to thigh—

Dani muttered in her sleep. He looked up in time to see her lift her arm over her face, stretch, then arch her woman's body, before relaxing back into the mattress. She wasn't naked.

It didn't help.

Matt swallowed dryly and tugged at his shirt collar.

Maybe this wasn't a good time to be reading her book. He tossed it on the floor, but without something else to focus on, his gaze did a homing pigeon back to Dani, deep in a restless sleep. It looked like neither of them was going get much rest this night, even if they were sitting in the small eye of a very big storm. There would be no peace while Hayes remained at large.

Tomorrow the storm would be on them again. Hayes was probably tapping his contacts right now. Matt was the only one who knew where Dani was right now, but in the morning, he would have to report in. He trusted his own people, but information had a way of leaking out when the incentive was big enough. If they were to have a shot at catching Hayes, they had to be in control of the field, the flow of information. Hayes would be expecting that. He would be making his move while they were making theirs. They would have to move her first thing tomorrow, but where?

Chapter Seventeen

She was lying in a bed that wasn't hers, staring at a ceiling that wasn't familiar. It was too ornate, carved into shapes she couldn't make out because the light wasn't bright enough. She heard movement in the shadows. Uneasily she turned toward it. "Who's there?"

"Willow."

She knew his voice, even before his face emerged from the shadows, she went from uneasy to terrified in a heartbeat.

Dark Lord.

The pale glow of his eyes pinned her in place, left her unable to move as she watched him walk toward her.

"I don't want to die," she told him.

He stopped by the bed. "Willow."

Slowly, as if she were a wild animal instead of his next victim, he bent and touched her hand. Her flesh shrank from his touch. He looked at her and she knew there was something he wanted her to understand.

"What? What do you want?"

He sat down beside her, his hand hovered next to her cheek, then drew back when she shrank away from him. "Soon, Willow. Soon you'll understand."

A low moan brought Matt awake in a rush. His hand closed around the butt of his gun before his eyes were completely open. Then he realized he was in his own bedroom. In his bed, Dani moaned softly, her head turning from side to side as if she were trying to escape something. Or someone.

Hayes. *How are you sleeping nights?* Still not good, it

seemed. He rubbed his face, then leaned forward and touched the hand twitching on top of the blanket.

"Dani? Dani, it's just a nightmare—" Her eyes opened so suddenly, so wide, he wasn't ready. Their faces were too close together. He needed distance to look at the fear in her eyes and not feel anything but responsibility for erasing the cause. "It's Matt. Matt Kirby. The—"

"—lonesome lawman. I remember."

He started slightly at being nailed so neatly, went to let her go, but her hand gripped his for a endless moment, then slowly relaxed so that he could sit back.

"What—time is it?"

He angled his arm. "Five am."

A wry smile shaped her mouth. "I had a feeling it was."

"It's too early to get up. Why don't you go back to sleep?"

A wry smile edged across her mouth, her voice was dreamy and slightly sad, "I don't think 'the repose of the night' belongs to me. It opens an 'inn for phantoms.'"

"What?"

"Bachelard. Gaston Bachelard. French philosopher." She looked at him. "Ironic, don't you think?"

"I'm not sure. What are we talking about?" How could she quote a French philosopher at five in the morning?

"Spook, the king of quotes. I wouldn't know why I can't sleep if it weren't for him launching the quote wars on the boards. Course, I wouldn't need to know why if it wasn't for him. That's the ironic part."

"Oh." He didn't know what to say. What she had done was damn stupid, but she knew that.

She sighed. "I guess I should have known he was a hit man." Her mouth drooped at the edges. "Real men aren't that sensitive."

Matt frowned. "After twenty years in the Marshals Service, I thought I'd seen all there was to see, but Hayes—well, he's in a class of his own."

"You're just saying that to make me feel better." Her eyes were losing their bruised look and her smile came more easily this time. "Thanks for being kind after I, you know, avoided you and everything."

Matt rubbed his face, mostly to take a break from looking at her in his bed, her hair spread across his pillow. "I'll admit it—annoyed me."

"It wasn't personal," Dani said, then, added with conscious honesty, "—until you told me to get my ass back into custody."

"Alice called me on it at the time," Matt admitted.

"Alice?"

"Alice Kerne, a member of my team. You saw Riggs at Boomer's and briefly talked to Sebastian—"

"The counterfeit smiley guy?"

Matt smiled slightly, the movement taking the harshness from his face. "That's right. He enjoyed the world tour you took him on."

"More than you did, I suspect."

Matt didn't answer, but his gaze was amused. "How did you learn to navigate cyberspace like that?"

Dani didn't want to tell him she had learned the good stuff from Spook, so she arched her brows. "Isn't it in my file? I thought you had all my sad, little secrets at your fingertips?"

"If I'd had all of them, we'd have had this chat four days ago—or less."

"Oh, really?" Dani punched up the pillow and tucked it behind her head. When she was comfortable, she donned her best innocent look, the one she used when being interviewed by jerks. "So it was simply a lack of information that complicated your hunting? Not seriously underestimating the romance writer?"

His stare tried to be hard, but he didn't get the twinkle completely under control. "I don't want to talk about it."

"Okay. Tell me about yourself instead." When he opened his mouth on a protest, Dani added, "It's only fair. You have my file. *Quid pro quo.*"

He sighed. "What do you want to know?"

Everything, she thought, but aloud all she asked was, "What do you do when you aren't tracking down poor, defenseless romance writers?"

The bushy line of dark brows shot up, but he didn't take the bait. "This is Colorado. Rock climbing, skiing, hunting, hiking, fishing—we have a cabin up by the Rocky Mountain National Park."

A mountain cabin. Why wasn't she surprised? "We?"

"Me and my brothers. Luke, the oldest, is a cop and little brother, Jake, who is also a Deputy Marshal, comes when he's around. He travels a lot."

"How law-abiding you all are."

Matt grinned. "Runs in the family, I'm afraid. My dad was a cop. His dad, too."

Against the odds, Dani felt herself relax, felt sleep trying to steal back in. Matt had taken the edge off the fear she usually used to fight it back. He was far too comforting for his own good. Or hers.

"Was?"

"He died in the line of duty when I was in college."

"My parents died just before I started college, but you know that already, don't you?" The words came out in pieces as her mind began to blur.

"Yeah, I do." Matt noted the signs of returning sleep

with a mix of regret and relief. The more vulnerable she was, the more dangerous she was.

"Your mom," she had to yawn before she could get the whole question out, "she's still—"

"Yeah, she lives not far from here in the house I grew up in. She's dating again. He was my dad's best friend. She's known him, well, since the wedding. He was the best man—"

"You don't like it," she said on a sigh.

"I do, too," the protest was automatic, "I'm glad—hell, I've known him forever." He shoved his hands into hair. How had he gotten on this subject? "He's a stand up guy—"

"I didn't say you didn't like him," Dani said, her hand covering his where he gripped the sides of the chair. Her palm was cool. His skin heated to warm it. "I just said you don't like the situation."

"I don't have the right—" To dislike the situation or to like her hand on his.

She smiled. "I'm glad you realize it. Though it's natural to feel like he's letting your dad down." She yawned again, taking her hand off his to cover her mouth. Her words came out in sleepy pieces, "With guys, it's about—territory. If you can see that, you might get over it—"

She yawned again, her eyes closing as her voice faded. She sighed, then turned on her side. She reached out and found his hand again. A strand of hair fell forward over her face, curling against the smooth line of her cheek. The hand she wasn't touching curled into a fist. He flexed the fingers of his free hand, then lightly, gently smoothed the hair back behind her ear. Where her skin touched his, heat flowed, igniting the age-old longing to mate.

She wasn't, he reminded himself, a short time girl. She was a lifetime woman—for a guy with regular hours and a job that wasn't dangerous. Someone who could be there when she needed him, not when he could fit her in.

She sighed, her body shuddering slightly as she slipped into a deeper sleep. He closed his eyes. If he could just get through the night, the need would fade. He was just tired, that's all. At this time of the night, everybody felt lonely . . .

Niall McBride was almost too easy to kill. The last five days had turned him into a nonentity that needed to be exterminated, Hayes decided with disgust, not sacrificed on the altar of pain. Hayes killed him slow. He wanted him to know he was dying and why. As life faded slowly from his eyes, he told him about Willow, told him why his betrayal was costing him so dear. Told him he wouldn't burn. Hayes would not make him a martyr. All he was fit for was to wallow in his own blood.

Hayes sat and watched until the blood stopped flowing from the gash in his neck, then used his blood to write, "Not worthy" on the wall by his head. There was still the problem of Copeland, but he had a plan for him, too. When he walked out, he was almost a free man.

Willow was safe. Her enemies were dead. Even Orsini, though he hadn't done the job himself. He smiled grimly. The hit man had put out a contract on the employer. Ironic.

Willow would like that. She liked irony. He couldn't wait to tell her about it. He could, now that it was time for them to be together.

All he had to do was find her.

Matt woke up hurting with the sun stabbing through a slit in the blinds right into his eyes. He was slouched deep in the chair, his back at a bad angle. Inch by painful inch he straightened. Good thing Dani was still asleep. Would not be good for the witness to see the marshal grimacing and wincing in pain because he slept in a damn chair all night. Not when he was trying to inspire confidence in his ability to protect her.

Standing was marginally better than sitting. A hot shower would increase the margin. All he had to do was get there—if he didn't meet a belligerent two year old in the hall.

At least hurting had killed horny.

Dani chose that moment to roll over, taking her covers with her. Her dress had ridden high on her thighs. Way too high. Her legs, still covered in black nylon, were dangerous in daylight. She sighed, then bent one leg, sliding it up the pillow she was hugging. This took her hemline to new heights, exposing the lower curve of her nicely formed bottom.

Good breasts, great legs, outstanding ass. That made her three-for-three on the lust scale. He could be in trouble here.

For the third time in twelve hours, he turned and stalked away from her. He would like to meet the idiot who said there wasn't life after forty, he decided grimly. Probably some kid who didn't know that if there was breath, there was life.

On the other side of a cold then hot shower, his stomach rumbled a reminder it wasn't just sex that had been in short supply last night. In the kitchen, the refrigerator was almost bare, a state easily corrected with a market just across the street, if it weren't for the damn stairs. He tossed back a couple of Tylenol. He scribbled a quick note, locked the door, then punched the buttons on his cellular telephone as he headed down the hall. When his assistant answered he said, "Let me talk to Alice."

Dani woke on her stomach facing a long, narrow window

that she didn't recognize. Hovering at the edge of full consciousness, her hand opened and closed, as if it missed something. She rolled onto her back with a groan. Above her was an unfamiliar ceiling.

"Where am I?" For a moment she felt like she had done this before. She frowned. In her book *Putting Love Away*, her protagonist, Gemma had wakened in a strange room, so in a way she kind of had done it before. Gemma, she recalled suddenly, had been naked when she woke up. Cautiously Dani lifted the sheet and examined her clothed body with mixed feelings. "Obviously I haven't done what Gemma did."

Dani sat up, pulled her legs to her chest and propped her arms on her knees. She couldn't believe she had slept past five. It was a breakthrough, even if her brain still felt like mush. Waking up was not something she was particularly good at no matter what time it was. She needed a Diet Dr. Pepper and/or chocolate to smooth the transition. With an instinct that was well honed, she sensed neither was available here. She had been in the lonesome lawman's den, he had been making coffee—then boom, morning to face.

Imagination filled in the details. He had carried her to his bed. Then, she looked around, sat in that chair pulled close to the bed and guarded her rest.

How heroic.

Kelly would be thrilled he was finally playing the part nature had so perfectly fitted him for. Too bad his heart wasn't in it. No, good thing his heart wasn't in it. Her heart was no match for a determined assault by someone who looked that good in jeans and didn't mind taking on the odd killer.

Dani had sampled the bed and found it good. Now she studied his room. It was surprisingly old-fashioned with its high, sloped ceiling and crisp, white walls. It wasn't a large room, but, like everything else she had seen, it was a decidedly masculine one.

The king-sized bed, the dresser and night stand were hewn in blunt, clean lines that solidly filled space without overpowering the small area. In the corner, a closet door stood partially ajar. The chair by the bed was rugged, but comfortable looking—

She straightened. She did wake at five. They had chatted about his mother—the details came back in bits—then she had fallen back to sleep. A vague memory rose up to tease her, of Matt holding her hand and smoothing back her hair—

Dani frowned. It was not good for a writer to mix fantasy with her reality. It was almost as dangerous as mixing reality with her fantasy.

The missed 5 a.m. bathroom trip needed to be taken care of urgently. That done, the open closet door was beckoning. She gnawed her lip as conscience battled curiosity. He had snooped extensively into her life, turnabout *was* fair play. It wasn't like she was *opening* it to snoop. He had left it that way, practically inviting her to peek.

Inside she found guy clothes sharing space with guy stuff, mostly sports-guy stuff like skis and fishing poles and a locked rifle case. Now she remembered him mentioning his vices and shuddered. Far more interesting was the total lack of anything female. It upheld her impression she had wandered into a confirmed bachelor zone. A photo album was shoved onto a shelf overhead just begging to be removed and opened. So she did.

Inside she found snapshots obviously taken outside the cabin he had mentioned. The men must be the brothers. One was an older carbon copy of Matt, the other only like him around the eyes. Others snapshots followed, some of Matt, some of the brothers, wearing snow skis atop steep slopes or holding up huge fish or lolling animal heads.

When she called Matt a hunting hound dog it had been an understatement of massive proportions.

She lingered for a bit over a picture of a younger Matt, his arm looped around a brunette with sad eyes. Bending close she could just make out what looked like wedding rings on both their fingers. There had been a woman in his life, but there wasn't now. They had a divorce in common.

The romance writer and the lawmen? She was, she told herself, examining the idea for fictional reasons. She turned the page and found a shot of Matt hanging over the side of a cliff, a slight smile edging his firm mouth, a predatory look in his eyes. He hadn't been exaggerating when he said he climbed rock. He had just neglected to mention how high the rock was.

Just looking at the photo made her dizzy. Not even on paper could she work the kinks out of a romance between a rock climbing marshal and a romance writer with acrophobia. If he kept wearing jeans in front of her, she would be mightily tempted to try for a sea level, rock-free fling.

Dani looked at the steep drop the camera angle revealed again and flinched. Nah, never happen. He was wedded to rock and job. Didn't need to be a rocket scientist or a romance writer to know that about him. She only needed to be hunted by him for five days to reach that level of enlightenment. She set the album aside. Time for a shower.

In the hall there were two doors to choose from. Lucky for her the one to the bathroom was open. She listened at the closed door, but didn't hear any sounds emitting from it. Either the roommate was out or a very quiet sleeper. In the bathroom, she showered quickly. It wasn't like she had a lot to do. No toiletries. No clothes.

There was a towel and a toothbrush in a package on the side of the sink. Did it mean the lawman wasn't always lonesome or just thoughtful? There was no way to know, but she decided to assume he was thoughtful and helped herself to a dark silk robe hanging on the back of the door. It smelled like him, tough and earthy and—good. She tried not to inhale—it had worked for Clinton—as she rolled up the sleeves, then headed for the living room. Time to beard the mighty hunter in his lair. No, that was mixing her metaphors. Time to beard him in his—what? Where did hunters lurk? The gun shop?

"Hello?" she said, relieved when there was no answer.

She had taken in the broad outlines of his home last night. Now she walked around, looking for details to fill in the outlines. She read the hastily scrawled note that said he had run out for supplies. The writing was typically bold and masculine.

She ran her hand across the worn covers of his books, glad they weren't there just for show. A small thing, but something in common. The titles tended toward action adventure fiction, sports, Louis L'Amour, and law tomes.

She turned her back on the books and discovered it *was* her laptop on his desk. The nerve of him snooping through her hard drive. Then realized she would have to pretend she wasn't tempted to snoop through his drawers. That was the problem with righteous indignation. It left you no where to go.

The telephone rang and almost put her through the high ceiling. She stared at it, fighting the peculiar compulsion to answer, that six months cut off from the world obviously hadn't blunted one bit. It rang again and she gave into temptation. It wasn't likely to be for her. "Hello?"

There was a pause, then a female voice said, "Is Matt there?"

"No. He stepped out for—" The phone slammed down. With a slight smile, she replaced it. She had never cared for "other woman" plots anyway. Almost immediately it rang again. With one success under her belt, she didn't hesitate.

A pause, then a deep, cheerful man's voice asked, "Is Matt there?"

"He stepped out for a minute. Can I take a message?"

"This is his brother, Luke—"

"Luke? Oh, the big brother." Odd to think of Matt as a little brother. He was so . . . un-little.

A moment of surprised silence, then a laugh. "That's right. Who are you?"

She hesitated. "Louise. This is Louise."

"Oh. Well, Louise, they told me at his office he was home."

"Yes. He is—or he was. He stepped out for . . . sustenance which seems to be in short supply. But I'm sure he'll be back shortly. I can tell him you called—"

"Maybe you can tell me, do you know if he's still planning on going to the cabin with me tonight?"

Dani edged aside the curtain. Down on the street Matt was looking at a bin of apples and talking to the grocer. She hoped he was asking the man for chocolate and her soda. She wasn't into apples. "I don't know what his plans are for tonight—"

Luke's rich chuckle startled her. "If he can't figure something out, yours truly is available."

Dani chuckled back. She was actually flirting. It felt weird but nice. "I better not. I have a feeling the testosterone level in a cabin would be worse than it is here."

Luke laughed out loud. "I like you, Louise. Tell my little

The Last Enemy

brother to bribe you into risking it. And tell him I'll be home soon. If he stands me up again, I'm gonna kick his ass up over his head."

Dani grinned. "I'll give him your message."

She hung up, the grin lingering. Not that it was a good sign that both brothers appeared to be unattached. Of course, Matt's lack of attachment might be so recent he didn't even know it. Her grin took on an evil edge as she watched the object of her thoughts go inside the grocery *sans* apples. She turned back to the quiet room, feeling suddenly uneasy as bits and pieces of last night's nightmare filtered back to her mind.

She didn't want to know what the dream meant. Didn't want to hear herself think. She needed sound. She pushed the power button on his stereo, heard a whir of parts, then Mary Chapin Carpenter's distinctive voice flooded out of the speakers, singing that song about taking chances.

Symbolism? Again? She glared at the unit, then shrugged. If it drowned out her thoughts, why not? She'd sure as hell taken more than her share of chances. Even lived to tell about it. Looked like she had herself a theme song.

The music soared in the refrain, inviting her to take just one more chance. She wasn't sure. Something about the Spook/Dark Lord combo worried at the edges of her mind. She turned up the volume until it drowned out the worry. She started to sway with the music. There was a reason people danced while Rome burned. It was called denial.

231

Chapter Eighteen

Matt felt the thump of music vibrating through the old building before he reached the landing on his floor. The music got louder as he approached his door. Either Dani was up, Luke was home, or all of the above. Not sure what to think or expect, he shifted the sack of groceries to his other hand while he unlocked the door and paced down the narrow hall. He stopped short in the doorway.

Dancing? She was dancing?

Wearing nothing but his silk bathrobe.

And wearing it very well.

The brown silk clung where it should, fell straight where it didn't matter. His only complaint—it covered her legs almost to the ankles.

If she had to dance, and it seemed she did, Mary Chapin Carpenter's in-your-face song was a good choice for her. She had taken her chances and then some the last five days.

And how long has it been since you took a chance that wasn't work related, Kirby? With a soundless sigh, he set the sack on the bar. He should have started unloading it, stayed busy until she was through shaking her booty, but he was no saint.

Dani took two steps to the side, wiggled her silk-covered ass, did a half hop, turned to face him and froze, one foot still in the air. Pink flooded her cheeks. She looked good in pink. Her hair was wet and slicked back from her face. She looked good wet. The collar of his robe wasn't stingy where it made a vee across her breasts. His robe had never looked better.

"You're back." She smiled nervously, lowered her foot, then turned to lower the volume. "I was—just practicing my—tush push. Fred, the cop who taught me, says you should practice every day or your—tush—won't push—right—"

"You know he was just hitting on you, don't you?"

A tiny smile curved her mouth. "I'm too old to be hit on."

His gaze did a sweep, lingering on the plunging neckline. "You're never too old to be hit on."

The smile expanded. "I don't know. I feel at least a hundred." Her pink tongue outlined her upper lip. Her hand crept up to close the vee. "I helped myself to your robe. I hope—"

"I don't mind." The words came out more forceful than he had planned. He quickly added, "It's almost as good as your biker babe outfit."

Dani chuckled. "I kinda liked her, too. How did you figure out it was me?"

"It's my job—" he grinned crookedly, "but your coconut shampoo didn't hurt."

Her eyebrows arched. "Very good."

He would like to show her how good. Color surged in her cheeks as if she had picked up on his want. Matt swallowed dryly. Good thing he'd called Alice.

There was a tiny silence.

"You did a sustenance run, I see?" She walked over to the sack he had put on the bar, then slanted a look at him that made him uneasy.

"What?" he asked, defensively.

"The grocery sacks don't exactly go with the gun."

"Not many things do." He turned and reached into the mouth of the sack, wishing he could pull out a case of temporary sexual immunity instead of milk and eggs. He didn't need his blood supply heading so obviously south.

"I guess not." She slid onto a stool next to him, smelling of his soap, his shampoo, and something that was just her. When she craned to peer into the mouth of the sack, his robe slid away from the silken length of her leg.

It looked even better than he remembered.

"My soda *and* chocolate. You're clearly—"

She stopped. He didn't care why until her hand came into view, carefully gathered the errant flaps of robe and pulled them together. He looked up then, found her blandly regarding him, a slight twitch at the edges of her mouth.

"—a man who notices the little details. Unusual."

"Hard not to notice some details," he said, dryly. "Everywhere you've been, I found empty M&M bags and soda cans."

The twitch turned into a smile that reached into his chest and gave his heart a painful squeeze. No relief for him when her attention turned to the soda he'd brought her. Her look of anticipation lit the gold in her eyes. She licked her lips, then lifted the can to the moistened, pink circle.

"It's warm." He brushed the back of his hand across his forehead. "There's ice."

He ought to go plunge his head in some, then apply it lower for as long as it took to get his detachment back—so he could step out from behind the counter.

"I don't mind. I learned to take it warm in England." She tipped her head for a long drink, laying bare the smooth sweep of her neck and the plunging vee of his robe. She gave a tiny murmur of pleasure, then sighed. "I think I might live now."

"Good." He was dying, but at least she would live. He walked stiffly around the counter into the kitchen, propped his hands on the counter with his back to her and asked, "French toast?"

Dani paused in mid-drink. He knew her favorite breakfast? "I wonder if Socrates would've been so sure the unexamined life wasn't worth living if he'd had the feds on *his* case?"

"What?" He looked at her over his shoulder, a frown drawing down his brows.

"Did any of my deep, dark secrets escape notation in my file?"

"As I mentioned last night, some critical items were missing." He turned back to his preparations, got a pan heating, then pulled a bowl out of a cupboard, setting it on the counter with the eggs and milk. He lifted his hand to crack the first egg against the bowl, then stopped. "Why did you call him?"

"Call who?"

"Your ex-husband. I would've thought—"

"—that he'd be the last person I'd call?"

"Yeah." He cracked the egg and dumped the contents in the bowl.

"You're right. He is the last person I'd call. That's why I didn't call him." She traced the rim of the soda can with her pinkie. "I called Liz. He answered the phone."

"You cried." His voice had a harsh edge to it as he picked up another egg. He hesitated, then looked her way, his brows drawn into a frown that might have been forbidding if it weren't for the trace of puzzled in his eyes.

"I did not." His brows went up. "Only a little."

"Who for?"

She hesitated. "For—all of us, I guess."

"I don't get it." He cracked the egg too hard and it disintegrated into a mess of shell and liquid. He tossed the mess in the sink and grabbed another one.

She wasn't surprised he didn't get it. Her feelings for and about Richard were complicated. She had spent the last six months trying to reconcile the Richard she'd known with the man who had died so violently yesterday afternoon. Six months sifting through years of association, trying to find a clue, a hint that he wasn't worthy of her trust and regard. Either she was a lousy detective or he had covered himself really well. "He must have hated dying like that."

Matt's face hardened. "Then he shouldn't have gotten involved with Bates."

"He shouldn't have done a lot of things." She looked at her soda can. The only downside of her favorite soda was the lack of leaves to read. If she had been a tea drinker, would she have known? "To you he's just a guy who killed someone and got caught. But—"

"Did you love him?"

She looked at him, her brows rising. He looked back, his face unrelenting, his eyes cool. Nice of the tinge of red in his cheeks to give him away. He hadn't meant to ask that question. Knowing that made it easy to answer.

"Not the way you mean. He was a big brother, long before he was an in-law, stayed one after my marriage crashed." Dani propped her elbows on the bar looking at Matt, seeing the past. "He taught me how to ride a bike, drive a car, and keep a date in line. I stood up when he married my best friend, he stood up when I married his brother. He bought cigars when Meggie was born. I bought Liz lingerie when their first was born. We cried together when Meggie—"

She drew in a shuddering breath and said with careful calm, "He stood by me when I divorced his brother and bought the champagne when my first book sold. Then—I'd really like to exorcise him from my head, you don't know how much I want that, but if I do, my past goes with him."

Matt cracked the egg against the bowl and added milk, then stared at it, his body tight and controlled. She didn't, she realized, want to know why he was so tense. It was better not to know some things—yet another lesson from Richard.

"I keep hearing his voice in my head at Meggie's funeral saying, *Bring out the coffin, let the mourners come. Let aeroplanes circle moaning overhead, scribbling in the sky the message that [S]he is Dead—*"

Matt watched a tear break free, track unnoticed down her cheek and drop onto her clenched hand.

"I don't have much family, just some cousins twenty times removed, but I never noticed. They, he and Liz, were all the family I needed. When that ended, I don't know, I didn't feel like I had the right to feel bad about it." Her sigh was a shedding of the burden she had carried. "I guess it's selfish, but now that he's dead, it's over. I think I've earned the right to feel what I want."

He nodded, let the bread hitting the skillet with a sizzling flurry of steam fill in the blanks of what he couldn't say. They ate quietly.

When Dani had swallowed the last bite of her French toast, she sat back with a satisfied sigh. The food was filling, the talk—freeing. She felt better on all fronts. "Thanks. You do a truly fine French toast."

"I'll pass your praise onto my mom, the author of my skills as a cook." Matt took her plate, rinsed it, and then inserted it deftly in the open dishwasher.

"You know your way around a kitchen, I see. Your girlfriend must be thrilled." Dani propped her elbows on the bar, her chin on her hands, frankly enjoying the view. Kelly had a thing about shoulders, but Dani was most definitely into butts, which were their finest when wrapped in snug fitting blue jeans.

He looked at her over his shoulder, his expression openly ironic. "According to my ex-wife, my job is tough competition."

"Not every woman is afraid of a little competition."

"No." He shrugged. "But when they realize it's a no-win, they give up."

"I see." She had already figured this out herself, so having it confirmed at the source couldn't be the reason for the tightness in her chest. There was a drop of syrup on the counter. She dabbed at it with the tip of her finger. "You got a call this morning while you were out."

"Oh?" He closed the dishwasher and started it.

"She didn't leave a message." Dani studied the thick brown drop. Odd how sweet things *looked* sweet, like a clue left by God. If He had known they would need the sweet in their lives and wanted them to know, who was she to refuse the gift?

Matt turned to blast her about the folly of answering his phone when she was supposed to be in hiding and saw her mouth close over the tip of her finger. Instead of the lecture, he gave a strangled, "Oh?"

She looked up, her look of inquiry fading into a wary yearning. She withdrew her finger, lowered her hand to the countertop and gripped. "I, um, know I shouldn't have answered, but—"

"It doesn't matter."

She swallowed dryly. "That's—good."

Not good. Not good at all. He couldn't even pull up a name, could barely remember his own name with Dani sitting there naked except for his robe and sucking on her finger. It felt too much like a morning after—minus the satisfaction. His control wavered, letting in the memory of the way she had looked in his bed this morning. Let in how hard it had been not to crawl in next to her. How much he wanted to kiss and touch her until she was as aroused as he'd been. Until she wanted what he wanted.

Man and woman created He them. A good idea it was, too, just not right now. Just because what he was feeling walked and talked and felt like something good, didn't make it so. A duck wasn't always a duck. Bottom line? This couldn't be about what he wanted. It had to be about what was *right*. If he crossed that line, he lost more than his principles.

Someone could die. Dani could be that someone.

God created life and death, too. Then He made Hayes and let him loose to prey on the innocent in a far from perfect world. That was Matt's reality. Fantasy was for teenage boys and romance writers.

This particular romance writer reached her hand under her hair and massaged her neck, a wistful curve on her mouth that tried to trump his logic. How did she manage to look fragile and strong, sexy and—sweet—

If God was kind, Alice was driving up right now.

Matt's eyes, Dani decided, were the canvas where emotion played, altering the harsh lines of his face in fractions by narrowing or widening. The desire flared in his eyes. She saw him try to put the fire out before it leapt the space that separated them. Saw him fail. Felt the slow sweet beat of passion's wings start inside her skin, like a phoenix rising from the ashes of the past.

She didn't fight it. It had been a long time since she had felt anything that wasn't vicarious and fictional. It felt good to desire a man. To be desired as a woman. To participate, not just observe and record. To feel warm and soft. To know he was warm and most definitely not soft.

There was no danger to her body. She wasn't about to act on the attraction flickering between them like a faulty light switch. There was, unfortunately, plenty of danger to her heart.

She was tired, dangerously tired, in body and in spirit. Kelly was right. Since Meggie died, she had been barely rooted in life. Here with Matt, she could feel her soul starting to grip deeper, harder. It wanted to fly high enough to feel the sun beating strong and warm. The poor, mended organ was in serious danger of wanting to beat with passion. Even worse, it was wanting to love again.

She couldn't walk away, couldn't flee the danger of feeling because she needed Matt if she were to have any chance of finishing what Richard had started.

It would be funny if it were happening to someone else. She had bolted from custody six days ago, determined to go it alone. She hadn't gone it alone. Even, and this was the really funny part, even Spook had helped her. There was no such thing as alone. Way back in 1624, John Donne had recognized the imperative of human contact when he declared that "no man is an island, entire in itself."

Only with Matt could she be "part of the whole."

She watched the curtain come down in his eyes and couldn't blame him. Why should he want the burden of her spirit, her heart? He was already responsible for her life, not to mention the lives of himself and his team. If this were one of her books, he would have no problem with leaping tall buildings, outrunning numerous locomotives, saving all their lives, and healing her heart without breaking it.

It was too bad that Lewis Carroll's White Queen could believe six impossible things before breakfast, but between them they couldn't *do* one itty-bitty impossible thing.

She took a drink of soda, then wiped the moisture from her lips, fighting the need to look at him. The silence was made out of rubber, stretching tight, tighter—

She had to look—

—but the doorbell beat her to it, it's buzz releasing the tension with a snap that made them both jump. Matt rubbed the back of his neck. "Alice. That's Alice. I called her. Asked her to bring your clothes."

"My clothes?" Dani fingered the lapel of his robe, felt silk move against her skin and swallowed dryly. "Good idea."

His crooked grin was unexpected and toe-curling cute. "Seemed like a good idea at the time."

It was a relief to chuckle, she was glad he had a sense of humor, but it put another notch in her need for him and started another round of rubber tension.

"Dani—"

The bell rang with greater insistence.

Matt rubbed his face. "If I don't let her in, she'll kick the door down."

"Oh. Be hard to explain." She pivoted on her stool as he came out of the kitchen.

"Yeah. Hard to replace, too. It's," he swallowed, "real wood. Solid."

"Oh. Solid is—good." Her hands curled into fists under the cover of his robe.

"Yeah." He swallowed. "I'll just get that."

"I would. For the sake of—your door." He stepped past without touching her. She was glad. Touching would not be a good idea. Well, it would be good, too good, which was bad, very bad.

She meant to be strong and not look, but if there was anything better than a nicely filled out pair of jeans coming at you, it was watching them walking away. No question about it. He had great buns.

She sighed. Wasn't there a country song about being lonely for too long? She shook her head. Yeah, there were probably a million of them. All sad. All about her.

Chapter Nineteen

Alice looked rested when Matt opened the solid wood door for her. She'd gone casual with jeans and soft boots. Matt was glad she'd left the heels at home. Made his feet hurt just looking at her. Right now his feet were the only thing that didn't hurt. He noticed she held a couple of bags and a white pastry box. His brows arched.

"Breakfast?"

"It is the most important meal of the day." She looked past him, then asked softly, "When did she get here?"

"Last night." He nodded for her to proceed down the hall.

"Really?" Her brows arched as she stepped past him.

He resisted the compulsion to explain for two whole heartbeats. "She was hammered. Didn't think she could handle a full-court press. Fell asleep before the coffee was done."

He didn't finish with, "Satisfied?" but it was implied. Alice wasn't the only one who could look what she was thinking.

She grinned. "Sorry. I was just a little surprised. I thought this was a female-free zone for the brothers Kirby."

"It is, but even we have to occasionally allow free passage," he waited a beat, "since our mom is a woman."

Her grin turned cheeky. "Thank her for plowing the field for those of us who aren't related."

"I will." Matt stepped back so she could pass him, then followed her into the living room.

Dani was leaning against the window frame in an unconsciously provocative pose, looking down on the street with a pensive expression. It was as pleasing as all the other expressions he had seen on her face. The light behind her emphasized all the things his robe didn't hide. "Probably not a good idea to show yourself in a window."

She turned, fear overriding pensive before she could bury it again. If his mom had been here, she would have given him a look. Since she wasn't, Alice did it for her. She didn't need to. He had finally found an expression he didn't like on Dani's face.

"If my neighbors see you in my window," he said, "wearing my robe, at this time of day, it'll raise my stock hereabouts and Alice wouldn't like it."

Payback was immediate and almost more than he—or his detachment—could handle when she smiled, holding nothing back. It opened her face, her eyes, and just for a minute, her heart. That gratitude was the main component didn't lessen the impact.

"I wouldn't want to make Alice unhappy." Her gaze shifted to Matt's companion and turned curious. She had heard their low-voiced conversation, the apartment was small after all, and she couldn't help but wonder about the woman Matt had such an obviously comfortable relationship with. She held out her hand. "You must be Alice."

"And you're Dani." Briefly they shook hands, studying each other with veiled curiosity. Dani liked what she saw. It appeared that Alice did, too, when her smile expanded. "Nice to finally catch up with you."

Dani laughed. "I guess I should apologize for being such a pain in the ass."

"But you won't."

"No. I learned in divorce court to never apologize."

Alice grinned. "A nicer way of saying that men are always wrong. I'll have to remember that."

Matt remembered why he hated being in a room with two women. It was like finding yourself alone with aliens, trying to figure out what they were saying—knowing all the time that you never would.

"Alice is a fan," he said. To his annoyance, they both looked at him like he had said something lame, then exchanged looks. He really hated it when women did that. "Alice brought you some clothes," he said, handing Dani the sack he had taken from Alice.

"And I thought you might be in need of sustenance. Bachelor pads are notoriously devoid of the creature comforts." Alice held up the white box she had brought with her.

"I fed her," Matt protested. They ignored him.

"I hope that's what I think it is," Dani said, getting that look of anticipation that was so hard on his parts.

"If you think its pastries, your hope is not in vain."

"I guess you've been reading my file, too."

She didn't seem to mind that Alice had been poking in her life, Matt noticed.

"They probably aren't as good as you can get in New Orleans, but I think you'll find them quite palatable."

Dani peeked in the box Alice held out. "Oh yes. This is very good. I think we're going to be friends, Alice."

Matt looked at Dani. "You can't be hungry."

Dani and Alice exchanged another one of those looks, then Dani said lightly, "If I only ate when I was hungry, I'd never eat." She scooped out a treat. "I'll just take this with me while I go change."

He couldn't argue with her. He needed her to get out of his robe before he imploded. He had a strict, non-implosion policy around Alice. She would enjoy seeing him in coyote position a little too much. Besides, it was time to get down to business. He didn't like it any better this time around. "Why don't you help her, Alice. I'm gonna call Anderson."

She nodded, her gaze meeting his for a brief, pointed moment. She was a smart girl. She understood he wanted her take on Dani's state of mind.

He shouldn't have, but he watched Dani leave. Then he went and found a cold beer to down before he made his call.

Dani changed quickly, then ate her pastry. While her palate enjoyed flaky pastry and rich filling, her thoughts circled like a vulture waiting for that last gasping breath from a dying corpse. It was an interesting sensation. "You married, Alice?"

"I was." Alice sat down in the chair. "Divorce is a bitch, isn't it?"

"Yeah." Dani stretched her legs out, missing the soft silk of Matt's robe sliding across her skin, the heat of his eyes even more. She didn't know how cold she had been until now. "How long for you?"

"Two years."

"Eight for me." She and Steven had tried to keep the marriage going after Meggie died, but it was too hard with liquor playing third wheel. And Steven had needed the time to make sure they had no community property to divide. "You started dating yet?"

"A little. My job gets in the way." Alice was quiet. "You were young when you divorced?"

Dani shook her head. "I was young when I married, but old when we divorced."

It was good to remember this now, good to remember the flip side of love and desire. Good to remember how bad love felt when it was dying. Was it just a sign of the times, or a product of their short attention span society? she wondered. People used to stay in love longer. Course they used to live shorter.

"Your books are about love," Alice said. "I've only read one, but I really liked the way the characters found hope when they found each other." She looked rueful. "Almost made me want to give love another crack."

"Almost. Let's face it, the older we get, the slimmer the pickings." Her smile was as rueful as Alice's. "In the eight years I've been single, I've only really known maybe ten guys."

"Ten is good. That's almost a dozen," Alice pointed out.

"Really?" Dani started counting down. "Six of them I made up. Two turned out to be killers. One's a married biker—"

Dani stopped counting and looked wistfully at the lone finger still up.

Alice chuckled. "And number ten? Any hope there?"

Dani sighed. "Him?"

A lonesome, mountain climbing lawmen and a romance writer who was afraid of heights might work in fiction—if the fiction was paranormal so that a liberal dose of magic could be stirred in—but this was real life. She wrote fiction, she didn't live it. She looked at Alice.

"He's a man. The odds aren't good."

Where was Willow?

The game was different this time, and yet almost the same, Hayes thought, trying to hold back frustration that would only confuse his thinking. He was hunting, but not for blood. Not this time. Now was he searching for the other half of his heart.

He could feel her out there, but he couldn't pinpoint her—yet. Soon, very soon, he would have a fix. It was harder this time. He couldn't use his usual contacts. Whatever fear they had of him would evaporate in the scent of all the money on his head right now.

Maybe he shouldn't have put the contract out on Orsini. He was pretty far up the food chain. Rattled the cages of some pretty serious sharks. The big ones didn't like it when their biters bit them. *Hubris* wasn't just a problem the Greeks had.

He grinned. "It's a fine thing to rise above pride, but you must have pride in order to do so."

If he couldn't find Willow the usual way, he would find her the unusual way. He would feel his way to her on his hands and knees if need be.

The real test of a man is not how well he plays the role he has invented for himself, he recalled, but how well he plays the role that destiny assigned to him.

Their destiny was to live—or die—together. For them both, he would play the role assigned to him.

Matt's face was grim when Dani and Alice joined him in the living room. What tiny bit of warmth she had been able to hold onto promptly turned to ice when he told her why. She wrapped her arms around her middle, but it didn't help. Inside, with a snap so loud she was surprised Matt and Alice didn't hear it, Willow failed to bend. She didn't break—not yet. She cracked slightly, a prelude to breaking. With no shock this time to cushion her against the ugly realities of circumstances.

Meggie was dead.

Stephen was a drunk who wanted her dead.

Richard, who'd wanted her dead, was dead.

Spook was Dark Lord. He wanted her dead, too—

A ripple of disquiet wound in, she sensed she was missing something important . . .

Soon, Willow. Soon you'll understand.

What—no. It was just a dream, she told herself, but the feeling didn't recede. She looked at Matt. He looked strong and hard—and very far away.

"What's happened?" It surprised her how steady, how calm her voice sounded. She must be a better actress than she had realized.

He looked at Alice before he spoke. There was something familiar about the look that they exchanged. She couldn't figure out why.

"They found McBride."

"I—" Dani swallowed dryly, "—didn't know he was missing."

"He wasn't," Alice said reluctantly.

Now she placed the exchange of looks. They were the precursor to bad news, the silent asking of, "How do we tell her? Can she take it?"

Dani sank slowly onto the desk chair, her back straight, her feet together, hands not clenched in her lap—but only by supreme effort.

"How?" She didn't look at Matt.

He didn't hesitate. "Throat cut."

There was no softness in his voice. Dani was grateful. Right now she needed him to be as hard as the rock he climbed. A hint of softness and she'd shatter like glass.

"Why?"

This time Matt hesitated. "I don't know." He looked at Alice. "Someone hit Orsini, too. Word on the street is Hayes bankrolled it."

Alice frowned. "Wasn't Orsini bankrolling the hit on Bates and Davis?"

"That was the general consensus."

"Well then—this is getting too weird." Alice turned away from them and slid onto a stool, propping an elbow on the counter. "Who's left—besides Copeland who may or may not care now that he won't get paid?"

Matt opened his mouth, but it was Dani who spoke.

"Spook. And me." She hadn't known all the players in Richard's little drama, but it didn't seem to matter, since they had all been taken out. "Spook and *me*—"

Suddenly Dani didn't like where her thoughts were going.

"What?" Matt asked, his voice and gaze sharp as they honed in on her.

For the first time since she had found out who Spook really was, Dani opened her memory and took out her three meetings with him and asked herself, with no awareness that she spoke aloud, "Why didn't he kill me when he had the chance? Twice, he didn't do it. Why?"

She looked up at Matt, her hand on a throat that still showed the marks of one meeting. "He could have so easily. But he didn't. He just wanted to know . . . about . . ."

"About what, Dani?" Matt crouched in front of her. If she really had a line into Hayes's head—"What did he want to know?"

She licked her lips. A small kick of desire tried to get a foothold in his concentration, but he wouldn't let it.

"He wanted to know about Willow."

"But—" Matt stood up. This wasn't what he'd expected. "He had to know you were Willow."

"No," Dani shook her head, "he didn't. When I asked him how he knew I was Willow—he went—nuts. The first time he left. Then in the alley, he practically howled. That's when I got him with the pepper spray. And hit him."

Her pride was so apparent, Matt grinned, but it quickly faded as her words sank in. "But if he didn't know you were the Willow he was chatting with—"

"—why did he want to meet me at the mall?" Dani finished. "I don't think I want to know." She stood up and paced away, then turned toward Matt, her face, her eyes asking him to give her an answer she could live with.

Matt didn't have one. "This is nuts. This—can't be."

"Dani," Alice said, "when Hayes asked you out the first time after you met him, what did you think?"

She hesitated. "I thought he was a girl." She managed a brief, rueful smile. "He was a little too sensitive to be real, if you know what I mean?"

Alice smiled. "I know what you mean." She sobered, looked at Matt. "This could get interesting."

Matt opened his mouth to blast the whole idea, then closed it. How could he assert that Hayes couldn't fall for Dani without seeing her? He might not like it, but he couldn't deny that he felt something looking at her picture the first time. After he had chatted with her, felt the charm in her written words easily bridge the space that divided them, it had gotten worse. Hayes hadn't seen her in a silk bathrobe, but with his imagination, he probably didn't need to.

"Have you noticed," he asked slowly, "what Hayes *hasn't* been doing since he found out you were Willow?"

Dani started to shake her head, then stopped, her body slowly tensing as her thoughts spun through her wide green eyes.

"That's right," he said, grimly, "no e-mail. No threats." To Alice he added, "We've got to get her out of here."

Alice started to agree. Dani started to disagree.

Matt held up his hand and opened his mouth, but they

all froze when they heard someone at the door.

It was like watching a ballet, Dani thought, seeing them in action together. No need for words. Each knew exactly what their steps were, did them with a minimum of fuss. Guns were pulled and checked, "at ready" positions taken on either side of the hall opening. In the silence, the soft creak of the door as it swung open was perfectly audible, as was the measured beat of masculine footsteps coming down the hall.

Chapter Twenty

A cheerful whistle made a counterpoint for the footsteps and took the tenseness from Matt's shoulders. He lowered his gun. Alice, still on alert, looked a question.

"Luke," Matt said briefly, shoving his weapon back in the holster.

"The big brother," Dani said. "I forgot to tell you he called—"

Luke stopped in the doorway. He also filled the doorway, Dani noted. He seemed determined to take his "big brother" designation to its physical limits. Their relationship was obvious, he looked very much like Matt, though he topped him by about four inches and was less closed, more cheerful in aspect. Hands on his hips he looked at Alice, who still had her gun trained on him, gave her an appreciative once over and said, "All this because I threatened to kick your ass, little brother?"

It was obvious that Matt didn't like being called little brother. Dani exchanged a delighted glance with Alice, who was stowing her gun.

"I forgot to give him the message," Dani admitted, pulling his dark gaze, so like Matt's and yet so not like him, in her direction.

"You must be Louise." His eyes registered curiosity first, then approval. "Nice to meet you in the flesh."

Sheridan, the attorney prosecuting Richard's case, had said something far less controversial during a deposition and she had wanted to go and shower. Delivery, Dani decided as she grinned at him, was everything. "I can only concur."

Matt might have choked. It was hard to tell. When Dani looked at him, his face was still locked up tight.

Alice extended a hand. "Alice Kerne. I work with Matt."

Luke took her hand and gave it a pat. "Lucky Matt."

"He doesn't always think so," Alice admitted, a smile lighting her face.

"I got a situation breaking here, okay?" the subject of their conversation snapped.

Luke sighed. It was a huge sigh. He couldn't manage small sighs with his big barrel of a chest, Dani decided with delight. Somehow he managed to look mournful and abused. "Why do I have the nasty feeling I'm about to be stood up again?"

Hayes stared at the computer screen with a frown. His tap into the security system at the federal building was proving to be a less than rich mine of information. No sign of Willow at all. It didn't make sense. She had to be with them. He had done a city sweep of his contacts just before they cut him off. She was out of the cold and in care. He was sure of it.

Had they already moved her to a safe house? It was possible. If they had, they had moved fast, even for them. The marshals had protected Willow and for that he was reluctant to strike against them. In a strange way, they had become allies, though they didn't know it yet. Of course, if they kept her from him, he would take them out one by one.

They couldn't be allowed to interfere.

No one could interfere.

He was a patient man, but his patience was running thin—no, it was turning into pain—so much pain, he could hardly think his way through it. He couldn't sleep, couldn't eat—only thoughts of Willow, of being with her, kept him functioning. He had to find her before the pain consumed him. She had to complete the pattern with him. It was the only way to save them both. If he failed—

He couldn't, wouldn't think about failure. Not when he was so close to having her. He touched her picture. How beautiful she was and how perfect for him. Not the flashy type, who trumpeted their surface flash to the world. No, her beauty was quiet and deep, like the heart of his mountain. Her words floated up to disturb his reverie.

I don't do heights.

He frowned. She was afraid of heights, of mountains. It didn't fit the pattern—like a voice from the mountain itself, he heard the whisper, "I lift mine eyes unto the mountains, from whence cometh my strength."

Of course, that was the answer. Just like the mountain had relieved his pain, her fears would melt away in completing the pattern. Willow would be free of past hurts and fears, free to join her life to his. She would learn to love the beauty of the mountain heights, and with him she would honor and preserve the pattern forever. It had been ordained from the beginning. Like truth, it took time and distance to see it whole. In much the same way he had thought he needed Bates and people like him to guide him to the sacrifices. He hadn't understood. He had been too close, too new to the pattern to see the whole. Now he understood more. When he joined with Willow, they would both understand all.

Tennessee Williams thought time was "the longest distance between two places." He was wrong. Time was the shortest distance between him and Willow. If he failed to close it before his time ran out, he would lose her forever. If they reached the peak, completed the pattern within the allotted time, then nothing would separate them in life or death.

He had to find her, he would find her—if he had to drown the whole city in blood to do it.

Like always, when he needed it, the missing piece of the pattern came to him. Kirby. Kirby was the agent in charge of finding her. Find Kirby, find Willow? He tapped keys, then frowned at the screen showing the log of who had checked in and out of the building. Kirby wasn't in the office. Hadn't been in since yesterday. Odd. Very odd.

"I'm not leaving," Dani said. "I've been there, done that."

Her gaze held the swift parry of a sword when he tried to stare her down. He wanted to shake her. He circled her where she sat in his desk chair, her knees together, her hands carefully relaxed on her knees. Since he couldn't shake her, he said with intense patience, "Hayes is a wild card right now. We don't know what he wants, what he's going to do. The only sensible thing is to fall back and regroup—"

"I thought you wanted him?"

"I do," he shot back, "but—"

"But what? When will you ever get a better chance to get him? When will you ever again have what he wants?" Dani asked, turning her head to stay with him as he circled.

Matt looked at Alice, then turned away from them both, shoving both hands into his hair. "Talk to her, Alice."

"It's our job to protect you, Dani—"

"You just want to hide me away somewhere until he gets too tired to care. At least with the trial I had a deadline to hang onto, but this, this is a life sentence to limbo! I won't do it." Her hands curled slowly into fists. "You want me to live. I want my life back. If you aren't willing to try, then," she took a steadying breath, straightened her hands into pseudo-relaxed and finished with quiet intensity, "let me talk to someone who will."

She almost flinched when Matt spun to face her, emitting anger in scorching waves. This heat wasn't sweet or comforting, but she refused to back down. She would never survive if she did. Her body might, but her mind would die. Her spirit would die.

Willow wouldn't bend this time. She would snap in two.

His gaze bored into hers for what seemed like forever. She let him see her resolve. Her need she kept hidden. He didn't want her need, only her cooperation. He didn't know he couldn't have one without the other. She didn't know how to separate them. Need was a package deal of all or nothing.

When he sighed, the release of tension almost collapsed her like a balloon. She shook slightly, dug her nails into her knees to stop it. He gave no quarter and she refused to ask for any.

Then he almost broke her when he crouched down in front of her. "You don't understand what we're trying to do. If you could . . . look, we're just taking this in steps, trying to get past reacting to his actions. The first step is to secure your safety. Then we're going to try and draw him in—"

"He won't decoy again," Dani said, softly. "He'll know. He always has. The only reason it worked the last time was because I was there." Her nails dug deeper into her knees, the knuckles turning white. Luckily her jeans provided a measure of protection. Too bad her heart wasn't wrapped in denim. It hurt to have his face close enough for her wanting hands to trace, his dark eyes a deep pool she wanted to sink into more than she wanted to breathe air. What twist of fate had made her need a man who didn't want it?

"How can he know whether it's really you or not, Dani?" Her eyes were a code he couldn't break, her words harder to decipher than code. "How could he know?"

"I can't—explain—he just does." She stopped, licked her dry lips.

It was a blow to his pride when he wanted to respond to her need, instead of what needed to be done. He tightened down the lid, but it was getting harder to do.

"Just like I—" Dani stopped and looked away. Alice stepped into the circle of their tension, but if she felt it, it didn't show on her face.

"Just like you—what?" she asked, in carefully neutral tones.

Dani looked up, hesitated, then said, "Just like I know when he's hunting me." Her gaze returned to Matt. "Don't you see? That's why the nightmares. Why I called him Dark Lord. Because I could feel him hunting me, just like Dark Lord hunted Frodo. Only Frodo could feel his eyes searching. I don't feel his eyes. I—I feel his heart beating. It's getting closer." She swallowed painfully. "I hope I'm wrong. I—hope he does want to kill me."

Now he understood. Knowledge left a bitter taste in his mouth, added tons to the weight of responsibility he already carried. His dad had taught him and his brothers two rules for dealing with the opposite sex: Do not harm. Don't let anyone else harm.

That covered a lot of territory, set a high standard that he hadn't always lived up to. He was human. He had hurt Judith. He had hurt her badly, although he hadn't meant to. That didn't change the regret he felt at letting his dad and himself down. He found it easier to keep from stumbling again by not getting too close.

He was too close right now. He could see all the way to her heart. It was a brave one. Damn, she had guts. Her fear beat against his need to stay cool and calm. All the feelings he thought he'd shelved when Judith left surged up, edging into the act, trying to trip him up. With Hayes playing wild card somewhere, this was not a good time to even *want* to wrap his arms around her and tell her it was going to be all right, that he would take care of everything.

It was going to be all right. He would do everything he could to make it all right. Except wrap his arms around her and tell her so. It wasn't in the job description.

His cell phone rang, giving "saved by the bell" new meaning for him. He stood up, an honorable retreat was the better part of valor. Hayes wasn't the only one who could pull up quotes.

"Kirby," he said into the telephone.

"You gotta get out of there, Matt," Sebastian said, urgently. "Someone's been tapping into building security, looking at your log in/log out record."

He bit back a swear word. "Anderson know?"

"Yeah, he says go. He's getting bad vibes, doesn't even want to risk the airport without a plan. If you can handle it, he'll wait for you to contact him. Only him. Wants this strictly need to know."

"Right." He had to think—not just react. That's what Hayes wanted. Out of the corner of his eye, he saw Luke, who had gone to shower away his night shift in Homicide, rejoin them.

"Matt?" Sebastian recalled his attention. "Be careful."

"I will. Thanks for calling. Tell him I'll be in touch." He shut off the telephone, thought for a minute, then looked at Luke. "We gotta move."

Without missing a beat he asked, "The cabin?"

"For tonight, then we—" he hesitated, then looked at Dani, "—you decide what you want to do."

She sighed like one shedding a burden, gratitude softening her eyes. "Thank you."

Matt was giving her control, nothing else. "Thank me when it's over. Then we'll know if I deserve it. Now let's get the hell out of here. You coming, Luke?" Luke nodded. Matt turned to Alice. He didn't like leaving her to pick up, but he didn't have a choice. It was her job. "Make sure she didn't leave anything behind, then go. This won't be a good place to be if Hayes is heading this way. I'll be in touch."

She nodded soberly. "Good luck."

Luke checked, then strapped on his gun. "Out the back?" Matt nodded. "I'll take point."

Chapter Twenty-one

Dani sat quietly between the two men as the sprawl of city fell away behind them. Ahead the road climbed steeply toward jagged, distant peaks lightly touched with snow despite the firm hold summer had on the plains below.

Was it just her imagination or did she already feel cold? How could she tell? She didn't like up, but here she was heading that way. Strategists always made such a big deal about the high ground. She couldn't see why. In the movies heroes and victims were always heading up, when it was obvious it would just get them cornered. Granted this rugged countryside was very different from the tops of buildings, but the principles were the same: always leave yourself room to maneuver and stay away from long drops.

The real kicker was she had brought it on herself. In a heartbeat Matt would have sent her right out of this very high state, maybe even to a low-lying one. Oh no, she had to have an attack of insanity and insist on staying to face the bogey man. And for what did she insist on this? For her life. The life, if Kelly was right, that she wasn't even sure she wanted to have.

She had heard that sleep deprivation had weird side effects. Obviously she had heard correctly. Now was the time to stop the madness, to tell him she had changed her mind and would prefer to run away and hide somewhere—now, before her ears popped again.

She peeked at Matt, sitting next to her like something hewn out of granite, except for the slight frown pulling

261

down his dark eyebrows. Granite was supposed to be good
rock, very hard. He could be its poster guy. She had only
been in his company just over half a day and already she
could tell how annoyed he was by how far his eyebrows
dipped.

When granite moved, she wasn't ready. He arched one
brow in a silent query and gave her one more reason not to
give up. There was just so much she didn't know about—
rock. It wouldn't hurt to enlarge her knowledge a bit. If she
ever did get home, she could be sure of one thing: the soggy
swampland of New Orleans was seriously deficient in hard
stuff.

"You don't by any chance play poker, do you?" Luke
took his eyes from the road long enough to grin at her.

"A little." One of her characters had been a compulsive
gambler.

"Strip poker?" he asked hopefully.

Beside her Matt stirred uneasily. "Luke—"

"Hmmmm. It sounds diverting, but I think I'd have to
watch it first, *see* how it's done." She smiled demurely at
Luke. Matt chuckled. It was a nice sound, just enough
rumble, hardly any gravel and lightly sun-warmed.

He was a nice man, a good man trying to do good things
in a world that often wasn't good—or sympathetic to the
good. She was, she realized, more worried about him than
herself. He was so determined to make things right, so idealistic in a tough, no-nonsense way. Sometimes determination wasn't enough to stop the evil that men do. She ought
to know.

*Take therefore no thought for the morrow: for the morrow
shall take thought for the things of itself.*

It was from the book of Matthew. She didn't usually like
symbolism, but this time it did seem like a good omen.

They stopped in Boulder so Dani could beef up her personal items for what could be a long haul. Matt looked at her curiously when she spotted a purse display and stopped to buy one. The gesture was more defiant than useful, since she didn't have much to put it in. It made Dani feel more connected to life. The only other stop was for gasoline. Luke stayed in the car with Dani while Matt paid with cash so Hayes couldn't track their credit card use. While they waited, Luke beat a tattoo on the steering wheel in time with the country song playing softly on the radio. He turned suddenly and asked, "Why do I have a feeling you've got eyes for my little brother?"

"Why would you think I have eyes for your little brother?" It surprised her she wasn't uncomfortable with him or his question. There was something steady and solid about him—like a teddy bear, a great big teddy bear, who just happened to pack a gun.

"Maybe it's the way you watch him?"

Dani looked at him innocently. "How could I not watch him? He has great buns. For that matter, so do you."

That surprised a laugh out of him and a slight blush. His eyes stayed worried. "Matt's marriage—"

"—broke up because he's job obsessed. And no, I don't have illusions that I can fix him. I'm a romance writer, not a masochist."

Luke laughed again. "I'm glad to hear it. I like you. I'd hate to see you get hurt. Not that he'd mean to. Matt, well, he's just not into personal. Screws his concentration. Can't have it screwed when lives depend on you. He'll do his best for you, we both will, but he'll do it from a nice, safe distance."

Dani nodded thoughtfully. He was only confirming what she already knew. Now if she could just convince her body to quit overloading on hormones when Matt was around. The problem, she found, was that thinking about *not* thinking about him had the same effect on her as thinking about him, as evidenced by the heat creeping up the inside of her skin. She decided a change of subject was in order. A blush right now would send the wrong message. "What about you? How long have you been keeping women at a distance?"

Luke acknowledged her bull's-eye with a smile that was tinged with sad. "Since my wife died a few years ago."

"I'm sorry." She covered his hand gripping the steering wheel. She had learned from her own loss that talking about the person helped, even if it hurt. "How?"

"Ovarian cancer. Seems like one minute we were talking about starting a family, the next I'm looking at a headstone with Rosemary's name on it."

"Rosemary for remembrance. She must have been a lovely person."

"Yeah." He reversed the grip of their hands. "How did you know?"

"You flirt the same way I do," Dani admitted, "with the surgical gloves on."

"Either you have damn good instincts or—you've been there, too."

"Been there, done that, and bought the tee shirt, I'm afraid." Dani gave him a wry smile. "At least I've been able to turn angst into a marketable skill."

He got her hand again, raised it to his mouth. "You're one tough lady, Louise."

The passenger door opened.

"Am I interrupting?" Matt's face was as inscrutable as ever but his tone had a sour edge.

Luke kissed Dani's hand before releasing it, then grinned

at his brother in a highly provocative way. "I don't think so, little brother, but if you do start to get in the way, I'll be sure to let you know."

Dani bit her lip and stared straight ahead as Matt clambered into the cab beside her. "Uh," she cleared her throat and asked, "is it much further?"

"Not much. Little bit more than an hour." Luke reached for the gear shift between her legs, bringing his face close to hers in the process. He grinned, then winked. "If you're tired, feel free to use my shoulder."

Next to her Matt jerked, emitting a sound suspiciously like a snort. The lonesome lawman wasn't as cool as he looked. It wouldn't change the future, but it was nice to know.

"Thanks, I will," she said, settling back in the seat between the rock and his soft-hearted big brother. Despite the guy/girl complications it wasn't a bad place to be.

If she had been alone, she would have started humming. As it was, she just let the words flow through her head.

> *Through many dangers, toils and snares*
> *I have already come.*
> *Tis grace hath brought me safe thus far.*
> *And grace will lead me home.*

Grace and a couple of lonesome lawmen in tight jeans. Almost sounded like one of those sad country songs.

Hayes slid silently into Kirby's apartment, then stopped, his senses stretched out for signs of life other than his own. The man watching outside hadn't posed much of a problem, though it disturbed him that Kirby had obviously been expecting him. He was proving to be an unexpectedly adept adversary. If the game had concerned anyone but Willow, he might have enjoyed this contest of wits.

His gaze shifted from side to side, his nostrils twitching as he tested the air for signs of Willow, while his eyes took in data for his brain to process about the man who had her.

Everything was orderly, neat, completely male. No sign of feminine occupation in either bedroom. He lived, Hayes knew, with his older brother, a widower whose wife had died. Amazing the information made so easily available on the Internet these days. Used to be much harder to dig it out.

Hayes completed his first pass through the apartment and frowned. Was he wrong? It wasn't Kirby's job to guard his Willow, but Anderson didn't have her. Or anyone on his team. They were all at the office trying to set up an out-of-state transfer for her. He couldn't let them do that. Someone had to know where she was. The only someone that made sense was Kirby, who hadn't come into the office since the explosion yesterday.

It wasn't like him. He had been there almost round-the-clock since the initial strike on the safe house. A look at his log in/log out patterns for the last year showed a similar dedication to the job. This wasn't a guy who missed work in the middle of the week. He wasn't home either. He could be on another case since Willow had shown up. Somehow he doubted it. He wasn't the kind of the guy to back off until the fat lady had sung her heart out.

Hayes stood in the living room and turned slowly, his eyes looking for anything, any place he hadn't looked. He almost passed it by again.

The refrigerator. If Willow had been here—

Bingo. Diet Dr. Pepper. Her odd addiction was useful— for now.

Okay. She had been here. Where had he taken her?

He started searching again, but this time he wasn't looking for Willow. He was looking for clues to the man with her.

In Kirby's bedroom, Hayes went methodically through his closet, and learned that Kirby and he had similar tastes without discovering where he might have taken Willow. He sat down on the bed, fighting past a rising tide of pain, frustration and the clock in his head telling him he was running out of time.

This was a dead end. That was clear, though not a complete wash. He had learned much about his enemy. He gathered himself together. It was getting harder and harder to keep going. He put his hands on either side, he needed to push up against the exhaustion dogging him, and felt something hard under the blanket. The tingle along his nerve endings told him it was important. This was the clue he had been looking for.

When he pulled out the album and it fell open to a picture of Kirby standing in front of a mountain cabin, he knew why. He even knew, within a few miles, where the cabin was. How could he not know, when it was *his* mountain rising in the background?

Kirby had taken Willow right where Hayes needed her to be.

He was so grateful, he might not kill him.

Unless he got in the way.

Chapter Twenty-two

"Here we are." Luke shut the motor off and looked at Matt, then down at Dani who was slumbering quite comfortably against Matt's side. "I'll go open up while you wake Louise."

Matt nodded. Each breath she took was like Chinese water torture against his resolve. He was only human, all too only human, he thought grimly. Lucky for him falling asleep was such a good deterrent. Unlucky for him he had to wake her up.

He lightly touched her shoulder. "We're here."

Her struggle up through layers of exhaustion was painful to watch. She was too tired. How could she do this? How could she face down Hayes like this?

The lashes making half moons against her white cheeks fluttered, then slowly lifted. Her eyes were so green and foggy, so bedroom, that they reached deep into his gut and pressed all the wrong buttons. He swallowed dryly. "We're here."

Above Long's Peak, the gold sun was making signs it might set. They would have gotten up here sooner, if not for the stop in Boulder to allow her to replace some necessary items. He had almost lost patience with her when she lingered over buying and stocking a purse, been ready to object, when something in the way she'd run her hand across the leather surface made him hesitate. For some reason, it seemed important to her. Weird, but if it helped her through the next few days, damned if he was going to complain. Back in the truck, she had removed the paper stuffing and stowed what she bought, tucked it against her side, and then disarmed him by falling asleep on his shoulder. Matt had endured this enjoyable torture because he hoped she would rest, but her sleep remained as restless as the night before.

"Here?"

"The cabin."

"Oh." She turned her head, her body still nestled excruciatingly against his side, and examined her surroundings.

Sometimes the mountain wasn't too welcoming, sometimes it was downright hostile. Right now, at the approach of evening, Mother Nature was playing it cool. Matt liked her best when she was cool. He knew Dani wasn't wild about heights, so he was glad she was seeing the mountain when the gold from the sun was making the color of sky, rock and trees as rich and crisp as the air going into their lungs. There was a majesty in the rugged sweep of rock that kind of lengthened the view, helped put things in perspective when life got too real, too close. It cut big things down to a more manageable size. Up here, even Hayes didn't seem that important.

While Luke paused at the foot of log-hewn steps to stretch his tired muscles, Matt let Dani quietly soak in his mountain.

She sighed. "It's very—high, isn't it?"

He looked down at her. "High? You—a writer—look out over one of the most spectacular views in the area and all you can find to say is that it's high?"

She regarded him warily for a long moment, then looked at Luke, bending to unlock the door. "Some of its inspiring."

Women. Who could understand them? Who would want to? He noticed Luke was having trouble with the lock and she was still looking. "Luke's not over his wife's death yet."

"Really?" She sat up and looked at him, something in her eyes made him shift uneasily. "Luke warned me against you, too."

"The hell he did! What'd he say?"

"That you'd do your best for me from a nice, safe distance."

"Oh." He stared at her, felt something inside him shift, something important that shouldn't be shifting. "He's right. I will."

"I already knew that."

"You did, did you?" She was doing that woman thing again, poking around in his head, figuring things out, and then looking wise about it.

"It's all right. I'm not looking to mess with this lonesome lawman life you've got going here." She gestured out the window. "I know I don't fit in here. Besides, I've already driven one guy to drink. And yes," her smile was slight, but dangerously tender, "it is very beautiful, but way too high for my blood. I'm sea level. You're sky level."

It should have made him feel better. If you took out the female variations, it could be the standard guy, "I'm not looking for a committed relationship" speech. He realized she wasn't looking at him anymore. She was staring straight ahead, her hands restless in her lap.

"For some reason my hormones would like our twain to meet somewhere between my sea and your sky. You've obviously picked up on my hormones and it's put you in a difficult position. You've been assigned to—look out for me—not provide copy for my next book."

How to feel like a bastard in one easy lesson. "Dani—"

"Please let me finish." Her hands curled into fists. "I just want you to know that I feel the same way you do about this—attraction. I may get the occasional urge to jump your bones, but I'm an adult and not so quick to—jump—as I used to be. Your bones are quite safe. All I want, need—" She stopped. "Get me home, please?"

"Okay." Why was it, that when a woman gave you the space you asked for, it immediately became the one thing you didn't want? Would she ever do or say something he could see coming? In the silence, he felt his conscience telling him she deserved better than a terse, okay. "Dani?"

"Yes?" She stopped sliding off the seat, but she didn't look at him.

"It wasn't you." He rubbed the back of his head and shifted on his seat. "It was me. I'm having trouble with me. My hormones."

"Thank you." There was a short silence, then she looked at him out of the corner of her eye, a tiny smile tugging at the edges of her mouth. "They say confession is the first step in overcoming temptation."

"What's the next step?"

She gave a tiny shrug. "Joseph fled Potipher's wife, but we can't do that."

"No, we can't." There was nowhere to run, nowhere to hide.

"You guys going to sit there all night?" Luke called from the open door.

He would like to, Matt realized. He would like to sit here with her and watch the moon come up. As a teenager when his hormones first started kicking in, he'd lie in bed at night dreaming about the front seat of a truck on a moonlight night and about unwrapping the mystery of a pretty girl. There'd be plenty of moonlight tonight, but he wouldn't be spending it in the front seat of a pickup truck unwrapping Dani.

"We're coming." He pushed open his door and went around to help Dani with her bags.

Some things didn't change near as much as you'd like them to. The dreams hadn't. Neither had the timing.

It was still off.

Timing was everything, Hayes decided, staring at the photo of the cabin he had taken from Kirby's apartment. The chair he sat in rocked slightly, keeping time with his thoughts and fidgeting feet. As soon as he grabbed her, the pursuit would begin. They would need time, more time than typical because Willow was a sea level greenhorn in the mountains. The hike would break her, then remake her. That took time.

How strong was she?

I bend, not break.

She would make it. She had to. She always did what she had to.

They would need supplies. And there was the problem of Copeland. He was hunting hard. Couldn't let him mess up things with Willow. Like a heartbeat, the pain in his head picked up the pace. He pressed a palm to its center, then pulled a sheet of paper toward him and started making a list of what he needed to do and how. Copeland was at the top.

"I've never seen moonlight like this." Dani stared dreamily into the night, safely in the bastion of Matt and Luke's cabin. This dark didn't bother her. It hid the steep terrain, let her pretend it was just a place, not a state of being.

"Where's the moonlight you usually see?" Luke bent to pick up a poker next to the huge fireplace.

"New Orleans."

"The Big Easy. Night is different without city lights screwing it up." Luke poked at the fire, then set the poker to one side and picked up his beer. "Anybody waiting back there for you?"

She turned around and leaned against the window frame, the night at her back now. "A few friends, my next book, a new breed of mosquito—"

He laughed. "I can see where you'd miss that."

"Hey, at least it's not ten thousand feet in the air."

"Worse and worse, in my book." He hesitated, then shot her an uncomfortably penetrating glance. "Would you like me to yawn and pretend I need to go to bed early?"

Dani grinned. "This isn't about that."

He arched his brows, for a moment looking eerily like Matt. "With guys, it's *always* about that. I'm surprised a romance writer doesn't know this."

She crossed her arms. "What the romance writer knows is that women don't want to read about men the way they really are. They want to read about them the way they wish they would be. It's less depressing and sells more books."

Luke grimaced. "Ouch. Guess I walked into that one." His gaze shifted behind her. "You arrived just in time. I'm taking a beating here, bro."

"I've never known you to mind a good beating." Matt sounded amused. He stopped next to Dani, not touching, but close enough for her to feel the heat from his body arc the distance with more potent force than the fire blazing up from the prod of Luke's poker.

Their little non-involvement chat should have cleared the air and put her hormones back in mothballs. It hadn't. The problem was compounded by Matt's admission he was feeling the heat, too. It wasn't the words, but the way he said them. The husky rasp had scraped across her nerve endings like sweet sandpaper, telling her what his words didn't, that he wanted her as much as she wanted him. Definitely one of those times when a little knowledge was a dangerous thing.

Dani looked at him. The worry in his eyes belied his light tone. "What's wrong?"

Matt hesitated, looking at Luke instead of her. "Hayes has been in my apartment."

Luke frowned. "They're sure?"

"Oh yeah." His gaze flicked to Dani. "He killed the cop watching the place."

Earlier she'd been grateful for his toughness in his refusal to temper the wind for her. It meant he respected her personal strength, that he scorned subterfuge.

Now it sucked big time dead toads, completely ruling out the option of going fetal, whining or fainting in his arms. Just as well, since he had his hands shoved in his pockets.

"Does he know where we are?" she asked.

Matt frowned. "I don't see how he could. There was nothing in my place to show you've been there, no one but Luke and I know we're here at the cabin. We should be fine for tonight at least. By morning Anderson should have a plan and a place for it to happen in."

"I see," she said. He was giving her what she had asked for. A chance to end it. Who was it that said be careful what you ask for because you might get it? She used to ask Spook the quote questions. There was that irony again. Good old Spook, the other account in her life she couldn't make balance properly. It was her math. Never could make things add up right, though even she could add one plus one. How many girls could claim *two* killers among her acquaintance?

When Luke again proposed cards, minus the stripping,

Dani accepted with relief, glad to have a distraction for her thoughts. She'd never actually played poker, but found her research on the subject stood her in good stead, not to mention her amateur acting experience. Several hands later she frowned down at her cards, sighed, then said doubtfully, "I guess I'll call."

"Lay them down," Luke said. She did. He looked at their faces fanned across the rough wooden surface, then at his hand. He tossed his in. "I can't tell if she's just damn lucky or playing us for suckers."

"Probably a little of both," Matt said, remembering the world tour she had taken him and Sebastian on. He had finally learned not to underestimate the romance writer. He tossed his hand in. "I'm out, too."

He rubbed his face, happened to see his watch. Damn, two a.m.? He looked up in time to catch Dani trying to hide a yawn behind her hands. Her eyes weren't smudged with exhaustion, they were black with it. How did she manage to look like hell and heaven at the same time?

Dani swept her ill-gotten chips out of the middle, then began adding them to the neat stacks in front of her. Neat and poker didn't go together. Trust a woman not to know that. She looked up and caught him watching her. She looked at his chips, then Luke's, scattered in front of them. He could almost see her struggle, then she slowly toppled her stacks and stirred them together. He had to smile.

Her answering smile was rueful. "My deal?"

"No." Matt pushed his chair back. "It's time for you to hit the rack."

She frowned. "You're going to torture me?"

Luke laughed. "This is that 'women are from Venus' and 'men are from Mars' problem, isn't it?"

Matt gave him a look, then said to Dani, "Go to bed."

Dani looked at Luke. "He must be from Mars if he thinks he can tell me what to do."

"I can see why Ralph wanted to kick Alice to the moon," Matt said, then added grimly, "Did you or did you not ask me to get you home? And did I just assume you meant alive?"

"The only thing worse than a guy who says I told you so, is one who claims you asked him to do it." She picked up the deck of cards and expertly shuffled it. She may not play poker, but she was seriously addicted to solitaire. "Have you ever wondered if this whole male/female interaction was actually a punishment for something we did before we came here?"

"Absolutely," Luke said. "Especially the part where we have to live in the same house, not just on the same planet. How can a man live with someone obsessed with picking up—"

"—guys' dirty socks," Dani shuddered, "the toilet seat, the empty cartons back in the fridge and that cooking— don't get me started on that. I mean, I know I write romances, but fiction aside, wouldn't it be so much easier if we each had our own place and could just get together now and then for sex and maybe a movie?"

Matt choked. He couldn't help it. Luke grinned. She ignored them both and finished, "I'll bet the divorce rate would plummet." She yawned delicately. "I'm feeling a little tired, Luke. Would you mind if I called it a night?"

It was Luke's turn to choke, though his sounded suspiciously like a chuckle. "No problem. Just pick a direction upstairs. Beds on both sides are made up. I'll try not to wander in and join you." Luke gathered the cards she had abandoned and absently began shuffling them. "So will Matt."

"Thanks." With only the briefest hesitation, she pushed her chair back. "I'll just wash before I go up."

Matt watched until the bathroom door closed her in, then shook his head. "Women."

"Yeah," Luke said too enthusiastically. "Why don't you try to get some sleep, too?" He started collecting the scattered chips. "I'll take the first watch. This has been so entertaining, I find I'm not that tired."

"Glad you're enjoying yourself. Really." What really pissed him off was that he felt like a kid who wanted to tell mom that Luke was being mean. He hated it when Luke did that, hated that he still could. "For that I'll let you."

He pushed back his chair, stopped when he heard water running in the bathroom behind him, the creak of wood as Dani moved around. Funny how peculiarly, instantly recognizable as female the sounds were.

Water sounds changed as she turned on the shower. It was all too easy to imagine her shedding her clothes, piece by piece, the room slowly filling with steam, the rattle of the shower curtain, a slight change as the water hit her instead of the tub. She would turn in it, wetting her body, then reach for the soap, rubbing up a lather between her narrow hands—

He took a shaky breath. This was not a productive line of thought. He didn't miss a woman in his life. He couldn't. Okay, showers and sex were the up side of having them around, but also the bait they used in the trap. Balance it against the constant hassle of trying to make an unreasonable woman see reason and it wasn't worth it. It wasn't. Take tonight, a classic case in point. She's tired. He notices and suggests she go to bed. Doghouse time. Why? He didn't know why. How could he know anything when what he wanted was to go in there and take over the soap—

The water shut off. The curtain rattled again. His thoughts turned to a towel moving across her wet body—

"I like your Louise," Luke said, breaking into his thoughts.

"Her name's not Louise and she's not mine," Matt muttered.

Luke dealt himself a hand of solitaire, then looked at Matt. "You're going to let her get away, aren't you?"

The door to the bathroom opened and Dani came out. She wasn't wearing his robe. She had purchased this one in Boulder. It was ankle length and made out of soft blue flannel. She'd cinched it in at the waist with a matching belt. She looked fluffy and soft, like a stuffed animal a kid curled up with. Matt didn't feel like a kid, though he definitely had the urge to wrap himself around her.

They both stood up at her approach. She appeared to find this amusing. She stopped, her scent wafting his way.

"Still with the coconut, I see," he said.

"Not for long, I'm afraid. It's been discontinued."

"Oh." The robe lay open at her neck. Her skin looked dewy and soft. Her face was scrubbed clean and pink from the shower. She looked her age, but she had aged really well. He tried to swallow, but his throat was too dry.

"Well, goodnight." She continued on her way, leaving behind a trail of coconut. He watched her mount the stairs, remembering the last time her hips had done that side to side sway. If anything, the flannel was better than the leather. He was so hot he could have heated winter run-off. When she was out of sight, he grabbed his beer and downed half of it.

Luke looked at Matt with awe in his eyes. "Since you're not buying, mind if I take a pass?"

Even if he hadn't been so damn tired, Matt wouldn't have risen to a fly that obvious. "Better wait until after your watch. Wouldn't want Hayes to catch you with your bare butt in the air, now would you?"

"Probably not." Luke leaned back in his chair and grinned. "What time you want me to wake you?"

Matt looked at his watch. "Two hours?"

"You look like hell. I'll wake you in three." He pushed back the chair and headed for the kitchen.

"Luke?"

"What?" He stopped and looked back.

"Thanks."

"Get your ass in bed before I do kick it up over your head."

Matt nodded, left him reaching for a cup and the pot of coffee. Brothers. Can't live with them, wouldn't want to manage without them.

Hayes wasn't standing behind the door when Copeland came after him. He knew the late Bates's second best hitter would expect him to be there. Hayes never did what was expected of him. He stood just past the expected place, a part of the wall, a part of the dark, with the needle between his fingers. He was wearing night goggles so he could see the door slide open. He usually hunted by scent. The smell of fear and blood helped him home in on his prey better than a smart bomb, but tonight he would take no chances. Copeland was good. Not as good as him, but good enough to treat cautiously.

Hayes wanted to take him alive.

He needed him alive. This was not the time and place to kill him. This time and place didn't fit the pattern. This time and place wouldn't relieve his pain.

He needed relief from the pain. He needed Willow more than that. When all the pieces were in place, it would fit together perfectly and he would get everything he wanted. Everything.

Upstairs Dani looked at the bed, but she couldn't bring herself to climb in and close her eyes. What good was sleep without rest? Why seek out her demons? Let them find her.

She opened the window, then sank onto the covered rustic bench beneath it and leaned on the casement. Crisp cool air flowed in, carrying unfamiliar night scents to tickle the inside of her nose. In the sky, the round silver moon hung low over the dark tree line between two snow-covered peaks. An owl hooted plaintively. For some reason it reminded her of Matt.

Probably because it sounded alone and happy to be that way.

Her problem, she decided, aside from lusting after him, was that she liked him, which meant she respected his need for some distance, even while deploring it. A pity sex had to rear its far too enticing head to complicate the mix, though if Luke were right, pity had nothing to do with it. What was it Kelly told her that time she dumped her drink down the lawyer's pants? Women need a reason, men just need a place?

Wanting wasn't a good enough reason when put next to all the many reasons she had for *not* giving in to her clamoring hormones, starting with Stephen and ending with Spook. What was it she and Liz used to say in college? Men were at least three credit hours. She may not be taking classes anymore, but there still wasn't room for a man in her schedule or her life. At least not a real one. There was always room for the fictional variety.

I take my chances. The words of the song that had followed her all week came back now. Her mouth twisted wryly. Easier to take a chance on something when there *was* a chance.

She heard footsteps on the stairs and turned in time to see Matt stop in front of her partially opened door. He pushed the door wider. "Dani?"

"Over here. By the window."

When he saw her sitting by the window, dangerously awake instead of safely asleep, frustration spiked again. "What the hell are you doing?"

"Admiring the sylvan splendor now that I can't see how far up I am."

How did she do it? How did she make him want to strangle her, laugh with her, and kiss her quiet, all at the same time? "You should be sleeping. You need the rest."

"Sleep and rest aren't always synonymous." Her bare feet were starting to chill and she pulled them up under the robe, leaning her back on the casement. "Let's just say that, like Shakespeare, my dreams give me pause."

Matt rubbed the back of his neck. He knew she was having trouble sleeping, had read it, had seen it with his own eyes. Part of it had to do with what she had told him this afternoon, about her feeling Hayes hunting her. He didn't understand it, wasn't sure he believed it. She was a writer. An imagination was her stock in trade. Didn't matter. People made their own reality. All that mattered was what she believed.

He sat down by her.

"You don't have to," she said, dreamily.

"Have to what?"

"Do this." She looked at him, her eyes gentle and sad. "You're tired. It'll be a busy day tomorrow."

He felt an icy chill take a run down his back. It was hard to match her calm, but he tried. "Like at the safe house?"

Her lashes covered her eyes. "No. Not like that. It's just that—" She stopped, her shoulders rising and falling in a sigh.

He had seen the Mars/Venus guy's commercials, too. Heard enough to know she didn't need him to tell her what to think and feel. She needed him to listen. Not exactly his strong suite, but he did have the ears to try.

"Tell me what happened that night."

She went tense. "The lonesome lawman does lonesome shrink?"

He smiled slightly. "If you want. Or you can think of it as two friends, one talking, one listening."

"Alice has trained you well." Her voice was too soft and husky for the attempt at humor.

Thanks to Alice, Matt knew when to keep quiet.

Her hands curled into fists, but her shoulders slumped slightly in surrender. "I don't—want to talk about it."

"If you can't face him in your head, you sure as hell can't face him for real." He waited, then prompted her, "You were awake when he came—"

She looked away, her hands twisting in her lap. "Yes." She swallowed, the movement briefly changing the way the shadows lay on her neck. The place where Hayes had cut her was a dark line just under the line of her jaw. "We were both awake."

"Doing what?"

"Just talking. Chatting, really. She—wasn't feeling well. She got—sick after we ate." She drew her legs up to her chest, held them there with her arms, and rested her chin on her knees.

This wasn't listening. This was a trip to hell. "Neuman took her to the hospital. But she came back. Why?"

She started rocking slightly. "She knew I didn't like—waking alone."

"Because she knew about your nightmares?" She was wound so tight he could have played a tune on her. The cracks in her control were starting to show.

"Yeah. She came back for me. And she died. If she'd stayed in the hospital—"

"If she'd stayed you'd be dead—"

"Yes."

One word, but it carried some heavy freight and a lot of mixed signals. Matt frowned. "Are you saying you wish you were dead?"

"You don't understand." She tried to get smaller, to keep the hurt and guilt localized, but it spread like a toxic spill through her veins. "I—she was sick. He was strong. I couldn't—I just—watched."

It was out. There was some relief in putting her shame and guilt on the table. She felt lighter. It hurt not to cry, but she wouldn't use tears to sue for Matt's mercy. He would give it. She knew that about him. Just like she knew he would never run or cower from a fight. He would never stand by and watch a friend die without trying to help. He would give his life for his friends in a heartbeat. His strict code of honor, his unflinching courage weren't situational. They were him. He did what he had to.

Words came faster now that the guilt/shame dam was gone, pushing past her lips in harsh gasps. "I just watched. That woman. Meggie. I had a feeling I shouldn't let her go with Stephen. But she wanted to so badly. And I didn't want to be over-protective. Strange how we're so afraid of that. I let her go. I didn't take care of her."

Hell turned into a minefield for Matt. She sat there, her back straight and her quivering chin lifted, waiting to be punished for something she hadn't done, needing absolution for something she couldn't have helped. No wonder she couldn't rest. He wanted to touch her, to tell her it was all right, but Willow wasn't breaking. She was detonating.

Hell and damnation. He wasn't a priest or the bomb squad. This was totally out of his league.

He wanted to back off, but here, in the room his mom had made into a temporary home for him and his brothers, he couldn't retreat. His mom would never forgive him. Damn, he wished she were here right now. She would know what to say.

"Dani." She didn't look at him. His hand shook slightly when he touched her chin, gently nudging her face his way. "You didn't kill anyone. Hayes killed Margaret Oliver. Your daughter, well, that was an accident. Accidents happen. You know that."

Dani shook her head slowly. "It was my job to take care of her. I should have reminded him to buckle her. He always forgot to buckle her—"

Her face crumpled slightly, but she fought it.

"It should have been me. It should—have been me."

"No, look at me, Dani. You're wrong. If you'd died your baby would have been raised by the brother of a killer. The way things are, well, they're the way they're supposed to be. I don't know how I know. I just do. My dad always told me you play the hand you're dealt the best you can."

The first tears breached the dam she had tried to erect, rolled hot and wet down her cheeks.

"As for Oliver, hell, she died doing what she was supposed to do. She kept faith with herself, with you, and with the Service. I can guarantee she's resting easier than that poor bastard McBride."

She wanted to believe him, but she didn't know how to get from where she was to where he was. There was no bridge, just a chasm gaping wide as hell itself that she was being pushed toward. "You would never do what I did."

"Because it's my job. Just like it was Oliver's job to keep you alive. She did it." He grabbed her shoulders and made her look at him. "With your help. Staying alive was your job. And you did it. If you hadn't, her death would have been for nothing. Because you lived, her death means something."

Dani stared at him, felt something shift inside. It hurt, but it was a good hurt, kind of like pushing out a baby, a really large guilt baby. She tried to make her mouth smile. It wobbled wildly. "My job sucks."

He looked so relieved she wanted to laugh, but when her mouth opened sobs, not laughs, were waiting in the queue. The attempted laugh broke in the middle and she fell into the chasm.

Matt caught her and held her against the solid wall of his chest. It was a relief to finally have her here against his heart, even if she was scalding the front of his shirt with her tears. The silent, racking sobs finally lessened. Still following his mom's lead, he lifted her onto his lap, glad when she burrowed against him. He kneaded the back of her neck, taking guilty pleasure in touching her, even if all she wanted or needed from him was comfort. He smoothed her hair back from her wet face.

Dani sniffed, used the sleeve of the robe to wipe her nose, then said thickly, "I really hate this angst crap."

He chuckled. He should have let her go then. He had done what he needed to. She would rest now. The problem was, he was tired, too. Tired made it harder for a man to do what he should, easier to do what he wanted.

Right now he wanted to hold her. She felt right in his arms, like God had made her for him. When she had turned the front of his shirt soggy, it had soaked right through to his willpower. "You should go to bed."

"Mmmmm." She didn't move.

His back hurt and his arm was going to sleep. It didn't matter. Everything else was pain-free and wide awake.

"I'll help you," he squeezed out.

"Can't," she muttered. "Double."

"What?"

She yawned. "Haven't you heard—song 'bout sleeping single—double bed? Ver' dangerous. . . ."

He grinned, felt tender rising and didn't even flinch. She gave a shuddering sigh, her whole body going soft. He held her, counted to twenty while he breathed in her coconut scent and memorized how she felt lying heavy against him, then he did what he had to. He lifted her, carried her to the bed, laid her on it and let her go.

For a moment he studied the way her wet lashes lay in spikes against her flushed cheeks, the tumble of her hair against the white pillow, the way her body rose and fell in all the right places. As need rose in him like a wild fire, he tucked the thick quilt his mother's mother had made securely around her body and turned away to close the window and the curtains.

He had to pass by her one more time to get out. In this room thick with memories of his mom and dad, he paused by the bed they'd tucked him in as a kid. It seemed right to bend and smooth the damp hair back from her face, then press a kiss to her to the soft, salty skin of her temple.

He straightened and turned, walked away with the taste of her skin in his mouth, knowing he didn't feel like a parent. He also hadn't let his folks down.

Chapter Twenty-three

Dani woke lying on her face, merciless sunlight streaming in the window, the smell of bacon frying, and Matt standing by the bed wearing nothing but a pair of hip-hugging jeans and holding out a can of her favorite soda with the tab already popped. She appreciated the soda and the bare chest. The sun she could have done without. It stabbed into eyes almost swelled shut from crying them out last night. One hand burrowed free of blankets, accepted the soda and applied it to one eye.

"What time is it?"

"Almost ten." The bed sank from his weight. "How do you feel?"

"Like I just woke up." She moved the can so she could see his muscled bare flesh and dark hair tapering into the waistband of his jeans. It was a reason to relent slightly. "Other than that, not bad."

Matt grinned. Luke, after learning Dani had cried all over Matt last night, had offered some brotherly advice. "Go carefully into her den, bro. She'll feel better, but, oh man, will she hate what it did to her eyes."

"Luke thought you might need this." Matt produced a cold pack he'd lifted from the first-aid kit, twisted it to mix the chemicals, then handed it to her. "Might be easier to apply than the can."

"Thanks." Dani rolled over and exchanged soda for pack, then took a drink out of the can.

"When you feel up to it, there's grub in the kitchen."

"Grub?" She lifted one edge of the ice pack. "Grub? You're a morning person, aren't you?"

"Isn't everybody?"

"No." She re-covered her eyes.

"So that would make you . . . a night person?"

"I used to be, when I could sleep. Now I'm not anything."

It was obvious she was in sad shape. She even looked good to him all grumpy and icing her swollen eyes. He looked down where her hand holding the soda can almost touched his. His hand was big, the fingers square and callused, the nails blunt and serviceable. Her hand was slim and graceful, the nails perfect pink ovals. His skin was brown from a summer of work and sports. Hers was safe house pale. Soft and hard. Man and woman.

Trouble, he reminded himself.

"Men," she murmured, "greet each other with a sock on the arm, women with a hug . . . the hug wears better in the long run."

Matt gave her a wary look. "What?"

"Just something someone once said." Dani lowered the pack. "Thanks. For the hug. And for letting me weep all over your chest. I feel like crap, but in a good way." Then she smiled.

He had taken a bullet once. It had felt less lethal than her smile going into his heart. He rubbed the back of his neck.

"Good."

Somewhere under her morning mood, something else started to simmer. She took a long drink of soda. It took the edge off the morning grump, but left the sizzle unchecked. It wasn't helping matters that his chest, his really fine chest, was practically in her face. She wanted to touch him more than she wanted chocolate. Not good.

She cleared her throat. "Where's—Luke?"

"Outside chopping some firewood."

"For real?" Matt nodded. Dani chuckled. "This is a bastion of rustic isn't it? I guess I should be grateful you have beds and a bath."

Matt grinned. "You can thank my mom for that. She likes her rustic tempered with a few amenities."

My mom. He had a mom. Of course she knew he had a mom. They had talked about her. But—he had a mom. The lonesome lawman wasn't as lonesome as the romance writer. For the first time it hit her how little, how very little, of his life she was a part of. It worked better than the soda at killing sizzle. She smiled stiffly. "Thank her for me, if you think of it."

His brows drew together. "What's wrong?"

Bad time to find out it was possible for a man to be too perceptive. "I was just trying to imagine you with a mom."

Matt examined her smile, found it missing the warmth and edged with strain. Her mom had died when she was eighteen. Tough time to lose a mother. Not that there was a good time to lose a parent, he thought, thinking about his dad.

"You'd like my mom. She's good with a gun." He grinned. "Had to be good riding herd on three boys and a husband." His mom would like Dani, too. If things were different—

"Something's burning down here!" Luke hollered up the stairs.

"Coming!" You play the hand you're dealt. He stood up. "Take your time. I'll keep your breakfast warm for you."

"Thanks. I won't be long." All she had to do was get up and face a day that could be nasty. She could do a "life in review" or she could watch Matt leave. Since the guy couldn't look anything but great in jeans, she opted for the latter. It was shallow, but she wasn't in the mood for angst or for deep. Shallow was better anyway. Her crying jag had practically drowned her and Matt, but she felt more buoyant and flexible again. Taken with her clean sweep at poker last night, she had to wonder if her luck was changing.

Dani shed the pajamas, pulled on jeans and a long sleeved shirt. After a detour through the bathroom, she settled at the table with a plate of food she didn't want, but would eat because he'd fixed it for her with his big, sexy hands.

"Do we have a plan for today?" She tipped her soda can back and felt the cool bite of it flow down her throat.

"Anderson won't be ready until late this afternoon, so I figured, this is a popular wilderness playground. If we stayed off the beaten paths, we could do a little hiking or rock climbing—"

She spluttered, then coughed to clear shock from her throat, fixed an incredulous gaze on him and said, "Excuse me? Rock *climbing?* As in going perpendicularly up the side of something high?"

Matt arched his brows as he briskly scrubbed the frying pan. "That's the general idea. Though I've never heard it put quite like that before—"

"You can't be serious?"

Matt looked at her. "I can't?"

"How could you know so much about me and not know I don't do up?"

"I know you don't like heights—"

"Saying I don't like heights is like saying that Clinton only waffles a little. I don't climb."

Matt's lips twitched. "Not even stairs?"

"Only under duress." She took another drink, looking at him warily over the can. "I wouldn't exactly call it a phobia, because I don't consider wanting to avoid plummeting to my death an unreasonable fear, but if you really need to climb something, I could watch. Probably."

He smiled, shook his head. "Luke and I thought it might make the waiting easier. You want some toast?"

She shook her head. "No thanks. This is great."

He looked like he wanted to say something, but Luke came in, his arms full of chopped wood. When Dani finished eating, the three of them went into the living room so the men could check their equipment in preparation for the climb they were putting off for her.

Dani settled in a rustic chair in front of a wall of windows, her position such that she had a view of the panorama of mountain and valley and the men at work. Despite her doubts about the sanity of it all, she took an interest in the equipment Matt and Luke were assessing for worthiness. Just because she was afraid of heights, didn't mean her characters had to be.

"What's that?" she asked when Matt pulled out what looked like an emaciated speedo.

"This is a harness," Matt held it up for her inspection. "It's what keeps you from plummeting to your death."

"Really." She ignored his ironic tone. "Doesn't look up to the job if you ask me."

"Oh, it is," Matt said. He stepped into the harness, then showed her how it worked, in concert with rope and carabiners, to forestall plummeting.

Dani was impressed—with the way it looked over his jeans. It emphasized all the right places. She looked up and caught him watching her, his grin one that told her he knew what she was getting out of the demonstration. She grinned back and felt her throat go dry with wanting what she couldn't have.

"I think I'll get me a soda. You guys want something?"

"I wouldn't mind a beer." Luke looked up from the rope he was checking for wear.

"Same here," Matt said.

"Two beers. Okay. Anything—else?" Two feet separated Dani from Matt, but it felt like they were chest to chest, heart to heart.

Matt stared at her for an endless moment, started to say something, stopped, then shook his head. "Just a beer, thanks."

"Right." She wanted him to say it, but how could he? The timing was wrong. It always had been.

Dani sidestepped around their gear to the kitchen door, had her hand on it to push it open, then hesitated. It didn't make any sense, but it felt like if she stepped through that door, she couldn't go back. There's nothing to go back to, she reminded herself. If you have any backbone at all, you won't look back. You'll just keep going forward until this is all over and you're home. Too bad backbone got cried out of her with the angst.

She looked back and was glad she did. Matt was still watching her, something buried deep in his eyes that erased the strange chill and made her feel warm and safe again. She would be quite happy to just stand there forever looking her fill. He didn't move.

If one of them didn't do something, she realized, they'd start looking like coffee commercial clones. She pushed the door open and stepped through, then let it swish back into place. It swung a couple of times, giving her several brief, diminishing glimpses of Matt before it stopped.

She sighed, then realized just how much she had been doing that lately. She would have to style herself a weeping willow if she didn't stop it. She started to turn around and felt something brush against her neck, feather-light, followed by a sting, like something bit her neck. She started to lift her hand to slap at it, but a strange numbness spread from the spot faster than she could think, let alone move. Like an onlooker of her own crash, she felt her knees buckle, saw the floor coming up to meet her—

Arms caught her, cradled her. Matt. Her hero. Her head fell back against his shoulder. Darkness spiraled in like a tornado, but it didn't touch down in her head until after she saw Spook in the center.

Her lips formed a cry that couldn't get out.

Spook smiled.

Matt turned around to find Luke watching him with that big brother look on his face. He stared at him, wishing he wouldn't.

He didn't. "You gonna be able to get off for the climb?"

"I'd better be able to." Relieved, Matt knelt and began stringing carabiners on a sling. "I need the rest."

"Good." He was quiet a minute. "I saw Judith the other day. She looked like Judith. Only happier."

"Didn't know she was back in town." Matt kept coiling rope. He didn't want to think about Judith. It reminded him how lousy he was at marriage.

"Parents having some big do. She asked how you were."

"What'd you tell her?" Matt packed the biners in a pack, then started coiling rope.

"I told her you were the same. She thought that was funny."

"I'm glad she's finally developed a sense of humor."

"She's developing more than that. She's pregnant."

Matt stopped coiling. "Now that's news. I thought she was afraid of overpopulating the world."

"Guess she changed her mind."

"Guess so." Matt started coiling again. It didn't bother him that Judith was willing to give her lawyer-husband what she wouldn't give him. Sometime during the seven days of Dani, that part of his past had lost its sting. He could look at the people they had been and see that their inability to stay married to each other had more to do with who they were than what they did, that he could have done what she wanted and they still wouldn't be married right now. Was he happy for Judith? He was. Odd. When she cheated on him, it hit him hard, but only in his pride. He could see that now. It didn't matter. Was this what the shrinks called closure? He almost shuddered. If he wasn't careful, he'd end up on one of those daytime talk shows sharing with America.

Whatever it was, he felt free—to do what? Let his hormones lead him into another mismatch? Take away the lust and what was left between Dani and him? He liked up. She didn't. He was sports, beer, and pretzels. She was romance, Diet Dr. Pepper and M&M's—

Dr. Pepper. Had Alice found the cans in the refrigerator? He frowned. He had been thinking of Hayes like a killer, but he was also a man who knew Dani very well. Don't go off half-cocked, Kirby. Just because Hayes found some soda cans, didn't mean he could find this place—

A climber. Hayes was a climber. Matt looked out the plate glass window at Long's Peak. It wouldn't be easy, but if Hayes knew the area well and had searched even half-way thoroughly when he was in the apartment—

"We need to move Dani—" He stopped, a chill heading down his back with dry ice fingers. "How long does it take to get a couple of beers?"

Luke looked at the closed kitchen door. "Not this long."

Fear kicked in, trying to mess with his head, but Matt knew how to block it out. He'd always known. He pulled his gun, signaled for Luke to go right. He went left. When they were on either side of the door, he mouthed, "Cover me."

Luke nodded. Matt kicked the door, waited a beat, then went in fast. He could have gone in slow.

The kitchen was empty.

Chapter Twenty-four

The pungent odor of ammonia burned into the fog that Dani drifted in. She tried to get away from it. There was a reason she didn't want to leave. A good reason. If she could just remember what it was. The smell followed her. She coughed. When she did, little spikes of pain made a headache crown for her head, digging deep into the fog.

"Come on, Willow. Open your eyes," a man's voice said. It was a nice voice, gentle and filled with love. God's voice? she wondered, remembering she was probably dead. That's why she didn't want to leave the fog. The Queen of Denial. She giggled.

"Cleopatra," she murmured.

The smell stabbed into her nose, sparking another cough. God obviously didn't have a sense of humor.

"Let me be dead a little longer. I'll get up soon. Promise."

She tried to roll to her side, but something—or someone stopped her.

"Open your eyes."

The ammonia zoomed in again. This time she jerked hard enough to do what he asked. And realized she probably wasn't dead, unless heaven was the cab of a pickup truck. "I guess for a redneck it might be, but I was kind of hoping for something more comfortable."

"What are you talking about?" the voice asked.

Not God. He would know. Whoever he was he sounded amused and a little puzzled.

"Let me help you sit up."

Hands slid under her shoulders and lifted. Her head did a spin that raised a nausea echo in her stomach.

"I think I'm going to be sick."

"Drink this. You'll feel better."

Hands guided hers around something circular, helped her spaghetti arms lift it to her mouth. Something cool flowed down her parched throat. It wasn't her favorite brew, but when it hit her stomach, she did feel slightly better. Now if she could just get her brain to behave. Instead of an orderly queue of questions waiting to be asked, she had the Sesame Street segment from hell going on inside her head. Words kept spinning off in little tangents, while question marks and letters did a really lame macarena—like Al Gore on Valium. She persisted and finally put together a sentence.

"Am I dead?"

"Of course you're not dead. You're with me. It's the drug I gave you. It'll mess with your head for a bit longer, then you'll have a little headache."

"A little headache?" The questions were dancing at the base of her head, right where it hurt the most. She tried to rub the spot, but her fingers were mushy. She shook her head, but that just started the dance going again. "Who are you?"

"Spook. I'm Spook."

She got the dancers to move left so she could turn her head toward his voice. Pale, malleable features. Blonde hair. Blue eyes, a little tired around the rims. Narrow mouth. Sure enough it was Spook, aka Dark Lord, the whacked-out hit man.

"Are you going to kill me?"

"No! I love you."

Even the dancers stopped to think about this. "Why?"

He grinned. He had a nice smile for a killer. "Why not?"

"Well," she frowned, "for one thing, you're a hit man and I'm a romance writer." She frowned. "I think. Whatever. It's weird. And probably illegal."

He laughed ruefully. "Most things are. Don't worry about it. We're together, the way we were meant to be." He lifted her hands to his mouth. At least, she thought they were her hands. They looked kind of familiar. "I won't let anything keep us apart ever again."

"I have to pee," she said.

He grinned. "Except that."

"You aren't the first person to underestimate Hayes," Luke said to Matt as they drove toward the highway. "As far as I can tell, we're only the second ones to walk away alive."

It didn't help. It wasn't his job to stay alive. It was his job to protect Dani. He hadn't done his job. Now they had to play catch-up.

It had been easy to find the place where Hayes had brought his four-wheel up behind the cabin. They even found his footprints coming and going. Made him feel like damn Daniel Boone when he noted that those coming weren't as deep as those leaving. So Hayes had followed his own MO by disabling Dani before he grabbed her. Would he continue to follow his MO and kill her? He usually moved his victims, but not this far.

It gave him reason to hope, though a lovesick Hayes wasn't much easier to contemplate than a murderous one. He couldn't think about what form Hayes's love might take. He told himself that nothing was as final as death, tried to believe it before pushing away everything but the hunt.

His team was coming in by chopper, meeting him at the

Long's Peak Ranger Station where they would coordinate the search. Throughout the area roadblocks were going up in a two hundred mile radius. The locals hadn't liked it when he told them to search every building, to look under every rock that moved. They hadn't like it but they agreed to do it. Big government had a long reach. Matt didn't mind beating them with it if they could stop Hayes from leaving the area.

He wouldn't let himself think about what would happen if Hayes got Dani out of the area. Just like he wouldn't let himself think about how she had looked when she asked him to get her home.

Hayes had put a closed sign at the entrance of the campground before driving in. He didn't want to be disturbed at his work. While Willow took care of her bodily functions, the sight of the pit toilet had cleared her head more than the ammonia, he unloaded their gear and moved it to a safe distance from the truck.

Copeland was still out. Hayes had made sure Copeland would be, just as he made sure he kept the dosage below lethal. It wouldn't be as much fun to kill him this way, without him knowing who had taken him out, but he didn't want any trouble with him. Not in front of Willow. This would be her first kill. He wanted her to enjoy it.

With luck, Copeland's body would buy them the time they needed to make their climb, then their getaway to a new life.

Hayes hadn't decided exactly where that new life would be. They would take it in stages, erase their old selves, make new ones. He did know it would be some place high. They would need a new mountain for their new life, for their new pattern. He lifted his eyes to his mountain, used his hand to block out the sun, and felt regret bite deep. She was magnificent. He would miss her.

The door creaked loudly and he turned eagerly as Willow came out. She was pale, a bit wobbly, but the hike would work the rest of the drug out of her veins. It had served its purpose, easing the transition between her old life and her new. Now it was time for her initiation to begin. Time to introduce her to the wonder of blood and fire. Time to introduce her to his mountain.

"Come on, Willow."

Dani looked at the gentle rise to the parking lot where Spook waited for her. He looked taller from her vantage point. She knew it was the drug humming in her blood that made it possible for her to stand and calmly look up at him. Instead of a killer and a romance writer, they might be a normal couple out for a day in the mountains.

"It's time," he said.

Time for what? She examined the rise doubtfully. "I don't think I can make it up there."

"You can," he said. "You need to try."

She didn't know why, but it was easier to do what he asked than marshal thoughts to argue with him. There was a well-worn trail. She followed that, felt gravity tug at her, then give way when she topped the rise.

"I made it." She looked down, then at Spook. "I went up."

"Of course you did. You're Willow."

She didn't feel like Willow. She felt like Gumby. His eyes were still filled with love, but something else had moved in there while she was in the toilet. They had a glow like a dude in a Stephen King thriller. Unease tried to make a move, but it was hard going against Spook's drug. The places inside her that hurt hadn't changed. They still hurt.

Still felt empty. She just didn't care. If this was how Steven felt when he drank, no wonder he kept pouring stuff down his throat. Spook's eyes looked like Steven's when he drank, with matching dark circles underneath. "Are you all right?"

"I am now. Or I will be."

He seemed to hesitate, then he took her hands, held them against his face. Their bodies were close. Too close, Dani decided, feeling slightly claustrophobic at his nearness. Matt up close didn't make her feel this way. Course, Matt wasn't a murderer, and he had that really great butt going for him.

"It's time for us to complete the pattern."

Pattern? Even through the fog she felt the intensity behind his careful words. Knew she needed a clear head. If only the dancers would finish their party. If only she had her soda. It would kick her into gear.

"You don't happen to have a Diet Dr. Pepper, do you?"

"No." A flicker of impatience altered his face before he controlled it. "You have to pay attention, Willow. I know it's not easy, but this is important to our future."

What future is that? her brain asked. Fortunately her mouth didn't. "Okay. I'll try. It's just my head—"

His smile was quick and strangely charming. "I know. Let's sit here while I explain."

He led her to one of the logs that bounded the parking lot. When they were seated, he pointed at the mountain rising against the stark blue of the sky. "Do you see that peak?"

He had the same tone in his voice that Matt had when he talked about all this mountain stuff. Good old Matt. She should have jumped his bones when she had the chance. Just because she'd never done it, was no reason not to, was it?

"Willow?" Spook's voice had an edge to it.

She hurriedly looked up, squinting against the sun. "It looks high."

She was repeating herself, but what did one say about a mountain, for Pete's sake?

"It's over fourteen thousand feet above sea level." He took her hand.

"That's a lot of feet. At least, I think it is. I'm not very good at math. Too left brain for me."

"Willow, shut up." His hand tightened on hers. "We have to go there."

Dani looked at him. "Go where?"

"To the top of that peak. There's a trail—"

That got through the fog. "I don't care if there's a four-lane highway. I don't do fourteen thousand feet. I don't do—"

"Willow," his tone was so sharp it cut through her foggy panic with the precision of a knife, a reminder he carried one and knew how to use it. "We have to do this. It's the only way we can be together."

He obviously didn't have a good grasp of motivation if he thought that would make her want to drag her ass fourteen thousand feet above anything. She hadn't wanted to date him before she knew he was a killer. She decided to tell him that—until she saw his eyes. They were the same as they had been in the safe house when he killed Peg.

"That's not the only thing we have to do."

Even the drug couldn't take the edge off the chill skating down her back with razor-sharp blades. "What?"

"The feds will come after us. I'm wanted, you know."

Duh. "I heard."

The side of his mouth lifted slightly. "It'll take us at least two days to do the hike, get down and get clear. It will be easier if they think you're dead."

The locals had just finished updating him on the search and disposition of the roadblocks when he heard the chopper coming in. Matt didn't mind cutting short the report. It was a depressingly familiar litany that could be summed up in one sentence: no one knew squat.

"You were right, Matt," Alice said. "When Hayes was in your apartment he found your photo album. They found it hidden in the blankets on your bed. Several photos, probably of the cabin were missing. Rotten luck."

"Yeah. Get set up. I want to move as soon as we hear something." He stared up at Long's Peak, every cell in his body straining for action. This time he had a solid hold on impatience. His week-long pursuit of Dani had reminded him that hunting was more than looking. It was thinking, too. Something he had let himself forget in the last few years when the criminals were stupider.

Hayes was a thinker first. Matt could call up a state full of cops, but if he couldn't figure out what Hayes intended to do, it didn't matter jackstraws.

Hayes had smoked him, no question about that. His pride had taken a hit, but it wasn't a knockout. Hayes was good. He knew the system inside out, knew how to exploit the weaknesses of it and the men tied to it. He was always careful to do what wasn't expected. Knowing that could help Matt now.

Matt paced across the parking lot, his mind turning with everything he knew about Hayes, trying to turn knowledge into an arrow pointing where he had gone. When he ran out of parking lot, he turned around and headed the other way. If he had to wear a groove from here to China, he was going to crack the bastard's brain. Then he was going to yank it out and stomp on it.

"Please don't do this, Spook," Dani whispered, the words grating against her fear-dry throat as Spook arranged the limp body, then began pouring gasoline over him and the truck.

"He's a killer, Willow, not worthy of your concern."

So are you! her mind screamed. "John Donne. 'Every man's death diminishes me.' "

He looked up with a quick smile. "Very good. Coleman Dowell. 'Life is a series of diminishments. A lightening of self that eventually makes our own death possible.' Do you want to live forever, Willow?" When she didn't answer, he said, "You're not even sure you want your life to go on, why care about his?"

He hit hard. Dani looked down, trying to absorb his words without getting knocked out by them.

"Did you think I didn't know? Did you think I wouldn't see the aura of death like a shadow in your eyes? Why would you sentence him to life, when you're not sure you want it for yourself?"

He was good. His brain and the way he could argue a point without bluster was what had drawn her to him on the boards. There was so much bluster in the world, so little thinking. She had barely held her own against him, even after sharpening her brain against his for six months. What chance did she have now, with her brain riding the drug train? She still had to try. "It's his life, not mine. 'At birth man is offered only one choice, the choice of his death.' I won't be the one to take that choice away from him."

"I love the way your mind works," he said, his smile tender, his eyes avid with delight. "You won't be taking his choice. I will. For you. Because I love you. You don't understand right now, Willow. But you will. When it's over and your pain is gone, then you'll understand."

She opened her mouth to tell him that if he loved her, he wouldn't do it, but he was through talking. His movements brisk and businesslike, he grabbed the man by the hair, pulled his head back to expose the neck and pulled his knife across the arched flesh in a horrible mimicry of a bow across the strings of a violin.

Chapter Twenty-five

A scarlet flood gushed across Spook's hand. He opened his hand and the man's head thumped against the truck bed. He stared down at it with a slight smile, then knelt and wiped his blade across the white shirt before sheathing it. Nausea joined shock when he thrust his hand into the slowing gush of blood. His eyes warmed, then glowed hot as he washed his hands with it, his breath coming in short, panting gasps.

" 'Other things are very well in their way, but give me Blood,' " he murmured softly, then looked at her.

Shock kept Dani still when he came to her and cupped her face with his bloody hands. Desire put an unholy glow in his eyes when he traced her features, the blood a lubricant between them. He followed his hands with his mouth, his tongue licking blood and skin. He murmured against her skin, "It's coming together, just like I planned it, Willow."

His thumb penetrated her lips. She tasted the salt of blood. Her stomach heaved. She jerked away from him, draped herself across a handy boulder and got rid of the breakfast Matt had cooked for her. It got the taste of blood out of her mouth, but didn't leave one that was much better.

When there was nothing left to hurl, she slid to the ground and huddled in a semi-fetal position against the boulder. It was warm from the sun. She was cold. Part of her cursed the drug that still fogged her thinking, kept her from feeling too much. The rest of her was grateful for it.

She didn't look at Spook. Couldn't close her eyes. That started the instant replay. She wanted to cry, but she was too dry, too brittle. He handed her a bottle of water with a hand still dripping red, then crouched down in front of her.

"Don't feel bad. I threw up the first time, too. It's part of the cleansing process."

She rinsed her mouth, then wiped the drips away with the back of her hand. "Pretty messy way to cleanse yourself." Her face felt sticky and she could still smell blood. "Can I wash my face or is that part of getting cleansed?"

"No, that was for me. I like you in red."

"Every guy I know likes a woman in red." She tipped her head back and squeezed the bottle, flooding her face until the bottle was empty. This was her idea of cleansing. She used her shirt sleeve to finish the job. Tried not to look at the red streaks it left on the fabric.

"Can you walk?"

Dani looked at him. Something in his face made her nod instead of shake her head. She ignored the bloody hand held out to help her stand, using the boulder instead. The boulder was her friend. She wanted to cling to it, maybe have its children. Anything but go with bloody Spook.

He pointed up. "I want to be at the top of that hill before the timer goes off so we can see the fire."

Dani looked at his hill. She had to tip her head back to see the top he wanted them to reach, almost fell backwards doing it. She didn't know a lot of math, but she did know a ninety-degree angle when she saw one. "Oh shit."

"This way, just over that rise," Spook said, as easily as if they were out on an afternoon hike instead of a kidnapping.

Dani didn't answer. It took all her energy to haul her "body by New Orleans" up the steep incline against gravity and her own fear. Spook's drug was wearing off. Now she could feel the dread lodged in her throat making it even harder for thin air to get into her straining lungs.

She was alone in the mountains with the ultimate Jekyl and Hyde. As they climbed, Spook smiled and talked, helped her when she slipped on the rough, loose surface, his quick reflexes keeping her from taking a nasty tumble more than once. He pointed out landmarks, identified flora and fauna and told her how glad he was to be with her. None of it made her forget he had just cut a man's throat as easily as she sliced bread.

There were rocks aplenty and she considered using one on the back of his head. Two things stopped her. She could barely lift herself, let alone a rock. If she missed, the nature of their interaction might change in a way she would like less than his devotion. Even if she did rally her resources to the task, she had a feeling that Spook wouldn't be easy to take by surprise. Peg was trained to take on killers. Peg had the drop on him at the safe house. Peg was dead.

Even if she did manage to knock him out, they were in the middle of nowhere. Instead of being alone in the wilderness with a Loony Toon, she would be alone in the wilderness period. The only thing she knew how to do in the wilderness was roll down a ninety-degree hill very quickly.

Dani didn't look back as she climbed. She didn't dare. Fear was only a motivator if living looked better than dying. Right now life and death were in a dead heat—no pun intended. After several more yards of crawling and slipping and pulling herself up using scrubby bushes that scratched her hands raw, death started to edge ahead. If the incline hadn't leveled abruptly, death would have won the prize. She rolled over onto her back, her chest heaving with the double whammy of gravity and thin air.

"Was that great or what?" Spook, barely winded by the climb, sat by her grinning like the village idiot.

"Or what," Dani said. It had been about as much fun as a fun run, an oxymoron if she had ever heard one, with heavy emphasis on the moron part.

He shed his pack and jumped up. "We can see the parking lot from that outcrop." He took her hand and pulled her up, then led her over and pointed down to the parking lot below. His truck looked like a Matchbox toy, an improvement since it kept her from seeing the dead guy in the back.

"It's almost time. I wish we could be closer. It's not the same when you can't feel the heat, when you can't see the blood sizzle as fire licks it up. But I promise you, next time you can experience it all."

Next time? Maybe she should just do a nosedive off this outcrop and end it now. Even better if he did the nosedive. She took a cautious look. It only looked high enough to piss him off.

"Here," he handed her binoculars, "you watch. I've seen it before."

It took her a minute to adjust the focus and find the truck, but her timing was perfect. She didn't know how he managed it, but the fire started on the man's chest. Looked like it burst right out of his heart, flowing across his body in both directions. In the time it took for her to take several unsteady breaths, the whole truck was ablaze, sending black smoke to paint doom across the blue sky.

"Isn't it amazing?" Spook whispered, his mouth close to her ear. Dani studied the dark column for a moment longer then lowered the glasses.

"I need to pee again." Spook's eyes looked the way her dad's used to when she said that. She shrugged. "Hey, it's a scientific reality that a woman's bladder is smaller than a man's."

He sighed. "This could take longer than I planned." He bent and dug a roll of toilet paper out of a pack. "Hurry."

She fingered the paper. How did she know he was the type to use the sandpaper variety? "I'll squeeze as fast as I can."

When she got back, Spook was fitting a tiny microphone in his ear. The wire from it followed down his neck, then disappeared inside his jacket.

"What's that?" she asked, uneasy.

"A scanner. So I can listen in when the feds talk on their radios. So we'll know what they're doing."

"Oh." Dani swallowed, but the tiny bit of spit she managed to suck off the sides of her mouth turned to dust before disappearing in the hollow pit of her stomach.

Matt, his face wiped clean of expression, stood watching water flood over the burning truck. The fire had been spotted when the smoke topped the trees. They got there before the gas tank could blow. When the flames died away, Henry and a couple of forest service firefighters moved in.

"Nothing in the front," one man called. Matt saw Henry ignore a warning from a firefighter and jump on the tailgate. He looked at Matt over a sea of heads. "We got a body."

"Damn." Alice rubbed a smoke-smudged cheek with the back of her flawlessly manicured hand. "I thought—"

"Let's sweep the area." Matt shoved his hands into his pockets, the fingers clenched so tight his shoulders ached. "He can't be that far. Even if he used some kind of timer, he didn't have that much time to play with. And let's keep radio traffic to a minimum. The guy was a damn spook. Assume he's got a scanning device with him."

Did this feel wrong, or did he just want it to feel wrong because he didn't want to accept the fact that Dani was dead? Just because he found Dani hard to resist, didn't mean Hayes would risk life and business for her. Didn't mean he would choose her over his reputation for always finishing a job. Logic said that Hayes would move to reestablish his reputation. Others would be happy to buy his killing skills in the absence of Bates.

"Somebody lost their breakfast over here," Luke said, looking at the other side of a big boulder. "I wonder if someone came on this before the fire?"

With a frown, Matt went to look. "Sign said it was closed and no hiking trails head in here."

Henry slouched over to join them. "Yuck."

Matt crouched down. Yuck was right. It also showed signs of everything he had fed Dani for breakfast a few hours ago. It didn't mean it wasn't her body in the truck. Lots of people probably had a country breakfast this morning. Or she could have lost her cookies before Hayes killed her. Hayes had to have drugged her to get her out of the cabin so quick and quiet. It was his MO. That would make her sick.

It all came down to the timing.

He stood up. "Give me your binoculars, Riggs."

He ignored the look Luke and Riggs exchanged when he took the glasses and started scanning the hillside. A guy who liked blood, who liked fire, wouldn't like to miss the finale. If he had wanted to watch from a safe distance he'd choose—that outcrop up there. He lowered the glasses and asked the ranger, "You got a tracker?"

"I got a man who's pretty good."

"Get him here. Have him see if he can find a trail to that outcrop up there. And don't say why on the radio. Just assume everything you say is being listened to, okay?"

"Okay." He turned away. Luke looked at Matt.

"Why would he head up there? He'd be ridged against the mountains. Not a smart move when he must know half the state will be looking for him."

"It doesn't seem smart, does it?" Matt started to turn away, then stopped and reapplied the glasses to his eyes. What had caught his attention? There. What—white, something white wrapped around a tree limb. He frowned, handed the glasses to his brother. "Look at the piece of white at nine o'clock from the ridge. Tell me what you think it is."

Luke did as he was asked, then lowered the glasses, his frown a mirror to Matt's. "It looks like—toilet paper. Tied into a bow."

"That's what I thought."

"And the significance would be—?"

"Not sure." He spun around. "How long until our tracker gets here?"

The ranger looked up. "ETA in fifteen. He's coming in on a chopper."

"Good." He could wait fifteen minutes. *He can feel me,* Dani had said. Matt quit fighting his feeling she was alive. Instead he closed his eyes and took out the logic and the reasons why it couldn't be so. *Dani, are you out there?*

He didn't feel any different. No warm rush. No voice in his head. Just a certainty deep in his gut telling him she still lived and breathed and was counting on him to find her.

"I've got to rest." Dani stopped on the trail and bent over, resting her hands on her knees as she labored for more air. They had kept a steady pace in the hours since leaving the ridge, a pace he had only interrupted once when a helicopter flew over. If the stretch was particularly steep, he had let her stop and catch her breath, not easy to do in thin air. He never let her sit down. He said she would stiffen up if she sat down. What he didn't seem to get was that she had never been loose. She wasn't Amazon woman. She was a romance writer. Sitting down was what she did best. Some time during their hike the effects of the drug, with an exquisitely ironic sense of timing, had worn away, leaving her in full possession of her senses and with all her nervous pain centers fully functioning. Didn't have to be a scientist to know there were a ton of the little suckers, all clamoring loudly. She glared at Spook's back.

"I have to stop. Now."

Spook spun around, impatience flaring. She was going to have to do better than this if they were to make it. Then he saw her swaying with exhaustion, her face drawn and pale in the swiftly waning light. If only they had more time. If only the world would leave them alone to do what had to be done. It wouldn't. He smiled at her.

"I keep forgetting you're not used to hiking."

"That's why I keep reminding you."

He looked at his watch, then their surroundings. "The feds don't have a clue where we are. I think we can safely take a short break." He added encouragingly, "Then it's only about five miles until we stop for the night."

Dani didn't feel encouraged or wait for him to tell her she couldn't sit down. With the sun almost behind the mountains, it was getting cold, not that she had felt warm since getting snatched by Spook, even when sweating buckets from the climb. Her middle felt as hollow as a politician's promises. Matt's breakfast may have sat heavily on her stomach, but at least it had sat. Now there was nothing but acid churning away in there, keeping the nasty taste going in her mouth. The up side was, she would soon be able to take him out with her bad breath.

He still had the earpiece in, but hadn't told her what, if anything, he had heard.

"So, did the feds fall for your decoy?"

"Looks good so far. Even if they figure out you're not dead, they won't figure on us heading into the mountains."

He dropped his pack, knelt and opened the top.

"I suppose not." So Matt hadn't found her bow. What did she expect? She wrote romance, not mystery. They would be looking in all the wrong places for Spook, leaving her on her own in this unnatural environment with Mr. Over-the-top Mountain Man. Great.

"You look cold." He tossed her a jacket. "And I'll bet you're hungry and thirsty. I wasn't going to eat until we got to Eugenia Mine, but there's time for a snack."

Dani wrapped the coat around and looked at him hopefully. "I don't suppose you've got M&M's in there?"

"I have something better."

Better than M&M's? Maybe he wasn't such a bad killer after all.

He pulled out a foil packet and tossed it to her. Her hands shook as she ripped it open and dumped the contents into her waiting palm. "Trail mix?"

"You'd rather have a power bar?" He held out a water bottle.

"No." Dani stared at the emaciated bits of fruit. How like a man. When he's courting, he promises you chocolate chip cookies and the moon, but once he thinks he has you, it's trail mix and hauling ass up a mountain. "How—healthy."

Spook grinned sympathetically. "I know this isn't what you're used to, Willow. But chocolate and caffeine only give you temporary energy. You need real energy if you're going to make this climb."

He still hadn't gotten that motivation thing down. It reminded her of a movie she'd watched with Kelly where a whacked-out terrorist kept trying to influence the hero by blowing up her own relatives. "Please tell me you'll have some nice, unhealthy energy food waiting for us at your cabin?"

He frowned. "My cabin? I don't have a cabin."

Dani had a bad feeling about this. "But . . . where will we stay tonight?"

"I told you. We're camping at Eugenia Mine." He stood up. "We should get moving again."

Dani got up, aware that Spook was right about one thing. It was possible for her body to get stiffer. "Define *camp*."

His pale brows arched. "Surely you've gone camping?"

"Surely I haven't. New Orleans. Swamp. Alligators. Snakes. Mosquitoes. Why would I camp?"

He chuckled. "Okay, what about the characters in your books? Don't they ever camp?"

Dani crossed her arms over her chest. He may be amused. She wasn't. "My imagination isn't that rich."

"Well, then think of it as copy." He took her arm. "Let's move out."

Dani dug in her heels. "This camping thing. Does this mean if I have to pee—"

"You find a tree."

"But it's dark. And there's already a moon."

He sighed. By the time they got up Long's Peak, she will have fertilized half the vegetation. "Is this your way of telling me you need to go again?"

She took the roll he held out and began gingerly edging her way through the underbrush, trying not to hear the rustling that preceded her. "I don't suppose any of these trees has a shower?"

Spook laughed, like she was making a joke. The joke would be on him if she bolted. She would have, if she could figure out where to bolt to. There was only one bright spot, aside from her bare butt mooning the wildlife. Kelly wasn't here to see her reduced to penis envy.

Sorely in need of some fresh air, Matt stepped outside the ranger station they were using as their command center, searching the sky for signs of a dawn that couldn't come quickly enough. Finally alone, he let himself feel the relief of knowing his gut was right. Dani wasn't dead. The tracker had quickly found their trail, with its two sets of footprints, heading straight up the hillside to the outcrop. One set matched the shoes Dani had been wearing. That same set had been easy to follow from the outcrop to the toilet paper bow. In the dirt under the tree, he had also found a simple drawing of mountains and arrow pointing toward them. At that point, the shadows were too long for the tracker to keep on the trail. In the dark, the risk was too high he would miss any other markers she might leave. He would be starting again at first light.

The area had been sealed as good as a mountain range could be sealed. Matt, Luke and the team had withdrawn to their command center and spent the next few hours bouncing theories off each other about what Hayes might be planning.

"It's possible he has backup transport stashed somewhere inside the park," Luke had suggested. "But it doesn't make sense. He should have gone for the quick getaway. Instead, he's boxed himself in. Let's face it, Dani will only slow him down. Unless he's figuring on them doing a Rocky

Mountain version of Tarzan and Jane?"

Matt cut off thoughts like that before they formed. He had to. It made him want to rip up the countryside to think of Dani in the control of that whacko. Hayes had a goal that only he could see. Dani had tried to tip them off about what it was, but it was obvious she had been interrupted, or wasn't entirely sure what it involved. He grinned slightly, thinking about her tying that bow to the tree. She was keeping her head, keeping her cool. If there was a way to leave other clues, she would find it.

"He has to have transport laid on. Hayes doesn't go in a place without a way out. He torched the truck to slow us down, convince us Dani was dead. Had to know that at the most, it would buy him twenty-four hours, probably less. Best case scenario, traveling at four miles per hour on foot, where would that put them?" Matt asked.

"This isn't best case," the ranger put in. "The terrain is rough, not easy even when you're heading downhill."

"Let's work with best case anyway. I don't want them to slip through because we didn't figure wide enough." Matt looked at his watch. "It's midnight now. First light is around 5:30. We're looking at a radius of about 100 miles fanning out from where he torched the truck. I want to know every highway, road, foot or mule track in that area. Every possible route they could take, no matter how far-fetched. And then we'll need men available to cover them."

"What about some guys to leap tall buildings and outrun locomotives?" Alice asked, wryly.

Matt looked up, a grin firmly under wraps. It would only encourage her to be a smart ass. "If they've got 'em, let's get 'em out there."

Chapter Twenty-six

Spook woke Dani just after midnight. It was the first time in a long time she didn't want to leave her dreams.

"Why?" It came out half whine, half wail. "I've only been asleep for two hours."

"It's taking us longer than I planned on and we have to be on top by noon at the latest."

"I'll bet the sunset is lovely up there—"

"Have you ever been in a thunderstorm on a mountaintop?"

She lowered her brows. "I've never been on a mountaintop, period."

"Well, you sure as hell don't want to be on one in a storm. Lightning is a bitch." He handed her a wet wipe. "Use this to wash. We'll have to start being careful with our water from here on out."

Dani looked at the wipe. It was smaller than the sheet gynecologists' nurses handed out. She sat up and washed until the scrap went dry, then crawled out, shivering as the chill air hit the few inches of damp skin.

It was at this point she realized that not only had she been seized by a crazed killer who claimed to be in love with her and was forcing her to climb up a fourteen-thousand-foot mountain into a possible lightning storm, but he was making her do it without her Diet Dr. Pepper.

He'd gone too far. He was a killer and she was only a pissed off romance writer, but he was about to find out that when a romance writer starts plotting, well, more people

318

take notice than listen to E. F. Hutton talk. They hadn't gotten that fifty percent market share just for writing sex scenes.

Matt hated starting an op tired. The tough part of the hunt was still ahead of them, the part that would require them to think on their feet, to react quickly and decisively. They couldn't afford to make mistakes on this one. The margin of error was too narrow.

He turned abruptly back to his team. "Give me an update."

Alice looked up from the map she had been bent over for the last three hours. "I think we've identified all usable tracks within the target area, but there are as many places they could veer off and still navigate."

"Wouldn't be easy, but it's possible in the lower foothills," the ranger added.

Matt spread his hands on the table to support his weight. "Let's start with the most likely scenario."

The ranger nodded. "I'm guessing he'll cut up toward Storm Creek Pass trail. He could hike cross-country from where he torched the truck and hit the trail in short order. The cover's good and they'd make good time on a well-marked trail."

"And then what?" Riggs asked, pale and bandaged, but upright and thinking.

"From that trail he's got a lot of options. He could head towards us here at Long's Peak Ranger Station. We got a parking lot for hikers. No problem leaving a vehicle parked there for several days."

"That makes sense," Luke said, crossing over to join the briefing with a fresh cup of coffee for Matt. "We can have someone start running the plates on what's here."

"Do it." Matt lifted the hot brew to his mouth, felt it kick his tired system into gear. "What are his other options?"

"He could drop down into Bear Lake here," the ranger touched it on the map. "Again, the hike isn't easy, but it's not impossible. If they hiked all night, they'd be there within the next hour or so."

Alice looked up from the map. "We've got people there."

"That's a busy area this time of year. Be easy for him to lose himself in the crowd. And there's a regular shuttle to the parking lot at Glacier Basin," the ranger said, pointing to an area on the other side of the park.

"We got people at Glacier Basin, too," Riggs said. He took off his glasses and cleaned them on his shirttail.

"What's this?" Matt traced another line on the map.

"That's the east portal of a water diversion tunnel that runs the width of the park. They could hike out on it. Put them outside close to the convention center." The ranger looked up. "He likely to have help?"

Alice shrugged. Matt frowned. "Unknown," he said, "but unlikely. He's not the trusting type."

Henry, a pencil threaded through his fingers like a cigarette, tapped a spot on the map. "That's the convention center there?"

"Yeah, it's not far from where the tunnel comes out. Another parking lot to check out." The ranger rubbed the back of his neck. "We've got people there, too."

"If he goes into the park, the perimeter road is going to be a problem." Alice pointed to a road that circled the park.

"If he has transportation waiting inside the park, he could circle around and try to slip out the Grand Lake exit over here. Or park it along the way and start hiking again." The ranger looked at Matt. "How experienced a hiker is your girl?"

Matt looked at Riggs.

"She's a romance writer from New Orleans." Riggs slipped on his glasses.

"Who's afraid of heights." Luke lifted a coffee cup to his lips.

"Holy shit. Even at this altitude she's gonna be one sick puppy. He tries to hike her higher—" the ranger looked grim. "He likely to ditch her if she gets to be too much trouble?"

"Probably," Matt said, without hesitation.

"We think he's got an obsessive fixation with her," Alice said. "I don't think he'll hurt her unless she does something to piss him off."

"Is she likely to do that?"

"No." Alice looked at Matt. "She'll keep her head. And keep trying to help us find her, like she did with the toilet paper."

"She's a regular little Gretel. Let's hope Hayes doesn't notice the roll disappearing," Riggs said.

First she had him staking out cookie counters, now he was following toilet paper bows. Had there really been a time when he thought the romance writer would be easy, Matt wondered?

"We gonna put choppers up?" Henry took the pencil out of his mouth to ask.

Matt hesitated, looked at the ranger.

The ranger looked doubtful. "Couldn't do it without him knowing it. If he's listening to our radio traffic—"

"What if we create a crisis, like a lost kid or plane gone down? We could put as many choppers up as we wanted."

"Hayes would see through that, Matt," Alice objected.

"Maybe, but we could insert chatter about the hunt for him, just him, into the traffic. He wouldn't know for sure and it would help us stay mobile without tipping our hand if we do get a lead on where he's headed."

"It could work," Riggs said, looking thoughtful. "Anything we can do to keep Hayes from knowing our moves can only help."

"Let's keep the number of people who know it's bogus to a minimum. I don't want any slip-ups," Matt told the ranger. "Have you warned your people that Hayes is extremely dangerous? I can't emphasis this enough. *No one* approaches him on their own, no heroics. We don't want dead heroes or the hostage put in unnecessary danger. Orders are to mark and follow only until backup is in place. Questions? Comments?" No one said anything and he was quiet, scanning for the weak spots in their planning. "Is that *every way* he could take her out?"

"If your hostage wasn't such a novice, he could head up Long's Peak trail."

"Wouldn't he ridge himself?" Luke asked.

"I thought there was a trail down to Wild Basin?" Matt said, trying to find the trail on the map.

"Yeah, there's a trail—of sorts. It's a real bastard. He'd have to know about it, have done it before to even find it, cause its not marked on the current maps." The ranger pointed at the map, tracing a line down from Long's Peak with his finger. "It would be crazy to try it with a beginner. Long's Peak is over fourteen thousand feet above sea level. The altitude would wipe her out before they made the timberline."

Crazy. It was the last thing they would expect him to do with Dani in tow. That trail was hard on seasoned hikers. Dani wasn't even a hiker. Hayes knew that.

"Let's put someone at Wild Basin, too."

Luke arched his brows. "That doesn't make any sense, Matt."

"I know. It's a long shot. But I'd rather err on the side of caution. One guy should be enough, have him check out any vehicles parked there."

"Right." Riggs nodded to Henry, who lifted his telephone. "You gonna stay here, Matt?"

"Yeah, I want one of the choppers so I can move once they're spotted. You stay with me, Alice. Riggs, Henry, I want you at Bear Lake with the other chopper." They nodded and moved off. Luke walked over to him, with a slight smile.

"You got marching orders for me, little brother?"

Matt looked up from the map with a quick grin at the mock-subservient tone. "Could you coordinate the license plate checks? I'll have Alice get you any gear you want and hook you up with Sebastian. He can run checks on the names. If we can find his transport, we'll know where he's headed."

Dani choked down a breakfast of trail mix, half a power bar and stale water, with an ibuprofen chaser, pretending to listen to Spook as he gave her some hiking tips.

"We have to take it slow, you don't rush a fourteener—"

"Fourteener?" The question was just an excuse to quit eating for a minute. Even to her it was obvious what the fourteener was.

"Our fourteen-thousand-foot mountain," he said impatiently. "The air'll get thinner the higher we climb. Makes your heart work harder. The trick is to do what they call the step-pause. Take a step, pause, then take another step."

"Can't I just do the pause part?"

He ignored her. "If you try to push the pace, you'll get sick."

"I'm already sick."

"It's worth it, Willow."

"Sure." And some day the literary world will take romance writing seriously.

He crouched in front of her, his face turning intense. It gave definition to its blandness, made him almost handsome. "When you get to the top, you'll be glad you made it. You'll know what matters, what doesn't. You'll know what I know."

She already knew what he knew. Nothing.

"Let's gear up."

"Excuse me?"

"You'll have to carry your own pack now, Willow. We need the supplies when we start down and I didn't have time to stash what we'd need at both places."

Great. Bad enough having to haul her ass uphill. Now she had to do it with a bunch of crap she didn't want on her back. He was lucky she wasn't premenstrual *and* soda deprived.

They started hiking, a slow plodding walk, using Spook's step-pause routine, with the pauses as long as he'd let her get away with. Since they were cutting across the mountainside, the hike wasn't too bad, though the ibuprofen barely took the edge off her headache. Her putrid breakfast sat uneasily in her stomach and the straps of her backpack cut into her shoulders. There was no kindly light up here, just the pale flicker of Spook's flashlight marking the trail for her between tall, ghostly lodgepole pines. At a junction of silvery Aspen trees, Spook stopped and looked at her. She started to sit down, but he shook his head.

"Don't. It'll just make it harder for you to start up again. Drink a little water and eat a little trail mix as you walk. It'll keep your energy level steady."

Her energy level was already steady—right down there at rock bottom.

"You're doing good. Just keep using the step-pause technique—and Willow?"

"What?" She ground a piece of dry fruit between her teeth and washed it down with a drink of water, trying to pretend one was chocolate, the other her soda, but her imagination failed her.

"This is a busy trail during the day. There'll be other hikers, both ahead and behind us. Don't call attention to yourself—unless you want them to die."

Suddenly the dry mix went dryer. Her lashes lifted, her eyes found his. "I'll hate you if you hurt anyone else, Spook."

His lids drooped and his mouth curved in pleasure. She was everything he had hoped for. And now the mountain was remaking her, just like it had remade him. She was exhausted, in pain, even frightened, though she tried hard not to show it. As she ascended the refining hell of the mountain, it just made her more beautiful. He could barely keep his hands, his mouth off her body. She was so perfectly formed for loving, for the thrusting of his body into hers. He had waited so long for her. It wasn't time yet. This wasn't the place. He was more than ready, but she wasn't. Wouldn't be until she reached the peak cleansed of her past and ready for the new life he had planned for them.

He reached out to touch her cheek. His hand trembled with the effort of keeping the caress light, when he wanted to dig his fingers into her bare flesh and taste her. "I'll love how you hate me, Willow. Just like I'll love how you love me when it's time. But no one has to get hurt—as long as you do as I say."

It was the first time since he had smeared her with blood and she tossed her cookies that she felt something sexual from him. Up to now there had been no passion in the restrained, almost fatherly way he shepherded her up his mountain.

Now he looked at her the way a man looks at a woman. His eyes stripped her, took her apart and probed the secret places of mind and body. Even as her skin and mind shrank from his touch, from the intimate invasion of his lust, she felt his strange attraction reach out to her, the way it had drawn her to him on the boards before she knew what he was.

It would have been more comfortable if knowledge had killed attraction, but this situation didn't allow for comfortable fiction. She wanted to fight him, to hate him, but passion of any kind was dangerous, too easily mistaken for love, by her own body and by the enemy that provoked it.

His goal was to break her, pitting his will against hers to control her body and her mind. She was his hostage, completely dependent on him for survival. He had isolated her, taken control of her food, limited her sleep and oxygen until she could barely think straight, then applied shock therapy every time she started to get her equilibrium back. If he forced himself on her, he lost the battle of her mind.

And if he mixed kind with the cruel? The stroke of his hand against her skin was dangerously comforting. Two steps to his shoulder and her burdens were his. It shouldn't be tempting. He shouldn't be tempting. But she was so tired. He was so close. It was a more terrifying combination than the thousands of feet above sea level he wanted her to climb.

She could quit now. Patty Hearst would understand, even if no one else did. If she could just figure out how to quit. It wasn't as easy as it looked. Especially when staring into the eyes of a killer.

"I'll—do as you say." She licked her dry lips, wished she

hadn't when the light in his eyes flared brighter. How much he wanted her, and his struggle to control that want, stabbed out of his eyes like his expertly wielded knife. "Shouldn't we go?"

Hayes didn't answer, didn't really hear what she said. He was too engrossed in what he saw. The defiant lift of her chin. The unconscious trembling of her mouth. She didn't yet know how futile resistance was. He had to show her. Now.

He slid his hand to the back of her neck. Her hair, soft as silk, brushed against the back of his hand. There was resistance when he pulled her toward him, but not enough to matter. Not enough to stop him from taking the shocked, moist circle of her mouth into his.

He only meant to take a small taste of her, but when pleasure speared deep in his groin, small wasn't enough. He wanted all of her.

With teeth and tongue, he forced her mouth open and bit the soft flesh he found inside. A small explosion of blood filled her mouth, then his. One hand held her head so he could suck and bite. The other hand fumbled, tearing at her clothes—

Her elbow went deep into his gut, exploding the air from his lungs. A last minute twist kept her knee from delivering more than a glancing blow to his rock-hard dick. Pain lanced through the pleasure. He shoved her away with a curse.

Dani staggered back, fell to her knees, blood dripping from her mouth. Her shirt was torn from one shoulder. The lace of her bra cupped her heaving breasts the way he wanted to. Pleasure pushed back the pain. Want rebuilt hard in his dick. He stepped toward her—

That's when he saw her eyes. Wide. Shocked. Void of want.

Damn her to hell. She had to want him. He had to see her want him. She would or he would send her to hell.

Every violated cell of her body screamed for her to run, but if she tried, he would be on her. His muscles were bunched to pounce again, his eyes those of an animal about to feed. She would never take him by surprise twice. If he got his hands on her again—

She moved carefully, slowly, so as not to provoke that attack, and wiped her bloody mouth. It was already swelling, the pain so bad it was all she could do not to weep her pain and fear. She wouldn't. She wouldn't give him the satisfaction. She rose, straightening her body bone by bone until her shoulders were back, her chin up. Then she zipped her jacket, shutting the flesh he'd bared from his view.

"I guess," she said so steadily she surprised herself, "those power bars do more for you than they do for me."

He rubbed his mouth, found her blood there and licked it. "Soon, Willow, you'll come to me. You'll open your legs, your heart, your mind—your soul if there is such a thing. You'll beg me to take you. I'll have you when I want, where I want, how I want. You can't fight what will be. If you don't know it now, you will by the time we reach the top."

The towering pines kept them in shadow, blocked what warmth there was from a sky just starting to be touched by the dawn. Pink, yellow, a touch of orange softened the velvet blue. It didn't soften him. He preferred the shadow to the light.

How was she going to escape his shadow except by dying? Dani had always understood why Alice stepped off that cliff in *Last of the Mohicans*, had even admired her courage. Now Dani understood this wasn't about courage.

It was about running out of acceptable options.

"And if I don't want you when I get up there, what then?"

He didn't hesitate. "I'll kill you."

"I—see." Between then and now she was going to have to answer Kelly's question. Did she want to live? Because Spook's offer sure as hell came under the heading of guilt-free passage to the next world. And if she found she did want to live? She had just sort of assumed, based on no evidence at all, that Spook could be reasoned out of his fantasy. Now she knew differently. This wasn't just about living or dying. This was about the survival of self. Dani's self. If she lived, only one person would come down that mountain again. The person she was. Or the person Spook wanted her to be. He didn't intend to lose, but she didn't know how to quit.

She lifted her chin, not enough to be provocative, but enough to show him she wasn't down yet.

"How nice to have a choice."

He looked amused. It was a better look on him than brutal lover, but it wouldn't make her want him. She brushed past, heard him fall in behind her. Still in shadow, they passed out of the protection of the timberline and into a world shrunk down to ground cover. Looming ahead of them she could see Spook's mountain peak waiting like Tolkien's Mount Doom for them to come up and play out the final stand off between the killer and the romance writer.

Too bad the lonesome lawmen couldn't be there, too. Or that last Mohican. She wasn't too proud to admit she could use a little help.

Chapter Twenty-seven

Matt paced back and forth in front of the Long's Peak Ranger Station, his mind turning over the information that arrived after the sun. He could only get the barest information from the tracker still following Hayes and Dani's trail. They had to talk in code to keep Hayes from finding out Dani was leaving clues for them. So far the license plate checks hadn't turned up a likely destination. Action was easy. Kicking ass perfection. Waiting sucked.

He saw Luke come out of the station carrying a sandwich and a cup of coffee. He held both out to Matt. Matt shook his head. "I'm not hungry."

"Eat or I'll shove it down your throat. And sit your ass down. You burn out before we find her, how you gonna help her?"

It was his big brother voice, his big brother face. Matt knew better than to argue with either of them. He took the food and propped himself on a railing. The coffee tasted good, the sandwich okay.

"You should know how to wait by now, bro," Luke said, watching him with his arms crossed, his feet planted.

"I should, shouldn't I?" He looked at the sandwich, wanting to toss it. Luke would just pick it up and shove it down his throat. "Never been any damn good at it."

"We should be experts," Luke said, his eyes going distant. He was quiet for a bit, then he sighed and looked at Matt. "Do you think she's a witch?"

"Who, Dani?"

Luke grinned wryly. "She'll always be Louise to me."

"Why witch?" Matt asked.

"We talked a bit while you were inside paying for the gas," he admitted.

"Is that when you warned her against me?" Matt asked dryly.

Luke chuckled, sat down next to Matt. "Think she's the one who should come with a warning." He hesitated, then said, "We talked about Rosemary. Rosemary for remembrance. That's what she said. That she'd been there and done that."

"She has. Her ex is an asshole."

Luke looked at his brother. "Ex's always are."

"I'll get you for that one later. Why does that make her a witch?"

Luke smiled slightly. "I didn't realize until later, that the shitty part was gone. Only the remembering was left." His mouth twisted. "Is this what the experts call closure?"

Matt winced. "Don't say that too loud or we're gonna find ourselves on Jenny Jones or Oprah."

Luke raised a brow. "You, too?"

"Yeah." Matt drank the last of his coffee and shoved the cup and the rest of the sandwich in a nearby trash can.

"So, is she a witch?"

Matt turned and looked at his brother. "I sure as hell hope so. It's a big, damn park and Hayes is a damn smart whacko. It's gonna take all we can do *and* a little magic to pull this one off."

"Let's go do this." Luke slapped him on the back. Matt nodded and turned to follow him, then stopped, looking at the mountains basking in the morning light. Normally the sight would have put peace in his heart. "What?"

Matt shook his head. "I keep thinking about what the

shrinks have to say about Hayes. That his killing has a religious edge to it."

"What about it?"

"Just that I have a feeling that even if Hayes hadn't grabbed Dani here, he would have brought her here. If I could just figure out why."

"I lift mine eyes until the hills from whence cometh my strength: from whence cometh my help," Luke murmured. "He will not suffer my feet to be moved—"

Matt frowned. "What's that?"

Luke shifted uncomfortably. "Something from the Bible Rosemary used to have me read to her when the pain got . . ."

"Oh." *My strength.* Some kind of religious fixation. Matt knew how he felt when he climbed. Like he was breaking free of everything that pissed him off down on the ground. Like he could see farther, see clearer how things were supposed to be. Was this the key to unlocking Hayes' brain? Could it be that simple? Hayes killed, then he climbed? Matt had wanted to show Dani his mountains. He had been sure when she saw them, she wouldn't be afraid of them. Might Hayes feel the same way?

"Who shall ascend into the hill of the Lord," Luke said. "She liked that one, too. I was glad her room looked out on the mountains."

"I'm glad, too." Matt swung around. "I got an idea."

It was almost eleven and they were just coming up on the Boulderfield. Spook looked at the sky, then back at Dani who had stopped looking at anything but her feet several hours ago. When she didn't need her hands to climb, she rubbed at her temples like she had a headache. For some reason the altitude at this point bothered some people. She seemed to be one of them.

"Let's take a break," he said. If she got altitude sickness, she would never make it to the top. He would have to risk the time, get some water and ibuprofen down her. Without answering him she stopped, dropped her pack and half leaned, half sat on a rock. She hadn't said much since he had kissed her, had withdrawn to someplace deep inside herself. He wanted to punch his way inside. Make her notice him again, make her give him her warmth and love. He needed her spirit broken, needed her to be rebuilt in his image. She couldn't do that if he broke her so completely she couldn't climb. He could bide his time for now. In the end, she would come to him. He would make her.

"Take these," he said. "They'll help your headache."

Dani looked at the tablets. She didn't want to take them. Didn't want him to know he was right, that she did have a headache, but the pain was getting worse, in her head and her mouth. At some point, Spook had given her an ice pack to put on her mouth. It reminded her of Matt, which started a different kind of pain, one located around her heart. Matt thought she was dead. If Spook had his way, by the time Matt found out he was wrong, there would be no trail for him to follow. They would be deep in the nether world that Spook inhabited.

If Spook had his way.

"Take them, Willow. You won't be able to plot your revenge if your head hurts." He sat down beside her. She tensed, but he didn't try to touch her. He was right, so she held out her hand. When she had taken them, he asked, "Are you still mad at me?"

Dani stared straight ahead. He might control the physical part of her, but he would find her spirit harder to force into line.

" 'Sex is only interesting when it releases passion,' " he said. "I'm sorry my passion hurt you."

"No, you're not. You—enjoyed it."

She was right. He ached to do it again. He could still taste her blood, feel the weight of her breast in his hand. "It was Camus that said we live to hurt others, Willow. He wanted to live his life without touching anyone. I don't. I—want to touch you every way a man touches a woman. I've wanted you so long, I can't remember when I didn't want you."

"What about what I want?"

"When this is finished, you'll want what I want."

How different he was from Matt, who had cared more about what she needed than what he wanted. She would take Matt's friendship over Spook's twisted love any day. Though here, where she was probably going to die, she could admit she would have liked more than friendship from Matt. And more than passion. If she wasn't already in love with him, then she had certainly been falling his way when Spook removed her so forcibly from temptation.

For a minute she let herself go back, let her imagination have free rein to write the scene the way she wanted, with the happy ending waiting in the wings. Hard body meeting soft. Want meeting need. Warm, then hot, then peace. Just thinking about him made her go soft, weak with longing—No!

She couldn't think about Matt. It was too dangerous. She couldn't afford to be soft. She had to be hard. As hard as the rock of these mountains that both men loved in their very different ways.

She wouldn't pretend they could have a life together if she could only somehow survive. She had to do this herself. She had to live or die herself. She had depended on others too much. It's what got her into this mess. If she hadn't chatted with Spook—

He would have killed her in the boardinghouse.

She would be dead already, without that time with Matt at his apartment.

There was that irony again.

Spook said in her ear, "You hear it, don't you?"

Dani had actually forgotten he was there. Not smart around a sexually frustrated killer.

"Hear what?"

"The silence. And the music in it."

"Music?"

"The music coming out of the rocks and valleys, the hills are alive with it. Don't tell me you can't hear it."

And here she'd thought they had gone about as weird as they could go. "I'm not damn Julie Andrews, Spook. Only thing I hear is my brain asking me what the hell I'm doing up here with a guy who apparently thinks he is."

As soon as the words left her mouth, Dani knew that calling a killer a girl wasn't the brightest thing she had ever done. It was hard to be bright at this altitude, with the sun reach-out-and-touch-me close. For really thin air, she was having a terrible time pushing her way through it. Getting oxygen out of it, a critical component for intelligent thought, was like pulling teeth out of someone who didn't have any. On top of that, gravity, which she should be getting farther from, seemed to be getting stronger, not weaker. She was having to tap into her energy store on credit, which didn't leave room for real bright. She braced for meltdown, choosing a spot to dig in what was left of the acrylic nails Mama had applied.

He started to rear back then he grinned. "Trust me. Before we get up top, you'll be hearing all kinds of music."

"Oh, joy. Just so I can separate it from my impending hallucinations, what exactly will I hear?" She didn't really care. It was just a reason to keep him talking, so she didn't have to start walking.

"It's not like anything you've ever heard—or will hear again." He sank back, his face lifted toward the peak. A beam of light cut through a cloud and lay across his face, lighting up the lines cutting deep around his eyes and mouth. "When we get to the Keyhole, the pain will be so bad, you'll think you can't bear it."

News flash, mountain boy, I'm there already. She didn't tell him that. She was pissed. She was miserable. She wasn't entirely stupid. To him that would be good news. It meant she was close to breaking.

"When it's the worst, then you'll hear it. Softly at first, like the first quiet notes of a great symphony." He stood up, his hands slack at his sides. "At first you won't realize the pain is leaving. You'll be lost in the music. Slowly, like dying, the music will fade. You'll miss it, the way you miss life. You might even think it took your heart with it. Until you realize your heart isn't gone. It's at peace. Finally, finally at peace."

He looked at her and there was a kind of peace in his eyes. She would rather live in torment her whole life than inhabit his kind of peace. She did feel something close to pity for him. Because of the strange place he lived his life and the pain he lived with. He was so alone. At least she had had friends she could turn to when her pain got too big to handle. Knew with certainty that she did have a soul and when it left her body, it wouldn't belong to Spook.

She would walk away from him, away from the bumps and bruises of this life into the light and join Meggie. She would lay down her burdens, float free of the weight of trying to live. She could fill her empty arms with her baby again. Smooth back her baby hair, smell her sweet scent, kiss that place on her baby neck until she giggled, and sing her the songs Dani's mom had sung to her. Then they'd go see her mom and dad and she could be the little girl again, be the one to get her hurts kissed better and told it was all right now, because mom and dad were here.

There were worse things than dying.

There would be no contest if it didn't mean leaving Matt behind, too. She felt the drag of feelings she didn't want to feel, holding her down, holding her here.

She looked around. Ahead lay a tumble of boulders, behind a barren stretch of mountain shaped by the howling wind that roared out of the sky. It was terrifying, but beautiful. Like life. She had never written a sad ending. Too literary. Had never not finished something she started.

Two choices so clearly laid out for her.

Go up and die. Descend and live.

Funny, it would be the first time down might be harder than facing high.

What was she thinking, Hayes wondered. Her eyes were so deep, so mysterious and sad. He didn't want her to be sad. "What are you thinking about, Willow?"

She looked at him, hesitated, then said slowly, "My little girl. I was thinking about my little girl."

He didn't like that. Why would she be thinking about the child she had made with another man? Would they make a baby together? The idea was unsettling, troubling almost. He didn't want to share her with anyone or anything. But to see her belly swell with his seed, to create instead of destroy? It might be interesting. Could be part of the new pattern. He would have to think about it, decide what they would do later.

"Let's go."

She nodded. Hayes watched her stand up, assessing how hard it was for her, how much energy she had left. It would be close, which gave out first, the path or Willow. Risk was part of the pattern. If she couldn't make it, she wasn't who he thought she was. It was that simple. Though his feelings weren't quite that simple as he watched her start through the Boulderfield.

"Tell me I'm right, bubba," Matt said to Sebastian, after what seemed like an interminable wait for the telephone to ring. He already knew he was right. When the tracker found the campsite at Eugenia Mine, Luke told Matt he was afraid he was right. They had to be sure before they pulled resources off other possible routes.

"It's not good for you, but you are right," Sebastian said. "I ran the plates like you asked and one is definitely a big time bogus. I know Hayes is a son of a bitch, but he does good work."

"I'll buy you a beer when I get back," Matt promised, before cutting the connection.

Luke looked resigned. "Don't tell me. Wild Basin."

Matt didn't answer, just bent over the map again. "Here's what we're going to do—"

"That's crazy," the ranger objected. "She'll never make it up that trail."

Matt looked up and said with calm certainty, "She's never quit anything in her life. If she hasn't shoved Hayes off a cliff, she'll be there sometime around noon. We have to be there before that without tipping Hayes that we know they'll be there. Pay attention, people. Here's how we're gonna play it."

Chapter Twenty-eight

Gravity was winning. Dani was losing. It wouldn't have mattered if gravity wasn't helping Spook. Unfair of it to take sides. As she grew weaker, she could feel him growing stronger, as if her waning strength was feeding his. She could feel his lust grow, too. It beat against her will, adding its demand to the other forces allied against her.

Each foot higher, with only trail mix for fuel, made it harder to launch a rallying cry to rouse flagging body and spirits. A good rally required some unhealthy, wholly satisfying junk food. Spook and his mountain were all there was, possibly all there ever would be.

Though the ear piece for the scanner had stayed in place during most of the hike, Spook hadn't told her what he was hearing and she had been afraid to ask. Afraid that if he thought she still had hope, he would move to take that away, too.

Dani saw Spook look at her and lowered her lashes against the invasion.

She was breaking, Hayes noted with a quick, fierce surge of elation. His body was about to explode from waiting to invade hers. It twisted in his gut like a knife against a neck.

He scanned the sky. They were late, but so far the weather was holding. He heard a flurry of activity on the scanner and turned up the volume.

"—no sign of him or the woman at all—"

So they knew Willow wasn't dead. He had expected that. The chatter was interesting, and just what he needed

339

Willow to listen to. It was time to administer another dose of reality.

He smiled. Did she think he didn't know the hope that lingered so stubbornly in her heart? Did she think there was anything he didn't know, or wouldn't soon know about her? Did she think he didn't know how to take her hope and turn it to his purpose?

"Listen to this." He pulled the headphones plug out and turned up the volume.

There was no warning for Dani. One moment Spook was speaking, the next she could hear Matt talking.

"—yeah, our expert thinks he found a likely vehicle at Glacier Basin. We need to start moving our resources that way, form a loose perimeter, get ready to close up the holes when they're spotted."

His voice was balm to her wounds, manna in her wilderness, a gift she never expected to have. Spook couldn't know how she felt about the lonesome lawman. That was something.

Alice answered Matt. "I just hope our girl knows enough to duck at the right time."

Dani licked her dry lips, as faint hope flared to a wild fire in her veins. Spook's gaze narrowed to an x-ray point and scanned her face. She had to dig deep to turn it back, wasn't sure she would entirely succeeded.

"Glacier Basin?" she asked.

"It's a long way from us. In the other direction."

The scanner crackled again, this voice unfamiliar to Dani. "We got a lost kid in the Arrowhead, Lake Solitude area. Do you think you can spring a couple of choppers and some men for us to use for a search?"

Spook frowned. "Arrowhead is just the other side of Long's Peak."

"I'll take care of it," Matt said.

His voice dropped out of the discussion replaced by a flurry of transmissions between rangers.

"—kid's name is Mary Louise Martin—" A description of the little girl followed, a description that sank slowly into Dani's exhaustion and added fuel to hope. A description that sounded like someone was reading it straight from her book *Don't Call It Loving*. Could it be? Had God answered "sudden and sharp" her prayer?

Damn Spook and his quotes. She shook it away and concentrated on the words, the hope-giving words.

"Mary Louise?" A voice broke in. "I knew a Mary Louise once. She was a Kelly girl that got fired for making a scene at Buns 'n Roses."

"Let's cut the chatter," the first voice snapped. "We got a kid lost, not a stripper."

"Too bad—"

The sound cut off abruptly.

Kelly. Buns 'n Roses. Louise. "A gauntlet with a gift in it," if she could just pick it up without Spook noticing.

"Something interest you about that, Willow?"

Dani looked out of her thoughts, found Spook watching her, his gaze still trying to penetrate her outer hull. Dani held his gaze with steady desperation. If he suspected the transmission was a fake, he might abandon their Rocky Mountain high.

"That girl's parents are sick with worry over their little girl and they're making jokes. It's tacky."

His gaze didn't change. He suspects I got a message, Dani felt, panic tightening its grip on her throat. The effort of holding herself still was almost more than she could bear.

Maybe he could feel hope beating in her heart. The only emotion that could mask hope from him was the one she feared the most: defeat. To show it was to let it in. Not to show it was to lie down with the enemy.

She could see it in his eyes, could see the barely contained lust, the violence threatening to break free of restraint. Only her spiral into defeat would hold him off.

Like Alice's leap off the cliff, Dani let go of her dark thoughts, let them wash over her in a dark wave. Her ghosts, past and present, rode the wave. They were glad to get out. Glad to dance on her hope.

"At least they have a chance."

"A chance?" Hayes stepped closer, a frown putting lines in the bland surface of his face.

"Of getting their daughter back."

Some of the tenseness went out of his body. "You won't have to grieve forever, Willow. Up there, you'll be free."

"Sure." Dani leaned against rock and closed her eyes against his high beam eyes.

"You don't believe me."

What had Matt been trying to tell her? "Why should I believe you?"

"Because it worked for me."

Now there was a yardstick to measure the world against. How could he take himself seriously, let alone expect her to?

"Why did you need all this high altitude healing? Where does your pain come from?" It had better be good. Catastrophic class shit—his whole family wiped out by cholera or a tornado—and that was just for starters.

He remained silent for so long that Dani almost forgot what she had asked. When he did speak, he sounded far away. "From nowhere, from everywhere. I was born—empty—and never filled with anything except pain."

I was born empty? What a whiner. He was more interesting when she thought he was a woman.

"I killed someone who wanted to kill me and I was afraid. I came up here to escape, to end it. And I came down renewed. I had purpose and peace."

Dani yawned. "Killing people isn't exactly a peaceful purpose, Spook."

"Life is 'a vapor, that appeareth for a little time, and then vanisheth away.' If it eases my pain, why shouldn't I be the one to make lives vanish?"

"Whatever happened to—" she yawned again, quit trying to fight her heavy lids open, "—no man is an island?"

"Don't you see, peace has always come at a price. I bought it, I bought you, with death."

Bought from whom? A mountain? Mountains don't buy people. Her thoughts were spinning now, like the merry-go-round the last time she had gone to the county fair with her mom and dad. She had been eleven . . .

"The mountain is hard for a reason. We shape ourselves against it and are renewed . . ."

The lights were spinning faster now. The music, loud and wild, drowned out his voice. The horse was hard between her thighs, but her dad was holding her so she wouldn't fall. She looked at him with a wide smile. No, it wasn't her dad. It was Matt. He was smiling, too. She tried to reach for him—

"Wake-up, Willow."

"Mmmmm. In a minute." She had to find them—

"You can't sleep now. We have to keep going."

"Yeah, sure," she murmured, "keep going in a minute—"

The slap knocked her head back against rock, shattering the merry-go-round and everyone on it. The side of her face stung. She tasted blood again, didn't like it any better than the last time. She touched the spot, looked at the red on her fingers, then looked at him.

"You hit me?" Steven had hit her once, but he had been drunk. He had only done it once. She moved out the next day. Richard, she recalled with a stab of pain, had helped her.

"Yes. I'll kiss it better—"

"I'd rather breathe, thank you."

"Willow—" He reached for her, but she flinched back.

"Don't touch me. Just—" She stood up. "Just leave me alone."

She turned and started up the trail.

"You shouldn't go so fast—"

"Shut up. You wanted me to move. I'm moving."

"Damn it, Willow, you'll burn yourself out. You can't—"

She rounded on him. "Can't. Got to. Do this. Don't do that. You've been calling the shots all the way up this fucking pile of rock. You want me to get to the top. So I'm going to the top."

"You'll make yourself sick—"

"News flash, mountain boy. I'm already sick. Now shut up and let me climb or kill me right now." She glared at him, her heaving chest wrenching the oxygen it needed from the paper-thin air.

"All right. Climb." His lips twitched as he gestured toward the trail.

She wanted to wipe the grin off his face. She wanted to wipe his face off his face. She threw herself at the incline. Almost immediately it blunted her drive. Spook's mountain wasn't generous. It would probably kill her if Spook didn't, but at least it wouldn't screw her first.

The weather started to turn on them just as the choppers dropped Matt and his team on the far side of Long's Peak.

It felt good to be on the move. Damn good. As soon as the chopper pulled away, he heard Luke, who was taking a team up another side, say in his radio, "Great. Looks like the afternoon storm is moving in early today. Gonna make the search for the kid real fun."

The pretext they had crafted to disguise their movements was also going to make it hard to coordinate the movement of the various teams toward the summit.

One of the climbers on Matt's team, an off-duty cop, said, "If he's a climber, he'll turn aside. He could take the old cable route, then head down into Wild Basin."

Matt slung his pack over his shoulder. "Maybe. Maybe not. Depends how bad he wants up there. Doesn't matter. We got it covered. I've even got people at the foot of the Diamond."

"No way he could take a romance writer down that, even by rappelling," the cop scoffed.

"I've learned not to take chances with this bastard. He's got more lives than a cat and more twists than a phone cord. And the romance writer? Well, let's just say she'd surprise you, too. Do not, I repeat, *do not* underestimate this guy. He's better than you'll see in your lifetime. You got any question about him or the safety of the hostage, shoot first, ask questions later. I'll cover your asses if there's heat later. That's a promise."

"Uh, I see something moving along the south side of Lake Solitude. Could be the kid," the voice of Matt's helicopter pilot came over the radio.

Matt lifted the radio. "Thanks, bubba. We'll try to work our way toward her from the south." A confirmed sighting. Now they were getting somewhere. He took his finger off talk and said to his team, "Okay, they're in the Trough. Let's gear up and try to beat them to the summit. Last one there buys the first round of beer tonight."

It was like drowning. If there was oxygen in the atmosphere, she couldn't find it. Dani wanted to quit but she didn't know how. Didn't know why she kept reaching for the next rock ledge. It was what she did. One hand, then the other. Feet to follow. Higher and higher, she inched her way up against the rising howl of the wind. She had to get to the top of Spook's world. Fourteen thousand feet below was her world. She didn't look up or down. She didn't dare. Like the opening salvo in her personal war with Spook, she heard the first clap of thunder overhead.

As exhaustion began to edge past her will, her mind spun slowly off into disjointed fragments, pictures from the past mingling with those from the present.

The look on Matt's face the last time she saw him in his mountain cabin—

Kelly dancing with that stripper to ABBA music—

New Orleans. Damp and warm. *Beignets*. The hum of cicadas and the scent of flowers drifting up from the courtyard of her French Quarter apartment—

Matt in his hallway asking her to come in—

Sunday dinner with Elizabeth and Richard, their babies and hers in highchairs throwing food—

The cold sun shining down on a tiny coffin—

Steven staring into a bottle instead of looking at her—

His fist heading for her face—

Richard's face disappearing in a ball of flame—

Matt holding her as she cried—

Where did the will come from to keep struggling up the side of the mountain, against the wind, against her own fears?

In some deeply buried place, Dani marveled at what she

was doing, even as she put one hand, one foot up on the next ridge of rock.

After a time she climbed into the swirl of dark clouds crowning the peak of the mountain. The pictures in her head swirled, too, with Matt's face at the center. Each time she reached up to him, he dissolved and re-formed higher.

Matt pushed the climbing cam in the crevasse and released the spring load, then tested it to make sure it was secure before looping his rope through it.

"Taking in," he called to his climbing partner, a guy named Malloy. He heard a faint, "Climbing," from below that the wind tried to blow away. Hayes and Dani would be close to the summit, too. Their last sighting before they disappeared in cloud cover, had them still climbing toward the Home Stretch despite the storm moving in. The wind was already making their climb more dangerous and difficult. When the rain came, it would be harder still. He blessed his training in search and rescue. Was glad the men joining him in this race against Hayes and the storm knew the mountain and were used to pitting their lives against it.

The wild passion in the building storm beat against detachment and cool thought, but Matt fought it back, pushing out thoughts of Dani up there with Hayes and a storm moving in. Instead he put Hayes in his mental crosshairs and started the next pitch.

The ground leveled out abruptly. Dani wasn't ready and sprawled onto the rocky surface, gasping for air that still wasn't there. Never would be there.

"You did it." Spook had to yell to be heard above the building wind. His eyes were wild, his face lit from within. The storm had cut off the sun and sky above, cut off the ground below, leaving only the mountain top.

Leaving her there alone with a wild man.

The wind beat against her as if it longed to throw her back down for having the temerity to climb up. Hair whipped her face in tiny, stinging lashes. Terror whipped her insides, but distantly, as if Spook had drugged her again.

"Can we go now?"

He shrugged off his pack, then helped her off with hers. "The storm is almost on us."

Almost? The guy had a serious problem with reality.

"We'll have to hurry."

Hurry? He was going to screw her brains out in a hurry? He must be a virgin. Incredibly, she felt the urge to giggle. Luckily, when she opened her mouth to do it, the wind rushed down her throat and choked her instead.

The air around them crackled and snapped like hyperactive Rice Crispies, making the hair on her arms stand up in between the brief moments of calm between fierce gusts of wind. Above her the clouds crashed together, sending the first drops of moisture smashing into her face like pellets from a gun.

Spook grabbed her arm and dragged her against wind and will to the center, the place where all the forces of the storm seemed poised to strike.

The rain picked up its tempo. The lightning flashes came with the thunder on their heels. Spook grabbed her shoulders, his face lit from within by fanaticism and without by lightning.

"It's time!" He had to shout to be heard above the wind.

"You're kidding, right?" He wouldn't, would he? No one could be that nuts.

Her hair soaked up as much water as it could hold, then

sent the overflow cascading down her face. Her clothes were soaked, her teeth chattered with cold and fright. The ground where she stood was soaked, too. If he really was looking for the ultimate boink, he had chosen a hell of a place for it.

He grabbed handfuls of her hair and yanked her against him. The bulge against her leg indicated he did indeed mean to do the deed here and now. If she had any lingering doubts he was seriously mental, he was putting them all to rest.

Behind him she saw a jagged flash of lightning sizzle through the rain and strike the next peak over from them.

"Holy shit! We're gonna get toasted. Spook!" She tried to twist free of his iron grip. "This isn't a good time! I have a headache! I have syphilis. AIDS. I have AIDS!"

For an answer he crushed his mouth on hers, his hands moving roughly over her body, grabbing, kneading. He tried to push tongue and teeth into her mouth, but she fought him.

His passion for her beat against her passion to resist. His was fueled by madness and the charged storm. Hers got a boost from adrenaline.

She twisted her mouth free. In a burst of lightning she saw his eyes. It was going to take more than elbows and knees to stop him this time.

Matt tried to call to Malloy, but the wind took his words as soon as they left his mouth, then brought them back with a roar as it tried to tear him from the rock face. He rode out the gust with his toes and fingernails, then reached up, feeling for the next crack. In a flash of lightning, he saw the rim. He was there. He looked cautiously over the edge, but it was too dark to see anything. He topped the rise and crouched behind a boulder, anchoring himself to belay for Malloy.

He had to lean over nothing to give him the signal to start. A grim-faced Malloy gave him a thumbs-up sign, then started his turn at the difficult pitch. Malloy was only halfway up it when Matt heard Dani cry out.

"NO!" What to do came naturally from the self-defense class she had taken with Kelly. "NO!"

The storm provided the perfect punctuation.

Spook's grasp loosened. Dani broke free. Spook's body was already bunching for round two.

She needed a flash of brilliance or a miracle from God.

The devil looked out from Spook's eyes. "What's it going to be Willow? Do I fuck you and let you live? Or fuck you then kill you? Will you live with me forever or die with my dick in you?"

It was only now, when she knew she was going to die, that Dani realized how very much she wanted to live.

It didn't matter that life hurt. It didn't matter that she mourned her baby every day and every night. It didn't matter that she loved Matt and he didn't love her. In sickness and in health, for richer or poorer, in sorrow and in joy, in all ways and all things, she wanted to live.

She wanted to see the sun rise and set. She wanted to turn the ideas in her head into books that would make her readers laugh and weep for people that didn't exist. She wanted to go to Kelly's hunky dentist and get her teeth cleaned, a cavity filled.

She didn't have to have a happy ending, as long as she didn't get an ending.

She wanted to live.

She was going to die.

If she was lucky, she would die before he got what he wanted.

" 'If thou must love me, let it be for naught, except for love's sake only,' " she shouted above the storm, trying one last time to reach the sane part in him.

For a moment, she thought she had done it.

He smiled tenderly, the lust in his eyes replaced by amusement. "Elizabeth Barrett Browning. You've learned much since we met, Willow. What about her *Sonnets from the Portuguese*? 'Guess now who holds thee?—Death, I said, but there the silver answer rang . . . Not Death, but Love.' Not death but love. I love you, Willow. Do you love me?"

He reached for her. She stepped back. The hand reaching for her curled into a fist. His eyes hardened.

"Love chooses it's own path. Don't you see? I can't. Maybe I can't love anymore. Maybe Steven killed the love I had left. I just know, I can't love you. I can't."

"You didn't try hard enough!"

The sky flashed again. Was that a movement she saw over by the edge? She saw Spook's eyes narrow and quickly yelled, "No, I didn't try. I didn't want to try! I didn't want to love you!"

That got his attention. "Why? Why didn't you want to love me?" He grabbed her arm, roughly pulling her against him, his face thrust into hers.

She had his whole attention and meant to keep it.

"Duh. You kill people!" His grip on her arm tightened until she almost cried out. "You don't love me! You don't know how to love! You only know how to lust. To want. To take. To hurt! That isn't love—"

"Shut up!" His rage found expression in the back of his hand against her face. She would have been knocked on her butt if he hadn't kept his grip on her arm. As it was, she saw stars wheel over his head.

The third time he had hit her. They say it's the charm. Dani didn't know about charms. She did know those wheeling stars had turned red.

"No! You can't make me!" Somehow she jerked her arm free. Maybe he let her go. He looked like he merged with his mountain, his face turning to cold, hard rock. "You didn't break me, Spook. You or your stupid mountain."

"Didn't I?" His eyes narrowed to knife points. "Then I'll send you to hell, you bitch!"

Lightning lit them up again. Now he held a gun. Behind him, near the edge, Matt was still tethered to his climbing gear, rope trailing from him over the cliff edge, trying to rip his gun clear of the holster.

"Hold it, Hayes!" His gun wasn't clear.

Hayes whirled, his gun already lining up on Matt.

"No!" Dani threw herself on his gun arm just as he fired. He shook her off with embarrassing ease. She rolled until she hit a boulder. Still dizzy from the blow, she scrambled around it and crouched in its shelter.

Spook had vanished into the raging dark, his silhouette lost against the darker rise of tumbled boulders.

"Where are you, Willow?"

Above them, the sky gathered itself for another electric discharge. Dani could feel it in the air, in the rising of the hair on her body. Something brushed past her shoulder. She thought it was Spook and flinched back. The rain sizzled. For an instant she saw Spook crouched a few feet away. Then light exploded between them, throwing her backwards.

"Son of a bitch!" Matt felt the coming discharge as Malloy started to scramble onto the ridge next to him. He turned, not stopping to think his thanks he hadn't had time to take his rigging off. There was only time to act. He shoved Malloy back, then threw himself with him, falling over the edge just before a shaft of light split the ground like the wrath of God.

He hit his head against a rock outcrop and saw stars against the dark clouds as he dangled from his ropes.

Matt shook his head to clear stars and water from his eyes, then grabbed Malloy.

"What did you see?"

"Didn't see jack shit." Blood ran down from a gash on his temple.

"Damn." Matt reached up. He had to get back up top before Hayes killed Dani.

Dani opened her eyes, not sure how long she had been out or even if she'd been out. Her sense of direction was gone. She didn't know where Matt and Spook were in this top-of-the-world hell. Her brain was saying, go!

She didn't stop to argue with it. If Matt was out there, maybe there were others. All she had to do was get far enough from Spook and close enough to them. Instead of sanctuary, Dani found the steep pitch of the Home Stretch.

Behind her she heard Spook cry out. He sounded close, closer than the shouts that answered him. The incline was steeper than the devil's nose, but it was away from Spook. Without stopping to think, she crawled over the edge.

The summit was the obstacle course from hell when Matt topped the rise again. Black as night, with pale figures darting here and there, he didn't dare shoot at one for fear it would be one of his men or Dani. Hayes, on the other hand, could shoot at anybody. Everyone was his enemy.

Keeping low and using the tumbled boulders, Matt started working his way across the top. The storm was moving away. A shaft of lightning hit the next peak over, illuminating theirs. He saw someone drop down the Home Stretch.

"Damn." He still didn't dare use the radio to mark positions. Might as well put a big arrow over his guys' heads if he did. He pulled it out, thought for a moment, then said, "Luke?"

"Glad to hear you're still with us, little brother. Didn't fancy facing mom and trying to explain all this."

"Any idea where our boy is?" And our girl, he mentally added.

"I saw someone heading home just a minute ago."

"Me too. What about—Louis?" Would Luke recognize this shortened version of Louise and realize what he was asking?

"I think he went down first."

"Shit." He rubbed his face. "Any idea how close the home-front boys are?"

"No," Luke's radio crackled with static, "but I don't think they're close enough to be of much use. At least the storm's bailing on us. It's gonna get real light up here soon. I say we get the hell out of Dodge now."

"Sounds good to me. I'll meet you at the exiting end of town." Matt stowed his radio, checked his gun, then rose and headed across the exposed top at a jog. Behind him, the first crack of sunlight broke through the dark clouds.

Chapter Twenty-nine

Dani had always been lost in rock and rain. Her other life was a dream. This was reality. She was vaguely glad she couldn't see anything as she scrambled her way back down the trail she had so laboriously climbed such a short time before.

Gradually the rain began to ease, the sky get lighter. Above she heard the scrape of feet against rock and knew, the way she had always known, that Spook was almost on her again.

Panic couldn't be resisted. Dani fled into the Ledges, a maze of twists and turns with no way out. She looked up, then down. In her other lifetime, this kind of up scared her. Now it was her only reality. Was that Keyhole she could see up there? Had she climbed down that far? She couldn't re-member. It looked right and Spook was getting closer. She reached up, found a foot-hold. In a few moments, she had reached the ridge, scrambled over it—

Instead of the trail, she found a slope to nowhere.

This wasn't the right place, was it?

It had to be. She scrambled down. Found an unequivocal dead-end. Now what?

As she hesitated, the now distant storm threw one last vi-olent salvo, then broke against the peaks and let the after-noon sun pierce its clouds. Her spirits rose. It was a good omen. Maybe she would get her happy ending—

Above her, she heard a rattle of stones. She looked up.

Spook stood at the gateway to freedom, looking down at her.

★ ★ ★ ★ ★

Matt faced Luke, frustration spiking in his veins. "Where the hell could they be? This damn mountain isn't that big!"

Luke looked around. "It's possible she headed for the False Keyhole."

Matt nodded. "I'll check it out. Why don't you head down to the Keyhole, see if you see them there. One of us spots them first, just radio it's a bust."

"Right." He started down. Matt looked up. The sky was clearing fast. He lifted his radio, "Bring in the birds, Riggs. I need some eyes up here."

He waited for Riggs to acknowledge the request, then started up the rock toward the False Keyhole, his mind blanked clear of everything but the hunt.

There was nowhere left to go, very little left to do, Dani realized. No energy left to think of something. Fatalistic took over from flight-or-fight. She had fought the good fight. It was time for a little dignity.

Her clothes were soaked. The wind had eased, but not enough. She wrapped her arms around her middle and leaned against the rock face so she wouldn't shiver herself off her precarious perch. No sense doing the job for him.

She didn't even flinch when, with a small flurry of stones, Spook dropped down on the ledge next to her.

"Willow."

The killer was still in his eyes. She didn't care. "I'm not Willow. I'm Dani. Just—Dani."

He stopped, a momentary confusion altering the cold blankness of his face into something more normal. Or maybe she just wanted to believe it had.

"Dani?"

"Yes. Dani." Water ran down her face from her hair, mercifully blurring her vision. Her teeth chattered with the cold. "Not Willow. Not Spook. Just Dani and Jonathan. Or do they call you Jon?"

He frowned. "Jon. Only my mother called me that."

"Oh?" Was that good or bad? Did she care?

Water poured from him, too, but it didn't seem to bother him. He frowned. "You're soaked. You should've put on your rain gear."

"Yeah." She rubbed her upper arms and stamped her feet. This was way weird, but she didn't fight the compulsion to respond to the strange script. "I should have."

"It was in your pack."

"I—left it up there."

"I tried to take care of you." Frustration pulled down his features. "Why are you doing this? I was only doing what was right for us."

It didn't matter if she pissed him off now, so she didn't pull her punches. "This had nothing to do with right. It was all about what you want. It's called being selfish, which can't make anyone happy. Didn't your mother ever teach you this? Or did you kill her, too?"

He looked at her. "My mother still lives in Connecticut. In the suburbs."

"Connecticut?" Dani felt an insane urge to laugh. "Was she a liberal?"

He looked sulky. "Actually, she was. What of it?"

"I'll bet she didn't spank you when you were a poor, empty kid." Dani sighed in frustration. "You're such a jerk. Your problem wasn't too much suffering. It's not suffering enough."

"Who are you to lecture me? You can't even decide if you want to live or die!"

"As usual, you know absolutely nothing about me. It just

so happens I don't want to die, okay?" Dani glared at him. Water ran into her eyes. She pushed her dripping hair back and saw blood running down her wrist.

"You're bleeding."

"Yes." Anger faded, leaving something that felt like peace. Had Spook's mountain delivered what he had promised?

"What do you want?"

Dani saw both the killer and the friend fighting for supremacy in Spook's eyes. "Remember that guy you quoted once, the one who said, 'We can believe what we choose. We are answerable for what we choose to believe?' "

"Newman," Spook said, absently. "Cardinal Newman." He nodded thoughtfully. "So you can't—choose to believe what I believe—even if it means you'll die?"

She shook her head, then amazingly, she smiled. "Can you really see me worshiping a fourteen-thousand-foot mountain?"

His answering smile was rueful. "No. I guess I can't." His face turned sad. "I'll miss you. You—lit up my nights."

No way to know if he just passed a death sentence—or given her reprieve. She pressed back against rock and made herself look down. At her feet the ledge sloped away to a really nasty fall. She closed her eyes. Be the final irony of her acrophobic life if she ended it by falling to her death.

"What's it going to be, Jon? Do you just push me or am I supposed to jump *a la Last of the Mohicans*?"

"You've got guts, Willow."

Unless he splattered them across a couple of feet of rock. She braced, digging deep for her last bit of courage, then looked at him.

"My guts want to go home."

Spook took the two steps to her side.

Now she could smell him, earthy and slightly sour. Could feel the heat from his body and see the steam rising from his wet clothes. Saw his eyes clearly reflect his battle for her life. Time slowed until she could feel the tick of each second passing.

"It would have been—amazing."

"Only if we were both different."

"Even all beat up you're beautiful."

Her smile wavered at the edges. "You are nuts."

He laughed. "Yeah. I guess I am—"

Together they teetered on the knife edge of his madness, then his eyes shifted. In them she saw her death.

He wasn't going to let her go.

Matt reached the ridge and crouched behind a boulder. He could hear voices, but he couldn't see them without giving away his presence. He lifted his radio and whispered the signal, heard Luke respond. Swiftly Matt checked his gun clip and loaded a bullet in the chamber with a quiet snap. There probably wouldn't be time to take a look-see, assess the situation. Down there was a ledge, a deadly fall and a madman who didn't like to lose.

When he showed himself, he would have the space of a heartbeat to find Hayes and act. He did a mental three-count, then stood up.

First he saw Dani. Then Hayes standing too close to her for a clean shot. Hayes shifted his weight toward the edge. Matt pulled the trigger.

Hayes leaned into gravity. His hand gripped her arm.

Dani heard the flat crack of gunfire, the shots so close she wasn't sure there had been more than one or just an echo.

Spook flinched once, then again. His eyes widened, then

turned dreamy. He tried to speak. Instead of words, blood bubbled out his mouth and dribbled down his chin.

He swayed, grabbed her arm as if to steady himself. It was instinct to try to help. Then he started to pull her toward the edge. He was dying.

He meant her to die, too.

Now she fought him, clawing with hands and teeth to get away as life surged back in her heart.

His grip on her tightened.

She tried to brace herself.

There was no purchase on the wet rock. Nothing to grab as he arched out over empty space, taking her with him. A last, desperate wrench broke Spook's hold. She fell to her knees far out on the curving rock.

Maybe gravity would be satisfied with Spook.

It wasn't. Even as hope made a brief appearance, gravity's hungry hold reached up to pull her forward as ruthlessly as if Spook still held her. She slid slowly forward, perfectly positioned to see Spook fall first.

At first he followed the line of the rock, his body a rag doll. Then he arched clear, falling in a graceful somersault that ended abruptly against rock. On his back against the mountain he worshipped, Dani saw his empty eyes stare up at her in a mute invitation to join him.

She wanted to refuse. Gravity wanted her to accept. She slid forward, faster now, clawing at the rock face, leaving bloody, fruitless trails against stone. An incoherent prayer whispered out her lips as she reached the point of no return.

Matt was over the ridge before Dani broke free of Hayes. Too far away to help her as she slid down the sloping rock, he leapt onto the rock ledge, went down on his stomach. His hand just missed her foot.

"Son of a bitch!" He tore the coiled rope from his

shoulder, all the while knowing it was useless. Hayes had lost his life, but won the final toss. He had finished what he started.

I'm going to die, Dani thought, surprised even after all that had happened. The thought splintered as a stray bit of sun caught on something sticking out of the rock.

A last, desperate stretch and her hand closed round it.

She felt the shock in her joints as her body slid past and down, then stopped with a jerk that almost broke her grip when she slammed into rock.

She wasn't falling. She wasn't dead. Not yet. Blood ran down her arm, warm and slick. The piton turned slick with it. And she was so tired.

Matt couldn't believe it when Dani stopped falling. How the hell had she managed to grab that old piton left in the rock years ago? The wave of relief left him lightheaded. He rubbed his face, then found something to tie the rope around. A few quick turns and he was back on his stomach looking down. He dug deep for calm control, then called her name.

She didn't move, didn't look up.

If he startled her, she might fall, but she needed to know he was here, that help was at hand.

"Dani!" He saw her body jerk. She didn't fall. Her head slowly tilted back until he could see her face. She looked like she had been in a street fight. Her mouth was bruised and swollen. A cut on her forehead bled sluggishly. Her eyes were wide and empty of recognition. "It's Matt."

Matt? She blinked. The lonesome lawman?

"What the hell you doing down there?"

It hurt when she smiled up at him. "Oh—" her grin wavered on both sides, "just hanging around."

"How 'bout I join you?"

"If you don't," she tried to get a better grip on the piton, "I'm gonna ask Luke to kick your ass."

Matt laughed, kicked the rope over the edge, and started rappelling down to her.

He had better hurry. Her arms were bunching with the strain of holding on. This wasn't over yet.

In a rush he dropped the last few feet, jerked back on his brake rope when he was slightly below her. She couldn't stop her hand from opening—

She cried out. Cried again when his hand closed round hers with punishing force.

Matt took the full force of her falling weight in his shoulder. They spun in a circle, first scraping, then smacking into the rock face. Matt tried to cushion Dani, but couldn't with one hand on the brake and the other holding Dani's blood-slick hand.

She grabbed his coat sleeve, twisted her hand around it. "We're going to die, aren't we?"

"Hell, no. Can you grab my legs, or even better, my belt?"

"I'd have to let go."

"I won't let you go. Brace yourself—"

They hit rock again. She let go of his sleeve, missed the first time, caught the edge of his pocket the second time.

"Good girl. Can you wrap your legs around mine?"

Dani laughed breathlessly. "This is hardly the time for that."

Matt's laugh was just as breathless. "I can't do this forever."

"I think—" Dani hooked one leg around his. "—it's very mature of you to admit that."

Matt chuckled. He could now that the strain on his shoulders eased. "I'm going spank your ass when we get out of this. Then I'm gonna prove I can."

"Promises, promises."

"I want you to get up where you can put your arms around my neck. Use my shoes."

"Shoes. Right."

Dani grabbed his belt, got one foot under her. Her weight came down on one foot, then his other foot. Her body scraped along his. Dangling over rock didn't slow his body's response one iota. He hoped to hell she wouldn't notice.

Her arms slid around his neck. She wrapped her legs around his middle, settling right where he didn't want her to. Okay, he would think the problem away.

It was hard to think with her face inches from his. She looked like hell. She felt like heaven.

"Hi."

"Hi." He cleared the husky out of his voice and added, "What are you going to do for your next trick?"

A smile broke across her face like the sun on his mountain. Before she answered, Luke dropped onto the ledge above them. They both looked up. He grinned.

"Gravity's a bitch, ain't it, Louise?"

"No." She laughed, a full throaty sound that worsened his problem. "Gravity's a guy."

Luke looked severe. "I think we've just been insulted, little brother." He looked over his shoulder. "The cavalry's arrived. How about we get you up here?"

Dani spun in a slow circle in Matt's arms. It was over.

The sun was back for a last hurrah before setting. Somewhere some birds were probably singing. She felt like singing. And laughing out loud. She was hanging by a rope halfway between earth and sky, and she'd never felt more at home.

The only thing that would make it better was Matt kissing her. Her kissing him back. His mouth, his hands erasing the memory of Spook's touch from her mind and body.

She stared into his eyes, knew he was thinking along the same lines and realized in one way she was almost as bad as Spook. If she could just figure out how, she would have been more than happy to help him do something about the desire humming between them.

When someone began pulling them up, the sun dimmed a little. It dimmed a little more when Matt's eyes turned professional and detached. Hands reached out to help her onto the ledge. She didn't want to leave the safety of his arms, but she did. She could still do hard things. Her poor lungs still weren't getting enough oxygen to satisfy and there wasn't a part of her body that didn't hurt, but with or without Matt, she was, she realized with something of a shock, glad to be alive.

Chapter Thirty

November 1, All Saints' Day, New Orleans

The miniature city of the dead was quiet as the morning sun crept across dew-damp grass and carved stone toward the Hastings's family crypt. Dani put a bouquet of daisies in the fixed vase on one side of the steps, then turned and traced her daughter's name where it was carved into the stone above Richard's name.

There were a few other family members filtering into the cemetery to pay their respects, but none were close by.

Dani slid her capacious purse off her shoulder and sat on steps still cool from the November night. In a few minutes the sun found her. She smiled wryly. She and the sunrise were still greeting each other, despite the seventy times she'd tried to miss it since she left the mountains and Matt's mile high city.

She was back in her apartment, back in her life.

Too bad she wasn't the same person. She didn't fit it anymore, her only hope that she would grow back into it in time.

She opened her purse and found the bag of M&M's and soda she had tucked inside, opened both and relaxed against the slowly warming stone, her cheek against her daughter's name. "I'm trying to do better this time, Meggie. I'm trying to live my life, not just trying not to break."

She put one M&M in the vase, one in her mouth.

"Liz is still pretending I don't exist. I miss her, but I'm

okay with it. Don't feel too bad about your dad. A short stint in jail is good for him."

She added some Diet Dr. Pepper to the vase. "I shouldn't let you drink this stuff, but you're ten now, so you can have a taste." She took a drink.

"Did I tell you that my book is going to be a Valentine release? The cover is awash with hearts and ribbons, but I'm trying not to notice. At least there aren't any breasts larger than mine pressed against a manly chest. They're in the step-back cover. That's right, a step-back cover. I've hit the big time. They're even talking about releasing my next book in hard cover. That's the one I just finished. Pat thinks it could make the NYT list." Dani smiled. "Kelly says if I make the list before her, she's going to have her dentist fill my tooth without Novocain. That's right, I have a cavity. At my age. You're lucky you don't have to worry about them." Dani saw movement among the crypts and her smile widened. "Speak of the devil, here she comes."

Kelly picked her way to Dani. "I thought I'd find you here. Trying to avoid the relatives from hell, are we?"

Dani moved over. "Watch your language in front of my kid."

When Kelly was seated, Dani offered her the bag of candy. They both munched quietly for a bit, then Dani said, "Isn't today your anniversary?"

Kelly smiled. "Three years. I'm telling you, Dani, dentists are the best kept secret of the modern world."

"It makes sense, I mean the guy is used to operating in small spaces—"

Kelly's smile turned wicked. "He operates like a pro, believe me. If he treats me any better, I might have to give up my beyond bitch status." She helped herself to a drink of Dani's soda, then asked, "Do you still miss him?"

Dani didn't look at her. She stared at the tomb across the path. Saw Matt's face the way it was when they were hanging in space. "Yeah. Silly isn't it?"

"You should have jumped his bones. At least you'd have some memories to keep yourself warm during our one cold night a year."

Dani smiled. "I have a good imagination. I'll make up some memories." Dani's smile faded. "I'm supposed to do a Valentine's tour. Six cities in seven days."

Kelly took the soda can. "Any city in particular?"

"The last one is Denver. I told them I didn't think I could do it and got a homily on getting back on the horse." She looked at Kelly. "I thought it was the hero that was supposed to ride the horse?"

"It's all this politically correct crap. It's messed everything up." Kelly hesitated, "So, are you going?"

"If I don't, they'll think I'm a wuss. If I do—"

"Matt will think you're chasing him."

Dani sighed. "Yeah. Maybe by February I'll be over him?"

"Yeah, and maybe all the world's men will figure out how to make us happy." Kelly twisted to look at Dani. "Have you ever thought about just telling the guy how you feel? It works in our books."

"I did tell him—kind of."

"So go beyond kind of."

Dani shook her head. "Love isn't about what you want— or it isn't love. I think he loves me, but is afraid of hurting me, of not being what I need. It's sweet, but if he can't figure out that as hard as it is to make being together work, it's still better than *not* being together. If he won't ask me to be part of his life, if he doesn't know I would in a heartbeat and that I want to be with him more than I want to be at sea level, then he isn't right for me."

Kelly sipped some soda and handed it back. "Too bad we can't mix a little more reality into our fictional men and a little more fiction into our real men."

Dani dumped out the last of the candy, offering part to Kelly. "Yeah, too bad."

Kelly chewed quietly. "What are you gonna wear in Denver?"

Dani smiled. "Something red."

"Good choice. If you can't get him to bite the big one with you, you ought to make him regret it for as long as he lives."

Dani looked at Kelly. "That's the plan."

January. Denver, Colorado.

It was the start of a new day, but the end of a long, hard night for Matt. He should have headed home, but he didn't. He didn't like climbing the stairs to his apartment. He didn't like looking at the window seat at the end of his hall and remembering Dani sitting there. He didn't like opening the door and walking down the hall to where she'd danced wearing his robe, hated walking into the bedroom where she had slept in his bed. He couldn't escape her in the mountains or in the cabin that had been his refuge. She'd even stopped by the office before she left, bearing chocolate chips cookies and thanks for everyone who helped her—leaving the fresh scent of coconut behind.

She was everywhere he went.

She was in New Orleans, he reminded himself, where she wanted to be. *Get me home,* she'd asked him with words and with her big green eyes. He had booked her flight and driven her to the airport. Watched her walk away from him, endured her last look back. He had kept his promise, though it had been a near miss. He still broke out in a sweat thinking about Hayes trying to take her with him to the rocks. Night after night, in his dreams, he tried to change the outcome. Night after night it played out the same. He had to watch her slide away from him. Then he had to hold her just long enough to get addicted to the feel of her in his arms and against his body.

And every time she slid away from him, every time she walked onto that plane, his heart followed, no matter how hard he tried to keep it in his chest.

It didn't make sense. He had known her one week, seven damn days plus one to say good-bye. Spent just over two days of that time face to face with her. She didn't belong to him. She didn't belong here. She was sea level. He wasn't.

So why couldn't he forget how it felt to spin at the end of a rope with her in his arms? Why had she felt so right when they were so wrong for each other?

He tossed his briefcase on his desk, dropped in his chair and looked at the pile of papers waiting his attention, saw them stretching out into a future turned bleak by a damn romance writer with a smart mouth and a sexy figure.

"Matt, what are you doing here?" Alice stopped in front of his desk, her brows bracketing the surprise in her eyes.

"My job." He grabbed a handful of paper, stared at it without seeing a word.

Alice shrugged. "Just thought you'd be catching up on your Zs. Heard you guys had a rough night."

He didn't look at her. She might notice how bloodshot his eyes were. "Got some stuff to do first. What the hell is this?" He shoved the papers at her.

Alice looked at them, turned them right side up and handed them back. "Try it now."

"Sorry," he muttered.

"No problem." She started to turn away, then stopped. "Do you remember Dani Gwynne?"

Did he?

He forced himself to look up and say casually, "Uh, yeah. The romance writer, right?"

"That's right." Her voice was laced with irony.

The look in her eyes made him want to shift in his chair and look away. His pride wouldn't let him do either one. Did she suspect the romance writer had almost made a believer out of him? He looked down at the sheets in his hand. "What about her?"

"I'm on her Christmas card list—"

The hell she was. Why wasn't he? He'd only saved her life.

"—just got this flyer from her. She's coming to Denver for a book signing."

She was coming back. She'd be here. Not New Orleans. Here. He could see her again. Yeah, and an alcoholic could walk into a bar. Didn't make it good for him.

"On Valentine's Day." She held out the pink sheet. Matt eyed it for a moment before accepting it. Was it his imagination that made it smell like coconut? Too many hearts and flowers mixed in with the copy. The book was called *One Near One*. Under it was a quote by Robert Browning: "If two lives join, there is oft a scar. They are one and one . . . One near one is too far."

In the margin next to the cover, she'd scrawled, "My publicist thinks I need to get back on this particular horse or be doomed to forever live in fear of your Mile High City. She obviously doesn't know her Kafka. 'My "fear" . . . is my substance, and probably the best part of me.' But she's the one who calls the tune, so the worst part of me is coming. Can we do lunch or cookies while I'm there?"

She had signed her name and inked in an emoticon grin. Her handwriting was like her, nearly indecipherable.

Sebastian came up and read the flyer over his shoulder. "Cool. Can I come, too?"

Henry, seated at his desk, looked up. "To what?"

Sebastian explained. Henry wanted to go, too. So did Riggs. Matt couldn't believe it. Dani brings them a box of cookies, smiles and thanks them, and they all forget how much trouble she was. Maybe Luke was right. Maybe she was a witch.

Less than six weeks until her broom landed here. Less than six weeks to figure out how not to care.

Easy. If you routinely did the impossible.

Valentines Day. Denver, Colorado

Dani wasn't the only author signing books in six cities. Her publisher was calling them the Valentine's Six Pack. By some strange twist of fate, she was the only one who chose to wear red, the others having opted for virginal white.

It was harder than she expected to land in the Mile High, to walk off the plane without hoping he'd be there waiting. Happy endings paid her bills. It was a good thing her finances didn't depend on the lonesome lawman. He wasn't there. Carolyn was.

"You don't look like you've been through hell," she had said with a broad smile after they had hugged.

"If you could see under the makeup you wouldn't say that," Dani had answered. There was a radio interview. She became an actress again as she assured the citizens of the city that she didn't hold them responsible for Spook's rampage and actually loved their city. When asked how she researched her sex scenes, she smiled and said, "Very carefully."

During the drive to the mall Dani played the part of a woman who didn't give a damn, catching up with an old girlfriend. Alice met her inside. She lunched with her and all the guys—minus one—still acting at a level worthy of an Oscar nomination.

Alice walked with her to the bookstore, both of them chuckling over how quickly the men sheared off, after giving Alice money to buy books for their wives and sweethearts.

She was running out of time to ask about Matt. Decided she wouldn't, her mother always used to tell her not to pick at wounds or they wouldn't heal, but the words came out anyway. "So, how's Matt and Luke?"

She endured Alice's glance with composure, but was glad when it was over.

"I hear Luke's dating someone. I haven't seen Matt today, but he's fine, too. I think he took some comp time so they could go climbing. A couple of real romantics."

Dani smiled, shook her head ruefully over the foibles of the male sex, and in her head plotted his castration. Couldn't even face her. The coward. She earned two Oscars signing and smiling, while internally cursing the cooling off period that kept her from buying a gun. She looked up to hand a woman her signed book and there he was.

Standing smack in the middle of a bevy of romantic women, holding a heart-shaped box of chocolates, a bottle of coconut perfume and a single red rose.

With a face like the storm on the mountain.

Their gazes connected like thunder on that mountain.

Dani rose to her feet, her mouth curving in a smile edged with evil. This was going to be good.

It was the hardest walk of Matt's life. Harder than walking into a den of Uzi-toting drug dealers. There were women everywhere he looked, all wearing that knowing look

that made him want to swear or worse. He wasn't a romantic guy. Didn't want to be a romantic guy. If he hadn't
finished her book, he probably would have just waited until
she was done signing and said something normal like,
"Want some dinner?"

If he hadn't read that damn book. Put a lot of pressure
on a guy to keep up with a hero straight out of a romance
writer's brain. As far as his could tell, the only thing he had
in common with the guy was that they were both male.

And they were both in love.

It still made him wince to admit it. He had given up
trying to get over it. It was an incurable disease. Probably
terminal, too. He'd almost bought a damn book of love
poems. Since he couldn't get over it, he might as well offset
the misery with some of the benefits.

He could still hear her voice on the radio saying she researched her sex scenes very carefully. She looked up and
saw him, her eyes widening into pleasure, sucking the air
right out of his lungs. She stood up and his heart stopped
beating, too. Her dress, so red it practically made his eyes
bleed to look at her, hugged her body everywhere he had
fantasized about touching her.

Her mouth, the mouth he'd dreamed about for six, damn
long months, widened into a smile that parted the waiting
women like the Red Sea. Made it easy to walk toward her.

When only the table separated them, Dani put her hands
on her hips. "Well, well. If it isn't the lonesome lawman."

His throat went dry with wanting her. He dumped the
crap he had bought on the table. Shoved the whole thing
aside, vaguely aware romance writers were scattering like
startled white chickens. He stepped in close, let his hands
settle on her shoulders. The relief of finally touching her almost took out his knees. He slid his arms around, pulled her

in that last little space that separated them. Her head tipped back so he could see all of her face.

He took a minute to compare memory with reality. Reality was better. All the things he had rehearsed, liberally plagiarizing from her book, went right out of his head. All he could remember was that he loved her. He wanted to marry her more than he wanted to live. He wanted to make a life and babies with her. Wanted to grow old with her. He opened his mouth to say it, but all that came out was, "I give up."

The sighs of thirty romantics ruffled Dani's hair. She had written, then rewritten this scene every day and night since she left him standing in the airport. She'd never written it like this. This was real. Matt was real. She could see in his eyes all the things that went with his surrender.

Awed by the tender desperation in the way he held her, she touched his cheek.

Because she finally could, she spread her fingers across skin, found it both soft and rough.

Felt how ragged her touch made his breath, how fast it made his heart beat. Hers accelerated to match.

"Of course you do."

When her smile turned cocky he had to do something about it. Her green eyes were sizzling with enough anticipation to melt rock. Fine. He could take anything the romance writer could dish out. First he was going to take care of that smile.

He bent his head and erased it.